Summer

at

West Castle

THERESA LINDEN

BOOKS BY THERESA LINDEN

http://theresalinden.com
Library of Congress Control Number: 2022921234

Paperback: 978-1734992953
First Edition, Silver Fire Publishing, December 2022

Cover: Theresa Linden

Editor: Carolyn Astfalk

SILVER FIRE
PUBLISHING

DEDICATION

This book is dedicated to the fans of *Anyone but Him* who asked me to write about the summer Caitlyn and Jarret fell in love. Thank you for inspiring me.

ACKNOWLEDGMENTS

I am so thankful for the encouragement and assistance I received from fellow CatholicTeenBooks.com authors Cynthia T. Toney, Leslea Wahl, Corinna Turner, Carolyn Astfalk, and T. M. Gaouette. And I am always thankful for the love and support of my husband and boys, who help and inspire me in countless ways. And let me never forget to thank Our Lord, from whom all blessings flow. I love every aspect of writing faith-filled stories, from the moment inspiration strikes through the first draft, editing, and final edition. And I particularly enjoy the prayer and study of the Faith that accompanies each one I write.

CHAPTER 1

May he grant you your heart's desire
and fulfill all your plans!
~ Psalm 20:4

Caitlyn

I stood engulfed in the shadow of the West family's castle-like house. Like on my first elevator ride, my heart seemed to float as my gaze traveled up two stories of gray stone walls to wrought iron windows and battlements that ran between two turrets. I'd never even known this amazing house was here, tucked away in acres of wooded land, until five years ago when I became friends with Roland, the youngest of the West brothers, both of us freshmen at River Run High.

Songbirds shared my joy, as did the breeze playing with my flyaway red curls, lifting them into the afternoon sunlight—where they blazed like fire in my peripheral vision.

My heart pitter-pattered as I searched from window to window on the second and then the first floor. Which room would I get to stay in?

I blinked once, hard, and rattled my head. Was this really happening?

Psalm 20:4 played in my mind. *May he grant you your heart's desire* . . . Mom had written the verse in a card for my high school graduation, and I'd loved it so much I'd memorized it, repeating it often while away at college. My heart's desire . . . I was not a materialistic girl, but the West family's unique home had always opened my mind and heart to adventure and possibilities. Butterflies zipped through my chest—

A body slammed into my back—Stacey!—propelling me forward, just as my sister Priscilla shrieked, "Let go!"

"Oh, sorry," Stacey mumbled. "Didn't see ya."

My knees scraped the edge of the circular driveway then both hands planted themselves in the well-maintained lawn— arms stiff, just the way I'd learned not to fall in the self-defense class I'd taken as an elective. To compensate, I relaxed my arms and rolled to one side, the momentum stopping once my thigh hit the ground, half in the grass. Red scratches stretched across both knees, but my flowy hunter-green skirt should just cover them when standing.

"Let go!" Priscilla shrieked again, yanking an armful of dresses from Stacey, neither of them acting their age, Priscilla sixteen and Stacey fourteen.

With an evil grin, Stacey released her hold on the last flowery dress, which then fluttered to the pavement. The crooked grin lifting higher on one side, she looked from the dress to Priscilla then toward the back of the van. Before Priscilla or I could do more than open our mouths in shock, Stacey raced to Andrew and David, ages six and eight, who stood peering into a flowering hydrangea bush near the front porch.

"There it goes," Stacey said, pointing to a bug or something as if she'd been playing with the boys ever since we'd all tumbled from the van.

I loved my family and wanted the happy chaos of a full home of my own one day, but this retreat without them—and in a house several times larger than ours—was going to be wonderful.

"Caitlyn . . ." Mom emerged from around the back of the van, my box of essentials in her arms. Her eyes shifted to— "Your nice dress is on the ground!"

With a glance toward the nearest window, hoping no one had witnessed the squabble or my mishap, I pushed myself onto all fours. I snatched up the dress and climbed to my feet— stepping on the hem of the dress for only a second. Ordinarily, I would've groaned and rolled my eyes, if not outright complained about my sisters' childish behavior, but nothing could shatter my happy, hope-filled mood.

It was only mid-May and for the entire summer, I would be living as a resident of the West house! I would wake up inside a home fit for a princess, with big empty halls, captivating rooms, and unexplored nooks and crannies. I would take strolls on the grounds and visit the stables and sit on the porch alone, finding plenty of time to think over my life. But I would not be a princess.

I'd be the maid of West Castle.

"Boys, come get the suitcases," Dad hollered out the driver's window. He shut off the baseball game he'd been listening to on the radio in the short ride from our house and slid out of the van. "Mr. West said we're just to let ourselves in, right?"

"Doesn't your laptop have a case?" Mom gaped at the contents of the cardboard box in her arms. The box's three remaining old flaps hung open.

An old man's voice came from directly behind me. "Let me get the door fer you."

I shivered, the skin on my neck crawling, and I spun around. "Oh, hi, Mr. Digby." Relieved it was only him, I exhaled and offered a smile.

The Wests' groundskeeper, thin and unassuming in dark work pants and a short-sleeved tan work shirt, did not smile back, only nodded. Gripping a little shovel in one hand, he looked our chaotic family over for a second.

As Dad approached, Mr. Digby offered his other hand for a cordial handshake. "Mr. West is expecting you." He led the way up the stone porch steps and stuffed the shovel into a tidy basket of tools. He held open one side of the double doors with its wrought-iron handle and invited everyone inside.

"Take your shoes off," Mom called as she kicked off her sandals and the kids rushed pell-mell into the house. Andrew and David immediately discovered how nicely they could slide in their socks on the hardwood floor. Stacey, already barefoot, must've taken her shoes off in the car . . . or maybe she hadn't worn shoes. She opened her arms to Priscilla as if offering to hold my dresses, but Priscilla turned away and used one foot to pry the shoe off the other.

I slipped off my used-to-be-white tennis shoes, tossed them on our new shoe pile, and stepped barefooted onto the cool hardwood floor. Though I'd visited the Wests' house many times in the past five years, I looked at it all anew.

Two hallways came off the large museum-like foyer with its glorious chandelier and framed artwork, one running straight back, past the kitchen and dining room to the great room that overlooked the back of the property. The other went off to the left, leading past various rooms I'd never explored and to the Digbys' suite on the far end of the house. Sunlight streamed from a few open doorways down both hallways. Then a shadow fell by the kitchen entranceway halfway down the hall, and a tall man stepped out.

Mr. West strode from the kitchen in cowboy boots and jeans—not in socks or barefooted like the rest of us. Of course,

Mr. Digby never did ask us to remove our shoes. That was Mom's idea.

"There he is," Dad said in a low voice, grinning the way he did before saying something silly. "The cowboy of the castle."

I didn't remember ever seeing the man without a cowboy hat. He'd grown up on a ranch in Arizona and never shed the cowboy image, making him seem somewhat out of place in his fancy home. He'd received this house as a gift—which was another story—and he likely remained because of how much his dearly departed wife had loved it. I couldn't help but think he'd be more at home in something modest and maybe out West, rather than here in South Dakota.

"Where's Roland?" Stacey came up beside me with a devilish grin, the sunlight from the long window beside the door glinting in her sneaky little eyes.

"He's taking summer classes," I answered defensively, heat rising up my neck. I tried to suppress the question that had popped into my mind at the mention of Roland's name. As a distraction, I picked up the suitcase Andy had set down while taking off his shoes.

"That's right," Mr. Digby said. "The boys won't be around this summer. All off doing their own things, Roland at college, Jarret on field study, and Keefe away at the monastery."

Dad laughed and rubbed Stacey's shoulder. "You know your sister wouldn't have this job if the boys were here." The boys . . . shy Roland and his older twin brothers, the haughty Jarret and humble Keefe.

I thought about Dad's comment. If they were here, maybe I wouldn't be, but maybe I would. Certainly by age twenty I could make my own decisions. Although, if Roland were here, I probably would have said no, uncomfortable with the thought of playing housekeeper and cook in the West house after the decision he and I had recently made.

Mr. West lifted his cowboy hat as he neared us. "Well, howdy, Summer clan." He shook Dad's hand, tipped his head at Mom, and offered a smile to the rest of us. Priscilla giggled and Stacey grinned, but the boys didn't stop sliding down the front hallway long enough to acknowledge him.

"We're right glad Caitlyn can be here." Mr. West's blue eyes sparkled, an easy smile on his lips. He must've heard Dad's comment about me not taking this job if his sons had been home. "Can't think of a nicer person for the job."

The heat that had risen up my neck when Stacey asked me about Roland now reached my cheeks. "Thank you." I felt honored to have the job and wished I could do it for free—except I really needed the money if I wanted another year of college. I was already a year behind Roland because I'd had to work and save before getting started—but Mr. West had offered to pay me well. I hoped I was the right person for the job. Mrs. Digby, the Wests' live-in housekeeper and cook, who everyone called Nanny, just had double hip replacements, so they needed temporary help. Could I do all the tasks she was accustomed to doing before her surgery?

"Caitlyn knows how to cook and clean and organize her time," Mom said, as if sensing my insecurity.

"Organize her time? I don't know if I'd go that far," Dad said, always the joker, a trait I didn't appreciate at the moment.

"I'm sure she'll do fine. She can settle in today and chat with Nanny in a day or so, see what her expectations are." Mr. West did a double take down the front hallway, glancing first at the spot where Mr. Digby had stood, though he wasn't there now, then at my brothers busy at their sliding games.

"How's Nanny doing?" Mom said with a tilt of her head and that motherly concern in her eyes.

"Just got home from the hospital yesterday. I reckon she's resting now. Mr. Digby's been taking good care of her. Stayed up at the hospital with her the entire time. Quite devoted."

At the last comment, Mom and Dad both offered compliments about the Digbys.

"Where's Caitlyn's room?" Stacey said with a crooked grin.

"She'll stay in the guest room nearest the Digbys' suite, in case Nanny needs her at night." Mr. West pointed. "You're welcome to check it out now. Door's open." He made a move to pick up my other suitcase.

"I got it." I grabbed the handle before he could and gave an appreciative smile. "Thank you."

"Y'all are welcome over anytime," Mr. West said to Dad and Mom, "stay the night if you like. We have other guest rooms, and the boys won't be needing their rooms this summer."

"Hmm, we just might take you up on that offer." Dad bounced his bushy brows. "It'd be like a vacation. We could play pool all day, go horseback riding, campfire out back . . ."

"Honey." Mom nudged Dad, probably not wanting him to get my siblings' hopes up. She was a homebody and would never go along with the idea.

"We could play a game of pool now if you'd like. I've ordered pizza. Should get here soon." Mr. West nodded for everyone to follow him.

Mom handed my box of essentials to Stacey and grabbed Andrew's arm before he could take off again to slide down the hallway. "Come along, boys," she said, eliciting a moan of disappointment from them.

She smiled at me, signaling that my sisters and I could check out my room without the disturbance of our brothers—which I really appreciated. As they followed Mr. West, Dad made some silly joke that Mr. West and Mom chuckled over, and their voices soon trailed off.

Priscilla, hugging my dresses protectively to her chest, looked at me with expectant eyes. The gleam in Stacey's eyes said she could barely wait another second to see my room.

Excitement again thrilling though me, I grabbed the second suitcase and smiled at my sisters. "Shall we?"

We pattered down the front hallway, glancing through every open doorway but not slowing until we reached the last one. The room just before the Digbys' suite. My room!

"Wow," Priscilla said, crossing the threshold. "Is this really going to be your bedroom?"

Sunlight streamed in through sheer curtains, the thicker drapes tied back, giving a warm and homey glow to the room of antique furniture and feminine flourishes—like the pile of lace-trimmed pillows on the big bed next to the window and the flowers painted on the baroque giltwood headboard.

I stepped from the hardwood floor to a soft antique rug. Centered under the bed, it came to within four feet or so of the walls, leaving bare hardwood floor under the off-white-and-gold antique desk and chair with curvy legs and the side tables that held vintage painted lamps and the old armoire with a carved *fleur-de-lis* pattern. This room did not have the distinctive medieval or Western flare of many of the other rooms in the West house, but I loved it.

Stacey set my box of essentials on the desk and stepped into the closet. "Wow, this is big enough to be my room." Her voice lowered as she spoke to Priscilla, who turned on a lamp. "Let's make beds along the sides," Stacey said.

Finding an outlet next to the desk, I pulled my laptop from the box and set it up. I'd promised Ling-si, my new best friend from college, and Roland that I'd email them once I got settled.

"Let's help Caitlyn unpack." Priscilla joined Stacey in the closet. "Oh, you put those on the floor?" She glanced over her shoulder at me.

As my laptop came to life, I shrugged to let Priscilla know I didn't mind. Stacey must've been using my dresses for their *beds* in the walk-in closet. Oh well. In an hour or so, they would go home, leaving me alone to begin my "retreat." I'd hang the dresses up nicely and finish unpacking. Then explore.

Before I could write more than a short message to each of my friends, a flash of light through the window captured my attention, drawing me over. A car with a glowing pizza slice sign on top crawled up the circular driveway. The car stopped and the delivery boy got out, his mouth hanging open as he gawked at the house. He must not have delivered pizza here before. It had been quite a shock when I'd first seen the place too, so I wouldn't judge.

Happiness bubbling inside me, I plopped down on the bed. My retreat would begin soon. At some point, not today, I'd start praying and thinking about things. About Roland and the decision we made. About my future and where God called me. Had I made a mistake? Was it irreversible? Or had I made the right choice? Was God calling me to something I'd never even considered? The possibilities were endless. Life was an open road, an adventure that could take me anywhere.

"Is it comfortable?" Stacey bolted from the closet and jumped onto the bed, next to me, but the mattress hardly bounced, and the bed frame didn't squeak like ours did at home. Still, she kept trying, bouncing on the mattress.

"Want me to unpack your suitcases?" Priscilla emerged from the closet, saw us on the bed, and joined us. "Oh, this is so comfortable! It's like those nice ones in the mattress stores."

I laughed. I loved my sisters. I loved my family. But I really loved this opportunity, this granting of my heart's desire. "Come on. The pizza just got here. Let's go eat!" I scooted off the bed.

When I swung open the bedroom door, I'd been looking back at my sisters, so I didn't notice the figure looming before me in the hallway—and I walked right into him.

"Oh, sorry." I stumbled back, bumping either Stacey or Priscilla behind me, both of them whispering now.

"Just gettin' ready to knock." Mr. Digby stood before me, lean and sort of glum-looking, a little book tucked under one arm. "Have this here for you." He handed me a black 5 x 7 notebook. "Since Nanny won't likely have the concentration to guide you for a while, I put together a chore list. It'll help you get started."

"Oh, great! Thank you." I spoke with enthusiasm. Mom used to give us chore lists, mixing things up each time, making it fun because we never knew what to expect—fun, until it got down to actually doing the chores.

"I've arranged the list by room . . . daily chores, weekly chores, and some things you'll only do once." He gestured as he spoke, ticking off chores in the air. "That sort of thing."

"Wh-what sort of thing?" I glanced from the notebook to Mr. Digby a few times. Why hadn't he simply torn out a page and given it to me? Unless the list was . . .

Anxiety gripping me, I angled my body away from him so he wouldn't see my initial reaction. Then I opened the notebook and flipped through the pages, finding rows and rows of chores: clean cobwebs, wipe down doors, spot wash walls, scrub windows and vacuum window tracks, mirrors, ceiling fans, baseboards . . .

As I flipped through the notebook, my retreat started drifting away, becoming a castle in the air. A list for the kitchen, family room, dining room, great room, library, hallway . . . Pantry cleaning and organizing! Oh yes, very thorough. Pages and pages of thorough. No-time-for-a-private-retreat thorough!

Not sure what to say—should I thank him for this horribly thorough chore list?—I tore my gaze from the notebook, but Mr. Digby was gone. He'd probably shuffled back to their suite, but I'd missed it. Hadn't even heard his footsteps. But then, Priscilla and Stacey had grown louder with their whispered exchange behind me.

"Where's the pizza?" Stacey finally said, poking her head over my shoulder.

I took a deep breath, tossed the notebook into my room, and closed the door. I'd face the list tomorrow and find a way to salvage my retreat.

CHAPTER 2

Jarret

With my toes on the chair I'd shoved against the wall by my bare bed and my palms on the floor, I decided to crank out twenty extra decline pushups. Maybe it would help rid me of the restlessness I'd woken up to.

Torso straight, I lowered myself to the floor and pushed back up. One.

Down, up. Two . . . three . . . four . . .

Unable to make regular gym visits, I'd had to find creative ways to work my muscles—various pushups, jogs around campus between classes, pullups on branches . . . I missed my weights and equipment back home . . . and the simplicity of life, though I hadn't realized it before college. It'd been so easy to keep a routine, start the day right: wake up, workout in the basement, grab a shower and something to eat . . .

Eight . . . nine . . . ten . . .

For close to the hundredth time, as I lowered myself to the laminate oak floor, I glimpsed a pamphlet under the bed, probably one for my field study in Pompeii. I made a mental

13

note to pick it up when I finished this last set. The question that had been nagging me for weeks came to mind. Should I really be taking this trip? Or was I gonna get myself into trouble?

Fourteen . . . fifteen . . .

Sweat dripped down my back and my muscles screamed, but I kept going. Maybe the workout would ease some of my growing anxiety. Why did I feel this way anyway? This gnawing in my chest at certain times. Granted, as a South Dakota boy, getting used to the Arizona temperatures hadn't been easy, but college life itself was more chaotic than I'd expected. Not quite feeling it with my original degree choice, I'd switched majors twice, setting me back a bit. How long could I keep this up? Working the rest of life around classes and assignments. Squeezing in grocery shopping and meals— which I'd never had to even think about at home. Trying to stick to some kind of exercise routine without totally ignoring friends . . . and her.

Nineteen . . .

I pushed up from the floor, arms ready to give out, lowered my chest down, and one more . . .

Twenty.

Satisfied that I'd completed the extra set, I dropped a knee to the floor, snatched the pamphlet from under the bed, and got to my feet, ready for a shower. My suitcases—four of them and a duffel—stood between the kitchenette and the door to the outside, blocking the little hallway to the bathroom.

Not wanting to leave anything important behind—a friend taking summer courses would be moving in—I scanned the little studio apartment again. The six cupboards above the kitchenette hung open, empty except for junk I didn't care about. I opened and closed the drawers next to the range one more time, old batteries rolling about in one drawer, taco sauce packets in another. I'd stripped the bed this morning and shoved the sheets and pillow into one of the suitcases that would stay in my car all summer while I went to Pompeii. Too bad I couldn't have washed them first.

I lifted one suitcase to the little table against the wall and shoved the others aside, leaving just enough room to get to the hallway off the kitchenette. Before I could step past them, someone knocked on the door, probably one of my friends dropping by to return something or say goodbye.

As I reached for the doorknob, I glanced at the digital clock on the microwave. I had about ten minutes for a shower then I had to pick up my girlfriend and get to the airport. A squirrelly sensation started in my chest. Excited about the trip? Or was it the thought of going with—

I swung open the door to a burst of sunlight, warm air, and *her*.

Rylee Brooks stood before me, a fashion plate in sandals and a short flowery dress that looked good against her caramel skin, a few blue streaks in her jet-black shoulder-length hair, and a tiny purse dangling from one hand. Her makeup, heavier today, drew attention to the playful look in her upturned eyes.

"What are you doing here?" I held the door with one hand and the doorframe with the other, blocking entrance. How'd she even find me? In the three months we'd been together, I'd purposely never given her my apartment number.

"Jarret, you are so rude sometimes. Aren't you going to let me in?" She wrapped her arms around my sweaty neck, kissed me firmly on the lips, and pushed me out of the doorway.

"I thought I was picking you up."

She stepped past my luggage crowded against the table and glanced at the bed and the window and the kitchenette. "Cute place. A bit stuffy"—she fanned her nose—"but why haven't you ever invited me over?"

I shook my head and huffed, irritated, the squirrelly sensation spreading in my chest. I had no intention of explaining my motives. She wouldn't understand. "Look, I gotta take a shower. Go back to your place and I'll pick you up in ten minutes."

She laughed and sat on the bed, tossing her purse aside. "I'm all packed, got a ride here, and set my luggage by your car. Go take your shower. I'll wait here."

"Uh . . ." The bathroom door didn't lock, and she'd always seemed to want more from me than I wanted to give. I'd sensed that about her before I'd asked her out three months ago, something in the way she batted her long lashes at me and the suggestive pauses when she spoke. But we got along so well in the few classes we had together, especially the Methods in Archaeology course. The playful banter and way we clicked . . . I couldn't *not* start something with her then. It'd been a hard row to hoe, as Papa would say. But I didn't want to make the same mistakes I'd made in high school.

An image of my first serious girlfriend came to mind and the secrets I'd never shared with later girlfriends. I shook the thoughts away. Why couldn't I meet a girl with the values I now wanted to live?

"Need some help?" Rylee got up and sashayed toward me.

"What?" Not trusting myself to acknowledge her remark, I glanced at the clock again. Time to implement Plan B. "Sit down. I'll just be a second." I grabbed my duffel bag and darted into the bathroom. After closing the door behind me, wishing I'd fixed the lock, I proceeded to wash up, rather than actually shower, and pull my hair back into a ponytail. Then I changed into the Oxford shorts and short-sleeved olive-green Henley I'd left out while packing everything else. I shoved my toiletries and dirty clothes into the duffel, gave the bathroom the once-over to make sure I hadn't forgotten anything, and then split.

She stood leaning against the kitchen countertop and glanced up from her phone. "That was quick. I didn't even hear the shower go on."

"Yeah, and since you're here, you can help me with my bags." I slung the strap of the duffel bag over my shoulder, extended the handles of the two smaller suitcases for her, and grabbed the last two suitcases. "Let's go."

"Well, you're no fun today. I hope you lighten up by the time we get to Pompeii." She gave me a flirty smile and fluttered her dark eyelashes as she dragged suitcases past me through the door I held open. "We're going to have so much fun, Jarret baby."

I led the way down the outdoor hallway, glancing over the railing at my cherry red Chrysler 300 in the mostly empty parking lot. Heat rippled off the roof of the car and the streets in the distance, though it was only mid-May. Not a cloud in the sky. We stomped down the shaded stairwell to our echoing footsteps, crossed the parking lot, and loaded everything into the trunk.

The car took its time cooling down on the way to the airport. I really liked the idea of going to Pompeii, my favorite professor leading the field study, many of my college friends there with me. But I had other reasons too . . .

Papa had enjoyed his time in Pompeii, back in the day, and often talked about it. Framed prints of the ruins hung on the walls at home. Detailed maps and photos in Papa's study. I almost hated to admit it but Papa's stories about Pompeii, more than anything else, had inspired me to pursue this field. Would I enjoy archaeology as a career? Was this really what I wanted to do for the rest of my life?

Maybe I'd find out on this field study. I'd love it or hate it. But it just might help me find direction in my life. As much as it seemed to please Papa, I really didn't want to simply follow in his footsteps. This needed to be my choice.

Thin trees with tiny leaves grew along both sides of the highway and the divider. Distant purplish mountains peeked between stand-alone stores and gas stations and bigger pale buildings with terracotta roofs. Soon palm trees and little spiky plants lined the road. The dry desert landscape often put me in a melancholy mood, but today that squirrely sensation in my chest wouldn't leave me alone. It was getting annoying. Made me worry I'd have a heart attack or something if it didn't quit.

Stopping at a light, I checked my phone and found a text message from a friend. *Prof Z not going. Had to cancel for family emergency.*

I read it again and then a third time, the squirrely sensation turning into a sinking sensation. No way. It had to be Professor Z leading the field study. No one else could replace him. The other professors didn't have what he had, the cool factor and relatability, along with the knowledge and zeal for all things archaeology.

"Light's green." Rylee placed her hand on my thigh.

As I reached for the steering wheel, my cell phone slipped down between the seat and the door. "I can't believe it." I grabbed her hand just as she started rubbing my leg. "Professor Z can't make it now."

Rylee shrugged. "Two other professors are going."

"Yeah, but . . ." I decided not to explain, gathering she didn't feel the same way about Professor Z, but all us guys got along well with him. He loved what he did, spoke in ways that made sense, and his enthusiasm motivated everyone. Plus, he'd hang out with students afterhours sometimes, telling stories over a beer or a cookout or a two-in-the-morning breakfast at a 24-hour restaurant, seeming to care about each of our futures and somehow bringing archaeology into the real world.

The airport stretched out before us, Saguaro cacti and trees with dusty green leaves flanking the road. Rylee reached into her purse and pulled out the envelope that held our tickets.

Thoughts flitted through my mind, all of them moving so quickly I couldn't pin any of them down. I drove past a huge parking lot, heading for the terminal.

"Are you parking in the garage?" Rylee turned her head as we passed the open parking lot.

"Uh . . ." I tried harder to pin down the thoughts zipping through my mind. "No, I'm not."

"Well, you just passed a parking lot. They have a shuttle."

"Yeah, saw it." I pulled up to the terminal, where cars sat parked along the curb and more cars crept along in either direction.

"Oh, you want to drop me and the luggage off and then park?" Rylee got out at the same time I did, both of us slamming the doors together. She met me at the back of the car.

A sense of urgency gripping me, I grabbed her bags from the trunk and set them on a luggage cart in the shade of the overhang. I'd pinned down one thought, the most urgent one: I couldn't go through with this. Not just the field study but *us*. It didn't feel right. I had to tell her, and I had to do it now.

She leaned into the trunk and straightened up, two hands on the handle of one of my suitcases, hefting it as if it weighed a hundred pounds. "What's in this thing?" She lifted it toward the luggage cart.

As she released her grip on the handle, I grabbed the suitcase with one hand and tossed it back into the trunk. "Hey, I don't want to have to say this," I blurted, the urgency inside forcing me to speak.

Her eyes shifted to me from the suitcase that I'd returned to the trunk.

". . . and you're not gonna wanna hear it, but I can't see you anymore." My heart seemed to stop for a moment, everything around me seeming to fall silent as I waited for her reaction. I hated breaking up with girls. If I ever found the right one . . .

Her mouth opened slowly, her cherry red lips wrapping around the letter "w" for a full second before she finally said, "What? Are you breaking up with me?" She darted a few glances to each side as people rushed to and from cars pulled up at the sundrenched curb. As if worried that passersby would know or care that she'd just been dumped.

"Yeah, sorry." I slammed the trunk and drew my keys from the front pocket of my Oxford shorts. "And I'm not going on the field study. I mean, I'd really love to, you know, Pompeii, but since Professor Z can't make it . . ."

"Professor Z?" Her eyebrows slanted together, and she shook her head. "Why are you breaking up with me? This was going to be the best summer ever, you and me in Pompeii, working and exploring together . . . We were really going to get to know each other."

Averting my gaze, I sucked in a breath through my mouth, regret rankling me. I really should've done this sooner. What kind of jerk breaks up with a girl at the airport? Granted, I'd only just realized I should break it off, that it couldn't possibly work in the long run. In addition to other reasons, I only had so much self-control and she seemed intent on wearing it down.

Turning to her, I tried to touch her arm, but she pulled away. "Look, all your friends are going. You're gonna have fun. Maybe you'll meet someone. I'm just not the one for you."

She huffed, irritation bringing a sneer to her otherwise pretty face. "Fine. Enjoy your summer." She put two hands to the luggage cart and rolled it through the automatic sliding glass doors.

Relief flooding me, I got back in my Chrysler and cranked the engine to life. Now I had an eighteen-hour trip ahead of me, but then I'd have all summer to myself. Time to think and find my own path. I took a deep breath and exhaled pent-up tension. I was going home.

CHAPTER 3

Caitlyn

I stopped just inside the Digbys' suite, transfixed by the lovely combination of medieval and French country styles in the sun-kissed living room before me. Decorative pillows with farmland scenes sat in the corners of a blue-and-cream plaid sofa and the solid cream loveseat across from it. Framed pictures and ceramic vases decorated the wooden mantle above the fireplace on the far wall. An airy kitchen came off to the right, with a little table for four and a wrought iron garden bench with pillows under a window with lacy curtains.

"Nanny's been so tired since coming home." Mr. Digby closed the door and shuffled past me, stopping a few feet from a half-open door.

"Yes, I'm sure she would be. I can't imagine having both hips replaced. Or any kind of surgery. Or the medicine you'd have to take, or the pain. Or being stuck in bed . . ." I shut my mouth before more babble could come out and looked to Mr. Digby for my next cue. I'd spent two days flailing on my own, trying to navigate using Mr. Digby's chore list, trying to locate the appropriate supplies for each chore, trying to understand why he had me cleaning things that no one would ever see—like the floor under the refrigerator or the tops of curtain rods.

Today would be different. Mr. Digby had come to get me at precisely nine o'clock this morning. Caught me raiding the refrigerator. It felt weird helping myself to someone else's food . . . in someone else's kitchen, but Mr. West had insisted I make myself at home and specifically said I could eat whatever I liked. I'd made myself scrambled eggs and toast but then returned to the fridge for something more. That's when Mr. Digby came into the kitchen.

"Well, she's lookin' forward to seeing you today." With one hand to the doorknob, Mr. Digby stuck his head into the room with the half-open door. "Miss Summer's here if you're ready to speak with her."

"Oh, yes, yes," came Nanny's tired voice. Then the hum of an adjustable bed. "Please send the dear girl in."

Opening wide the door, Mr. Digby nodded at me. "I'll leave you two and get on with my own list."

I could only imagine what chores filled his list. He did all the outdoor chores, including landscaping and stable work. Was his list as thorough as mine? As Mr. Digby shuffled through the living room, I took a breath, pressed the notebook to my tummy to calm the quivering inside it, and stepped into the Digbys' bedroom.

"Oh, so good to see you, my dear." Nanny sat half-reclined in bed, dressed in a floral nightgown with a lacey neckline and covered to her waist with a white sheet folded neatly over a plaid blanket—Mr. Digby's doing, I guessed. With a smile that contrasted with her tired eyes, she motioned for me to sit in a nearby armchair angled toward the bed. "Are you all settled in, dear?"

"Yes, thank you!" I thought about telling her everything I did since arriving, about the pizza and games with my family before they left me on my own. Then how I'd wanted to stroll the grounds outside, but the sun had set by then. I'd basically just cleaned up after my family and gone to my room then spent the next two days navigating through the chore list . . . with no time for my retreat. Not wanting to babble on when she probably needed rest, I simply said, "I love the guest room I'm staying in."

"Yes, Mrs. West picked out the furnishings for that room." Her eyes held a distant look. "Many years ago." When she returned her gaze to me, her demeanor turned businesslike with a hint of drowsiness. "I'm not sure what Mr. West told you the job would entail, but we can go over it now."

"Okay, yes, I can't wait to help you more, in addition to the chores. He said something about helping you get around and such." I sat stiffly in the chair, back straight and hands folded on the notebook on my lap, my full attention on Nanny—although I wanted to look around. I imagined this room, while darker because of the drawn drapes, had even more interesting decorations than the rest of their suite.

Nanny shifted, winced, and rested her head back, her gray curls pressing against the pillow behind her. Then for the next hour or so, between stories of her recent experiences and questions she had for me about family and college, she explained the help she would need: assistance with little daily walks, encouragement with exercises, and help with minor tasks when Mr. Digby was not available. She even wanted me present when the therapist stopped by tomorrow so I could learn the exercises.

"Okay, you can call or text whenever you need me." I sunk my hand into a pocket in my skirt but came up empty. Not wanting to check my phone every few minutes, I'd been leaving it in my room. "Would you like my number?"

"Oh sure. That's a good idea." She squinted at the nightstand, where a glass table lamp cast warm light on a tissue box, a clear glass of water, a puzzle book, a folded grabber to help her reach things, and her phone.

"I got it." Happy to help, I picked up her phone and added my number to her contacts. When I returned it to the nightstand, my attention dropped to the notebook on my lap, Mr. Digby's list. My heart sank a bit. I loved the idea of helping Nanny through the difficult days of her recovery, and I didn't mind cooking and chores. But so many chores . . . would I have any free time at all?

"Thank you, dear. I'm feeling a bit drowsy now, so I'll take a nap. But would you mind making an early lunch, maybe soup and sandwiches? Once it's ready, maybe eleven-thirty or noon, you can help me to my wheelchair and take me to the kitchen. I'd like to eat out there today."

"Okay." With a smile, I stood and ran my thumb along the edge of the notebook, flipping through the pages. "In the meantime, I'll see what chores I should be doing today."

"Chores? I can't think of anything that needs done today, especially with the boys away and Mr. West hardly around. Why don't you have a nice stroll around the property? Forecast calls for lovely weather."

"Oh, but Mr. Digby gave me this list." I opened the notebook randomly and turned it so she could see two pages overflowing with items. In order to add "helping Nanny" to my day, I'd have to get to work the second I left the Digbys' suite. I could do this. I'd just have to change my expectations, think and pray while I worked instead of counting on free time. It could still be a retreat, right? Like a working retreat with no leisure time . . . but in a super nice castle-like house.

Would I find answers to my questions this summer? Would I get the guidance I needed in making life choices? Certainly God would accept my work as a prayer and guide me even if I didn't have the time or energy to think things through. Kind of like when someone accidentally fell asleep while praying the Rosary and their guardian angel finished it, right? Was that really a thing?

Nanny took the notebook from me and turned a few pages, a smile growing on her face. "I do try to keep up with the housekeeping, cleaning every nook and cranny, but I certainly don't expect you to do that. You're here to help me and prepare a few meals, especially when Mr. West is home. I like for him to have something nice to eat when he's here. And I'll ask you to do a little light cleaning, but nothing like this." She handed the notebook back. "You can toss that."

"But won't Mr. Digby be expecting—"

"Don't you worry about Mr. Digby. The outside is his domain; the inside is mine." She grabbed the remote and lowered the bed, a grandmotherly smile on her lips. "I'll see you around noon then."

"Okay." I practically bounced from the room to the door of their suite and into the hallway. My original retreat was back on! Exploring the house and grounds, maybe petting the horses and going for long walks, plenty of time for prayer and contemplation, time to think over the changes in my life and my future direction.

Dancing inside and eager to begin the day, I started down the hallway. I no longer had to worry about a major chore list, but I did need to clean up after myself in the kitchen. Mr. Digby had interrupted my breakfast, so I'd left quite a mess and I was still hungry.

A burst of light and footfalls then movement at the opposite end of the long hallway pulled me from my thoughts. A figure stomped through the sundrenched foyer, coming into view. Mr. Digby probably. He carried something, luggage maybe, one suitcase in each hand . . .

My heart stopped beating in my chest, shooting instead to my throat, and I froze in place. Not Mr. Digby.

Athletic build, confident stride, designer shorts and shirt, and curly hair pulled into ponytail. Jarret West had come home.

I'd act the same as if a skunk had found its way into the house. Avoid sudden moves that might rattle him, and he'd be on his way without a stink.

Forcing my heart back into place and ungluing my feet from the floor, I continued down the hallway. He must've been stopping home for something before going on his little fieldtrip. That was all. If he were staying longer, Roland would've known. He would've warned me.

As I got within two rooms from him in the long hallway, his gaze found me, and he did a doubletake, making me extremely self-conscious. After staring at me for a full two seconds, he shook his head as if in disbelief, dropped the suitcases, and faced the adjacent hallway. "Roland!" he bellowed.

Before he could turn back to me, my hand shot up to fix my hair. His always-so-stylish look, even when a bit rumpled, like now, made me feel so thrown together. Had I even looked at my hair this morning? I forced my hand back to my side before I spoke. "Roland's not here. He's taking summer courses."

His mouth fell open and a hopeful look replaced the hint of irritation and weariness in his eyes. "Keefe?" he whispered as if unable to actually say his twin's name aloud, not daring to hope.

I giggled at how his brain worked. If Roland wasn't here, then I must've been here as Keefe's guest. Maybe a part of him hoped Keefe had changed his mind about his vocation. "Doesn't he live in a monastery?" I didn't imagine any of the Franciscan brothers went home for the summer.

He looked me over from head to toe, his eyes narrowing with suspicion.

One thing I'd learned about him in high school, his expression always gave him away before he spoke. He was not happy to see me.

"So what are *you* doing here?"

"Nanny." Taking my last few steps toward him, I jabbed my thumb over my shoulder, in the general direction of the Digbys' suite. He must've known her situation, how she'd need help for the summer. I'd assumed all the West boys knew. His rude tone made me unwilling to explain it for him now.

"Oh." His brown eyes turned upward and then to one side as if trying to collect a memory from a back closet. He must've had more important things on his mind when he'd been informed of her situation, things like himself.

Standing two yards away, I looked him over for a clue as to why he had come home. No broken limbs. Didn't appear ill. His rumpled olive-green shirt and shorts told me he'd been driving for a while. And the luggage . . . Wouldn't he need his things for the summer-long fieldtrip? I had to ask. "So . . . what are *you* doing here?"

"What am I—" His brown eyes went dark. He shouted, "It's my house!" Then he stomped back out the front door, which he'd left open after first stepping inside. His cherry red luxury car sat parked in the circular driveway, the trunk open. He grabbed two more suitcases and a duffel bag and slammed the trunk.

Debating whether or not to help him, I watched as he stomped back inside, kicked the door shut, and piled his luggage in the hallway. I could imagine myself trying to help, my high school klutziness returning, stumbling over one piece as I picked up another, looking absolutely ridiculous under his conceited gaze.

Jarret glanced at me as he dropped the last item—the duffel bag—onto the pile, and then he walked away. Leaving it all just sitting there. At the end of the foyer. Blocking easy access to the hallway that led to the kitchen.

"Um, Jarret," I called after him, climbing over the pile, disbelief overcoming me. Probably heading for the stairs, he hadn't gotten too far down the hallway that ran toward the back of the house. "Would you like me to carry these upstairs?"

I couldn't believe I was offering, but why in the world would he just leave his things in the way?

He stopped and turned, shaking his head. "No. I'm sure Papa didn't hire you to carry my luggage. You're here for Nanny, right?"

"Well, yes, but"—I waved my hand in the direction of the barricade—"it's blocking the hallway."

"Don't worry about it."

Was he expecting poor old Mr. Digby to do it? "But . . . I need to get Nanny to the dining room for lunch."

"It's not lunchtime." He turned away and strode to the stairs.

I stood for a moment, one hand on my hip, the other clutching Mr. Digby's chore notebook so hard that it curled. *Don't let him bother you,* my inner voice said, *you have your own work to do.* So I stomped to the kitchen, to the mess I'd left on the bar counter and the dirty skillet on the stovetop. I hadn't even returned the eggs to the fridge.

Before long, I washed, dried, and put away the last of my dishes, gave the marble countertop a final wipe, and hung the washrag and dishtowel to air dry. Not sure what to do before starting lunch, I stepped into the hallway and glanced both ways, at the great room on my right and the pile of luggage down the hallway, on my left. Then a shuffling sound came from the stairwell roughly across from me. A door creaked shut. And a shower came on.

Hmm . . . I tapped my chin, turning toward the pile of luggage. He'd be in there for quite a while.

CHAPTER 4

Jarret

Under the pelting water of a cool shower, I didn't want to think about anything. Just wanted to wash the day's stress down the drain. After a moment, I turned and let the shower beat against my neck and shoulders.

That eighteen-hour drive had taken its toll on me. After dropping my girlfriend—ah, ex-girlfriend—at the airport, I'd driven until my eyes wouldn't stay open any longer, stopping only once, outside Denver. I grabbed a miserable three-hour nap in my car at the darkest end of a truck stop. Giving up on rest, weary and with a stiff neck, I made the final stretch, which seemed longer than the first stretch, but maybe because I'd grown anxious for home.

Sleep beckoned me, but I wet my hair and grabbed the shampoo. Scrub. Rinse. I needed a nice long nap in my own bed with no distractions. I needed a break. From everything.

A calming ocean scent filled the air as I combed conditioner through my hair with my fingers. I hadn't seen it coming, but I'd made the right move breaking up with Rylee.

I really should've done it sooner. She didn't like Mexican food—okay, maybe not a dealbreaker. But still. She didn't want kids—okay, maybe she'd want them later. From my experience, almost every girl said the same thing, so maybe immaturity had something to do with it, but what if she never changed her mind? And she argued a lot. Not usually with me, but the bickering with her friends rattled me sometimes.

I took a deep breath and grabbed my washcloth. Relief had accompanied me much of the way home, and a healthy sense of freedom that had me appreciating the landscape and the weather and my Chrysler 300 and even little things like ice-cold fountain drinks, favorite tunes on the radio, and sandals that made long-distance driving a bit more comfortable. And I'd actually been able to pray, which hadn't been easy lately, for whatever reason. But disappointment kept returning too. My friends would be landing in Italy soon, embarking on an adventure that should've been mine too.

I squeezed pine-scented body wash onto a washcloth. If only I could wash my emotions away as easily as sweat and dirt. I didn't want to think about anything, but a jumble of emotions tormented me. In the weeks before the field study, I'd been walking on air, looking forward to the overseas experience of working the same site Papa had worked over twenty years ago.

All the while, unease had grown inside. My girlfriend hinted at her own plans for our summer together in Pompeii, and self-control had never been my strongest virtue. Not wanting to be caught off guard, I'd tried visualizing potential challenges with the intention of planning my defensive moves, but that had only increased my problems—bringing temptations of a different kind.

After rinsing the soap from my body and conditioner from my hair, I shut off the shower and grabbed a towel, my gaze shifting to the door. I sure hadn't expected a homecoming like this. I'd sailed through more emotions in one brief moment than over the entire year. First, irritation. Whenever I saw any of Roland's friends, I thought of Peter, the brat who loved pranking me . . . a confetti shower over the pool table, Limburger cheese in my car . . . But Peter wasn't here, just Caitlyn, and I'd assumed Roland was too. But no.

Keefe? It made no sense for me to think Keefe had come home. Keefe loved monastery life. But I'd almost dared to hope. The thought had pulled my heartstrings hard and given me a little ache inside. I missed Keefe. I'd never found anyone I could talk to the way I could talk to my twin. But of course Keefe hadn't come home. Caitlyn was here for Nanny. That made sense.

Then guilt had tugged my conscience. I should've called to ask Nanny how her surgery had gone, but I hadn't thought about Nanny once since Papa had told me about her situation weeks ago.

I dressed in my bathrobe and opened drawers in the vanity, looking for something to keep my curls from frizzing. Pushing aside products that didn't work, I found a nearly empty tube of my favorite leave-in conditioner, squeezed a dollop into my palm, and rubbed my hands together.

Dark circles hung under my eyes, too much stubble on my chin, and the tired look wasn't just from the long drive. I'd been on an emotional roller coaster. Irritation, confusion, hope, heartache, guilt . . .

The first emotion to hit me at home . . . I almost didn't want to admit it. I hadn't recognized Caitlyn at first glance. Coming from the opposite end of the hallway, she'd appeared more like a vision, long ginger-red hair framing a feminine face and a flowy pale-blue-and-white flowered dress that draped past her knees . . . and something else . . .

The aura that surrounded her had spoken to my soul, unsettling me in a way no girl had done before. Then I'd recognized her. Caitlyn Summer. She'd changed since I'd seen her last.

I gave my hair another glance in the mirror. Satisfied with the way the curls hanging to my shoulders held together, I rinsed my hands and opened the door. No more thinking about girls or emotions. Now I needed a nice long nap. Drying my wet hands on my linen bathrobe, I stepped into the shadowy hallway, the light from downstairs not quite illuminating my path. Something was off, but—

With my next step, my toe rammed into something hard, my shin hit something, and I was going down. I crashed onto a heap of—my luggage? In the middle of the dark hallway, between my bedroom and the bathroom.

What the—?

I stifled a curse, but the familiar beast of anger rose up inside, threatening my self-control as I climbed to my feet.

Who would've—?

Seething now, I shoved suitcases out of my way and stomped toward the steps. I'd told her to leave the luggage alone. As my foot landed on the first step, an invisible wall came up . . . or maybe my guardian angel, wanting to stop me. I readied myself to shove it aside but then paused. If I went down there now, I'd confront her with uncontrolled anger. I'd make the already uncomfortable situation of having her in the house even more uncomfortable. I should turn around and cool off first, wait until my heart stopped slamming against my ribs and I could form a coherent thought.

I glanced down at my bathrobe. Maybe get dressed first or take a nap, but then I was confronting her. I had a few questions that needed answered.

--*

No sooner did my head hit the pillow when a surge of panic overtook me. *I stood in a courtyard under a darkening sky, limestone houses with Greek columns all around, birds flying erratically and too low—Mount Vesuvius looming nearby.*

"Jarret, this way!"

I turned toward the feminine, oddly playful voice, my heart screaming a warning.

Dressed in a long white toga and with tiny flowers in her hair, Rylee stood with a hand reaching for me, a flirtatious smile on her painted face.

The earth shook, making me throw my arms out for balance. Terracotta tiles rattled on nearby roofs. Dogs barked in the distance. Babies wailed. Screams ripped through the air all around.

"Hurry!" Rylee grabbed my hand, smiling, still playfully unaware of the danger. "What are you waiting for?"

Squeezing her hand, I ran.

Lightning flashed in a massive gray cloud belching from Mount Vesuvius. The pungent odor of rotten eggs gagged me. People raced past in the opposite direction, fleeing Pompeii with their families. A wave of heat nearly knocked me down.

Wait, no! We headed toward Mount Vesuvius, not away. Wrong direction! I wanted to scream, but oppressive heatwaves prevented me. I tried pulling Rylee to a stop as billowing clouds of smoke rolled toward the city at terrifying speed.

Panic mounting, I wrenched my hand from Rylee's and turned. Bursts of heat blew holes in roofs and walls. Chunks of limestone toppled into my path, under my feet, breaking my stride, tripping me up. A redheaded girl ahead moved them out of the way—no, she moved them into the path . . . wait, not limestone—luggage!

My eyes snapped open as I jerked awake, sweaty from head to toe. A warm breeze fluttered the curtains. Throwing the sheet back, I got up to close the window. I shouldn't have opened it with the air-conditioning on. Lingering scenes from a stupid dream slithered to the recesses of my mind, something about Pompeii and Rylee and—luggage!

Yeah, time to talk to Caitlyn.

Caitlyn

"Oh no!" At the sound of something crashing upstairs, I froze. I dropped the knife and celery to the cutting board, tiptoed to the kitchen entrance, and listened. More thumping noises then angry footfalls that got louder . . . and then stopped.

I sucked in a breath and darted back behind the bar counter. Jarret must not have seen the little path I'd left between suitcases. Was he coming down here to give me a piece of his mind? Maybe I could offer him lunch and he'd let it go. I'd made enough egg salad to feed a family of eight—my usual quantity—but Mr. West had gone out this morning, so I only needed to feed three: the Digbys and myself.

Working quickly now, I chopped a few more celery sticks, arranged them with carrot sticks and green pepper slices on a ceramic tray, and scampered with the veggie tray to the dining room. I'd already brought out plates and napkins and a bowl of green grapes. Would the Digbys like potato chips with their sandwiches? We always did.

As I passed the entrance to the kitchen, I glanced into the hall. Still no sign of Jarret. Maybe he'd gone to his bedroom. Judging by the state of his clothes—all sweaty and wrinkled—and the circles under his eyes, I'd say he drove all the way from Arizona, where Roland said he'd been attending college. So he must've been tired. Maybe he even appreciated that I'd carried his luggage upstairs for him . . . instead of being angry that he'd tripped over them.

I stacked dirty dishes in the sink, wiped off the kitchen countertop, put refrigerated items away, and washed my hands. Had I done it on purpose? Piling everything where I knew he had to walk, wanting Jarret to trip on them? Maybe in retaliation for his inconsiderate decision to leave it all in the middle of the hallway?

Thinking it over, I left the kitchen and tiptoed past the stairwell on my way to get Nanny for lunch. The upstairs remained dark and silent. I picked up my pace, walking silently in my socks on the polished hardwood floor. I scurried toward the foyer, rounded the corner, and then stopped. Did I hear something . . . footsteps maybe, in the hallway I'd just left?

Not ready to see Jarret so soon, I practically jogged down the front hallway to the Digbys' suite.

Fifteen minutes later, after helping Nanny into her wheelchair, I set out to bring Nanny to the dining room. As we neared the foyer, I braced myself for a Jarret encounter, but we rounded the corner to an empty hallway. A moment later, I pushed her past the stairwell, my gaze sliding upstairs but catching only shadows. Jarret might still be resting after the long drive, but then again, he could've come down and might've been looking for me. Would he yell at me in front of Nanny? Nah. He probably didn't think twice about the incident with the suitcases. He wasn't a moody teen anymore. Accidents happened, right?

My mind filled with past experiences I'd witnessed in high school, Jarret angry over this or that, yelling at his brothers or friends. He had a temper for sure.

"Mr. Digby will likely join us." Nanny pushed a few short gray curls into place and smoothed her flowered top, as if wanting to look nice for her husband. "We can sit at the little table in the kitchen area. We'd love for you to join us."

"Oh, I set everything up in the dining room, but I can move it." I probably should've asked first. Of course they'd have their own routines. And I'd likely make a lot of little mistakes over the next few days. Maybe my entire time here. As long as I didn't break anything . . .

"No, don't bother. We'll enjoy eating in the dining room. We typically eat there only when Mr. West is home."

I made a mental note: dining room only when Mr. West was home. But how would I know when he planned to be home? I doubted he'd update me with his schedule. "Will Mr. West be here for dinner?"

"He'll be here tomorrow." She continued speaking, saying something about me not worrying about making dinner unless Mr. West was home because she'd made a few meals in advance of the surgery and frozen them.

But my mind turned over other questions. Did Mr. West know Jarret had come home? What would he think about it? Would I still have a job? Jarret wouldn't likely be willing to help with cooking and cleaning, but he might help Nanny into her chair and hang out while she practiced walking a little each day. Maybe they wouldn't need me now.

I guided Nanny's wheelchair to a place at the long dinner table, having moved a chair out of the way earlier. Mr. Digby soon joined us, somehow sneaking into the room while I had my back turned. After seeing what kind of bread each wanted, I made three sandwiches and dumped lightly salted potato chips into a big bowl. We said grace together and ate with a bit of small talk between bites.

When almost done with my sandwich, a second crashing noise came from upstairs, but no one else seemed to notice. Then more sounds. A thump, then another thump, three . . . four . . . Jarret must've been tossing the luggage into his bedroom. Finally. After maybe tripping over them twice, once after his shower and then now. *Oh dear.*

I tensed at the sound of footsteps. Someone padding down the stairs. Then nothing. After holding my breath for a long moment, and no angry Jarret showing up, I continued eating.

When I finished my plate of food, I realized that the Digbys still had half of their lunches to go, so I excused myself and went to wash the dishes I'd piled in the sink. I held my hands under the warm water as bubbles multiplied in the sink and a citrusy scent surrounded me. As a child I had often lost myself in the rainbow swirls on dish soap bubbles.

As the biggest bubble in the sink popped, a male voice spoke over my shoulder. "There you are."

I shuddered, the skin on the back of my neck crawling, and whisked around to face the peculiar Mr. Digby—no, not Mr. Digby.

Jarret West stood two feet away, peering down at me through fiery brown eyes. Long damp curls made wet spots on the shoulders of his sea-blue trim-fit t-shirt. "You moved my luggage."

"I know," I said with an attitude, folding my arms across my chest, my hands all soapy and wet— making the undersides of my arms all soapy and wet. My cheeks burned as I looked up at him, wishing he'd back up a few inches at least. I should probably apologize, but I hadn't meant for him to stumble over the things . . . unless maybe subconsciously.

"I told you to leave it," he barked as if reprimanding a dog. "I'd take care of it myself."

"You didn't tell me you'd take care of it yourself." My defense fired out at a rapid speed. "If you had, I might've left them, but Mr. Digby wasn't around to help, and I had to get Nanny through."

"About that . . ." Finally backing away, he dropped car keys onto the counter and opened the fridge. "I just pulled my car into the garage and didn't see your car anywhere."

"I don't have a car."

Pushing milk and juice aside, he searched the top shelf. "Parents dropping you off and picking you up every day?" His casual tone said he expected that was the answer.

"No." I should've just told him, but I felt entirely uncooperative. He'd figure it out. Yes, I was living here. Like it or lump it, as Dad sometimes said, ever so annoyingly, but the saying had popped into my mind anyway.

He emerged from the fridge with a tall bottle of iced tea. "So who's giving you a ride?"

I couldn't help making a face as I shook my head, the kind I made when weary of Stacey's taunting games but when I didn't feel like arguing.

"What? I'm sure you're not walking." He twisted the lid off the iced tea, which was probably meant for everyone, and took a swig directly from the bottle. As he lowered the bottle, understanding dawned in his eyes. "You're not staying here."

"Bravo. You figured it out. Nanny needs help and wants someone available, so I'm staying here."

He wiped his mouth on his sinewy arm. "For how long?"

"She just had double hip replacement surgery."

"Yeah, I know. So how long?"

"The summer."

All emotion and a bit of color drained from Jarret's face. Moving in slow motion, he set the bottle on the countertop and turned away. Then back. "So you're just helping Nanny? Like helping her get around or . . ." His dark brows twitched.

"Yes." Feeling a smidgen of pity due to the anguish this seemed to cause him, I decided to give more of an answer. He obviously had his own plans for how this summer would go and my presence in the house must've thrown a wrench in it, so he'd have to get used to me being here, just as I'd have to get used to him being here. "I'm also helping with chores and meals whenever she wants me to make something, like when your father is home."

"Oh-h-h-h, Papa," he moaned, his eyes opening wide. "This is never gonna work out. Why can't you just stay at your house? It's not that far. Have someone drop you off for a few hours a day." He swung his hand about as he continued expounding upon how he thought things should go. Shaking his head. Some frantic look in his eyes. And then a little brown tag peeked above the front collar of his shirt.

I didn't want to stare but . . . it almost looked like Our Lady's Brown Scapular? Same color brown, anyway. Couldn't be. I dismissed the idea with a shake of my head.

"Jarret, is that you?" Nanny's voice came from the dining room.

Mouth hanging open, he turned toward the dining room, visible through the doorway on the opposite side of the kitchen. "Yeah, Nanny, hey." Grabbing the bottle of iced tea, he gave me a final look before going to her.

Relieved for the interruption, I turned back to the sink-full of dishes. I continued working in the kitchen to the sound of Nanny's and Jarret's voices, and occasionally Mr. Digby's. Though I couldn't tell what anyone said, the conversation sounded pleasant enough and I didn't hear my name once. I couldn't imagine how Roland put up with him for all these years. He must've been much more tolerant than I felt willing to be. I was not going to put up with his attitude.

My thoughts shifted back to the brown tag. Could Jarret West wear the scapular? I'd have to email Roland to see what he thought. He wouldn't like that Jarret had come home. Did Jarret plan to stay for the entire summer?

CHAPTER 5

Jarret

Deciding to work my upper body after a restless night, I planted my feet on the floor and lay back on the workout bench. The strip lighting created a blue glow around the bars, handles, chains, and weights of my home gym equipment in the otherwise dark basement, and a pumped-up song from my old weightlifting playlist resonated through the open space. The familiar setting and cool air, and even the action of stretching out on the bench and reaching up for the barbell, brought some level of contentment to my agitated soul.

Conscious of keeping my shoulders back, I gripped the barbell and, inhaling, eased it to my chest. Exhaling, I pressed the weight back up. Inhale, down. Exhale, up. I had come down here later than I'd wanted, but tomorrow I would start on time. I needed some sort of routine for the summer, some sort of order for my life. Maybe I'd work out my upper body today, lower tomorrow, then go for a run the next day, and repeat, leaving Sunday for a day of rest.

Sunday . . . *Have you been fulfilling your Sunday obligation while away at college?* Nanny had asked yesterday. She was always looking out for me, wanting to encourage me in her own little way to stay on the right path. A smile forced itself onto my face on the next exhale, as I pressed the barbell up. I hadn't always appreciated her, but she'd been good to me, especially after Mama died when I was young. I was glad Nanny had someone to help her out over the summer while she healed.

After talking with Nanny and escorting her back to her suite yesterday, I'd made certain to avoid Caitlyn on my way back to my room. Once Papa came home—today, Nanny said— the less I crossed paths with the girl in the house, the better. He wasn't gonna like the arrangements but, oh well, he'd have to deal with it.

While struggling to complete my tenth press, my phone lit up, someone calling. Wouldn't be Rylee but maybe another friend on the field study. I wanted a three-minute break between sets and wouldn't mind knowing how it was going in Pompeii, so I secured the barbell, sat up, and reached for my phone.

Roland's name and number filled the screen. I huffed, a bit irritated, and decided not to answer it. Caitlyn had probably told him the situation.

I took a few swigs from my water bottle and wiped my hands on my shirt, wishing I'd remembered to grab hand towels. Before I could stretch out on the bench for a second set, another call lit up my phone. Roland again. Was he going to bug me all day? *Tough luck, little brother, I'm not answering. You'll have to get all the details from your girlfriend.*

I lay back and reached for the barbell. What *would* Roland think about this situation? Seemed he always wanted to give me the benefit of the doubt, but knowing his girlfriend and I would live under the same roof for the summer . . . with my history, that might be a bit of a problem even for him.

With my next set of ten bench presses, my mind wandered . . . to Caitlyn strolling down the hallway when I'd come home, looking like a vision, triggering a deep longing inside. I hadn't known it was her. Or I would not have felt that way. I'd somehow associated the ultra-feminine image with my own desire for a good woman, not someone shallow like too many girls I'd dated, girls who lacked the values I wanted to live, but someone I could grow with, one day build a family with.

Why did I always attract the wrong kind of girls? Was it the way I dressed? My muscles? My confidence level? Surely I didn't have to change any of that to find the right girl. Given my experiences so far, I struggled to believe I'd ever find the one.

The basement door squeaked open, and a growing beam of light pierced the semidarkness. Familiar footfalls sounded on the steps. Papa in his cowboy boots.

"Howdy, Jarret," Papa said when halfway down the steps. "Just got home. And as the garage door opened, it revealed quite the surprise."

"Yeah? Did I park over the line?" I said for fun. The roomy garage allowed for plenty of error.

"Didn't expect to see your red Chrysler this summer."

I set the barbell in place and sat up, cool air hitting my sweaty neck, making me wish again that I had a towel. "Yeah, me neither. I mean, I wasn't expecting to come home."

Papa stood at the foot of the steps, making a quick scan of the basement, dark everywhere except for the beam of light from upstairs and the blue lights around my equipment. "Field study canceled?"

"Nope. I backed out," I blurted, wishing I had my twin's diplomacy skills. Keefe's manner of answering would've satisfied Papa at once, but I almost couldn't help sounding confrontational.

Eyes squinting and head slightly tilted to one side, Papa stood silent for a moment, likely figuring the best way to deal with me. I had a history of messing things up for him on assignments and even at home. Now I was doing it again.

"Look," I said, wanting to cut short his judgmental thoughts, "I changed my mind about going this year. I'm just gonna wait till next time."

"Did you cancel in time to get a refund? That cost me a pretty penny, Jarret."

"Yeah, I know." *Crud.* I hadn't thought about that minor detail. He paid for everything concerning my education. Maybe I should've just gone. "I'll pay you back."

"It's not the money." Papa shook his head, probably worrying I'd change my major yet again and that I'd become a permanent college student. "You should be taking every opportunity available to you for field study."

"You know I've been on plenty of digs, so if it's a matter of gaining experience—" I took a swig of water to keep myself from blurting out every cocky thought that came to mind, but it was true. I had a lot of experience. Papa had taken us to archaeological excavation sites many times, growing up. Granted, I was a kid then and not a college student, so it wouldn't count toward my degree, and I'd never wanted to go—caused a lot of trouble and only cared about amusing myself. But we went once in high school too, to some dig site in Mississippi where we uncovered artifacts from Native Americans who probably lived there from 360 BC to 110 AD. Not that my heart had been in that dig either. "Look, it's not that big of a deal."

The blue light emphasizing crevices on Papa's otherwise dark face made clear his disapproval. "It is a big deal, for more reasons than you think. What are your plans now?"

Sensing the direction of our conversation, I snatched my phone and stood up. I'd have to finish my workout some other time. Papa and I had the potential for one or two more strained exchanges before this all fell apart. "Don't have any plans. Just gonna enjoy the summer." I moved toward him, only because he stood at the foot of the stairs, but the way I moved likely came across brash. To compensate, I decided to address his concern. "I didn't know you were gonna hire live-in help. A girl. Maybe you should've told me."

As I moved past Papa, he said, "Son, you'd better think about getting a summer job. And I've gotta see if our arrangement will hold."

"Why wouldn't it?" I stopped on the bottom step and looked at him. "Think Caitlyn's gonna leave because there's a boy in the house?"

"I assured her parents that you boys would be away. I like to keep my word. And besides, Caitlyn's not like other girls."

"Right." We both agreed on that. Caitlyn Summer was in her own category, a little nerdy, a little carefree, didn't dress like other girls with their tight tops and leggings, didn't talk like other girls with their gossip and games, didn't even date like other girls. Practiced something like courtship, whatever that looked like in our generation. But even if I were still a girl-crazy teen, flirting with every female that crossed my path, I would be no temptation to her whatsoever. Girls like her didn't like boys like me.

"She's not like other girls," I said, jogging up the stairs, "so you've got nothing to worry about, and neither do her parents." Once I reached the top, I turned to him.

Papa followed me up. "That's not exactly my point. I think we need to talk, Jarret." His gaze flickered toward the kitchen and back to me.

"Here's the deal," I said, my voice too loud and my self-control waning. I needed to end this conversation. "My favorite professor backed out, so I backed out too. I'll go another time. World's not gonna end tomorrow. And unless Vesuvius strikes again, Pompeii will still be there."

The earthquake, heatwaves, and billowing clouds from my dream flashed into my mind, making me cringe. Needing relief, I turned to dash off and nearly bumped into the redheaded girl living under our roof, coming from the kitchen with a basket of laundry.

"Oh, sorry," she said, sidestepping me, her green eyes stealing a glance.

I watched her walk away in her bare feet, some flowery pink-and-green skirt flouncing around her legs. How much had she heard? I wasn't quite up the steps when talking about her, was I?

CHAPTER 6

Caitlyn

The next day, having completed my chores—even from the Digby list, which I now challenged myself to complete—I strolled barefooted along the border of the wooded area of the Wests' property. With trees on one side and cool grass under my feet, I inhaled deep breaths of fresh woodsy air and appreciated everything nature had to offer—and also the meticulous work Mr. Digby did about the grounds: the edged driveway, weedless lawn and backyard, mulched trails, trimmed bushes and deadheaded flowers, and the impressively-sized vegetable garden. He also worked in the stables, which I had yet to visit. How did he accomplish so much all by himself?

The sound of a screen door swinging open drew my attention. Mr. Digby, with a bucket dangling from one hand and garden gloves in the other, emerged from a side door, the one off the laundry room and kitchen area. He took long strides toward the garden.

Not wanting him to see me lazily strolling, I dashed across the lawn toward the big circular driveway in front of the house and followed it to where the gravel driveway began. A canopy of leaves stretched over the long driveway, inviting me to walk further in the shade, but the gravel poked the soles of my feet with every step, so I plopped into the grass and nursed my wounds.

Before I could pick all the tiny rocks off one foot, my phone, tucked away in the pocket of my skirt, vibrated. Maybe Nanny needed me!

Excited for the opportunity to help, I pulled the phone out. But the screen showed Ling-si's name and number. *Oh! Why would she be calling?* She, Roland, and I all agreed not to call or text except on Sundays because I wanted to make this a sort of retreat. I'd been glued to my phone lately, texting about the silliest things and disappointed if someone didn't reply right away. I needed to return to a simpler life where my phone did not rule.

As her name and number pulsed for the fourth time, I answered the call. She wouldn't have called without good reason. "Hi, Ling-si. Is everything okay?"

"Hi, Caitlyn," Ling-si said in a cheerful voice. "I know we agreed not to call, b-u-u-u-t you didn't reply to my email."

The sound of her voice made me smile. I'd emailed her and Roland the other day, telling them about Jarret's arrival and asking Roland his opinion on the likelihood of Jarret wearing the Brown Scapular. Roland had emailed back almost immediately with a bunch of questions. *Why is Jarret there? How long is Jarret staying? If he's staying for the summer, are you still going to live there?* I hadn't emailed him back yet, but now I couldn't get Roland out of my mind. Maybe it was time to think about our decision.

"Sorry, Ling-si. I saw Roland's reply but not yours. When did you send it?" I stretched out both legs in the grass and arranged my old pink-and-green flowered skirt in a semicircle, noticing a threadbare section near my knees and dangling threads along the hem.

"Oh, well, I didn't actually email you back," Ling-si said, making me picture her with apologetic eyes and biting her bottom lip. "I helped with Roland's reply, though, and—since we aren't texting or calling—we were both waiting on pinecones for you to email back."

"Pinecones and not pins and needles?" I smiled, remembering the day we first met. Shortly after starting SDU, Roland and I went to a picnic held by a group of Catholic college kids, a meet-and-greet for new students interested in joining their off-campus club. Ling-si had stood off by herself, toeing a pinecone on the ground and playing with the end of her single black braid that hung over her shoulder, not seeming to know anyone.

Then she ducked under the cascading branches of a weeping willow tree and turned in a circle as if admiring the tree from that perspective. Curious as to what it looked like from that vantage point, I joined her. We both talked reluctant Roland into joining us, and we all became instant friends. She was reserved, like Roland, but with a fun sense of humor and curiosity that matched mine.

"Is Roland with you now?" I said into the phone.

"No, I'm at the dorm. I wanted to call you alone. I thought maybe . . . did you need to talk? I mean, with Roland's brother home, does that blow your summer retreat?"

I could almost see the kind little smile on her perfectly round face and the arch of her thin eyebrows over small, angled eyes that reflected her thoughtful and inquisitive mind. "I don't know. As long as my parents don't give me a hard time, I don't think it changes anything. It's not like we cross paths all day long."

"Okay, well, keep us posted on how things go. But . . . since I have you on the phone, I really need to ask you something."

"Oka-a-a-ay."

"I have to ask, maybe should've asked sooner, and you have to be completely honest."

"Oka-a-a-ay." I pulled my legs up to sit cross-legged and braced myself for her question. Ling-si was perceptive. She must've realized some of the reasons I needed a retreat.

"Do you regret the decision you and Roland made at the end of the schoolyear? That you and he were just meant to be friends?"

And there it was. The question that had been bouncing around my mind since the end of the schoolyear. Did I regret it? Had I made the right choice? Since the moment I met Roland in ninth grade, on the steps of Saint Michael's Church, I liked him, finding him mysterious and interesting and wishing he liked me back. Years later, he finally admitted he liked me too! We didn't start courting, exactly, not quite feeling ready for that, but we did spend more time together, always with friends, and the idea of a future courtship hung between us. But then what happened?

"I just need to hear you say it again, because he and I might start seeing each other, and I would never want to stand in the way—"

"No, Ling-si, you're not in the way of anything. I love Roland and feel really close to him, but somewhere along the line, he became like family to me, more like a brother than a potential boyfriend. And you're like my sister. It would make me so happy for the two of you to be together."

Ling-si once told me the story of how her parents came together. They'd met in China at a young age and fallen in love. Then her father's family had emigrated from China to the United States. Years later, when Federal policies eased immigration restrictions, her mother had come. They found each other in California, their love still strong, and married right away. *Nothing can break the invisible thread between two people who are meant to be together*, she'd said, quoting some ancient Chinese proverb.

"Okay, then I won't ask you again," she said. "And I'm so happy that you'd be happy for us to be happy together."

We giggled and talked for a few more minutes then I stuffed the phone away and strolled back toward the house, smiling. Over the months, I'd noticed something between Ling-si and Roland, something special that they didn't seem to notice. It truly made me happy to think of them together because of how much I loved them both. But it left me with questions: What was wrong with me? Was I even capable of developing romantic feelings for a guy? Was I too closed off? Ever since childhood, I'd dreamed of marriage and family, with many children running around the yard and happy chaos bursting from the seams of our home.

Was my career choice compatible with family life? Mom didn't think so. The year I spent earning money for college, she spent trying to talk me out of pursuing a degree in criminal justice and police science. But I really wanted to be a detective. Maybe I just needed time to find myself. Then I could worry about finding my husband.

I climbed the front porch steps and shuffled into the warm foyer, ready to start on dinner preparations. Mr. West still hadn't left for his trip, so Nanny wanted me to throw something together for dinner. He was probably worried about Jarret being here. Yesterday, I heard Jarret and Mr. West arguing out in the backyard, maybe even fighting. A big archery target got toppled over and a quiver of bows lay in the grass. Not wanting to be nosy, I'd moved on before anything more happened.

As I swung into the kitchen, footsteps pounded down the stairs across the hallway. Had to be Jarret. And I'd just told Ling-si that we didn't cross paths that often. Of course, Jarret didn't have to be headed this way. There was a whole house for him to haunt.

I went around the bar counter to wash my hands, but movement in my peripheral vision drew my gaze.

Jarret strutted through the doorway in black shorts and a yellow shirt with black palm trees, hands behind his head, fixing a ponytail maybe. Before I looked away, he gave me a funny look, yanked the hairband out of his hair, and shot it across the room—at me!

The hairband hit my shoulder and flopped onto the counter. Good aim, but how rude!

"Don't let Nanny see you like that." Moving toward me— or toward the bar counter, really—he spun his index finger, motioning toward his own long curls now resting on his broad shoulders.

I flicked the black elastic hairband to the end of the counter, but then . . . should I put my hair up? Probably. Kitchen help never wore their hair down on the job. Not wanting to use his dirty old hairband, I slid open the drawer that I recently discovered held odds and ends. Maybe I'd find a rubber band or a ribbon or a tie wrap . . .

He came around to the refrigerator. "Ain't nobody want to eat your hair," he muttered, searching through bottles on the top shelf.

"Oh yeah?" Not finding anything I could use, I slammed the drawer—too hard—then leaned against it and gave him a snarky look, but I couldn't think of a better answer. *Oh yeah* didn't really fit his comment. My brothers always gave those silly nonsense retorts back and forth, like, for hours. *Oh yeah? Make me. You make me. Dork. Am not. Are too. I know you are, but what am I?*

"Uh . . . really, yeah." Jarret leaned against the counter across from me, between the stove and refrigerator and tipped back a bottle of juice. "You ever pull a strand of someone else's hair out of your food?"

I stared at him for a moment, no snotty and appropriate answer coming to mind, my cheeks warming as he stared back through his cool brown eyes. Of course, I've pulled hair out of my food. Everyone has. Usually my own hair, though, so I decided not to answer.

"Need help?" His crooked smile and cocked brow showed his lack of sincerity.

He'd tidied up his facial hair since I'd seen him last, clean along the sides and just stubble on his chin and over his upper lip. A goatee, right?

Ugh. Why was I looking at his— "No, of course not." I snatched up his stupid hairband. Eyes locked on his as if I had something to prove, I slid the hairband onto my wrist, gathered my thick mane, and pulled the band off my wrist and onto the ponytail. Not wanting my ponytail to fall out right away, I twisted the band and tried stuffing my hair through again, but strands pulled and got loose and bunched up.

Jarret's lips parted as if he might say something—or laugh—then his eyelids fluttered, and he averted his gaze.

Oh dear. I couldn't imagine how horrible my hair looked, but I patted the ponytail and the hair barrettes I'd put in this morning, gave a satisfied nod, and turned to the sink.

"Nice," he whispered then took another swig of juice.

Scrubbing my hands vigorously under the faucet, I ignored the . . . compliment? Ridicule? Whatever. He was used to model-type girls who wore makeup and contemporary outfits and had perfect hair. It probably took his current girlfriend hours to get her look right, and I . . . really should work a little longer at my hair before leaving my room.

"Hey, you're not cleaning upstairs, are you?"

"Today?" I shut the faucet off and grabbed a towel. I'd finished my chore list for today. After dinner, I planned to relax. Maybe visit the horses.

"I mean any day."

"I'm sure it's on my list—"

"Well, don't. In fact, don't even go upstairs. Except maybe to clean the bathroom. Yeah, like Mondays and Thursdays, so I know when you're gonna be up there."

"Mondays and Thursdays, huh?" I huffed, amazed by his arrogance. Wasn't he the bossy one? Well, I wasn't going to let it bother me. If I got to his bathroom, fine, but—

The kitchen phone rang.

I glanced at it, but Jarret didn't. He still looked at me, as if waiting for an answer.

The phone rang again. I wanted to get it, but it wasn't my house. So I tipped my head in the direction of the phone.

"No one's calling me on that phone." Jarret strutted from the room, taking the bottle of juice with him.

Watching him go, my conscience niggled me. I really should've apologized about the luggage, but the phone kept ringing, so I snatched up the receiver and blurted, "Hello, um, West residence." I almost said, "Caitlyn speaking" but the caller shouted my name into the phone, sounding way too happy to hear my voice.

"Hi, Dad, why are you calling the Wests' landline?"

"Oh, your mother said you weren't using your cell phone, said I should call the house. So anyway, got a second? I'd like to talk to you about your new living situation."

CHAPTER 7

Jarret

Sometime after the Digbys, Papa, and Caitlyn ate dinner, I changed from shorts to comfortable jeans and my tall riding boots, and I tramped downstairs. The savory aroma of baked chicken still hung in the hallway outside the kitchen. Wonder what she made for sides? My stomach growled, complaining as if I hadn't eaten in days. I'd skipped dinner to avoid Papa's ongoing "advice" on how to spend my summer.

Dishes clanked in the kitchen, but I exercised self-restraint as I passed by, not even allowing myself the slightest peek.

Still. I could see her in my mind. Caitlyn reaching overhead to put glasses in the cupboard. Caitlyn running a washrag under the faucet, squeezing the excess water out, wiping countertops with the washrag in her wet hand . . . a messy ponytail with a few red curls hanging free. Green eyes . . . *icy* green eyes that would likely never warm up to me. She knew about too many of my mistakes.

I could only imagine the playful and sweet looks she had for Roland. Yeah . . . Roland. Roland's girlfriend. Why was I thinking about her at all? I was not some girl-crazy teen, and even if she were free, Roland's friends annoyed me. I forced myself to think of the Limburger cheese Peter had hidden in my car one summer. Maybe Caitlyn had even known about it, laughed about it, went along with it.

Lord, send me a nice girl, won't you? Even as I mentally prayed the words, I knew I wasn't worthy. I didn't deserve a girl who'd stuck to the right path. I'd take a reformed girl though, one who'd made mistakes but regretted them, changed her life the way I was trying to change mine. We'd understand each other, help each other. *How 'bout it, Lord?*

I cut through the veranda and stepped outside to a cool sixty-degree evening, not a cloud in the sky, nice evening for a long ride. Once inside the barn, the scent of fresh hay and horse all around, I grabbed a rubber curry comb from a hook on the wall where Mr. Digby kept all the grooming supplies. Bottles, sprays, and a neat stack of towels stood lined up neatly on a long shelf, various brushes and hoof picks hanging below it.

Desert whinnied then snorted, turning to see me over his stall. He must've recognized my gait as I'd clomped into the barn. "Hey, ya, Desert. Ready for a brushing and a ride?"

I led him from his stall, tied him in the grooming area, and brushed him down while murmuring a few sweet nothings, using circular motions on his creamy buckskin hair, as Papa had taught me. When done, I'd saddle him up the way I'd been taught too. Never even thought if there was a different way, a better way to do the things I'd grown up doing.

Halfway through the grooming, Desert leaning into me and practically purring, really enjoying it, someone clomped toward the barn, footfalls just audible over the soft brushing sounds. I cringed inside. Papa had found me.

"Howdy, Jarret. Missed you at dinner." Papa lifted his cowboy hat and ran a hand through his graying hair. He wore a vest over his gray-and-blue plaid shirt. The one he often wore riding.

I took a breath before answering and quickened my work, moving the comb easy on Desert's hips. "Yeah, I'll eat later."

"Mind if I ride with you?"

I clamped my jaw to keep the honest but somewhat snide retort from flying off the tip of my tongue. Then I took another breath, working on an answer that Papa's ears would find less offensive.

Without waiting for my answer, Papa opened a stall and led his Pure Spanish Horse—which we always called the Spaniard or Spanish—to the grooming area, bringing it alongside Desert. The Spaniard stood a hand shorter but had a more compact, muscular body. The two horses greeted each other with sniffs and snorts while Papa grabbed another curry comb. "We should talk."

"Actually, I was wanting to ride alone," I replied, eyes on my work and not him. I pounded the curry comb against the heel of my boot to clean it, hung it on the wall, and grabbed the hard brush for a few areas of Desert's coat that needed more attention.

Apparently not concerned with what I wanted, Papa continued brushing his horse and finished the job just before I did. We both grabbed saddle pads and saddles, him securing his to the Spaniard a moment before I secured mine. He untied both horses, handed me a lead. Then I shoved my boot into the stirrup, and to my annoyance we mounted in sync.

We rode from the stables to the shady path that led to the back of the property. I admired many things about my old man, and I liked what he did for a living—the freelance archaeology assignments that took him all over the country and even overseas—but I didn't want to become him. I didn't want to simply follow in his footsteps. I wanted to take my own path.

I wished I could pour out my confused thoughts to Keefe. No one could listen, no one could offer advice that made sense to me like he could. But I knew what Keefe would say now. *Seek the path God has for you instead of finding your own path. God knows what'll make you happy.* But what exactly did that look like? God's path for me was not the same as God's path for Keefe, or anyone else on the planet.

I'd prayed, asked God for direction now and then. Okay, less often lately, but my studies and the business of life . . . Eh, those were excuses. It didn't take any time at all to simply lift my gaze to God. I'd just been too focused on other things, how I wanted things to go. Same old temptation to have things my way.

"So, Jarret . . ." Papa rode Western style, one hand on the reins, eyes on me. "Tell me about this professor you like so much."

Well, this was a new strategy. Instead of telling me over and over what I should be doing, he wanted to know about Professor Z. I gathered my thoughts for a moment, not sure where to start, then realized he and Papa had a lot in common. "You'd like him. Loves what he does. An expert in archaeology. Geology too, seems like. And his enthusiasm rubs off. I'm sure we're all better students, more eager to learn, because of him."

As the horses trotted along, I told a few stories about Professor Z to better explain. Papa nodded and chuckled now and then as he listened. Then he shared stories from his college years and field study experiences. He briefly mentioned Pompeii, but then we both fell silent.

He wished I would've gone. I wished I *could've* gone.

We neared the neighbor's farmland, where rows of winter rye stretched out, the wispy flaxen ears swaying in a breeze, almost ready for the late May harvesting. The neighbors would get something else in the ground next, soybean maybe.

The trail curved around and the horses galloped for a bit, then we slowed them down to walk for the last ten minutes.

Papa looked my way before speaking again. "You stopping at a bachelor's or in for the long-haul? You'd have a lot more options with a couple more years."

"Not sure." If I wanted something other than museum work or some boring cultural management job, I'd need a master's or doctorate. Could I stick with college for that long? I'd already been going for too long and had only three years toward my degree to show for it. What kind of work would I get afterward? Even with the degree, I'd never get the interesting freelance jobs Papa got, unless maybe I worked with Papa for a while and people got to know me. These were the things I wanted to sort through this summer.

We dismounted outside the stable, and Papa filled two buckets with water from the spigot. "Let's get these beasts some of Adam's Ale," he said, his goofy way of referring to water.

While unbridling the Spaniard, Papa said, "I'm fixin' to go on assignment, and I want you to come with me."

Bristling inside, I hefted my saddle onto the saddle rack and grabbed a sweat scraper. The conversation had started nice, but I'd expected it to take this turn: Papa telling me what to do.

"Granted, it's not archaeology work, no field study." Papa rubbed the Spanish down, glancing at me sideways. "We'll be doing a bit of geological prospecting instead."

I held a towel under water from the spigot then wrung it out, ready to wipe down Desert. From Papa's past assignments, I knew some of what geological prospecting entailed. Studying rocks, looking for specific minerals, trying to find the best place to mine for something. Could be interesting, but not this time around. "No thanks. Look, in one year I'll have my bachelor's degree so, unless I go for more, this might be my last free summer. Why can't I just enjoy it?"

Papa stopped grooming his horse and squinted at me, disapproval surfacing in his piercing blue eyes. "If you're dead set on sticking around, at least get a job. No reason for you to be a coffee boiler, bumming around the house all day. You're a grown man. And grown men work."

"Eh, I'll think about it." I finished wiping Desert quickly now, ready to light a shuck back to the house, as Papa sometimes said. He'd likely start using a few more cowboy phrases if he got even more agitated. Desert sensed my hurry and flicked his tail a few times, turning his head toward then away from me.

Papa had resumed wiping down the Spaniard but then whipped the rag with excessive force in the general direction of the stable laundry basket. "You'll think about it? You expectin' me to leave while you're still here—"

"You wouldn't care if we didn't have a girl in the house." I led Desert back to his stall, promising myself to bring a carrot out to him later.

"Sure I would. I mean, the girl adds to my concern, especially since I've given my word to her parents, but honestly, Jarret, I'd like to see you working hard to get the things you want. Too many today just lying around taking their ease, letting everyone else provide for them. A man needs hard work and perseverance to feel good about himself."

I strode to the barn door, his words sticking in my craw. Or maybe pricking my conscience. Sure, I'd been a bit lazy, bossy, and self-serving growing up. But that wasn't me now. Was it?

"What are you made of, Jarret?"

His question broke my stride for one moment, but I had no answer, so I kicked it back into gear, eyes on the veranda and no intention of stopping again.

"I'd like to see you stay in the saddle," he hollered after me.

CHAPTER 8

Caitlyn

With a pail of cleaning supplies in one hand and a broom in the other, I left the sundrenched laundry room with one more chore for the day: clean the upstairs bathroom. Once complete, I'd have the day to myself—until dinner time. Passing through the kitchen, I thought of the ice cream bars I'd discovered in the freezer, and I stopped for a snack.

I'd fallen into a wonderful routine. Every morning I woke with the songbirds, said hello to Jesus, and got ready for the day. I made breakfast-for-one and took it either to the front porch or the veranda to enjoy with a view of the property. It always put me in such a wonderful mood. After cleaning my little mess in the kitchen and throwing in a load of laundry on certain days, I helped Nanny with physical therapy and little errands. Before and after making lunch, I had plenty of time to complete Mr. Digby's chore list—minus the upstairs bedrooms.

The thorough cleaning allowed me to discover new things in the West house. Today I enjoyed dusting artifact display cases on the side of the family room closest to the veranda. Each artifact had a little tag with the discovery date, location, and brief description. A journal, also in the case, likely gave more details about the items and their history. I'd been curious, but a note on my list said not to open display cases.

I also got to dust family pictures hanging on the wall and arranged between decorations on a long console table, pictures from before Mrs. West died. Some pictures had been taken in this house or on their property, while others may have been taken on Mr. West's trips. A tent in the background of one, camper trailer in another. Roland once told me they used to all go with their father on assignments.

Roland was always easy to identify in the pictures, being the youngest of the three boys and the palest of the lot, but the twins . . . I tried guessing which one was Jarret and which Keefe based on their postures and expressions, assuming Keefe to be the more laid-back one.

I gazed at little Keefe in one of the pictures. He and I had courted for a time but, oddly, it felt like a chapter in someone else's life. I remembered it not as a courtship so much as a brief and special friendship where I came to learn from his example what it meant to follow God regardless of the challenges. Where was God calling me?

With my imagination wandering, I'd cleaned that side of the family room thoroughly, dusting, polishing, sweeping, and washing every nook and cranny. I'd also cleaned and organized a few kitchen cabinets, appreciating the quality pots and pans and casserole dishes, getting more ideas for meals I'd like to make—for as long as I continued to live here. However long that might be . . .

Dad's phone call last night popped into my head.

"I'm not sure how I feel about you staying over there now that Jarret's home."

"There's nothing to worry about," I tried to assure him, *though he certainly understood that at my age I would make*

my own choices. *"I barely see him in the house. And it's Jarret, so . . ."*

"Yeah, so he's the one who got your best friend pregnant."

"Dad! You have nothing to worry about, even if he were my type. Which he's not."

After stuffing the last bit of ice cream bar into my mouth, I threw the wrapper and stick away, grabbed the pail and broom, and set off to finish the final chore. What would I do later today?

I crossed the hall and climbed the steps. As I reached the top, Jarret's bedroom door flew open, and he burst into the hallway.

My heart shot to my throat.

Not wanting shock to propel me down the stairs, I zipped out of the way and slammed into the wall across from his bedroom. The pail of cleaning supplies bounced against the wall, and my fingers slipped off the plastic handgrip on the little metal handle. The pail landed on its side, cleaners, gloves, and rags half dumping out.

Jarret jumped back, as if equally startled, and glanced from me to the mess on the floor, his jaw twitching. "What are you doing up here? I told you—"

"It's Thursday." I pointed to the half-open bathroom door.

He shifted a glance toward the bathroom as if not sure what I meant, as if not remembering the cleaning schedule he'd given me himself.

Then I remembered his other bossy command, and I grabbed a hairband from my apron pocket, leaned the broom against the wall, and gathered my frizzy mane to make a ponytail. Over the past couple days, rather than let his bossiness bother me, I'd decided to make a game of it, putting my hair up every time we crossed paths, sometimes looking both ways and saying, "Oh my, oh my, I hope Nanny doesn't catch me with my hair down."

Before I could get the words out this time, he let out a breathy chuckle and a smile played on his lips. "You keep doing that. Doesn't matter when you're not in the kitchen. You can shed all the hair you want up here."

"Well, just in case." My hair wouldn't go nicely into the band, making me struggle with it for too long, all under his amused gaze.

As a grin started to stretch across his face, he turned away, maybe to conceal a laugh, then he dropped down on one knee before me.

My breath caught, and I almost lost the final lock I was working through the hairband. Then I realized what he was doing.

He righted the pail and shoved the cleaners back into it then stood up and offered it to me.

Stunned, I was barely able to whisper, "Oh, thanks," as the handle of the pail transferred from his hand to mine.

His hair pulled neatly into a ponytail reminded me that I still had one of his hairbands, the one he'd shot at me the other day, so I grabbed it from my apron pocket. "And thanks for letting me borrow this." Not wanting to end on a completely civil note, for reasons I couldn't quite place, I added, "Hope I didn't leave any hairs in it."

He accepted it in his open palm and stuffed it into the front pocket of his jeans. "Don't worry, I'll treasure them." As soon as the comment came out, he was shaking his head. Then he sucked in a breath, turned, and galloped down the stairs. He disappeared down the hallway but then swung back, one hand to the wall. "Hey, I could use some towels in the basement, by my weights." Without waiting for my reply, he took off.

Well, that was weird. Not sure what to make of the encounter, I grabbed the broom from where I'd leaned it against the wall and darted into the bathroom. I stopped just inside the door, looking over the mess. Towels and clothes on the floor, half open drawers and cabinets, an empty toilet paper roll, hair products and a full roll of toilet paper on the vanity.

"Oh wait."

I gasped, not expecting to hear Jarret's low voice again, and the pail slipped from my grip as I turned toward him.

He set the pail on the vanity, having somehow grabbed the handle as he came up behind me, maybe knowing I'd drop it. He pushed further into the bathroom, scooped up the towel and clothes, shoved hair products into a drawer, threw me a glance, and then left.

Heart racing a bit, I closed and locked the door. Awash with relief, I leaned back against the door and a laugh escaped me. He probably left the big mess for Nanny but didn't want me to see his personal things.

Half an hour later, after cleaning the bathroom from top to bottom, including organizing the drawers—which Jarret would probably frown upon—it was time to do some exploring. With the pail in one hand and the broom in the other, I stepped into the quiet hallway and my gaze snapped to a door that I hadn't paid attention to before.

It stood at the end of the hallway, taller and thicker than the bedroom doors, with vertical wooden planks instead of a single sheet of wood, swirly black metal decorations near the top and bottom, and a big sliding lock near the handle. What did it open to? Maybe a closet but . . . who needed a cast iron slide bolt on a closet? I set the pail and broom down again, tucking them away in a corner at the top of the stairs, and I turned to the door.

CHAPTER 9

Jarret

Smooth red locks hung loosely around a pretty face, half hiding one eye and wrapping around an alluring smile. I stood mesmerized by the girl on the hair color box. Most of the reds I knew had fiery personalities, so I'd developed a sort of stereotype in my mind. And I avoided dating redheads.

Did Caitlyn fit the stereotype? Maybe it felt so weird between us—kind of tense and awkward—because we'd known each other but never been friends . . . or even friendly. She'd tolerated me once, as her best friend's boyfriend, but I'd always sensed her disapproval. She wouldn't know that I'd changed. How could she? I dressed the same, wore my hair the same . . . a little older and a bit more facial hair, maybe, but to any outside observer, I was the same old Jarret. And she'd caught me arguing with Papa a few times at home, heard my sarcastic remarks. And I could still come across as a bit bossy. Maybe I shouldn't have told her to clean my bathroom.

What did I care what she thought about me? I shook myself from my dazed state and continued down the aisle. I wasn't here for hair color. I needed shampoo.

Our last encounter . . . Couldn't believe I actually said, *Shed all the hair you want up here.* What the heck did that even mean? I pictured a golden retriever blowing its coat. And what about the flirty comment I'd made when she'd given my hairband back. I'd treasure the strands of her hair I found in it? For real, man. Like I was some dwarf and she Galadriel in *The Lord of the Rings.*

I huffed and shook my head then focused on the shampoo before me. She'd blushed when I said it. She'd blushed when I picked up the cleaners and pail. Her in that little white apron over a pale blue dress with peach flowers. Did she think I was coming on to her? Was I flirting?

My mind just turned all silly around her, the result of that tense and awkward thing between us, maybe related to her being Peter's friend. Peter, my archenemy, if I ever had one.

After scanning too many shampoo choices, I found something that had worked for me before and added it to the merchandise in my arms: vitamins, energy bars, air freshener for my car, batteries for gaming remotes, lip balm, vitamin drink, and other impulse items. Should've grabbed a basket.

"Hey, Jarret!" some guy called as I neared the checkout.

I dumped everything onto the counter and drew out my charge card before turning to see who'd called me.

My one-time best friend Kyle—a redhead with short, tousled hair—came up to me with a big grin and wanting a fist bump. He wore a t-shirt with a faded saying that I didn't bother reading, flip flops, and rumpled cargo shorts. "Haven't seen you in forever, not since you abandoned us for Arizona. You home for the summer?"

We bumped fists then did a quick handshake-to-hug.

"Yeah, taking the summer off." I grabbed my bag and stuffed my wallet in my back pocket then headed for the door.

"You've been going ever since high school? Working on your master's degree or what?"

"Something like that." I felt no urge to explain how often I switched my majors. On the way through the drugstore lobby, I glimpsed another "Now Hiring" poster. While not intentionally looking for them, I'd noticed three others on my little trip to the store, two at fast food restaurants and one for a factory—not jobs I'd take anyway.

"That's great for you, but I just can't see myself sitting in a classroom so soon after high school." Kyle walked with me, emptyhanded, to the parking lot.

"So what'cha been up to?" I said.

"Let's talk Friday night. All the guys are meeting up at Guy's Place, some girls too. You oughta come up there, tell us all about your conquests at college." Grinning, he bounced his reddish eyebrows.

"Nah, I'm busy." I neared my red Chrysler, thinking about some of the stupid things we used to do together. Skipping classes to smoke outside. Wandering the streets till two in the morning. Pranking kids we didn't like. I hated being pranked, but I hadn't minded pranking others. Once I'd decided to turn my life around, I'd stopped hanging out with Kyle and a few other friends to avoid the temptations. I didn't want to be that person again.

"Come on, man, you gotta. Unless you want to invite us over. Haven't been to your place in forever." Some look flickered in his eyes, a good memory or a bad one? "We really ought to catch up."

"Yeah, maybe." We'd had some good times too. Eating out, playing sports, wandering around parks. It hadn't all been stupid. And it would give me something to do, some reason to get out of the house—other than to go to a menial job. Maybe I should hang out with my old friends this summer, have some cookouts or something, didn't always have to meet at a bar. "What time?"

"Probably get there around seven or eight, give or take."

As I opened my car door, my cell phone buzzed, so I pulled it from my pocket and made like I'd been waiting for a call.

Taking the hint, Kyle lifted a hand for a lazy wave, said, "Can't wait to catch up," and returned to the drugstore.

After tossing my bags into the passenger seat, I answered the call, realizing too late that it was from Rylee. "Hey, what's up?" I put the call on speakerphone and pulled onto the road.

"Hi, Jarret." Her voice held a note of sadness. Then she sighed into the phone. "I can't stop thinking about you. I don't know what led to your breaking up with me, but if you want to talk about it . . ."

"I don't know." Hearing her voice gave me mixed emotions, but she didn't sound angry. "Sorry I broke up with you the way I did. Shouldn't have done it like that, at the airport and all. I just don't think we're meant for each other."

"Oh . . . well, I'd still like to talk about it. And I hope we can remain friends, maybe catch up in the fall, you know, when school starts back up."

I took a deep breath and exhaled hard. We could be friends, but . . . she wanted a closeness that I no longer wanted with anyone . . . except my future wife.

"Are you still there?"

I pulled onto Forest Road. "Yeah, I'm here. How's Pompeii?"

"Oh, you'd love it. It's incredible." She went on to explain the field study work and lectures and lodging, then the sights and the night life.

A wee ache of jealousy formed in my chest. Couldn't I have gone anyway and just kept the relationship platonic? How weak was I?

As I ended the call, I passed the Brandts' house and bed-and-breakfast, the Forest Gateway B&B, a sneer coming to my face. Was Peter home for the summer too? Roland had mentioned something about him going to some institute of technology for electrical engineering. Hope Caitlyn never decided to invite Peter over.

To avoid spoiling my mood, I stopped thinking about Peter the moment I turned off Forest Road and onto our gravel driveway. I took it slow, not wanting to kick up rocks and ruin the finish on my car, and I appreciated the woods on either side of me, the canopy overhead as it shifted in the wind, and our big house as it eased into view.

Movement and something out of place on the roof drew my eye to the battlements.

I leaned for a better look, driving ever closer. Realizing what I saw, my heart skipped a beat, and I stepped on the brakes and stared. Caitlyn stood gazing over the battlements, facing the stables, not seeing me watching her.

The wind played with her hair, tossing long red locks with abandon, and ruffled the sleeves of her pale blue dress with the peach flowers. Tilting her head to the sky, maybe even closing her eyes, she seemed to be in another world . . . seemed to *come from* another world. A fantasy world with romance and adventure and goodness. Caitlyn, some princess in a fairy tale. Caitlyn, the maid of West Castle.

The sight made my soul ache for someone pure and good. Not her, of course. I needed to stop thinking about her, put some kind of wall up. She was Roland's girlfriend. And Peter's friend. And we didn't get along in the least. And the biggest obstacle of all: girls like her didn't like boys like me.

Caitlyn

A warm breeze tousled my dress and hair and carried fresh nature scents, green things, growing things, flowering things, and—eww. I wrinkled my nose. Hay and manure. Running my fingertips along the rugged tops of waist-high stone battlements, I paced to the opposite side of the roof and stood in the shadow of a turret. I peered out over the garden and the side lawn and the trees bordering it. Thick clouds crept across the blue sky, though it wouldn't likely rain today.

This new perspective transported me to the realm of possibilities. Would I marry one day and have a brood of children, as I'd always hoped? Would I marry young or later in life, like maybe after a few years of detective work? Was I called to something else, like a vocation to the religious life? I could work as a missionary in some other country—or here, for that matter. I could bring joy to the homebound or imprisoned or sick. I could work with children, orphans maybe, possibly fulfilling my desire to nurture little souls in a way I hadn't previously considered.

I closed my eyes and leaned my head back, almost sensing the Holy Spirit on the breeze, beckoning me to trust in His plans for my life. Then I opened my eyes and saw Mr. Digby down by the garden, looking up at me.

I had to force myself not to jerk back and hide. He'd already seen me. I waved instead, offering a smile. I wanted to like him but really didn't understand the man. He never smiled, seemed to expect a lot from me, and had the uncanny ability to suddenly appear when least expected.

Squinting up at me, Mr. Digby tapped his wristwatch and said something that the wind carried away.

I was about to shout back, "What?" when it occurred to me. I should be starting dinner right about now. After nodding to show I understood, I headed back to the steps that led down to the second-floor door.

Maybe I could visit the roof again for lunch sometime or watch the sunset in the evening. No one would care, would they? Mr. West had told me to make myself at home. *If a door's unlocked, you're free to open it.* Of course, this door had been locked—with a strange, medieval-looking black iron sliding contraption. But it was an outside door, and all the outside doors were locked, so they didn't count. Right?

I opened the door with caution and a bit of apprehension, but sunlight fell on an empty hallway floor and the pail and broom I'd left in the corner. Closing the door behind me, I cut off the main source of light and had to wait a moment as my eyes adjusted. Then I slid the lock in place, gathered the pail and broom, and carried my refreshed and peaceful mood downstairs.

As I returned the cleaning supplies to the laundry room and glimpsed a stack of folded towels on the dryer, I remembered something else Jarret had asked me to do. So I grabbed two hand towels and headed for the basement.

Thinking over the steps I'd take to prepare dinner, I crossed the hallway and opened the basement door.

Just then, footfalls sounded in either direction. Clomping boots from the front of the house and a softer plodding from the back. A man came from either direction, Mr. West in his long-sleeved button-down shirt and cowboy hat and Jarret in jeans and a slim gray t-shirt.

A rush of apprehension or maybe foreboding washed over me, though I couldn't wrap my mind around the reason for it, so I continued down the stairs without acknowledging either one of them. I'd only descended a few steps when I heard voices.

"What's she doing?" Mr. West said.

"You're asking me?" Jarret replied.

"I told you not to boss her."

"I'm not."

"Looks like she's bringing hand towels down for you. Isn't that what I see?"

Their back and forth continued, voices elevating, as I padded down the final steps and placed the towels on a table next to Jarret's exercise equipment. I scanned the shadowy area with only the light above the stairs, looking for used hand towels but couldn't find any. Then I turned toward the steps and hesitated.

I didn't want to step out in the middle of their argument. They'd been arguing every time they crossed paths, but I felt responsible for this skirmish. If only I'd remembered to bring the towels down earlier . . . or forgotten until later.

I crept toward the stairs and placed a hand on the rail, the bickering continuing above me. The topic had gone from housework to Jarret getting a job. Maybe I could say something to make it better, like, that I didn't mind running towels down here. And Jarret hadn't really been bossing me much lately, not since he'd asked me to clean his bathroom.

Their voices quieted. Then footfalls moving away.

I hurried up the steps, eased the door the rest of the way open, and peeked each way.

"There you are, Miss Summer." Mr. West, by the little table in the kitchen, tipped his cowboy hat. "Just wanted to be clear. Nanny's your boss. No one else. So don't worry about anything upstairs or in the basement. Jarret can clean his own bathroom and bring towels or whatever to the basement."

"Oh, okay." I shut the basement door and shuffled into the kitchen. "I don't really mind—"

"No, no. You make time to enjoy yourself, ya' hear?"

I nodded, a tight smile on my face, and headed to the pantry to get what I needed for dinner. No more cleaning Jarret's bathroom. No more hand towels for the basement. I was to enjoy myself.

--*

A pattern developed over the next couple of days . . .

Between washing the dinner dishes and sweeping the dining room floor, my cell phone rang—Mom calling—so I took my phone outside, going through the exterior door in the laundry room. I stood on a sidewalk not too far from Mr. Digby's garden. Drops of water from the sprinkler glowed in angled sunbeams above the young plants. I'd seen a rabbit near the spinach the other day, but today a little fence surrounded the entire area. How high could a bunny jump?

After asking how things were going, Mom turned to the subject of my youngest sister, Stacey, again. "She's been skipping her chores and not coming home when she's supposed to. I don't even know where she goes."

"Mom, I'm sure it's nothing to worry about. I used to walk all over town when I was her age." I loved those days, hiking down paths in the woods behind Peter's house, traipsing off to the city center, sometimes meeting Zoe, other times meeting Peter or other friends. And then the day we'd discovered this place, the castle nestled in the woods . . .

"Yes, but I always knew where you were going. And you did more than your share of chores. You were more responsible."

"Not really, Mom. I mean, I tried to give you a general idea where I'd be, but sometimes my destination changed."

"Still, dear, you had good friends. I'm not so sure about Stacey's friends."

"You just knew my friends better, some of them, anyway. Other friends of mine got in a bit of trouble, if you remember, but I turned out all right. Didn't I?" I wanted to comfort Mom, but I did worry about Stacey. She had a bit of a rebellious streak, seemed a bit lost. Maybe this was just a phase she'd outgrow.

After Mom's call, I went back inside, picked up the broom and dustpan, and headed for the dining room to finish my last chore of the day.

At the far end of the table, back to the wall, Jarret sat hunched over a plate of the chili enchilada casserole I'd made. He glanced up and shook his head, no sign of friendliness at all. "You'll have to sweep later."

"Oh, well, can't I just sweep around you?"

"No," he said around a mouthful of casserole.

I stood dumbfounded. Okay, so he wasn't supposed to give me chores to do, but he sure shouldn't stand—or sit, in this case—in the way of me doing my work.

Still hunched over the food, he lifted his brown eyes to me. "Look, I'm not getting in trouble because you want to clean while I'm eating."

"Why would you get in trouble? I just want to sweep the floor."

"I dunno." He leaned back with his fork gripped in a fist. "Apparently, my father's real worried about me being in the same house as you, so if I'm in a room . . . stay out."

I wanted to argue with him, but then pity won out. This probably wasn't how he'd planned to spend the summer. He was supposed to have gone on some fieldtrip. But here he was. And here I was. And there wasn't much anyone could do about it.

"Okay, enjoy your dinner." I spun back to the kitchen. I'd skip the chore tonight and worry about it tomorrow.

--*

The next day, after lunch, I sat on my knees on the floor behind the pool table, studying the vacuum cleaner I'd found in a corner of the rec room. I liked how easily it moved across both floors and rugs, but I couldn't figure out how to remove the hose so I could use the attachments. *Oh there*—I found the right latch.

As soon as I secured the wand and crevice tool on the hose, someone stepped into the rec room, so I stood up.

Jarret, just inside the door, let out a breathy "Ah-h-h" and jerked back. Then he composed himself, shifting his weight to one leg in a casual stance, and glowered over the pool table at me. "What are you doing?"

I couldn't help but notice how puzzled he often seemed about ordinary things. I lifted the vacuum cleaner wand to give him a clue.

"You'll have to clean in here later." He snatched the triangular ball rack from the wall and tossed it onto the pool table then proceeded to retrieve balls from the pockets. "I need to unwind."

Unwind from what? I was tempted to ask. He sure hadn't gone out to get a job yet. Would he ever? I was starting to agree with his father.

"On second thought"—he continued drawing balls from pockets and rolling them toward the rack—"don't worry about this room. Nanny always made us clean it."

I looked at the crevice tool in my hand and back at him. Once I vacuumed the edges and nooks and crannies, I'd be done with the room anyway. Couldn't he give me five minutes? Deciding not to press the issue, I picked up the pail of cleaning supplies and returned the vacuum cleaner to the corner of the room. "Okay, fine," I said, flipping my hair as I passed him.

He ignored me, dropping balls into the rack with both hands, but as I stepped through the door he said, "Hey."

I paused and glanced at him over my shoulder. He wasn't about to boss me, was he?

"That Mexican casserole you made last night . . . it's really good."

"Oh, thanks." Shock stole my regular voice, allowing only a whisper to eke out.

––*

The next morning, happy to start a new day, I pranced from my room and down the long front hallway. I'd come to enjoy the quiet mornings. As I passed through the sunny foyer, I decided I'd carry my breakfast out to the front porch, maybe make French toast and sausage today. I slowed a bit as I traveled down the next hallway, stepping softly in my slipper socks past the stairwell and into the kitchen. Where I skidded to a stop.

What was he doing up so early?

Jarret sat at the bar counter in slate gray pants and a long-sleeved black t-shirt, a cup of coffee and a plate of scrambled eggs before him. He threw me a glum face over his shoulder then shook his head. "I won't be that long."

My stomach growled in response, and I think we both heard it. I had to say something to Mr. West to get him to lighten up on Jarret. Jarret's behavior was throwing a wrench in my routine. But then Mr. West would probably not lighten up until Jarret got a job. Any chance that's why he was up early today?

"So . . . what are you doing up so early?" I remained near the doorway, not pressing my luck by entering the room further.

He twisted around on the bar stool and looked me over before answering. "I always get up early." He continued staring, fork in hand, one eyebrow arched as if waiting for me to leave so he could finish eating.

Feeling a bit self-conscious from the once-over and simmering a bit because of his attitude, I pulled a hairband from my skirt pocket and gathered my hair. "Well, you're not usually down here so early."

The hint of a smile passed his lips. "I have things to do."

"Job hunting?" I dared to ask, still fumbling with my thick hair.

He huffed, smirked, and turned back to his plate of food. "I'll be back in five minutes. Is that enough time?"

"Maybe." He threw a smile over his shoulder.

I did not smile back.

--*

Later in the morning, following the Digby list, I carried dusting rags and dragged a vacuum cleaner down the hall, toward the family room so I could dust everything on the fireplace and suit of armor side of the room then vacuum under the couch cushions. Maybe I'd even get to the windows, a chore slated for tomorrow.

As I stepped through the double doors to the family room, I stopped.

The TV was on, showing some old Clint Eastwood Western. And Jarret was sitting on the couch, hugging a bowl of Doritos, a can of Coke next to his feet on the coffee table. He'd said he had things to do today . . . his reason for eating breakfast so early.

I rolled the vacuum cleaner behind the couch and stood there. Jarret didn't seem to notice. Should I just come back later, switch some of my tasks maybe? Who watches TV in the late morning?

Irritation rose inside like bubbles just before water boils. "Excuse me," I heard myself say.

"Oh, hey, not now, huh?"

"Look, I have a list of chores I'm supposed to do, and I don't have all day to do them." I shut my mouth before saying, *some of us work around here.*

"So do something else on your list." He shoved a Dorito into his mouth and laughed, maybe at something on the TV, but it was a Western so . . . not really funny.

I groaned nice and loud and flung the dust rags into the air.

Jarret slid his snack bowl onto the coffee table and got up, facing me. He stood with one hand on his hip and the other hanging at his side, the sleeves of his black t-shirt, pushed up past his elbows, revealing toned forearms.

Not wanting him to think I was checking him out, I averted my gaze.

"Just skip it. Nanny don't care if you clean every room, every day. But if Papa finds me and you in the same room"— he gave me a crooked grin and quirked a brow—"he'll knock me galley west."

"He'll do w-what?" Suddenly the bubbles of irritation turned into laughter. I wanted to cover my mouth but settled for holding my tummy as I practically guffawed. Galley west?

He smiled too then laughed with me, though in a more reserved manner.

I surrendered. I would worry about vacuuming couch cushions next week when it showed up on the list again. "Okay, I wouldn't want that to happen. I don't even know where galley west is. So you win." I picked up the dust rags, one from the back of the couch and two from the floor.

"Thanks, and hey"—he blinked a few times, his glance darting to and from me—"sorry I was a jerk the other day."

A bit stunned, I opened my mouth to reply, but what could I say to that? Was he seriously apologizing? A sarcastic comment came to mind. *Oh, really, which day are you sorry about?*

"About the luggage, when I first got home," he clarified before I could say anything. "Just threw me for a loop seeing you here."

"Oh, that's okay." Heat slid up my neck, the way it seemed to do whenever he spoke more than two words to me. Fanning myself with the rags, I rolled the vacuum cleaner back to the closet. Jarret apologized to me?

CHAPTER 10

Jarret

Dressed in a white linen Calvin Klein shirt, faded wash straight leg jeans, and white sneakers that I'd really paid too much for, I stepped into Guy's Place. The place brimmed with energy tonight, tables full and people milling around, loud hip-hop music competing with conversations. An eruption of laughter came from a group off to the right, a mix of guys and girls. Didn't recognize them.

The place was fairly dark, despite the variety of lighting. Industrial type fixtures with dark pipes and exposed lightbulbs hung from the high ceiling, string lights over the bar, and track lighting along the walls, highlighting the steam punk and Americana artwork.

"Over here, Jarret," a guy shouted from the long table nearest the dartboard.

I recognized half the dudes at the table as I strutted over: C.W., who'd called my name, Sherman and Ken from high school, and of course Kyle, who'd convinced me to come out tonight. Some of the excitement zipping through the air transferred to me, making me glad to see my old friends. New friends could never replace the ones made in high school. Regardless of the trouble we got into back then, they'd have a special place in my heart.

"Hey!" Kyle stood for a fist bump then introduced me to the ones I didn't recognize at the table, two guys and two girls, and to another girl standing nearby, none of them looking familiar.

Upon glancing a second time at the girl standing nearby, a blonde, I decided she almost looked familiar. Might've known her from high school. Maybe she'd colored her hair. She wore a white shirt and jeans, just as I did, and old me would've wanted to see if we clicked.

"Lemme buy you a beer." Kyle motioned for me to take a seat.

I pulled out my wallet to let him know I'd get my own drink and strode to the bar counter, where the bartender—an overweight dude in a patriotic t-shirt—turned from another customer he'd been talking to, ready to take my order.

"I'll take a Coke."

He grabbed a glass and scooped ice into it. "A rum and Coke?"

I shook my head. "Just a straight Coke." I had no intention of drinking tonight. Just wanted to catch up with the guys and have something to do other than make Papa suspicious at home. I took my drink to the table and sat between Kyle and an empty chair, although the coaster with the wet ring said I might've taken someone's seat.

"What'cha been up to, man?" C.W. reached across the table to bump fists and slap hands, the way we used to do in high school. He looked exactly the same, greasy blond hair parted down the middle and hanging in his face, a crazy-troublemaker gleam in his eyes.

We talked about college and jobs and Arizona, everyone around the table chiming in now and then. Kyle worked at a factory, C.W. did construction, Sherman worked part time and attended the community college, and Ken was between jobs. Then the conversation turned to trivial things with a lot of laughing and sarcasm, just what I needed right now.

"Let me get the next round," Sherman said. He stopped playing with his meticulously styled, blond-streaked short hair and motioned a waitress over.

Everyone ordered but me.

Kyle noticed, of course, and took a sip from my glass. "Thought you were drinking a rum and Coke. Just getting ready to see if you wanted to do a shot with me."

"No thanks, not for me."

"It's Friday night, man, and you're on summer break." A wild look crossed his face as he shouted, "Let's have some fun!" and lifted his empty beer mug overhead. Everyone lifted their drinks and cheered.

After a couple minutes of him needling me about not drinking, I grew weary and pushed my chair back. "Who wants to try to beat me at a game of darts?"

The girl whose seat I inadvertently took—the blonde—played the first game, C.W. the second game. I beat them both, to my satisfaction, and turned to see who else wanted a try.

"I'll play but only if we make a bet." Kyle sauntered over, a grin stretching across his freckled face, and draped an arm over my shoulders. "You win and I'll by you another Coke or some of Guy's killer jalapeno poppers. I win and you do a shot with me."

"You are persistent. I'll give you that." Since I beat Kyle at every game I ever played him, *and I mean ever*, I handed him a set of darts. "You can even throw first."

We bumped fists, and he stepped to the throwing line.

When his first throw landed dead center, I wondered if I should worry. Then his second throw hit the 18 in the triple ring. The third . . . no way. A 16 in the triple ring.

I should've gone first. Then I wouldn't have had this unease as I readied my dart for a throw. As my third dart landed, I stood dumbfounded. I lost. How'd Kyle get so good?

Kyle laughed and slapped my back. "Awesome, dude! You owe me a shot."

"Yeah, yeah. You won." One shot wouldn't kill me. I was a grown man and hadn't had anything to drink all night.

Not wasting a second, maybe not wanting me to back out, Kyle made a beeline for the bar and soon returned with a tray of shots that he offered to whomever wanted one. The girl whose seat I took—couldn't remember her name—grabbed one, along with Sherman and C.W. And Kyle personally placed one in my hand.

We all tipped our heads back together and whatever it was didn't taste half bad, barely burned as it shot down my throat. So maybe it had low alcohol content anyway.

Kyle and I played another game. I lost. We did another shot. I couldn't remember if we'd made the same bet, but the shots didn't seem to affect me. And Kyle, though he'd been drinking all night, proved he could walk a straight line and touch his nose with his eyes closed. Must've been weak shots, so I didn't mind doing another.

As the night wore on, I laughed like never before, played pool with my buddies, even danced with the girl whose seat I took.

"He's tricking you, you know," she said, leaning close while we danced to some stupid song with repetitive lyrics but a good beat.

Tricking me? Who is? Not sure what she meant, I shrugged and kept dancing, started thinking about some traditional Mexican dance I'd tried to do years ago . . . hands behind my back, stomp, stomp, turn.

She leaned in again, a look of warning in her eyes. "Every time you take a shot, Kyle's just drinking water. He's playing you."

Still thinking about the Mexican dance, I cracked up laughing.

Sometime later, slumped over a beer but not feeling like drinking, music still playing but bar half empty, Kyle's face appeared in front of me.

"Hey, we gotta get going. Want me to drive your car?"

"No one *dries* my car but me," I slurred, shoving my beer back, clinking it against empty mugs and shot glasses on the table, not wanting another sip. Shouldn't have drank so much. What was I thinking? Room spun as I went to get up. Shoot. How drunk was I?

"Sorry, Jarret, you're in no condition to drive." Kyle laughed and grabbed my arm, hefted me to my feet. "Up you go."

"Don' choo touch my car." Headlights turned this way and that in the dark parking lot. Cars pulled onto the street. The fresh air felt good. Carried a hint of cigarette smoke. I wanted to slap my face to make the numbness go away. Where was my car? I dug my keys from my pocket, but someone snatched them from me.

I opened my eyes to a rush of nausea and Kyle standing outside the car. My car? "Who drove my car?" I slurred loudly, vaguely aware that I'd been in a moving vehicle. I forced one foot out of the back seat and onto the driveway, then the other, grabbing the door to steady myself, and turned to see whose car it was. Not mine. Some lame hatchback.

"Chill, bud. Nobody drove your car. We took you home. See?" Kyle pointed to something.

Staggering forward a few paces, not sure toward what, I turned to see what he pointed to, but nausea forced me to my knees. Doubling over, I puked in the grass, not nauseous now, face still numb. "Where's my . . . ?"

"It's still at Guy's Place. You can get it in the morning."

"M'not leaving my car parked at some bar," I bellowed. "I love that car."

Kyle grabbed me roughly and hoisted me to my feet, escorted me toward the house, up the porch steps . . . "Sleep it off, Jarret. Worry about your car tomorrow. It'll still be there in the morning." He unlocked the door—with my keys? Opened it part way and slapped the keys into my hand. "You got it from here?"

While the world tilted over and over, I shoved the keys into my pocket and stepped inside. Get my car in the morning? I couldn't leave it sitting at some bar all night. All morning. What time was it? I thought about checking the time on my phone but didn't do it, just stood swaying in the middle of the foyer.

Then I felt someone watching me. My guardian angel? A twinge of remorse made me drop my head. *Sorry, angel dude. I let you down, huh? Don't give up on me.*

This wasn't me. So stupid. What was I thinking? I was stone-cold drunk.

Someone continued to watch me. Not my guardian angel. It was her, Caitlyn—Roland's girlfriend, standing in the dark front hallway, blending in with shadows. "Stop hiding an' step into the light," I slurred as I shuffled toward the wall opposite the open front door.

In eerie silence, Caitlyn moved forward, but then she took a breath, her exhale peaceful. Barefooted. Pale robe tied with a fuzzy belt. Hugging herself as if she were cold. Her unruly mane of curls hung freely over her shoulders, and moonlight fell on the contours of her face. She looked at me, her head tilted humbly, her eyes conveying . . . judgment? Condemnation? No, not a trace, just genuine concern and something else, something unique, some quality other girls didn't have. Not the ones I'd known.

"Are you all right?" she said, her voice soft.

I stared for a moment. What made her different? No dark red lips or thick black eyelashes. A little pimple or something on her chin. Did she ever wear makeup? I kind of liked that she didn't. Kind of liked that she didn't dress or fix her hair in the style of the day. But the difference that spoke to me . . . it was more than physical. She had this aura of joyfulness and generosity, a girl at peace with herself, even when irritated at me over hairbands or chores. It made her more than pretty. She was so . . .

"D—, you're beautiful."

Her mouth opened slightly in evident surprise, but then she giggled and pressed her lips together as if to suppress her smile. "You're drunk. Or you wouldn't think so."

"Oh yeah?"

"Yeah."

A moment passed, her looking at me, me looking at her. "I think it all the time, just never tell you. Can't help but notice . . . the older you get, the prettier you get." I lifted my hand to my mouth, to shut myself up, but my heavy arm fell back to my side and a wave of warmth wrapped around me. I'd said enough, maybe too much, to a girl who would likely be my sister-in-law in the near future. Needed to stop flirting.

Sadness . . . regret welled up, some icky feeling that made me feel alone, made me want to give up trying to be good. How easily I fell. *You're a fool, Jarret. That's all you'll ever be.* At the same time, I hungered for the joy and peace she possessed. *Don't give up, Jarret. Start over.*

How many do-overs did a person get? I took a deep breath. Needed to get to bed—oh, wait. Needed to rescue my car.

Everything continued to tilt around me, the open door, Caitlyn on my right, darkness on my left. But I was steady enough leaning against the wall, so I pulled out my phone to find myself a ride.

"Do you need help getting upstairs?"

"No, need'a get my car first." I tried downloading some uber app but got confused and went back to the browser to find a cab.

Meanwhile, she was talking, saying something about me not driving tonight. I shook my head but kept working on getting the ride. Next time I looked up, she was gone. She must've gotten frustrated and given up on me. I'd be okay once I stepped outside and took some deep breaths, maybe jogged around a bit.

. . . drowsiness weighed down my eyelids as I walked, my arm over someone's shoulders . . . Hair smelled nice, like orange blossoms and coconut. Caitlyn?

She mumbled instructions as we climbed the steps, then she turned on the faucet in my bathroom, made up my toothbrush, and gave me more instructions.

. . . a knock on the bathroom door pulled me from sleep. I sat on the floor, slumped against the vanity.

"Here, let me help you." Caitlyn slid her arm underneath mine and lifted.

"Where's my car?" I whispered, almost too tired to speak.

"We brought it home, remember?" She sat me on my bed and removed my white sneakers then reached for the buckle of my belt, actions she'd likely done for her little brothers countless times. "Sleeping with a belt on will give you acid reflux, my dad always told us."

Her motherly care reminded me of Mama and my heart ached, missing her. Why'd she have to die so young?

"Maybe I can find you some pjs." Caitlyn opened my dresser drawers. "You can change when I leave." After turning my blue-and-black striped bedspread down, she set a t-shirt and shorts next to me.

Her kindness . . . her care of me . . . "Don't leave." A harmony of loneliness, loss, and longing played in my heart, overwhelming me, pulling me under. And I found my arms wrapping around her waist and dragging her into my bed.

Caitlyn

As I landed roughly on Jarret's bed, I whispered harshly, "What are you doing?" in the tone I used with my younger siblings when they misbehaved on my watch. Did he seriously think his pathetic, drunken attempt would work? Attempt at what? Certainly not seduction. I laughed inside. Jarret, always so cool and coordinated, had flipped me onto the bed with such lame and awkward movements, then he clung to me the way my little brothers would cling to Mom's leg when they didn't want her to go.

Not wanting him to think he could get away with it, I struggled to sit up.

"Don't go." Jarret draped one arm and leg over me.

"I'm going to my own bed now. I'm tired and so are you." I shoved his arm away and maneuvered out from under his leg.

He shifted his limbs back over me.

I shoved again.

He tried yet again.

Oh, Lord Jesus, help me to see You in Jarret or let the test end already! I grabbed his hand, and we did some awkward arm wrestling for a moment.

"Don't go yet. Not yet." His eyes closed, but he still worked on keeping me by his side.

"Jarret, I have to go. Your dad will knock you galley west if he finds me in here." I freed myself again, this time pinning his arm with two hands, then scooted off the bed and knelt on the floor, still within arm's reach.

He lamely attempted to grab me again but then dropped his hand to the bed. Then his eyes fluttered open, and he gave me a sorrowful look before closing them again. "Please, just . . ."

"Please, just *what?*"

"Sing something."

A giggle escaped me. "You want me to sing?"

"Yeah, and pet my hair." He mumbled something unclear as he grabbed my hand and lifted it to the dark curls resting against his neck.

I pulled my hand back. I'd never even run my hand through Roland's dark wavy hair. Touching Jarret West's hair? Way too odd.

He reached toward my hand but didn't take it this time, just rested his next to mine on the bed, his fingers barely touching mine. ". . . like Mama used to do, used to sing to me when I was little, 'fore she died. Can still hear her voice sometimes."

I had to admit, I felt a bit sorry for vulnerable Jarret, so I didn't get up to leave even though he wouldn't likely try to stop me now. He wanted me to sing to him *like Mama used to do.* My chest tingled at the sweet, childish request. He'd probably burn with embarrassment tomorrow, maybe try to avoid me and pretend he'd never said it, but he really wanted this now. Should I? Could I?

"So what do you want me to sing?"

"Mmm . . . how 'bout . . ." And then Jarret West sang to me with his eyes closed, his voice low and soft. *"Arrorró mi nee-ño, arrorró mi sol, arrorró peda-a-azo, de mi corazón."*

It pulled my heartstrings to hear this grown man—who seemed so vain and even arrogant at other times—singing a lullaby, even though I couldn't understand the words. I let him go on for a moment before admitting, "I don't know any Spanish songs, Jarret."

"Mmm, right. Okay, okay . . ." He waved one hand back and forth, humming, maybe trying to find another melody. Then he sang a line of some other song I didn't recognize. He stopped and opened his sleepy eyes. "Know that one?"

I shook my head, trying not to laugh. My heart softened toward him as he tried another song and another. Such a sentimental young man. His thoughts turned to his mother when most vulnerable. I had no idea.

Then, just as I was thinking he'd never find a song that I knew, he sang, "Sing o-of Mar-e-e, pure and lowly—"

"Yes!" In my excitement, I grabbed his arm and sang along, ". . . vir-gi-in mother un-de-filed."

We sang the next line together then he sighed and sank his head into the pillow. He dragged my hand up to his hair and closed his eyes.

So I remained kneeling next to the bed, and I sang to him and stroked his hair, filling in for his mother while sentimental Jarret likely returned somewhere in his mind to his childhood. To the years before life had become complicated and he'd gone down so many wrong paths. To the days when his mother loved him and regardless of the mistakes he'd made during the day, never let the sun go down on her anger. And she tucked him in and sang to him and stroked his hair and let him know he was unconditionally loved.

And I sympathized. Regardless of the number or size of our mistakes, we all wanted to experience that unconditional love.

Once he fell asleep, his breaths coming deep and regular, I stood up but stopped before walking away. His stylish white shirt had something really yucky on it. He did wear t-shirt underneath. I could just slip the outer shirt off. Should I . . . ? I would never leave one of my own brothers like that, so I shouldn't leave him that way either.

After sliding open three buttons, I saw it. My hands trembled on the next button, and a degree of awe filled me. There before my eyes lay proof that Jarret West had faith. Our Lady's Brown Scapular—well-worn and stitched up on one side— rested on the snug t-shirt on his very manly chest.

I'd suspected that he wore one before, when I'd noticed something brown peeking from the neckline of his shirt, but it still surprised me. So Jarret was not only sentimental and missing his mother, but he also had faith and some connection to our spiritual mother. I could hardly believe it.

As I finished removing his shirt and covering him with a blanket, I made a personal commitment. Regardless of what Jarret said or did, I would work even harder to see Jesus in him. I would go out of my way to be kind to him, to befriend him. Maybe somehow I could make a difference in his life.

CHAPTER 11

Jarret

I crept toward consciousness, a headache pounding to the beat of my heart. Thirsty and with a dry mouth. Pushing a blanket off my sweaty body, I sat up, swung my legs off the bed, and slouched. Still wore the jeans from last night. My white shirt lay folded on my sneakers, which sat neatly by the dresser. Didn't remember putting them there or folding my shirt.

Too tired to get up right away, I gazed in the direction of the shirt, just resting before I made the trip to the bathroom to quench my thirst from the faucet. A bit of brain fog lifted, my thoughts returning to last night.

I'd played a few games of darts then some pool, right? Kyle smiling and happy most of the night. C.W. flipping his stringy blond hair around and playing air guitar to his favorite songs. Sherman doing a lot of talking. Ken more serious than the others until something made him laugh. Why do I remember dancing with some girl? Head spinning, nauseous. Why can't I remember the entire night? And driving home—

Panic coursing through me, I jumped up and crossed the room to the window, yanked the curtain back and squinted against the brightness. My red Chrysler 300 sat parked in the circular driveway, gleaming in the sunlight. Looked okay. I breathed easy now, but I remembered being really worried about my car . . .

I let the curtain fall and paced to the bed. Something little lay in the tangle of sheets. As I drew closer, I tried to make it out. Was it a . . . hair clip?

I picked it up, a turquoise blue barrette with little white fabric flowers and iridescent beads attached to it. Why would it be in my—?

My stomach sank and head grew light. Suddenly off kilter, I made a move to sit down but then steadied myself and glanced wildly about the room, looking for other signs of . . . girl.

Had I brought a girl up here last night? *Please, God. No.* I didn't want to be that person again. Next girl I brought to my bed would be my wife. But . . . had I?

Hand to my forehead, I paced around to the other side of the bed, to where my shirt lay folded atop my shoes neatly placed by the dresser. I wouldn't have done that. And a belt lay coiled on the dresser. I checked to see if I still wore a belt— no, I didn't.

God, no. God, no.

My head throbbed. I'd been easy prey last night, laughing and losing at darts and pool. Kyle's stupid challenge and the shots. They'd gone down smooth, though, no punch. How could I have gotten drunk off them? Kyle had said they were weak, even proved they barely affected him by walking a line and touching his nose. But someone had told me he was playing me, drinking a shot of water to every one of my shots.

Regardless of how it affected him, why had I assumed I could handle it? Didn't want Kyle to show me up or make me look weak. Stupid. Stupid.

I was weak. Thought I'd changed, wasn't that guy who did what he wanted, when he wanted, because he wanted to. I thought before I acted and avoided situations that might drag me down. But here I was, messing up again . . . two steps forward and a mile back.

Squinting through my headache, I looked down at the hair barrette resting on my palm. Turquoise blue with white flowers and little beads. Looked familiar. Maybe the blonde at the table. The one I'd danced with?

My stomach sank again. I needed something for this headache. Maybe then I'd remember more. I stuffed the barrette into the front pocket of my jeans and left the room.

A glass of ice-cold water calling my name, I swung into the kitchen, tidy except for a full bottle of blue sports drink on the end of the bar counter. Nanny always kept a little tray of common medicine on a shelf in the pantry.

I slowed as I neared the bar counter. A bottle of ibuprofen and a glass of water sat next to the sports drink. Just what I needed. Sitting right where I couldn't miss it.

Pushing my confusion aside, I opened the bottle of pain reliever, shook a pill onto my palm, and popped it into my mouth with a swig of water. The sports drink would help rehydrate me, so I cracked that open and took a swig of that too. Wonder who got it out? Maybe I shouldn't have drank out of the bottle.

"Feeling better?" Caitlyn stepped into the kitchen through the doorway to the dining room. She wore a purple knee-length t-shirt type dress, her hair pulled back in a fairly tidy ponytail. Probably fixed it in front of a mirror this time.

"Better than what?" I drained a quarter of the bottle with one long gulp.

She didn't exactly smile but the look was sweet enough as she strolled toward the laundry room, probably to get supplies for whatever chores old Mr. Digby had her doing. "Better than last night?"

I stopped mid-swig and forced a gulp down to avoid choking. "You put this out for me?" I pointed to the bottle of ibuprofen with the hand holding the sports drink.

"I thought you might need it."

"Y-you saw me come home?" Okay, that was a stupid question. Of course she saw me.

"Well, yes." One hand on the laundry room doorframe, she gave me a funny look, eyebrows twitching with her momentary confusion, probably wondering why I didn't remember.

"Di-i-i-d I come home alone?" As the question came out, I almost regretted asking. I hated that she'd seen me come in drunk, but I loathed the thought of her seeing me come home with a girl. That wasn't me anymore.

"No."

"No?" I repeated, whispering, ready to hate myself. Did I want to ask her for specifics, like whom I'd come home with?

"Well, not really. Your friends dropped you off. I'm not sure how many were in the car, just saw the one, some guy you used to hang out with in high school, I think. He helped you to the door." She smiled and darted into the laundry room, her long red ponytail swinging.

A great exhale escaped me, and I set the sports drink down. *Thank you, Lord.* She probably saw Kyle. No girl. But wait . . . that didn't explain the hair barrette in my bed. Could some girl have given it to me last night? A harmless gift, a token to remember her by? And what about my car? If Kyle dropped me off, how did my car get here? And if I'd needed help getting to the door, how did I get upstairs?

I found myself walking to the laundry room, stepping into the doorway, and nearly bumping into her, now wearing her little white apron, a pail of cleaners in her hand.

"Oh, sorry." She backed up two steps and glanced at something to her right, maybe the stack of folded towels on the washing machine. "Did you need something?"

I couldn't stop staring at her hair . . . and the flowered hair barrettes on the sides of her head, one turquoise blue, the other orange. Dumbstruck, I pulled the barrette from my pocket and held it up. It matched the blue one in her hair.

"Oh, there's my hair clip." She lifted one hand.

I drew my hand back. I'd give it to her once I understood how it ended up in my bed. The only explanation I could come up with couldn't possibly be true, not with a girl like her. She would never. But it had been in my bed all the same, and for whatever reason, the mystery irritated me. "Wanna guess where I found it?"

She shrugged. "I suppose I could've lost it anywhere. I'm all over the house. And sometimes they don't stay in my"—she tapped a barrette and ran her hand over her ponytail, a shy look in her eyes now— "my wild hair."

"It was in my bed."

She giggled. "Oh, okay." Then she put out her hand again.

I dropped the barrette into my palm and closed my fingers around it. "Wanna tell me why?"

"U-u-um . . . 'cause it fell out?" she said, mirth in her green eyes.

"In my bed?"

She raised her brows and shrugged again. "Are you going to give it back?"

"Yeah, sure, after you explain how it got there."

Before she could answer me, footsteps sounded in the hallway, Papa clomping toward the kitchen. Wasn't he going away on assignment? Not wanting to get into a discussion with him, I gave Caitlyn a last glance and took off toward the back of the house. I'd have to ask her another time.

Possibilities ran through my mind. She'd helped me upstairs and stumbled, falling into my bed. She was kinda' clumsy, but she wouldn't have landed up by the pillows, where I'd found the barrette. So maybe I was the one falling over and reaching out, accidentally knocking the barrette from her hair.

It could've sailed anywhere. Or—worst case scenario—I forced her into my bed. In which case, I'd have some major apologizing to do even though she wouldn't have let anything happen. I had some apologizing to do regardless. Coming home like that, her having to help me . . . she didn't have to help me, I guess. Why'd she do it?

CHAPTER 12

Caitlyn

A fter dinner, I accompanied Nanny with her walker—push, step, push, step—through the halls of West Castle, though she only needed help when doing an about-face. I also assisted with her daily ankle and leg exercises. Every day she pushed herself a little more.

I'd come to appreciate the perseverance of the Digbys as they fulfilled their separate responsibilities and personal goals. I also appreciated their respect and care for each other, even though I still didn't understand Mr. Digby any better than I did the first day here. Too often he appeared in places I didn't expect him, and he still didn't smile.

We passed through the double doors off the family room and then by the great room and turned the corner. "I'd like to do a few steps tomorrow." Nanny looked toward the stairwell. "Dwight said I should be ready, especially after all my practice on the exercise step."

Dwight, her handsome young therapist with an athletic build and a charming personality, stopped by twice a week and always seemed pleased with her progress. He made sure I understood the exercises, too, and gave me pointers and advice to know when she needed a rest.

"I see you looking at those stairs," I said, "but I think Dwight wants you to climb something with fewer steps, like maybe the front porch." Once she got stronger, maybe we could go out on the roof!

Nanny gazed up the stairs as we passed. "Roland used to be terrified of that door at the end of the hallway. A strong wind makes the door creak, sometimes even rattles the old lock." She glanced at me with a little grin. "Once the twins noticed how little Roland hated walking past it, one of them used to sneak outside, onto the roof, and rattle it on purpose."

Seemed like something Jarret would do.

Nanny chuckled. "Poor Roland. I think he still dislikes that door, always hurries through the hallway."

"Some fears are hard to outgrow," I said in Roland's defense. We neared the sunny foyer now.

"Yes, such a shame." Nanny winced with her next few steps. "You know, the age difference between the boys and the closeness of the twins made it hard for him sometimes. The twins had such a special relationship, so close they seemed to read each other's mind. Probably made little Roland feel left out. But they've grown closer the past couple years, especially Jarret and Roland, which I never thought possible. But, as they say, God works in mysterious ways."

"Yes, he does." I loved hearing Nanny's stories, learning new things about the family, things Roland would've never shared. Some stories made us laugh so hard we had to stop walking until we recovered. Others touched me. And still others made me realize every family struggled, just in different ways.

"Well, I'm about done for the day." Nanny fixed her eyes on the door to their suite. "Once you've helped me to my chair, please enjoy the evening."

After getting her settled, I stepped outside through the veranda. Mr. Digby groomed a horse, so I walked softly past the stables, heading for the nearest path.

Halfway to the woods, my cell phone rang—maybe Nanny forgot to tell me something. I glimpsed the number, not recognizing it, but the veranda door swung open at that moment, startling me into answering the call anyway. "Hello?"

"Hey, sis, what'cha doing?"

"Stacey?" I stopped walking, glanced at the number again—Stacey didn't have a cell phone—and checked to see who was coming from the house. *Yup.* Jarret strode toward me with purpose, dressed in a short-sleeved gray tracksuit and the white sneakers he wore last night. While tempted to pretend I hadn't seen him and continue on my way, Stacey's phone call had me rooted in place.

"Yeah, hey, can you come get me? And can you not tell Mom or Dad?"

Red flags went up in my mind, but I suspected I needed to proceed with caution. She'd called me and not home for a reason. "Stacey, where are you?"

"Near the t-shirt shop. Can you hurry?" Her casual tone did not convey panic, did not even sound rushed.

"What t-shirt shop? Are you okay? Who took you there?" My heart thumped harder, either from worry about her or from Jarret approaching, though I'd expected him to try to catch up with me sooner or later.

"Come on." A little chuckle with a hint of nervousness. "I just need a ride."

I turned away from Jarret, wanting to focus on my sister. "Stacey, you know I don't have a car. How can I come and get you?"

"I can give you a ride."

My stomach leaped and I turned back.

Jarret stood a few feet away, reaching into a pocket. He pulled his keys out, lifted them chest-high, and dangled them on one finger. "Is that your sister? You need a ride?" He gave a little head tilt, maybe in the direction of the garage. "Let's go."

I bit my lip. *Should I?* "I don't think your father would approve. Would you . . . maybe . . ."—I dared to ask—"let me borrow your car?"

He jerked back, his eyebrows twitching. "No one drives my car but me."

"I drove it last night."

"You"—a few rapid blinks and a glance over his shoulder— "that's how my car . . ." His jaw clenched, chin tilting upward. "Look, I can give you a ride. My father doesn't need to know. And"—a humbler tone and something intense in his eyes—"you didn't finish telling me about last night. It's killing me that I can't remember."

"Yeah, that'd be frustrating. I can't imagine what it'd be like to lose my memory. But I don't know anything about last night. I only saw you when you got home."

"Who are you talking to?" Stacey's impatient voice came through the phone. "Are you coming or not?"

"Right now, that's all that matters to me," Jarret said, his voice low.

His vulnerable, pleading look made me want to tell him everything. But I didn't want to embarrass him, kicking him while he was already down. Plus, I didn't know how he'd react once he realized he'd sung to me and begged me to sing to him, him being so full of himself sometimes. Maybe he'd make life harder on me to compensate for the humiliation.

I turned away from him again and cupped my hand to the phone as if that would make our conversation more private. "Sorry, Stacey, I—"

"Aw come on," she whined. "You have to."

"Your horse needs exercise, Jarret."

I startled at the sound of Mr. Digby's voice. Jarret did too, judging by the way he squirmed.

Mr. Digby came from the direction of the stables, leading a tan horse with pretty eyes and a dark mane and legs. The horse greeted Jarret with a snort and bumped him with its nose. "Since you ain't working, might as well exercise the horses."

"What, all of them?" Jarret shifted his weight to one hip, one shoulder drooping.

"Got something better to do?"

Jarret flipped his hand in my direction. "I'm talking."

Mr. Digby placed the reins in Jarret's upturned hand and strode away, mumbling and shaking his head.

With a huff, Jarret pressed his keys into my palm and turned to his horse. He shoved a sneaker into the stirrup and with a little hop mounted the horse smoothly and settled into the saddle. He looked down at me. "Maybe we can talk later."

I nodded, clutching the phone in one hand and his keys in the other, appreciation tingling through me. Maybe I could come up with a simple explanation by then, something honest but that wouldn't embarrass him.

--*

Forty minutes later, after retrieving Stacey from outside an ice cream shop in a touristy town with old Western false front buildings lining the road, I pulled into our local library parking lot.

"See ya." Stacey stuffed a cell phone in a pocket of her faded denim skorts and grabbed the door handle.

"Wait! You haven't explained anything to me." Once I'd gotten her into Jarret's car—which I still couldn't believe he let me drive—I'd barraged her with questions. She'd replied with, *Can we not talk about it?* and *Let me think for a minute.* That minute stretched out for the rest of the twenty-minute ride back to the local library, where Mom probably expected her to be.

"Thanks for the ride. Tell Jarret I like his car, except for the funny smell." She wrinkled her nose, opened the door, and swung one foot, in a black tennis shoe, out of the car.

"Oh, no you don't." I grabbed her arm. "If you don't want me to say anything to Mom or Dad, I need to know why."

With a sigh of defeat, she leaned back in the seat and glanced at me sideways. "I met friends at the library, but we decided to go shopping. Only they didn't bring money, so they were just gonna take stuff."

"Shoplifting?" I blanched, struggling to believe her little friends would do such a thing. "Who did you go with?" I didn't realize she had friends old enough to drive.

"I don't wanna say. Can't you just be happy I left outta there? I didn't take anything." She grinned. "Except for my friend's phone. But I'll give it back." She got out of the car, shouted, "See ya," and slammed the door.

Feeling compelled to give her advice, I rolled the passenger side window down and shouted, "Maybe you need to find better friends!"

--*

The next day, my family picked me up for Sunday Mass, and I spent my day off with them. Mom complained about Stacey's behavior again, but I kept Stacey's secret. When her friends decided to do something wrong, she left, so maybe she just needed a bit more time to come fully around to making right choices. If not, I'd have to convince her to tell on herself.

Monday, Jarret's questions started back up. And over the next few days, he asked me several times and in several ways to tell him about that night. The irritated glint in his eyes said my vague, somewhat evasive answers didn't satisfy him. Then he stopped asking. Even if we ended up in the same room, he only stared at me while I cleaned.

I had to give him more.

CHAPTER 13

Jarret

A lmost a week after my night out with friends, I sat in an armchair in the great room with an old book open on my lap, something about the history of Spain. Twice I checked to make sure it wasn't upside down. And I tried to decide if the afternoon sunlight streaming in between the open heavy burgundy drapes would be enough light to actually read by. Maybe I should've turned on a lamp.

I should've been doing something else, making the most of my summer or trying to get my thoughts together about my future or even getting a job like Papa wanted me to do. But here I sat, pretending to read a book while really *watching the girl in the house* do some cleaning and trying to figure out how to get her to talk to me.

On the opposite side of the room, Caitlyn stood on a stepladder by the two-sided fireplace—the other side open to the family room. She wielded an ostrich feather duster, running it over and between decorations on the mantle. Wearing that little white apron tied around her slim waist over a dress with artsy gray, pink, and orange flowers. A loose ponytail of wild red curls resting on her back. And those sparkling green eyes occasionally sliding a curious glance my way. Man, she was cute. She . . . Roland's girlfriend . . . Roland's girlfriend was cute.

I dropped my gaze to the book, chastising myself for thinking it.

For the past few days, I'd tried like mad to get her to explain what happened last Friday, Saturday morning, really. I needed to curb my obsessive tendencies, give up, move on, but her reaction to messed-up me last Friday compelled me to uncover the truth. Even if I'd hate myself for whatever I discovered. Better to find out as soon as possible. Rip the Band-Aid off, find a way to repair the damage, and get on with my life.

I didn't feel capable of moving on without knowing. The other day, wanting to start over on the right path, I'd pulled up to Saint Michael's Church in time for confession, but I couldn't get out of the car. How could I confess when I didn't remember everything I'd done?

Mumbling to herself, Caitlyn stopped dusting and looked up at the medieval battle painting over the fireplace. Then she glanced to either side as if trying to figure something out.

Why wouldn't she tell me? It couldn't have been that bad or she'd be glaring and giving me the cold shoulder, the way she did the first few days after I returned home. But she was nicer lately, since last Friday, smiling when she saw me and exchanging pleasant greetings. *Good morning. . . . Enjoy your day. . . . See you later.*

With one hand on the mantle, Caitlyn lifted the feather duster, directing it toward the top edge of the framed painting. Not quite reaching it, she stood on tiptoe and bumped the green-and-gold double-handled vase from France, a late 19th century antique. Then she gasped and her hand flew out to save the vase, the feather duster falling to the floor.

I jumped up, dropping the book onto the nearest end table, and fetched the black feather duster. Maybe I'd been going about this all wrong. Papa had changed his strategy with me, asking about my professor instead of bossing me around—although he got around to bossing later. Maybe I needed to change my strategy with her.

Once she steadied herself and regained her composure, I handed the duster to her.

Her cheeks flushed pink. "Thanks."

"Sure. Want me to dust it?" I nodded to indicate the picture frame. She wasn't the most coordinated girl, but she obviously tried to do a good job. I wouldn't mind helping.

"Okay." She handed the duster to me and backed down the stepladder.

I stepped up and dusted the ornate frame from top to sides to bottom. As I jumped down and handed the duster back, a question popped into my mind, a new strategy for learning more. Caitlyn with her strong conscience . . . "Hey, so, what were you doing up so late last weekend, when I came home in the middle of the night?"

She didn't answer right away, probably wondering what angle I was coming at her with now. She was likely on to me. "Well, it's not like I stayed up that late. I wanted fresh air, so I went to bed with the window cracked open, and all that noise outside woke me. I peeked out the window to see what was going on." Standing a mere three feet from me, she twirled the feather duster one way and then another. "After a moment I realized it was you out there"—she paused, a smile playing on her lips—"lying in the driveway"—she paused again, pressing her lips together— "wailing about your car."

"Wailing, huh?" My pathetic behavior embarrassed me, but she seemed amused, so I decided not to let it bother me. I liked seeing her smile at me even at my own expense.

"Then your friend helped you up and got you to the front door." Immersed in the retelling, her voice grew louder and eyes less focused. "I couldn't see you from my window anymore, and I wanted to make sure you were okay, so I tiptoed down the hallway. Kind of watched you from the shadows, just wanting to make sure you got to your room okay."

She kept emphasizing that she only wanted to make sure I was okay, so I nodded to assure her I understood. She'd told me more today than ever before, and I didn't want to mess it up. Didn't want to move. Didn't want her to move as we stood facing each other, three feet apart in the great room.

"You really don't remember anything?" she said softly, returning from the memory to me.

"I remember up to a certain point, like, when I sat down after playing a game of pool, then bits and pieces of other things"—a game of darts flashed in my mind, then dancing with that girl, then beer sloshing in my mug as I shoved it into empty glasses and mugs—"and I remember feeling nauseous and my head spinning. Kind of remember getting out of a car, Kyle's car, I guess, and . . . I think I threw up."

"Oh, that's what was on your shirt." She glanced at my chest as if I wore the same shirt.

I rubbed my chest, disgusted with myself again and wishing she hadn't seen me come home that way. "Yeah, pretty gross. But it wasn't entirely my fault, getting drunk, that is. Kyle duped me, had me drinking shots while he drank water. I'm not a drinker." I shook my head, feeling lame for trying to excuse my behavior. "Anyway, so there you are standing in the shadows, watching to make sure I didn't hurt myself, right?"

"I didn't think you could see me"—her eyelids fluttered with another amused look, or maybe not amusement but something else—"but you told me to step into the light, so I did. Then you told me I was . . . beautiful."

Shocked, I jerked back. "I-I said what?" *Great.* I was drunk and hitting on my brother's girlfriend.

A huge smile stretched across her face, as if she might laugh outright, then she added, "Don't worry. I know the alcohol made you say it." Face beet red, she looked at me for a moment, still suppressing that laugh. "Really, don't worry. I know I'm not your type."

"Oh yeah? So what is my type?"

"Oh, I don't know. The kind of girl that would make a good model, perfect body, perfect hair . . ." She laughed, twirling a stray lock of her hair, and paced around the room with the feather duster, staying within a few yards of me. "Stylish clothes, knows how to walk without tripping." She pretended to trip and flung the feather duster into the air.

I caught it and handed it back. "You think I'm pretty shallow, huh?" I resented her judgment, but every girl I'd dated fit the description. Was it my fault I only attracted hot girls?

Her smile fell, and she stopped in front of me again. "Oh, sorry. Am I being judgmental? It's just that every girl I've seen you with has been so . . . perfect, lovely."

"And you're not?"

She shrugged. "Maybe to a drunk." She laughed, covering her mouth.

I laughed too, her indifference about her appearance making her even prettier to me. She was beautiful, and it wasn't just skin deep. I didn't need alcohol to see it, but I wouldn't tell her . . . my brother's girlfriend. Best not to think about her that way. I had to think of her as Peter's friend. Probably went along with his pranks. Secretly despised me for getting her girlfriend pregnant. And why shouldn't she? I despised myself. So incredibly selfish.

Still laughing, she staggered around the room pretending to be drunk, mumbling something like, "You look lovely, my dear. Simply lovely."

Amused by her silliness, I snapped from my condemning thoughts. "So then what happened? After I hit on you." I hoped that was the worst thing I did, but I had found her hair barrette in my bed. Still, whatever I did couldn't have been too bad. She wouldn't have tolerated bad behavior. Plus, she didn't seem angry with me.

She took a dust rag from her work pail and sat on the couch, a fancy piece of furniture with a tufted back, rolled arms, and clawed feet. Then she removed decorations from the coffee table, wiping each one. "You *really* wanted to get your car. I tried talking you out of it, but you were determined, so when your ride came, I went with you."

I paced toward the armchair but didn't feel like sitting so just stood resting one arm on the decorative carvings along the top. "I figured you drove it, after what you said the day after." The revelation had shocked me and probably accounted for me letting her drive my car. I'd questioned my decision until she finally brought it back unscathed.

She wiped the coffee table from end to end. "At first, you didn't want me to drive it, but you didn't stop me when I took your keys. And you got into the passenger seat on your own."

"Well, thanks. I'm sure I was in no condition to drive."

"So after we got your car home, I helped you to your room." She replaced the decorations, an old carved box, a vase of fake flowers, and two candleholders, positioning each one just so. Then she got up and went to the end table nearest me.

"And . . . ?"

She glanced while dusting. "That's all really."

I stuffed my hand into my pocket and pulled the barrette out. "Can't be all. You haven't explained this."

"Are you ever going to give it back?"

"Sure, when you tell me."

"It just fell out of my hair, Jarret." She paused with the dust rag halfway up the lamp and her green eyes locked on me, turning my insides to mush, her face all soft and serious now as she practically whispered, "Don't let it bother you. You're worried you did something wrong. But you didn't."

Suddenly I could hear and feel my heart thumping in my chest. "Then why won't you tell me?" I whispered back.

She stared at me for a long moment as if trying to decide whether to trust me with something, and I really wanted her to trust me.

Footsteps broke the silence and deflated my hope of finding out. Papa's footsteps. Whatever happened to the assignment he kept talking about? Shouldn't he have left by now?

With a sigh, I backed up a few steps, moving toward the double doors to the family room. "Thanks for telling me what you did. Even if you won't tell me everything." I stuffed the barrette into my pocket.

She smiled, that sweet little smile that had to melt Roland's heart whenever he saw it. It sure melted mine.

Then I swung the double doors open and took off. She'd trusted me with a lot. What kept her from trusting me with the rest of the story? Maybe I could earn her trust.

CHAPTER 14

Caitlyn

After a breakfast of waffles and sausage links, I assisted Nanny with her morning exercises then set out to complete the one chore on today's list: clean the veranda. I got my cleaning supplies from the mudroom and as I stepped into the hallway, I noticed a door across from me that I had never tried before. It probably opened to a closet, but I found my hand reaching for the doorknob just to be sure.

As the door swung open, crystal sconces on the walls blinked on, creating a warm, welcoming atmosphere, and my heart delighted at my discovery. A prayer closet! Well, "closet" didn't seem like the right word. It was probably bigger than my bedroom at home. Granted, I did have the smallest bedroom in the house.

Setting the cleaning supplies down, I stepped inside, and the door closed softly behind me. A beautiful crucifix hung on the back wall, not the sanitized kind but one with blood painted on the body and a crown of sharp thorns. I dropped to my knees on the velvety cushion of a carved prayer kneeler under the crucifix. My heart stirred to see this expression of the love of my Lord, and I couldn't look away for a long moment. When the moment passed, I sat on one of two benches and took in the rest of the little room. One could step away from the world and be alone with Our Lord here.

A unique statue of Our Lady of Guadalupe stood under the cross on one side of a mantle that stretched across the back wall, little battery-operated candles flickering at her feet. Saint Joseph stood on the other side, with more flickering candles. Dozens of photos, both framed and unframed, leaned against a lower shelf that ran the length of the mantle. Unlit candles in little glass cups had been placed here and there too, between pictures and around smaller statues, along with other mementos: scraps of paper with handwritten notes, a tiny booklet, a miniature ceramic horse, dried flowers, a hunk of fool's gold, and a pair of very old earrings.

Paintings of saints hung on the side walls, between the sconces. And white string lights ran along the perimeter of the ceiling, even though they hadn't turned on, as the other lights did, when I'd opened the door.

Resting in the peacefulness, I gazed from one old photograph to another. These must've been relatives, the Mexican- and Spanish-looking ones from Mrs. West's side of the family, the rugged Western-type from Mr. West's side. The much larger portrait in the middle of the shelf—of a dark-eyed woman with a red flower in her long curly hair—might have been Mrs. West. Such a beautiful woman with love in her smile. The Wests cherished their family members even after death, probably prayed often for their souls. How lovely.

I wanted that. I wanted a big family full of love that would last for generations, each of us caring for one another, praying for one another, never forgetting anyone. I wanted to remain close to my parents and siblings and grow close to my future husband's parents and siblings. I wanted to know their history and my history . . .

The flickering candles drew my gaze to Our Lady of Guadalupe, to her head bowed humbly and her eyes gazing downward. Tradition held that she'd consecrated herself to God at a very young age. While she prayed constantly for the Savior, she'd never expected to become His Mother. But God asked that of her, and she set aside her own plans and gave Him her unconditional yes.

What if God wanted something else from me? Not marriage and family. The questions I'd wondered overlooking the battlements came to me again, more intensely. What if He called me to enter religious life, to live in a cloistered convent or as a missionary sister? Or what if I remained single all the days of my life? Single people could accomplish things, make great sacrifices of time and treasure, that married people and priests and religious couldn't. Or what if God called me to intense suffering, making no other vocation possible?

I pondered these things in silence, Jesus tugging at my heart, waiting for my answer. I sensed He wanted me to stretch my way of thinking. Maybe He wanted me to let go of something . . . of my hopes and dreams? Or maybe He wanted me open to something I'd never considered.

Would I say yes no matter what He asked of me? Or would I only consider the vocation I've wanted since childhood: marriage and family? I needed to contemplate these things further on my "retreat." What a blessing to have found this little prayer closet!

Twenty minutes or so later, I said a quick but heartfelt prayer for my sister Stacey, genuflected on the stone floor, and offered a final prayer. "Holy Mary, help me to say yes to whatever God calls me to. Help me to trust that I'll find happiness when fulfilling Our Lord's will rather than my own."

Filled with peace and still a bit contemplative, I padded softly in my bare feet to the veranda with my pail of cleaning supplies and a long-handled duster. Indirect sunlight filtered through big, tinted windows all along one wall, falling on circular glass-topped tables and the cushioned chairs around them. Thin white curtains hung on either side of the windows, puddling to the floor. In the back of the room two couches flanked a coffee table, and a hutch stood against the wall. It all created such a romantic setting. Just needed bouquets of hydrangeas or candles on the tables.

Not sure where to begin, I set my bucket down. The windows would need to be washed, especially the ones on the outside wall but also the windows connected to the family room. I'd need to dust the overhead light fixtures and wall sconces and the pictures decorating the two windowless walls.

I extended the handle of the duster and decided to start from the top.

Halfway around the room, my arms ached from holding the duster up and brushing away cobwebs along the edges of the ceiling. As I lowered my arms for a break, the outside door swung open.

"Oh, you're in here." Jarret stood in the doorway, dressed like a jockey from the waist down, with tall boots and slim brown breeches. From the waist up, he was all Jarret, with long curls tucked into a ponytail, more curls on his forehead, a neatly trimmed goatee of stubble, and a loud blue muscle shirt.

"You sound disappointed," I teased, though he did seem irritated. I still felt awkward every time we crossed paths, but I'd grown used to him popping up in whatever room I was cleaning.

"Disappointed?" He huffed and almost smiled. Then he made his typical glance over the shoulder before stepping further into the room. "Why are you cleaning in here?"

"It's on the list."

His gaze dropped to my hands, as if he might find me actually holding the list. "No one uses the room."

When he looked for the list a second time, I realized my apron had come untied and hung awkwardly. I crossed the extra-long ties behind me and made a bow on one hip. "It still gets dusty, and the windows could use a good washing."

"Why not wait until someone wants to use the room? Clean it then. Nanny won't care, and who's gonna tell Mr. Digby?" He did a doubletake in the direction of the windows behind me then choked on a laugh.

There was Mr. Digby, washing the outside of the window at the furthest end of the room.

I laughed too. "He's everywhere."

"Yeah. More so lately." Jarret watched Mr. Digby for a few seconds then turned to me. "Want some help? We can get it done in half the time."

"Really? You want to help?" Did I want his help? He likely wanted to spend time with me in the hopes that I would continue telling him about that night.

He shrugged. "Ain't got nothing better to do."

"Think your father will care?" I glanced at Mr. Digby, who just might say something to Mr. West.

"Nah. He'd probably be happy I'm doing some work. Where's your water bucket?" He glanced around. "Or are you using Windex?"

"I didn't get the water yet."

A few minutes later, Jarret returned with a bucket of water, a spray bottle, and no boots, just socks on his feet. "I added the dish soap. And here's the vinegar water you asked for." He lifted a spray bottle and tilted it from side to side a few times.

"Okay, we'll wash the windows with the soapy water in the bucket then spray them with the vinegar water. And dry with these." I grabbed the microfiber cloths from my pail of cleaning supplies.

"I'll do the windows. You finish whatever you were doing." He took the cloths from me and set to work, starting on the opposite end of the room from Mr. Digby, who continued washing the outside of the windows.

We worked in silence, me wiping down tables and chairs, Jarret washing windows, sort of keeping pace as our work took us from one side of the room to the other. Before long, Mr. Digby, on the outside, and Jarret, on the inside, washed the same window. I completed the tables and went to my work pail for clean rags to wipe down the couches.

I'd expected Jarret to ask me more questions, a deeper interrogation, but he didn't. But I had promised myself I'd be kind to him, so as he worked opposite Mr. Digby, I decided to start a conversation. "I gathered by your boots that you were out riding. Did Mr. Digby tell you to do it, or did you just want to?"

Standing on the stepladder, he pushed a wet rag to the top of a window and water dribbled down his bare arm to the oversized armhole of his muscle shirt, drawing my gaze right along with it. "Both, I guess. I like riding but sometimes I need motivation. Mr. Digby can be a very motivational man." He smiled at me then titled his chin at Mr. Digby, as if greeting him.

Mr. Digby's eyes shifted to Jarret just then, though he probably hadn't heard him through the window. He didn't smile back.

"Nice work, Mr. Digby." Jarret nodded at him and put his thumb up. Then he lowered his arm and shook the water dribbles off, glancing over his shoulder at me. "What about you? I know Roland taught you to ride. Did you like it?"

I turned my eyes back to my work, brushing off one of the two couches. "Yes. It's been awhile, so I'd probably need to learn all over again, but it was fun."

"While you're here, you'll have to go riding sometime."

With all the scrubbing and wiping down furniture, I'd worked up a sweat, but my face burned at his suggestion. He hadn't even asked me to ride with him, so why the blush?

Having buffed the top section of a window to perfection, Jarret leaped off the stepladder and dipped a rag in the bucket of water. "So what are you taking at SDU?"

"Me? Honestly, I thought you wanted to help me clean so you could ask questions about that night."

Jarret threw me a smile and shrugged. "You're not gonna tell me anyways."

"So you really want to know what I'm taking?"

"Yeah, that's why I asked. What does a good girl like you want to be when she grows up?"

"Oh, you're making fun of me." I finished one couch and started on the next, wiping the tops of the cushions on the back. Considering the type of girls he always dated, I was probably an anomaly to him.

Jarret stopped working all together, dropped the rag, and strode toward me. He stopped a few feet away, all seriousness with a hint of remorse. "No, I'm not, really, I'm not."

A bit shocked, I dropped my cleaning rag too. Why the whispery voice? Why the serious look? I didn't know how to take him, but silence would only make the moment more uncomfortable, so I decided to answer with cheerfulness. "I'm hoping to get a degree in criminal justice and police science so I can be a detective one day. I like solving mysteries."

Once I answered, I picked up the rag I'd dropped—and I wished I could take my words back. He was probably thinking what a big nerd I was. Or that I was some silly girl who watched too many detective shows, which might not have been far from the truth. Why was I pursuing a degree at all when I really wanted to marry and have children? But couldn't I do both?

"That sounds interesting. Maybe kinda why I like archaeology, digging to solve a mystery."

"Hm. Yeah." I glanced upward, thinking that over. Then I got back to work.

He still stood there, watching me. "How many years for your degree?"

"Probably two. I'll just get an associate. Roland's going for four, but I don't think I can afford that. That's why I'm trying to earn money over the summer."

"Trying? Ain't my father paying you well? 'Cause I've never seen anyone work like you."

Mr. Digby reached the last window, his brisk movements making both of us look at the same time. Then Jarret laughed. "I take that back."

I laughed too. The man was everywhere and got so much accomplished.

"That dude works hard." Jarret scrubbed the window he'd abandoned when coming over to me. "And Nanny too, like, man, how clean does a house need to be? And my father, he don't ever seem to rest. Doesn't want me to rest either." He shook his head, a sulky look coming over him for a moment, passing quickly. "Okay, never mind, but you do work hard. He should be paying you well."

I laughed again, enjoying his rambling answer. It's the kind I would give. "Yes, your father is paying me well. It'll really help." Then a question came out before I considered whether I should really be asking it. And I probably shouldn't have, but there it was, hanging between us. "Do *you* plan to get a job this summer?"

He stopped working, a spray bottle in one hand and dry rag in the other, and his eyes narrowed and jaw clenched as he turned to me. "Oh. You're on Papa's team too, huh?"

"What team?" I shouldn't have asked. I knew he wouldn't like the question.

"Team *Jarret Needs a Summer Job*." He slid his head from side to side.

"Sorry. It was just a question. I can't help but hear him asking you every time he sees you." Having just dusted the insides of the couch, I flipped the cushions to put them back into place. Somehow I tripped on the last cushion and landed on one knee on top of the squishy thing, with my skirt wedged in such a way that I couldn't get back up easily.

"So you think I should?" When I didn't answer—busy trying to right myself—he added, "I'm an adult. I don't need my father telling me what to do."

Getting to my feet at last, I shrugged then stuffed the final cushion in place. "It's always good to respect our parents and listen to their advice, right? And there's that Bible verse in Exodus: *Honor your father and your mother, that your days may be long in the land which the Lord your God gives you.*" I suddenly felt odd having quoted from the Bible to a guy like him. "Besides, wouldn't the tension between you two go away? Or maybe you'd enjoy going with him on his assignment, whatever it is. I've always thought his freelance work seemed fun, what little Roland's told me about it."

"Trying to get rid of me?" Washing the window faster now, he threw me another grumpy scowl.

"No, of course not. I just . . . want everyone to be happy, I guess." I went to the hutch, the last thing to clean before vacuuming the room. A lovely set of pale turquoise dinnerware filled the shelves behind glass doors. Maybe I shouldn't have started a conversation with him, or maybe I shouldn't have let him help me in the first place. But I'd promised myself I would be a friend to him, try to see Jesus in him. Was I going about it all wrong? Maybe I just needed to change the subject. "So what are *you* taking at college? What was your fieldtrip about?"

He didn't answer right away, maybe still offended by my previous question, maybe concentrating on polishing the window. "Archaeology stuff. And the field study was in Pompeii. My father went on a field study there before he got married. I was looking forward to it."

"Why didn't you go?"

With the vinegar-and-water spray bottle in hand, Jarret turned to me and bit his lip, his gaze shifting to the floor with an insecure look uncharacteristic of him.

Sensing his discomfort, I said, "Never mind. I overheard you saying that your favorite professor couldn't make it." My detective mind understood that he had other reasons, ones he didn't want to share, so I blurted, "How many years will you go?"

"Four at least. Six if I want a more interesting job. Can't see myself stuck in a museum or doing cultural resource management. I've already got three years done, so maybe three more to go."

"Oh that's great." I hated to turn on the vacuum cleaner and end our conversation, but I ran out of things to dust, and he'd almost finished the windows.

Over the next few days, he joined me for breakfast, obviously familiar with my routine now, and told me his plans for the day, offering to pick things up for me or the household whenever he was going out. Then he'd find me later in the day, always making it seem unplanned, and he'd talk to me while I worked, sometimes even helping.

Was this just a new tactic, a way of hopefully finding out more about that night? Regardless, it made me happy to hear about his plans, what he wanted to do with his life, or about some incident from his past. And it always surprised me when he asked me questions about things I'd done or what I'd like to do, as if he cared. Sometimes while he spoke, my mind went back to him singing in bed with his eyes closed and drawing my hand up to his hair. Maybe Jarret West was a lonely man, and maybe our conversations would help him feel less lonely.

CHAPTER 15

Jarret

Papa's study had always piqued my interest. An old-world globe on a carved hardwood stand, map tables that displayed Papa's next adventures, shelves of books about ancient civilizations, foreign languages, and archaeological discoveries. And the tall glass case with artifacts and mementos, including a hunk of gold some relative had discovered as a 49er, and other things of value to him . . . even if not to the rest of the world.

I sat in the king's chair, a seventeenth-century antique of carved oak wainscot, across from Papa's cluttered desk, one ankle crossed over my knee. I'd never wanted to sit in this chair growing up, the chair Papa forced us to take when he had a lesson to teach, and he always had lessons for me, few of them sinking in until maybe the past couple of years. The chair didn't bother me now . . . maybe 'cause Papa wasn't in the room.

I thumbed through one of his oldest books on Pompeii. The newer books had better pictures and more discoveries, but I loved the mystery that came through the pages of the old ones. I even loved the yellowed pages and sweet, musky smell of the older books. I'd take this one to my room, along with a few others that might help me decide if I really wanted to go in this direction at college. Was I just following in Papa's footsteps? I'd never thought of myself as a follower. Keefe, yes. Me, no.

Caitlyn liked solving mysteries, huh? We had that in common.

My gaze had shifted from the page to the clutter on the desk, though I didn't focus on any of it. That's one thing I really liked about archaeology: the detective work, uncovering secrets from the past, every artifact and feature another piece of a puzzle slowly coming together, discovering the similarities and differences of ancient cultures to our own, and coming up with theories that might explain why people did what they did.

I liked to find proof that, as different as our world today was from the past, people still faced the same challenges. Not just providing food, clothing, and shelter. They lifted their gazes above, longed for an understanding of things outside themselves, creation and a creator. And they wanted love and family, even if some cultures went about it wrong.

No one could go back in time for a do-over—if that were possible, I'd be the first in line—but maybe we could learn from their mistakes and benefit from their accomplishments.

My attention back on the book, I studied a speculative layout of Pompeii, but then my phone vibrated in my pocket.

Rylee? Last time we spoke, she'd wanted more of an explanation from me about breaking up. I didn't have a better explanation for her any more than Caitlyn had one for me. Rylee wouldn't understand where I was coming from. And Caitlyn probably thought I wouldn't understand whatever she was keeping from me.

I pulled my phone out. Not Rylee. Roland. Did I want to talk with him? No doubt Caitlyn's been talking to him since she got here. Maybe he'd know about—

Worried it had rung too long and would switch to voicemail, I swiped my thumb across the screen to take the call. "Hey, Roland, what's up?"

"Oh, wow, so you finally answered your phone." Roland sounded ticked, which always amused me. He'd tolerated so much from me over the years, but since my grand apology a few summers ago and my ensuing attempt at being a decent human being, he'd become increasingly bold with me. His boldness tempted me to knock him back down . . . I mean, I really had to fight the urge sometimes. But I wouldn't let myself do it. He'd shown me mercy in a big way. And it changed my life.

"Yeah, so what's so important?" I tucked a couple of books about Pompeii under my arm and left Papa's study. Didn't want him coming back and finding me here. He wouldn't mind if I borrowed the books, would he?

"I've been trying to call you for days."

"Yeah, well, you got me. What's up?" I strolled down the front hallway.

"What's up with you? You were really looking forward to field study, but you backed out, Caitlyn said, because some professor couldn't go."

"She told you that? What else has she told you?" I rounded the corner, wishing I'd kept my voice down. If she were in the kitchen, she might hear me and know I was talking about her. But she'd obviously been talking about me, so . . .

"Uh . . . I don't know."

"Yes, you do. It's why you're calling. So out with it." I doubted Roland would breach the subject, so maybe I had to go stronger and force him to admit what she'd told him.

"I'm just wondering how you're doing. How's the job hunt going?"

Okay, so Papa had been talking to Roland too. After glancing into the empty kitchen, I took the steps by twos and swung into my bedroom, closing the door behind me. "You must talk to Caitlyn every day, right? Her being your girlfriend and all." I set the Pompeii books on the dresser.

"Oh, well, you know how I hate talking on the phone. But we email each other, not every day, and she's not my girlfriend . . . We're just friends."

My brain repeated Roland's last words even as I said, "What? You're not seeing her?"

"I just started seeing a girl I met here at SDU. Her name's Ling-si."

Roland said more about his new girlfriend, but I could hardly move past this revelation. Who broke up with whom? "Did you dump her?" The thought made me angry. No one should dump a girl like her.

Roland stopped mid-sentence, whatever he was talking about. "Did I dump her? You mean Caitlyn? Well, no. She kind of . . . well, she didn't exactly dump me. It's not like we were actually dating or anything. She just told me . . . never mind. We're friends, like best friends even. But I'm calling to see how you're doing."

"Oh, yeah." Wanting off the phone now so I could think over this new development, I tried to provide a satisfactory reply. "Just been riding Desert, working out, hanging out with my buddies, that kind of stuff. And I'm sure I'll be getting a job soon. Nothing to worry about here. But I gotta go now."

"Okay, answer your phone now and then."

"Yeah, you too." I ended the call, tossed the phone to my bed, and stood looking at myself in the mirror over the dresser. Caitlyn wasn't seeing Roland. Was she seeing someone else? I should've asked Roland. Should I call him back? No, bad idea. He'd wonder why I wanted to know.

My gaze raked over my reflection in the mirror, my olive-green cargo pants and off-white t-shirt with the y-neckline, clothes that looked good on me. My hard-earned muscles, my goatee of stubble, and long hair pulled into a ponytail. Chicks liked that. All of it. They liked me. But not the kind of chicks, the kind of *girl*, that I wanted. What did Caitlyn think of me? Looks probably didn't matter so much to her. She probably just cared about substance, the inner man, what a guy said and did.

The futility of it hitting me hard, I slammed a half-open drawer. She'd never like a guy like me, and I didn't deserve a girl like her. Why was I even thinking about it for a second?

Rubbing the back of my neck, I paced toward the window, thinking, thinking. I needed to find something to busy my mind. Something to get her out of it. As I flung open the closet door to get my riding boots, I remembered leaving them in the mudroom when I'd fetched a bucket of water to wash windows in the veranda. With Caitlyn. I'd really liked that, working with her, talking with her. Had she liked it too?

Argh. Stop thinking about her! I thrust a hand into my hair and stomped from my bedroom.

--*

Wind whistled in my ears and made my eyes water as Desert took the wide, partially shady trail at a full gallop, burning the breeze. I'd left my favorite saddle back in the barn, cinched up instead a bareback saddle pad, one with stirrups, for a better connection with Desert. Leaning forward some, sucking in air, I kept my body relaxed, moving with my horse. Holding the reins loosely, my hands followed the hypnotic, rhythmic motion of Desert's head. I was one with my horse.

Mr. Digby may have had to force me a time or two, but I loved to ride. Missed it when away at college. Found it an adrenaline rush that I didn't want to end. It cleared my mind, sometimes allowing no other thoughts but those of me and my horse, my body floating along, Desert moving under me. His black mane flapping and licking at my face, ears laid back, muscles bunching and releasing as his hooves pounded the ground, galloping down a forested trail. Free.

As we neared the sunny farmland at the back of our property, Desert didn't need my command to slow from a four-beat gait to a three-beat canter. Sitting lightly on the saddle pad now, I directed him down a dirt path between new crops for a little exploring. Couldn't tell what it was, but they'd harvested the rye already, planted something else. Desert snorted, puffing his breath out his nostrils. He liked to explore.

We rode up and down a few sunny rows then returned to our shady, treed property, slowing to a trot. Tugging up the neckline of my t-shirt, I wiped the wind tears from the corners of my eyes. Then I ran a hand through my windblown hair. I'd worn it down for the ride. Nothing like wind through your hair while flying on a horse. But it probably looked like a wreck now.

Long red locks streaming in the wind. Caitlyn turning her head, throwing me a playful smile. Her skirt fluttering around her legs . . .

I groaned and threw my head back. I had to stop thinking about her. I'd never even seen her on a horse, so where'd that image even come from? There could never be anything between us. I'd made too many mistakes. She knew about many of them, and if she asked me about the others, I'd tell her. I'd tell her anything she wanted to know about me, no matter how humiliating. And she'd know with great certainty that she'd never want a guy like me.

She was pure. She deserved someone equally pure, like Roland. Why exactly had they broken up? Was it his fault? Was it hers? Roland hadn't explained it at all, said they weren't actually dating. What'd he mean by that? I couldn't imagine a conversation between me and Caitlyn where I'd get to ask her those questions. I should stop talking to her altogether. It was messing with my mind, maybe my heart. Besides, she thought I should get a job so . . . maybe I should.

Desert bobbed his head and let out a friendly nicker, ears forward and eyes alert as if excited about something up ahead.

I peered down the trail, glancing from tree to tree, when I glimpsed something pink. In the next second, Caitlyn emerged from the trees, her hair loose around her shoulders, her pink gypsy skirt billowing about her legs as she walked toward me, not looking up, maybe not even aware that in one brief moment we would meet. As if by Divine Providence. Making it impossible for me to deny my feelings for her.

Desert may have sensed the change in me, the clashing of my hopes and fears that penetrated to my very core. He slowed even more, walking now. And when he snorted again, Caitlyn looked up and stopped in her tracks.

Since she just stood there, I closed the distance between us, my mind skipping from thought to thought as Desert's hooves clip-clopped down the trail.

. . . standing under a canopy of trees, shadows and sunlight dancing on her pale skin . . .

. . . Roland was not her boyfriend . . .

. . . a breeze playing with her hair, flinging one red lock across her cheek . . .

. . . she went out of her way to help me, a girl like her helping a guy like me . . .

. . . an aura of goodness surrounded her, something more than skin deep . . .

. . . but what surrounded me?

Reaching her, I shifted my weight, signaling for Desert to stop. I hadn't a single coherent thought in my mind. Should've at least said hello.

"I thought I heard a horse," she said, gazing up at me through green eyes that seemed even more gorgeous out here under the trees, "but I didn't realize you were right . . . here. On the same trail."

I still couldn't get a greeting out, couldn't get my mouth to work, but I could no longer resist inviting her to ride with me.

Not sure how to ask, I simply slid back on the saddle pad and offered my hand to help her up.

She looked at my hand but said nothing, did nothing, for a whole two seconds, making me feel stupid and self-conscious. "Get on the horse," I said in a commanding tone.

And to my surprise, she did.

CHAPTER 16

Caitlyn

Having no reason to hurry but feeling rushed all the same, I scooped up the corn muffin ingredients I no longer needed, and my upper arm brushed the stand mixer—instantly transporting me to the horseback ride yesterday and Jarret's arms around me, brushing me as he held the reins, his chest against my back, his chin in my hair.

My insides fluttered from my neck down to my toes, just as they did then. My goodness. Did I really? I'd just wanted to take a walk, enjoy the lovely day. When I'd heard the clopping of a horse further down the trail, I'd expected to see Mr. Digby—not Jarret in his off-white t-shirt, olive-green cargo pants, and high black boots on a creamy buckskin horse.

I ran my hands under warm water then rinsed out the measuring cups and spoons, set them aside, stuffed the corn muffin pan into the preheated oven, set the timer, checked on the chili simmering on the stove.

I . . . climbed onto a horse with Jarret West.

Get on the horse, he'd said, his voice so deep and commanding, making me want to obey. *Ugh.* I'd felt like I had no choice. Some part of me wanted to do just what he asked.

The way I'd mounted the horse . . . *Ugh, ugh.* So clumsy. I'd lifted the wrong foot to the little stirrup but then realized it before he had to correct me. Then I'd struggled to stuff the correct foot into it. He'd only smiled a bit as he yanked me up. Then he'd guided me onto the saddle pad, seating me in front of him. So close to him. His scent, some calming ocean smell, surrounding me.

I wiped off the countertop with a wet washcloth.

Ugh. Ugh. Ugh! Was I developing a crush? This was just not possible. The girls in high school couldn't get enough of him, some even dropping everything just to watch him strut down the hallway between classes. Him in his designer clothes. His long hair. His confident stride. His attitude. He thought so highly of himself. Who could like a guy like that?

I glanced at the wall clock as I carried blue-flowered ceramic bowls and plates to the dining room. Mr. West was home so everyone would eat in there. Would Jarret join us for dinner? He hadn't so far. Would today be any different? He didn't think I liked him, did he? Me and Jarret West . . . Ha! How silly. Of course he didn't. I was so not his type. He wouldn't be caught dead with a nerd like me.

Getting a date with him in high school had been a big deal for so many girls. My best friend, Zoe, once she started seeing him, had been the envy of girls all through freshman year— even after she got pregnant. All that just made me not like him more and more. Sure, I'd tried to remain civil. He was, after all, my best friend's boyfriend. But it didn't stop me from warning her about him and encouraging her to find someone else. And what was happening now?

Ugh. Ugh. Ugh. UGH! My decision to be friendly to him was not permission for my heart to go wild. What exactly happened to me yesterday? *Get on the horse,* he'd said, and I obeyed. Then the silent ride down shady paths, the clip-clop of the horse's hooves, the rustle of wind through the leaves, the pitter-patter of my heart, and nothing else. Neither one of us had spoken until after he dismounted back at the house and helped me down.

That was nice, I'd said, practically spellbound as I gazed into his eyes, the sunlight hitting them in a way that reminded me of a tall, bubbling glass of Coca-Cola on a hot summer afternoon.

Yeah, he'd said and nothing more.

I arranged plates and bowls on the table . . . one, two, three, four—and a fifth set? Jarret never came to dinner. With a sigh, irritated by my mistake, I carried the extra dishes back to the kitchen and opened the cupboard.

As I slid the plate back onto its stack, footfalls came from the hallway. It didn't sound like Mr. West's cowboy boots or Mr. Digby's . . . well, he never made a sound, just showed up here and there. It certainly wasn't Nanny's footfalls. She'd been using a cane and taking it slow, but the quick pace was not Jarret's either.

I peeked around the cupboards over the bar counter just as Jarret breezed into the room . . . all dressed up in a slate-gray button-front shirt and white chinos, his hair pulled back neatly, his goatee trimmed. My heart thumped somewhere in my neck, and a heatwave rolled over my skin.

As our eyes met, he practically slid to a stop. An arrogant appraising look, one brow arching and eyes roving over me, morphed into a big smile. "Well, I did it."

"Did what?" His smile made me smile. He was genuinely happy about something, proud even.

He took a few measured steps closer. "Landed a job. First place I applied."

Thrilled for him—he'd taken my advice to listen to his father and he'd actually gotten a job!—I fairly lost my mind and raced around the bar counter, almost threw my arms around him. Regaining the slightest amount of restraint, I stopped myself, grabbing one wrist and twisting my arms in front of me. How inappropriate would that be, hugging him like that? "Congratulations! I'm so happy for you!"

His face . . . a stunned little smile transformed into that big smile he'd first had, and he whispered, "Thanks." Then he cleared his throat and glanced away, then back, then away.

"Your father will be glad." I bounced on my toes, still having to suppress the urge to hug him. I was way too proud of him. It shouldn't have mattered so much to me.

He rolled his eyes, shifting to stand more casually now, his weight on one hip and hands loose at his side. "Yeah. He'll be glad alright. Haven't told him yet."

Stirred by the realization he'd told me first, another heatwave washed over me. "So tell me about your new job. Where is it? When do you start?"

"Well, I was thinking maybe you'd go celebrate with me. We could get dinner at that new Thai restaurant I'd been meaning to check out. I'll tell you all about it then."

"Oh." I pressed my lips together. His father wouldn't like the idea, but maybe Jarret didn't care. He didn't seem worried about being in the same room with me anymore. But . . . dinner? That sounded like a date. The horse ride had meant something more than it should've. Did he like me? No, not possible. Not in the girlfriend way. Speaking of . . . "I'm sure you'd rather celebrate with your friends or your girlfriend."

"No, I wouldn't." Shaking his head, he stepped past me, further into the kitchen, and opened the fridge. "They'd just want to drink."

"And your girlfriend?" He'd never mentioned one before, but I was certain—

"No girlfriend." He turned around with a half-full bottle of juice in his hand and leaned against the counter.

"Really?" Could that be true? I'd assumed he always had a girlfriend.

"Yeah, really." He took a swig of juice. "Come on, I got no one else. Please." He tilted his head down a bit and looked at me through puppy-dog eyes. "It's not a date, if that's what you're worried about. I'm just happy and want to celebrate with someone . . . with you."

His puppy-dog look—oh so irresistible. I glanced away, trying to think of reasons why I shouldn't, why I couldn't, but my mind drew a blank.

"Please," he whispered again.

Well, other than taking the cornbread out of the oven, I'd completed dinner preparations, so I could easily get away, face the dinner dishes later. Jarret said it wasn't a date, so I didn't have that to worry about. I'd wanted to befriend him, and he seemed to think of me as a friend, so . . .

"Come on, it'll be fun."

A bit of excitement tingled through me. "Okay. I'll go see if Nanny minds. If she doesn't, I'll go change."

A self-assured smile stretched across his face, and he lifted his chin. "Good."

Jarret

I held my menu at an angle and searched through it a second time. None of the entrée names sounded familiar. Krapao Talay and Pad Krapao . . . Could they come up with worse names? Preaw Wan . . . made with a sweet & sour sauce, might not be bad. Teriyaki Thai Style sounded kinda good. Pad See-Saw . . . ? No, no, it was Pad See-ew.

Caitlyn, sitting across from me, glanced up from her menu, which she also held at an angle. She bit her bottom lip and giggled. "Some of these sound . . . horrible."

"I was just thinking that." I liked that we both thought the same thing, at least about the menu. I usually didn't step foot in a new restaurant until I heard from someone else that they had good food. But I'd wanted to try something new. New job. New restaurant. New girl—no, no, slow down. She's just a friend. But we'd never had dinner together, so that was new.

The placed looked nice anyway. Orange lanterns hung from high ceilings over tables with fancy bamboo chairs. Potted oriental trees lined one wall. A golden-yellow screen with bamboo framework and light behind it formed another wall. The tables had enough space between them to allow private conversations.

We sat in a booth. I kind of wished I'd asked for a table so we could sit adjacent instead of across from each other. Didn't matter. She came out with me. Not a date, but still. Never in my life would I have imagined such a thing possible. Until recently, I wouldn't have even thought about it anyway. Caitlyn Summer sitting at a restaurant with me.

Caitlyn lowered her menu again and leaned forward to whisper, "Do you think it all tastes like Chinese?"

"I dunno. There's got to be some difference."

"Look." She turned her menu so I could see it then pointed and whispered clearly, "You can get a hamburger." That made her giggle, a little scraping sound in the back of her throat. Then she pointed to something else. "Or you can get a Tod Man, a Tod Man Pla." The last word came out with emphasis, like she was spitting something yucky from her mouth. She giggled harder.

I cracked up. She was funny out of the house, all silly and secretive. Not like the girls I've dated, with their perfectly made-up faces and styled hair, glancing at themselves in reflections and careful with the way they moved their mouths, as if they'd practiced eating and laughing and talking in a mirror. It had always annoyed me and pleased me at the same time, mostly because I thought those kind of girls helped maintain my image.

As soon as Nanny said she could go, Caitlyn had changed into a feminine beige dress that tied at her thin waist with a big bow. And she might have felt too rushed to do anything different to her hair. It looked kind of windblown and wild, and I really liked it.

I set my menu down and found myself staring at her thick red lashes, natural, pale, pretty—she looked up, and the room got a few degrees hotter. "I've decided," I announced. "I'm gonna try the kapow." I swung my fist and smiled.

She returned to the menu, pressing her lips together, then smiled and shot me a look. "I'm gonna try this." She pointed and said, "Yummy Yum Nua," before collapsing in giggles over her menu.

We discussed English words that Thai people might find funny and laughed until a waitress came to get our order. I ordered for both of us, taking her wide-eyed glance as a plea for help, hopefully not insulting her by taking over. Some girls hated that.

The food was good, the company better. We talked about our favorite foods—both of us loving Mexican food—and our other favorites: movies, books, places to visit, music, snacks, sports, activities . . . I didn't want it to end. She was interesting and fun to talk with, and she had some inner freedom and joy that I couldn't wrap my mind around but that made me want to listen to her talk all night.

And then, while talking about our favorite colors, my heart stopped at her answer.

"The blue I love most is like the blue in your bedspread." Caitlyn's eyes popped open wide, and a blush bloomed on her cheeks.

I nodded slowly, with a look that said I caught her. "Yeah, my bedspread. That's a good blue."

She smiled, stabbed a piece of steak on her plate, and stuffed it into her mouth. Our continuous conversation had left little time for eating.

"So, I kinda feel like we've become friends."

She looked at me, her cheeks bulging as she chewed. Then she lifted one shoulder and nodded, adding an "Mm-hm."

"I stopped asking you about that night, but I haven't stopped wondering. Any chance . . ." I let the question hang, while giving her a mildly pleading look. I wasn't going to overdo it, and if she still didn't want to tell me, fine. I'd get over it. I'd try not to ask again. I kind of wished I hadn't just asked—made me seem desperate—but the comment about my bedspread . . . mm. I could almost see her in my mind . . . in my bed. And I really shouldn't go there, not even in my thoughts.

She swallowed her food and gulped her water, downing almost half the glass. After wiping her face, first with her hand, then with the napkin she only just seemed to remember placing on her lap, she said, "Okay. I'll tell you."

Caitlyn

Jarret sucked in a deep breath, his chest rising, as if bracing himself for what I had to say. I really, really didn't want to embarrass him, but when he said we were friends, it warmed my heart so much that I wanted to confide everything to him. Well, maybe not everything. But at least this.

After scanning the tables around us, and certain no one paid us any attention, I began, "So after we got your car, I helped you upstairs and to the bathroom—"

"Huh?" He blinked a few times and shook his head, maybe wanting to shake the thought away.

I needed to explain. "I got your toothbrush ready and suggested you, you know, do all those things we do before we go to bed, and I then waited in the hallway while you . . . took care of business."

Eyebrows climbing up his forehead, he nodded and took a breath. Was he really ready to hear the rest?

"After a long while, when you didn't come out, I went in to get you, and I helped you to your room." While he gazed at me intently, I explained the rest step by step, how I took off his shoes and belt, how I got out something for him to change into and turned down his bed, and then how he pulled me into his bed. I laughed a bit when I said it, not intentionally, but it all played out in my mind again, especially the awkward way he'd manhandled me.

"Tell me I didn't." He paled, his head moving a bit from side to side. A disgusted look on his face. He was mad at himself.

"It was nothing. Just you being silly. I mean, you didn't try anything. You just wanted me to"—*and here it goes*—"sing to you and stroke your hair."

His eyebrows shot up this time, not just a slow climb up his forehead, and he glanced around the restaurant as if worried someone he knew might've just heard what I said. He squirmed a moment in his seat, his mouth half open, his face turning every shade of red.

For whatever reason, I found his reaction terribly endearing. Jarret so cool and confident on the outside was just a little sentimental softie on the inside. Missed his mother. Wished he could hear her sing to him one more time. It was touching and a bit heartbreaking and oh so adorable.

After a moment, Jarret cleared his throat and refocused on me. "Okay, so did you?"

I smiled. "Yes. I stayed with you, and you sang a few lines of songs I didn't know, and then you found a song we both knew, one your mother used to sing to you: 'Sing of Mary.'"

He nodded and a sentimental expression colored his face.

"So I sang to you and combed my fingers through your hair—"

He rolled his eyes and huffed, embarrassed again.

"—until you fell asleep. Then I removed your designer shirt because something gross was on it, left you in your t-shirt, and wouldn't you know, I found something out about you." I hadn't planned on telling him this part, but somehow it slipped out anyway.

"Yeah, what?" Looking a bit defeated—like, what could be worse than what I'd already told him?—he lifted one hand lazily, dropped it back to the table, and shook his head.

"You wear Our Lady's scapular." I wasn't smiling as I brought up something that should've remained private to him. Maybe I shouldn't have mentioned it at all, but it touched me more than anything. It proved things about Jarret that I still struggled to believe. Jarret was a man of faith.

He rubbed his chest through his shirt then dropped his hand to the table, sitting more relaxed now. "So?"

"So, that's cool. That's all."

He looked down then back up. "Keefe talked me into it in high school. I was going through a tough time."

"Oh, I didn't know. You've been wearing it since then?" Dozens of questions popped into my mind. Was I really about to discuss faith with Jarret?

Before I could ask another question, his gaze snapped to some point behind me, and he mouthed a curse word—at least that's what it looked like. Then he grabbed the dessert menu and held it in front of his face.

"What's wrong?"

"Don't look now but Erik Hill just came in with two, no make that three others we knew in high school. At least I knew them. Wait, is that—?" Jarret sucked in a breath, something close to panic on his face.

"Who's Erik Hill?" Regardless of his warning, I glanced over my shoulder. I didn't recognize most in the group, but there was Dominic the Gossip! We had to get out of here now.

Just then our waitress blocked my direct line of sight. "Here's your check. No rush—"

Lunging forward, Jarret snatched the check and yanked out his wallet. "Where do we pay?"

The waitress pointed toward the entrance, where the group still stood . . . next to the cash register. Suddenly the group was moving forward, directly towards us.

I sucked in a breath and slid down in the booth, my skin tingling at the thought of people we knew catching us together. Then I laughed. What difference did it make? Then I wondered . . . did it really bother me for people to see me with Jarret? What did that say about me? Or him?

"Come on." His expression serious, he nodded toward the opposite end of the restaurant. "We can go this way."

As we weaved around tables, another thought crept into my mind, stirring up a bit of indignation. Was he embarrassed to be seen with me? Maybe it would damage his reputation to be spotted with a girl like me. But he'd practically begged me to come here with him.

We made it to the cash register unseen, and Jarret settled the bill. Stuffing his wallet into his back pocket, he glanced over his shoulder . . . and visibly shuddered.

"Oh, hey, amigos." Dominic came up behind us, a big smile on his face. "I was not expecting to see anyone I knew at this place, much less the two of you. Are you together?"

CHAPTER 17

Jarret

Pleased with myself for making my third sale of the day, I led a couple that had decided on our most expensive dining room set to the finance area, where Julie would help them. Julie, a sturdy, no-nonsense woman in her forties, worked with them while I waited on the opposite side of the big wraparound counter, in case anyone needed me.

Five minutes later, Julie came toward me to make copies of something, the copier being just under the section of the counter I leaned on. "You're on fire today, Jarret. Great work for less than two weeks on the job." She smiled. "Why don't you go get a cupcake in the break room? They're from the new bakery downtown, and they're delicious."

"Okay, maybe I will." I tapped the counter then saluted the couple, who glanced up at me just then, and headed off to the breakroom. For a cupcake.

After my first day on the job, I'd come home to a grand welcome, as if I'd accomplished something extraordinary, rather than finally getting my butt off the couch to get a part-time job. Caitlyn and Nanny had made cupcakes. Mr. Digby and Papa had asked me twenty questions about my job then reminisced about their first jobs.

I liked how they'd all made a fuss over me, even though it made me realize I didn't care like I should about anyone but myself. Should've thought to check on Nanny the day of her surgery. Should've taken my own luggage up to my room. Should've shown more interest in Papa's assignment, the one he'd been putting off. Should've acknowledged Mr. Digby's hard work now and then, especially since he always cared for my horse when I was gone.

Stuffing the last bite of a caramel vanilla cupcake into my mouth, I stepped from the cramped breakroom to where two other salesmen stood talking by the carpet samples.

One of them, Parker, looked at me and a smile slithered across his face. "Your regular customer is back." He stretched a hairy arm way out to point me in the right direction.

"Come on, boss, do I have to?" I clasped my hands behind my head and turned my face to the ceiling, my neck cracking. This woman never bought anything, just wasted my time, and I didn't know how to handle her.

"You know how we roll, Jarret, my boy." Parker, a quirky middle-aged man, was not my boss, though I called him that, just one of the more experienced salesmen who helped me out a lot. He could turn "the salesman" on and off on a dime, boldly fake but with impressive results. And he knew how to handle every type of customer. Too bad he wouldn't take this woman off my hands.

I sighed, checked for icing on my face, and tugged my dark-red button-front shirt straight.

Parker waved his brows and slapped me on the shoulder. "You've made a killing tonight. Keep the streak going. Another two hours to go."

"But she never buys anything." I ran a hand over my hair and started off in the direction he indicated.

"Maybe tonight you'll get lucky."

I took my time, strolling down the aisle between dining room sets and living room arrangements. *Maybe you'll get lucky.* So said the guys I hung out with in high school whenever one of us had a date. The guys from high school . . .

I stopped scanning for Ms. Sadie as something else came to mind: my and Caitlyn's exit from the Thai restaurant. Dominic the Gossip had seen us together. What rumors would he spread? I should never have gone anywhere with Caitlyn, not with my reputation. People always thought the worst. And I'd hate myself if I tarnished her reputation by association.

Returning to the present, I scanned the areas on either side of the aisle and spotted her three arrangements away on the chaise lounge of a blue sectional. She waved. I nodded. I just wanted to go home.

Home. My heart warmed at the thought of stepping into the house. Caitlyn would be waiting for me. I'd seen her every night since starting the job. Had she always been up and about the house late, like, before I started working? I didn't remember seeing her, but I'd been avoiding her then.

"How are you, Jarret?" Ms. Sadie slid off the chaise lounge and sidled up to me with her shoulder-length hair of streaks and highlights, her hot pink lips, and her tight skirt straining against her thirty-something-year-old curves.

"Hello, Miz Sadie." I nodded again. I had only myself to blame for her obsession with me, not that I'd done it intentionally. On my first day at the store, not knowing how this salesman thing worked, I'd fallen back on the only skills I had with women. In my defense, I didn't understand that thing I felt around women—of any age, really, depending upon how one presented herself—that made me either flirtatious, annoyed, or protective—something I felt more often lately. Anyway, my attempt at rapport-building must've reached a very needy part of this woman. And she kept coming back and asking for me.

"Sadie is my first name, silly, not my last name." She actually touched me, just my arm, but still.

"So what is your last name?" I glanced then looked away, trying to learn from my mistakes here and not overdo the eye contact and familiar attitude.

"Please, just call me Sadie."

I didn't want to call her Sadie, didn't like the way she flirted or studied me while I tried explaining the features of this or that piece of furniture. I'd since promised myself never to check out girls the way I'd grown comfortable doing, scanning them from head to toe. If I ever planned to find the right one, I needed to change the way I thought of and acted toward women.

"You still looking for the right accent chair for your living room?" That's what she'd wanted the first couple of days. Then she'd wanted to explore bedroom sets. Then dining room sets. She did buy a vase that day, not that it helped me out. Commission on a vase? Pathetic.

"I am. And other things." Ms. Sadie returned to the sectional, sinking into it and closing her eyes.

Last Friday, I'd found Caitlyn on the couch in the family room, watching a movie by herself . . .

Caitlyn paused the movie and jumped up. "How'd it go at the furniture store?"

I recognized the movie, one of my old favorites. "I didn't know you liked Westerns."

"Well, I saw you watching one the other day, thought I'd give it a try. I just started this one twenty minutes ago."

Then she offered me snacks and I'd watched the rest of the movie with her, sitting on a separate couch and not next to her, which hadn't bothered me at all. I just liked being with her.

Suddenly Ms. Sadie jumped up, her mouth falling open and the color draining from her face.

I turned to see what bothered her.

A red-faced man in stained jeans and a dark work shirt stomped toward us, the name Gordy on his shirt pocket. "So who is this?" He looked at her and jabbed a finger at me.

"What are you doing here?" She slung the skinny strap of her purse over her shoulder and gripped her purse to her abdomen, as if trying to protect herself with it or at least get something between her and the man, Gordy . . . her husband, I presumed.

The man's scowl deepened. "Uh-uh. The question is, what are *you* doing here? Stopped across the street for burgers on my dinner break and seen your car parked here every night for a week. Thought it was time I came in to see the attraction." His angry eyes cut to me now, and he looked me up and down.

This had nothing to do with me. I should give them some privacy. I started to back up but bumped into a curio case or something.

The man lunged toward me, as if he might physically try to block my escape. "You're not going anywhere until you answer a few questions. What's your name, boy?"

Heart pounding like an animal that wanted loose, I glanced around for the boss or at least another salesman. *What should I be doing in a situation like this?* "Name's Jarret. I'm j-just a furniture salesman."

"Are you the reason my wife's coming up here every day?"

I glanced at her, wishing she'd answer his question. What did I know? Then I just shrugged and shook my head. "I'm just trying to sell—"

He grabbed the collar of my button-front shirt and pulled me close. "Are you having an affair with my wife?"

"Wh-what? No!" Keeping my cool, I pried his fingers from my shirt then lifted my hands in a gesture of peace. "Really, I'm new here." I worked to keep my voice calm, tried not to look arrogant, cocky, or offended. "Just trying to sell furniture."

"I know your type," he growled, "but you're messing with the wrong man, or his wife—my wife!"

Okay, my cool was slipping away bit by bit, and the old me was creeping back in. I resented his accusations, his attitude, his nerve . . . he could at least find out the truth before attacking some random salesman who happened to be standing near his wife. "Chill, dude. Is your name Gordy?" I pointed to the nametag on his shirt. "Listen, Gordy, I'm not messing around with your wife. She's, like, ten years older than me, and it's not my fault she comes up here."

One eye twitched, then a sneer, then he snapped, grabbing my shirt again. "Are you saying it's my fault? If I were a more attentive husband . . . ?"

"I'm not saying anything." Prying his fingers from my collar, I glanced again for a manager but only glimpsed a couple of salesmen watching from safe distances. "Listen, why don't you talk to her and leave me out of it?" I barked out the last words. And if he didn't drop it now, my temper was likely to blow. I could only keep the old Jarret down for so long.

"Leave you out of it, huh?" He curled one hand into a fist. "I'm gonna leave you with a warning—" Then he swung for my chin.

I leaned back, avoiding his fist but brushing the curio cabinet behind me. I couldn't stand here and take this for another second. "Okay, Gordy, you've made your point." I stepped to the side, away from the cabinet, my fists coming up.

He grabbed my arm. I jerked it from his grip. He swung again, this time low, aiming for my gut.

Having practiced fencing and fighting with my brothers, I could avoid a shot easily enough . . . most of the time. So my pivot kept him from making his mark and kept me from having to strike back.

"You know what?" I said, fists again at the ready. "Maybe you oughta head home and talk to your wife instead of me."

Gordy's face turned a deeper shade of red, looking ready to pop, when he swung again, and if I'd been watching his shoulder, I could've predicted where his fist might land. But movement in my peripheral vision drew my attention, my boss—the real boss—approaching.

And that glance away from Gordy cost me.

His fist ripped across my jaw, with a crack and a jolt of pain and a knock to my pride.

Upon impact, red hot anger burst inside, and the old Jarret took over. I lost control for one split second. But that's all it took.

I knocked that dude galley west.

Caitlyn

"It was not a date!" I shouted into my phone. I stood gazing over the battlements on the roof, overlooking the front of the Wests' property. The warm eighty-seven-degree day had cooled to low eighties as early evening drew on and a good breeze blew through. I didn't remember early June being so warm last year.

"Sorry. Sounds like a date to me." Ling-si wasn't giving up.

I'd emailed her, Roland too, the day after Jarret and I went to the new Thai restaurant, but she felt it vitally important to revisit the subject now. Maybe I shouldn't have called her. I'd decided no texting and phone calls while on my West Castle Retreat, but I had so much time to myself lately . . . with Jarret at work and my chores all complete and no retreat-type contemplative thoughts stirring in my head. So I'd decided to suspend my no-phone-call rule for the evening.

"Just try to see it from my perspective," I said. "Ever since Jarret got here, his father's been hounding him to get a job. Then three weeks later, I suggest he do what his father wants and boom! He got a job. It seems like I helped him to do what he felt he should've been doing all along." My heart sang. I'd promised myself, that night he came home drunk, that I would try to be a friend, as impossible as that had been for me previously. And here I'd done it. He thought of me as a friend and took my advice.

"I don't know, Caitlyn. Roland's worried that you're developing feelings for his brother, although he won't tell me why that would be such a bad thing."

The wind blew my hair over my face, right into my mouth, so I turned into it and leaned my back against the rough battlements. Sweet Roland. Never wanted to betray anyone with gossip.

"You can tell him there's nothing to worry about. We rarely cross paths anymore." Since Jarret started this job, he woke late, followed a strict exercise routine, showered, grabbed a bite to eat, and was out the door. Meanwhile, I stayed busy helping Nanny with her daily exercise goals and seeing to my chores. By the time I went to prepare lunch, he was gone.

I decided not to mention that I saw Jarret every night. I couldn't help myself. Wanting to support his efforts, I hung out in the kitchen or family room around the time I expected him home. Plus, the more we talked, the more I realized my negative impressions of him did not always match the real him. Granted, over the years, Roland had claimed that he'd changed but I never took him seriously. Now Jarret and I talked for at least an hour every night, except for the one night we watched an old Western together . . . him on one couch, me on the other, both of us snacking, him laughing at parts that didn't seem funny, making me like him even more.

A glance at the time on my phone told me he'd be home in about two hours. What snacks could I make tonight?

At some point, while my thoughts lingered on Jarret, Ling-si had turned the conversation to my retreat, so I told her about the prayer closet I'd found. And she wished she could see it.

"Roland doesn't tell me all the interesting things about his house," Ling-si said. "He acts like it's nothing, just an ordinary house, but you give quite a different impression."

"You really must come and see for yourself." I remembered when I first saw the place, how it stole my breath away and whisked me off into a fairytale. Now here I was, the maid of West Castle—at least for the summer.

"So your parents are fine with you being there, even with Jarret home?"

"They're okay with it. Dad had a long talk with me, and Mom calls regularly to check up, but she's mostly worried about my youngest sister, Stacey. She's fourteen now, that difficult age. And, really, she's always been a bit of a troublemaker, but now it's worse. I suggested Mom send her to Fire Starters. That's our parish youth group. It always helped me gain perspective." And maybe she'd make some good friends and abandon the ones that liked to sneak around . . . and shoplift.

"Yeah, I liked our parish youth group too. I made so many good friends. And it made me think about angels and miracles and other supernatural things."

"Well, the first meeting is tonight, so I hope she goes."

The sound of a car crunching over gravel rose above the rustle of leaves in the breeze. I looked out over the battlements just as a red car rolled into view. Jarret's car.

With a gasp, I backed up so he wouldn't be able to see me.

Then I found myself breathing faster, a hint of worry slithering in. Why would he be coming home so early? One possibility after another presented itself in my mind, each one supplanting the previous one. He got tired of working and quit. Or maybe he just wasn't feeling well and left early. He received bad news and had to come home. Or maybe good news, a bonus for exceeding sales expectations. He got fired for some big mistake. Or he'd simply come home to grab something he forgot to take with him.

"Ling-si . . ." I interrupted whatever she was saying, something about how she and Roland planned to visit their families one weekend this summer. "I'm sorry, but I have to go. Something just came up."

"Oh, okay. Well, call me again if you get bored. And remember, I'm praying for you, that God will guide you and give you direction."

We said our goodbyes and I ended the call. Then I rushed to the steps that led to the second floor. If I hurried, I'd get back inside before Jarret could catch me up here. Not that it mattered. Why would he care?

I stepped inside through the door at the end of the hallway, greeted by silence. Then I secured the lock into place with a heavy metal clang and tiptoed down the stairs. Before I reached the last step, voices came from a distant part of the house, escalating voices—Mr. West and Jarret, at it again— but I couldn't make out what they said. Mr. West must've met Jarret just as he'd come in from the garage.

Even as my feet drew me down the hall and toward the great room, my conscience told me to go the other way. This wasn't my business. But I rounded the corner anyway and pushed open the double doors to the family room. Maybe somehow I could help.

On the opposite side of the house, near the veranda, Jarret stood with his hands on his hips and his head bowed and shaking while his father shouted, "You haven't even been there two weeks."

"As if this is my fault." Jarret jerked one hand in the air, a bold gesture, an arrogant look.

"It's time to acknowledge the corn, Jarret." Mr. West stood calm and still, even as he spoke in a voice that could reach the far corners of the house. "Your attitude gets you in more trouble than—"

"But he hit me first." Jarret jabbed his index finger at his father.

"You can't act on every impulse. Especially when you're on the job. Things don't always go the way—"

"Oh, right. And what would you have done?" Jarret took one step forward, gesturing with both hands, the tension in his body palpable. "Just gonna stand there while some dude punches you? I highly doubt that."

"You do have a way with girls, Jarret, that another man might not appreciate, especially when the girl is his wife."

Jarret huffed, head shaking, and turned away. "I was *not* hitting on his wife. I was just trying to sell furniture. Can I help it she developed some *thing* for me, kept coming in every day?"

I stopped a good distance away and gripped the back of the couch in the family room, where I'd sat the other night when watching an old Western with Jarret. I wanted to help, wanted to say something, but I didn't understand what had happened. Maybe Jarret would talk with me later, once his father cooled down.

Mr. West shoved his cowboy hat back and scratched his head. "I don't know, Jarret, trying to reach you, keep you on the right path . . . it's harder than breaking in a wild horse."

Jarret shook his head again, his gaze tripping on me this time, his mouth opening for a breath, and his face paling with some needy look in his eyes. Then he turned away, raising both hands. "I'm outta here. We can talk about this tomorrow. If we have to."

And he flung open the door to the mudroom and blew out of here.

Anguish gripped me for one moment and an urge to tear off after him. Maybe I could catch him before he pulled out of the garage. Maybe we could talk.

But Mr. West was still standing there, his hat now in his hands and his head bowed.

Chapter 18

Jarret

I had to force myself to keep to the speed limit as I drove down Forest Road. Wind blew through the open windows, making my ponytail flap against my neck and curls scoot along my forehead. I alternated between gripping and slamming the steering wheel as trees and houses flew by. Easy on the accelerator . . .

My life was falling apart quicker than imitation Wii remotes from China. Lost my temper for one little second . . . cost me my job. Lost my resolve to avoid old temptations at the bar . . . cost me several hours of my life and a good deal of my dignity. And that look in Caitlyn's eye . . . I could see it even at the distance. She'd lost faith in me, what little she'd developed over the past month. And my paper-thin hopes of something more with her were now scattering in the wind.

Should I get another job? Try again? Over two-and-a-half months of summer left. Everyone had been so proud of me. Now this. Wasn't my fault.

I rubbed my shirt, feeling my Brown Scapular against my chest. *Lord, why do you let things like this happen? Blessed Mother, thought you had my back.*

Eh, I couldn't blame heaven for my own faults. But heaven help me, I didn't know what road to take right now.

Easing on the brakes, I turned down a side street . . . heading downtown? I had no plans. Just wanted to get away from the conflict. Maybe I'd go see what some of my friends were up to. Or maybe not. A Friday night . . . they'd be on their way to Guy's Place or some other dive.

Maybe I should've talked to Caitlyn before storming from the house, tried to explain what happened. How long had she been standing there? How much had she heard? She'd probably heard Papa's accusations. *You do have a way with girls, Jarret, that another man might not appreciate, especially when the girl is his wife.*

That painted a bad picture of me for sure. My own father saying it.

Frustration and anger simmering together, I sucked in a nice deep breath and exhaled through my mouth. I'd had no intention of getting a job in the first place. Never wanted one. Didn't need it. Couldn't go to Pompeii, so I just wanted to chill this summer.

Caitlyn had changed my mind, made me think of the Ten Commandments and a man's responsibility to honor his parents regardless of his age. The child in me kept saying, you're an adult now, Jarret, do what you want. But I knew that didn't fly. I had to do the right thing. So I got a job.

Or did I get the job to prove something to her, to prove I could be responsible, reliable? Why should I feel the need to prove anything to her?

The answer came quicker than the question. Ever since she'd helped me and I knew it, the feelings had started. And the past few weeks, talking to her almost every day, getting to know each other . . . She wasn't like other girls. Maybe I'd hoped the job would change her opinion of me. She'd see I wasn't the same guy she knew in high school. Then what? Did I think I had a chance with her?

Reaching the downtown area, I waited for a stream of minivans flowing from Saint Michael's Church then I cranked the wheel and pulled into an angled spot along the square. It was hopping here tonight, a man walking a dog, couples sitting on benches, teenage girls standing in a huddle, kids playing in the grass. Maybe a band was scheduled to play in the gazebo.

I shut off the engine and rested my arm on the open window frame and my head on the headrest. From this angle, the parking lot of Saint Michael's School showed in my rearview mirror. Lots of cars and minivans. Must've had something going on. I almost glanced away from the mirror when quick movement pulled my gaze back.

A girl, maybe thirteen or fourteen, raced from the parking lot toward the busy street.

Feeling a bit protective, I sat up and peered out the window, one hand to the doorhandle. Was that Caitlyn's little sister?

The girl—*yup,* Stacey Summers in a knee-length t-shirt dress and sneakers with no laces—walked halfway across the street with a tomboy stride and ran the rest of the way. Reaching the other side, she threw a glance over her shoulder, the wind blowing her in-need-of-combing shoulder-length hair from her face. The look in her eyes as she turned back . . . she didn't want anyone to catch her escaping.

She passed my car without seeming to recognize it, her eyes on something in the park—oh, the huddle of teenage girls, two in frayed jeans shorts, the third in leggings. As soon as Stacey reached them, one of the girls shoved her and another ripped into her verbally, though I couldn't make out what she said. Stacey shoved back and two of the girls grabbed her.

My protective instinct spiked. Not waiting to see what the third would do, I jumped out of my car, stuffed my keys into the front pocket of my denim-blue chinos, and I strode toward them. "Hey, Stacey," I called, making them all turn my way.

The two girls let her go, and Stacey shoved her tangle of shoulder-length hair from her flushed face, revealing eyes narrowed to slits. "Yeah, what?"

The oldest of the three girls mumbled something to the other two, and they took off.

"Where ya' going?" Stacey called after them. "Losers." Shaking her head, she stomped to a big boulder surrounded by flowering bushes, the one that always attracted me at this park too. She placed one sneaker on the side and climbed up, her knee-length skirt hiking up, revealing long shorts underneath.

I followed her.

She twisted around and plopped her bottom onto the boulder, her legs dangling over the side and her rectangular eyes glinting. "Thought that was your car."

"Those your friends?"

She shrugged. "Sometimes."

I reached for a thick overhead branch on a nearby tree and did a pull-up, leaves rattling. As I landed back on my feet, my car keys dropped from the pocket of my chinos and clinked to the ground. "Yeah, I got friends like that. I'm better off without them. I do fewer stupid things."

Her eyes shifted to my chin, to where Gordy had probably left his mark, and she gave me a crooked grin. "Your friends do that to you?"

"No, not a friend." I laughed and snagged up my keys. Not trusting the shallow pockets in my chinos, I looped the key ring over my finger. "Parking lot's full at church. Got a youth group meeting or something?"

Mouth curling up with a look of distaste, she shrugged. "Or something."

I knew how she felt. No one could've made me attend any of those churchy things at her age, but in my senior year I came to realize I'd been wrong about them. Maybe if I had gone sooner, I'd have figured a few things out quicker and not gone down so many bad paths. Maybe not. But still. It might do her some good. "Any of your friends going?"

She lifted one shoulder in a half-shrug, turning toward where she'd stood with the three teen girls.

"Ain't your sister there?" I couldn't remember her sister's name, but she was a year or two older than Stacey.

"Yeah . . . with her prissy friends." A mean little giggle churned in her throat.

Okay, I had her figured out. "What are you, thirteen . . . fourteen now? Getting ready for high school next year, right?" Stuffing my key in a back pocket, I did four more pull ups then leaned against the tree.

After giving me a sly grin, she nodded. "Yup."

"So that's the first youth group meeting of the year, welcoming the freshmen students, getting you connected before fall." I remembered Roland, before his sophomore year, going to the first meeting sometime in the summer, and the name of the group just came to me. "Fire Starters, right?"

She scooted back on the boulder and placed her sneakers down flat, knees up and arms wrapped around her legs— shorts visible to all passersby. "I can start a fire with a magnifying glass."

"Oh yeah?" I rubbed the stubble on my chin.

"And I can do it with the flint and steel I got for Christmas last year."

"Oh, you're a regular nerd, huh? Taking after Peter Brandt?" I didn't exactly smile when I said it, but I meant it in fun.

She snickered, giving me that devious look again. Then she stood up on top of the rock.

"Not exactly what the youth group's name means, though, huh?"

She focused on overhead branches, maybe wanting to try a pull-up after seeing me do it. "No, that's just boring stuff, more catechism."

"Nah, you learn your catechism growing up," I blurted, not sure what I was saying. "In Fire Starters you learn how to make it real."

"What does that mean?" She reached for a low branch, one much too thin to hold her weight, and pulled it down past her chin. Then she let it snap back up, leaves swooshing and rustling.

"Well"—I struggled to think of a way to explain—"you know God is everywhere, right, even though you don't see him?"

She shrugged.

"But do you know it in here?" I pointed to my chest then pushed off the tree, stepping closer to the boulder and looking up at her. "It's like when you try to start a fire with your magnifying glass. Without the sunlight, no fire."

"So God's like the sunlight?" She smirked, humoring me.

How to explain something I struggled to live day by day . . . the turning to Him for direction, the choices made to stay on the right path, the relationship, the awareness of Him from moment to moment . . . Maybe it had to start there, with the awareness of Him. "Sit down for a second."

After giving me her lopsided grin, she complied, sitting cross-legged on the boulder, a sunbeam falling on the peach fuzz on her legs.

"I want you to close your eyes. And don't open them till I tell you. I'm not going to say anything. I'm just going to stand here."

A suspicious laugh. "Why?"

"You'll see. Ready? Close your eyes."

She did as I asked, her arms resting on her legs and a little smile on her face. Trusting me.

I wished Papa trusted me that way. And Caitlyn . . . Had she lost all trust in me tonight? "Okay, open them."

She did and then looked around. "So?"

"So you knew I was right here even though you couldn't see me, right?"

"Yeah. So?"

"Well, God's here too, even though you can't see Him. I mean, you already learned that He's everywhere, right? With you every day. Well, He wants a closer friendship with you, but you gotta want that too. So close your eyes again and pay attention to Him, to God, right here with us. Ready?"

"I guess."

"Now." I closed my eyes first, assuming she'd do it too, and a rush of warmth enveloped me, throwing me off guard. Jesus stood so close I could feel it, and I wanted to rest in His presence, but when tears threatened to come to my eyes, I opened them. This was for her, not me. "Okay, open them."

When her eyes fluttered open, a little frown replaced the smirk. Then she rolled her lips inward as if to control whatever emotion she experienced. God must've spoken to her heart or maybe just whispered, but she'd heard it. "So that's what they do in Fire Starters?" she said, "They make it real?"

"Yeah, they make it real. And Father Carston's a good guy. You'll like getting to know him, not just seeing him at Mass." A part of me wished I could see Father right now. I'd put off going to confession after my drunken escapade, using the excuse that I didn't know exactly what I'd done. But now I knew, so I had no excuse.

She pursed her lips and twisted them to one side as she turned her head in the direction of the church. "I'm late now."

"Eh, who cares? I'll go with you." I offered her my hand, though she didn't seem like one to accept help she didn't really need.

One eye narrowing and the crooked grin returning, she took my hand and leaped down, dragging me forward roughly. We crossed the street together, her talking about other dorky survival skills she'd learned. Then I held the door for her, and we both stepped inside the old school building.

Familiar scents and sounds and the summer stuffiness brought back memories of my time here, especially of the days I'd been struggling to open my heart to God. So much had stood in the way, but God never gave up on me. And even though I'd messed up a few things now, He still would not give up on me. I needed to get back to grace.

Father Carston, with his glowing white beard and youthful face, stood at a table for six on the far side of the room. He looked up as we entered the room of old bookshelves, armchairs, and couches, an eclectic mix of furniture not much different from when I saw it last. "Well, hello there, Jarret. And Stacey Summer, welcome."

She turned to me and whispered, "He knows my name."

I nodded and whispered back, "You'll like him."

Stacey ambled over to a smiling girl her age and squeezed next to her on the couch.

"You're welcome to stay." Father approached me, reaching for a handshake, barely glancing at the bruise Gordy gave me at the furniture store.

"Yeah, why not." After shaking Father's hand, I found an old wooden school chair with metal legs in the back of the room, behind a group of teen boys on similar chairs. I turned the chair backwards and straddled it. "Let the fun begin," I mumbled, the nearest boys chuckling.

It was something to do, anyway. I doubted I'd be ready to go home even after the group ended. But I couldn't hang out with Kyle or that gang. I was better off without them . . . did fewer stupid things.

CHAPTER 19

Caitlyn

After helping Nanny with her morning exercises, I stepped into the mudroom for cleaning supplies. Oh, who was I kidding? My chore for this Saturday—dust and vacuum the library/piano room—was clear on the opposite side of the house. It made no sense to get cleaning supplies from here rather than the much closer laundry room.

I strolled toward the back of the tidy little mudroom anyway, past spotless cabinets that stored cleaning supplies, past the unreasonably clean utility sink, and past the little wooden bench across from a neat row of shoes and boots under hanging coats and jackets. Did the room ever really see mud?

With my sweaty hand frozen on the knob to the garage door, I took a deep breath. If I didn't see his car, I wouldn't check again. Last night I'd waited and waited for him to return home, wanting to be there for him, to help him get through this, ready to trust everything he said and offer consolation. After having checked the garage late last night, I'd finally rested my head on my pillow with a sort of numbness, in a state of limbo. Where had he gone?

Bracing myself now, I twisted the knob and opened the door to the smell of oil and car wax. A light popped on automatically, revealing Mr. West's silver Lexus, his full-size pickup truck, and Mr. Digby's big black car. No shiny red luxury car in the final spot of their four-car garage.

I shored up my heart as I closed the door. Questions whispered in my mind, but I didn't want to listen to them. It didn't matter. It wasn't really my business what Jarret did or whom he turned to when in need. It's just . . . the way we'd been getting along so well lately . . . maybe I'd read more into our friendship than he intended. Maybe he connected that way with every girl he spent time with.

As I stepped out of the mudroom, my gaze landed on the prayer closet door across the hallway, but I ignored the little tugging in my heart and walked toward the front hallway instead, to return to my room.

I unplugged my laptop and carried it from the off-white-and-gold antique desk to my bed mounded with frilly pillows. From here I could see a section of the long driveway through the window or possibly hear the crunching of tires on the gravel. Silly thought since I no longer cared. I propped the laptop on pillows and scrolled through my emails.

Ah yes, I hadn't replied to Roland's email about our dinner at the Thai restaurant. He'd seemed upset. Thought it was a mistake to go out with Jarret because he would assume that I liked him.

Well, Jarret must not have assumed I liked him that much, or he would've trusted me with his troubles, instead of running away.

Back to the email . . . Roland thought Jarret might ask me out again. Then he warned that Jarret could be insistent with girls. Would that insistence apply to other men's wives?

I sighed, annoyed with myself for even thinking such a thing. Maybe I didn't know Jarret as well as I thought I did—even after talking with him for the past few weeks—but I couldn't believe he'd hit on a married woman. Still, why would she come up to see him every day? Maybe he made her feel special the way he made me feel special.

Okay, next email. Roland sent me another this morning, wanting to know what was going on with Jarret. Was he still working? Still living here? Was something wrong?

Too bad Roland didn't just call Jarret for himself. On second thought, he probably tried. Maybe Jarret didn't want to talk to Roland any more than he wanted to talk with me. So whom did he want to talk with? The only explanation I could come up with made my chest ache. Frustrated with his father's response to his bad news, he'd gone out with friends. On a Friday night.

I'm not a drinker, he'd said. If he did have a drinking problem, he might not be honest about it. Maybe I could look for signs when he finally comes home. I hated to think that was how he handled life's setbacks. Running away. Drinking. Definitely not good qualities for a husband and father.

Stunned by the direction of my thoughts, I shook my head. Husband and father? Where had that come from?

I set the laptop aside and stood gazing out the window at the trees, their leaves a darker shade of green on this overcast day. The melancholy mood nature created brought an image of Jarret's eyes to my mind . . . such a lovely shade of brown, such long lashes, and when he looked at me . . .

My cheeks burned to think how I'd come to crave his attention. Like every weak girl in high school, had I fallen for Jarret West?

No! I'd come here to help Nanny and have a little retreat where I could sort out the seeds God had planted in my heart. I wasn't here to fall in love with a troubled man. Maybe this was a much-needed wake-up call. I needed to get my feelings under control, and to do that, I would have to stop spending so much time with Jarret.

I paced back and forth between the window and the bedroom door, frustration growing. I should've listened to the stirring inside and taken this whole issue to prayer, but I'd come to my room instead. *Oh, Jesus, help me.*

Jarret

Mentally exhausted and weary from an uncomfortable night's sleep, a bit of peace returned as I pulled into the garage. The garage door hummed as it lowered behind me, cutting off the outside and leaving me under the yellow light from the single fixture on the back wall that flicked on whenever a door opened, not the big bright lights that stretched across the ceiling and illuminated every nook and cranny. Regrets and wishes and responsibilities rushed back into my mind, but I pushed them aside for the moment. Only wanted that little light on the back wall, that little bit of peace.

As I climbed out of my Chrysler, the smell of campfire tickled my nose. I tugged my shirt collar up to my nose. Yeah, I reeked. Hope the smell hadn't gotten into my car seat. I hated foul odors in my car. Maybe I'd wash the thing later. That'd give me something to do. But first I needed a shower and to set a few things straight.

I stepped up to the mudroom door, the regrets and wishes and responsibilities returning. Maybe I'd find Caitlyn first. She'd looked concerned last night. Or maybe disappointed, like she'd lost faith in me. Any chance I could regain her trust?

I clicked the door shut behind me, kicked off my navy leather boat shoes, and crossed the room by the light of a nightlight over the tidy row of shoes and boots. The silent hallway gave no clue where I'd find her, no telling light or movement or sound coming from either direction. Should I find her now or shower first? My ego insisted upon the shower. A girl might get a bad impression, hard to erase, of a guy who'd slept in his clothes in a stuffy tent and reeked of campfire.

Stomping on my ego, I strode toward the back of the house. Caitlyn wasn't like other girls. She'd rather see me now than all freshened up later.

Not finding her in any of the rooms between the veranda and the great room, I almost passed up the music room on my way to the kitchen. Another room no one used. But there she was, standing on a stepladder by a ceiling-to-floor bookshelf, reading the spine of an old book. Sunlight through sheer curtains over the window behind the grand piano muted everything in the cozy little room—bookshelves, artwork, accent tables, and the rocking chair—making her tangle of red locks and hunter-green shift dress the focal point.

"Hey, Caitlyn." I stood in the hallway, reluctant to get too close . . . maybe because of my campfire scent but also because of the tense vibes I picked up as soon as she turned toward me.

She sucked in a breath and exhaled as if greatly relieved to see me, but her eyes showed something several degrees colder.

The icy look made me stagger, so I grabbed the doorframe, propping my hand chest high.

She flinched at my uncoordinated movements then turned away, slid the book she'd been holding back into place, retrieved the black feather duster from where she'd stuffed it on a row of books, and climbed down the stepladder. "Just getting in?" She glanced at the sculpted wall clock.

A bit of guilt pulled my gaze to the floor. "Yeah." I didn't know what to say next, where to begin.

"Glad you're okay." Her cold voice came out just above a whisper, as if she'd made considerable effort to get the words out. She dropped the feather duster and two cleaning rags into a pail of other cleaning supplies then folded up the stepladder.

"You got a minute?"

"Not really." With the ladder tucked under one arm and the bucket in her other hand, she came toward me, her eyes on the hallway and not me.

I swung out of her way and followed her into the kitchen. "Are you mad at me?" If I'd had her phone number, I would've called, we could've talked, but we'd never exchanged numbers. And I'd hesitated to ask her, afraid of rejection. It's not like we were seeing each other.

"Why would I be mad at you?" She spared me a glance over her shoulder as she entered the sunny laundry room. Windows lined the back wall, overlooking Mr. Digby's kitchen garden, ripe tomatoes visible from here.

"Well, you seem mad." I stopped in the doorway and grabbed the doorframe again, needing it this time to support myself against rising frustration. And the fear of losing our friendship. I could hear Papa's accusation in my mind. *You do have a way with girls, Jarret, that another man might not appreciate, especially when the girl is his wife.* She'd believed Papa, huh? Thought I'd been hitting on a married woman. After all the time we'd spent getting to know each other, when it got down to it, she couldn't trust me. But could I blame her? She knew enough of my past mistakes.

After leaning the folded stepladder in a corner of the room, she stood on tiptoe and opened a cabinet above the washing machine. She lifted some bottle of cleaner up to a shelf, but it started to slip from her hand.

I snatched it from the air on the way down and shoved it into the overhead cabinet for her, standing close for that one second, brushing her arm with mine.

"Thanks." Backing away and rubbing her arm where it had touched mine, she looked at me for one full second. Then she returned to her pail of supplies.

"Caitlyn." My voice came out low and insistent, but I still didn't know where to begin. Maybe if she started. "Tell me what's bothering you."

She dropped dirty cleaning rags onto a laundry pile, grabbed more things from the pail, and then took a breath. "Jarret, I'm sorry you lost your job. It didn't sound fair, but I don't know anything more than what I overheard. And it's really none of my business. Just like it's none of my business where you went last night." She faced me with a bottle of furniture polish and angry emerald eyes that glittered like jewels in the sunlight. "It just upsets me when people I care about turn to destructive behaviors when things go wrong in their lives. We should be turning to God and to each other."

I grabbed the doorframe again, irritated at the accusation. Would anyone ever see me for who I was trying to be and not as the person I once was? "I wasn't out doing something destructive. Wasn't out drinking if that's what you think. I don't drink. That was a one-off. It was stupid and I regret it. I got drunk intentionally only once in my life, and that was at a monastery."

She smiled but then her brows twitched and lips flatlined. "At a monastery," she repeated, not asking but showing disbelief.

"Look, I just needed to cool off last night. It's hard talking to my father sometimes."

"So where'd you go to cool off?"

"A friend's house."

One reddish eyebrow arched over an accusing eye. She pushed past me, leaving the laundry room.

"Not Kyle, another friend." She probably wouldn't remember Fred from high school. He came to the first Fire Starters gathering as a volunteer and invited me to his house afterwards. "He had friends over his house, tents set up, a campfire, food. It was just what I needed."

169

"I'm glad you found just what you needed." She gave me a fake little smile and sauntered from the kitchen to I don't know where.

I didn't follow her this time. I'd been hoping for too much, for things I didn't deserve, and it was high time I release the ashes of my paper-thin hopes.

CHAPTER 20

Caitlyn

A unique dinnerware set could do wonders for a person's mood. While cleaning earlier, I'd found in the bottom of the hutch a set of Western-styled plates, turquoise in the center with brown scroll around the edges. I'd also found a stack of colorful Navajo-inspired placemats and simple turquoise cloth napkins to tie it all together.

I set the table for five today, intentionally this time. Mr. West—his place at the head of the table—had asked everyone to come to dinner. Including Jarret, whom I set a place for to Mr. West's left. The Digbys would sit at the opposite end of the long table, as they always did. Where should I sit? Not across from Jarret. That might make us both uncomfortable. And it might seem odd to sit on the Digbys' side of the table. *I know—*

I placed my set in the middle of the table, close to the entrance to the kitchen. I'd be bringing dishes back and forth, so it only made sense.

After folding the napkins the only way I knew how, into little pyramids, I returned to the hutch for silverware. I'd barely seen Jarret around the house, not since the day after he'd lost his job. He'd only tried talking to me that once then must've decided I wasn't worth it. Maybe I should've given him the benefit of the doubt and not been so cold.

Part of me regretted my behavior, but the other part decided it was better this way. He wasn't the one developing feelings deeper than friendship. I was. And I needed to get them under control before he realized it. Me waiting around for him every day after work . . . What had he thought about that?

Satisfied with the table setting, I bounced back to the kitchen to check on the meatloaf. Savory aromas filled the air, and my stomach growled. Nanny had requested a dinner of total comfort food: meatloaf, mashed potatoes and gravy, and green beans fresh from Mr. Digby's garden.

The Digbys arrived in the dining room first, Mr. Digby escorting Nanny with whispered words of encouragement as she walked with her cane. Mr. West arrived next and exchanged pleasantries with the Digbys. I placed the last dish on the table just as Jarret sauntered into the room.

Oh brother. My breath caught as I laid eyes on him, and I hurried to take my seat. He wore a plaid shirt with a turquoise stripe—matching the cloth napkins—hanging open over a white t-shirt and faded denim jeans. Only a hint of facial hair today and the neat ponytail with one curly strand tucked behind his ear. Oh, he was handsome.

He glanced at me. Just a glance. Not checking me out at all. Not interested that way, of course. Had I ever thought he would be? I didn't want him checking me out anyway. Although . . . I'd known he would be at dinner tonight, so I'd spent a little more time picking my dress, a cotton blend bohemian style with blues and pinks and a wee bit of turquoise . . . that matched the napkins. And the little stripe in his shirt.

"Shall we say grace?" Mr. West removed his cowboy hat.

"What?" I blurted, distracted. I turned to Mr. West, glimpsing Jarret out of the corner of my eye. He smirked, maybe laughing inside.

After saying grace, we passed the food around. Everyone except for Jarret. He was busy staring at his plate, tilting it up even. "Man, I love these plates." Then he looked at Nanny. "Remember these?"

She laughed. "I remember. That's why I had to put them away. You broke a couple of them. Remember that? Goofing off with your brothers."

"Oh right." With the slightest glance in my direction, he set the plate flat and loaded it up, all the dishes near him now.

Everyone ate in silence for a moment. Then the saltshaker made its rounds, and a hot flash came over me. Had I forgotten to add salt to the meatloaf? *Oh, I think so.*

My next bite confirmed it. The meatloaf needed salt. I bit my lip, my eyes popping wide open against my will, my cheeks burning.

"Dinner's delicious," Jarret said, fork in hand, gazing across the table at me, some sweet look of concern on his face.

"Really?" I whispered across to him, mortified by my mistake while also touched by his attempt to lessen my humiliation.

"Best I ever had." He shoved another bite into his mouth, smiled at me while he chewed, and then turned to his father and asked over a mouthful, "So what'd you want us all here for?"

After wiping his mouth with the cloth napkin, Mr. West replied, "Well, Jarret, I know you were fixin' to get another summer job, but why don't you hold off."

That was news to me. But how would I have known his plans. We weren't speaking.

Mr. West continued. "We're going to have houseguests for a couple of weeks."

"Uh . . . what?" Jarret said.

Other questions and comments came from the Digbys' side of the table.

"I've invited the Zamoranos to spend some time with us this summer." Mr. West's cheerful eyes shifted from face to face as if he'd found the perfect solution to make everything right in the house.

"Really? You're just telling us now?" His eyebrows showing discontent, Jarret sat back in his chair.

"That's right. It was just decided," Mr. West said.

The Zamoranos . . . The name sounded familiar and suddenly I realized why. "Does that mean Selena is coming too?" The question flew out without my permission, so I slapped my hand over my mouth, but then I found myself laughing with joy and practically bouncing in my seat. Roland had told me so much about her. I'd always hoped I would meet her. I just knew we would like each other. And now . . . it was happening!

The discontent on Jarret's face vanished as his gaze connected with mine. And he may have given me the hint of a smile.

Nanny shared my excitement, and over the next two days we worked together planning everything, which guest rooms they would stay in, what towels they would use, and what meals we'd make, along with the complete grocery list. Mr. Digby even offered to take me to the store for grocery shopping. My retreat at the West Castle was about to take on a whole new dimension.

CHAPTER 21

Jarret

The full-on euphoria I'd experienced on my ride, taking
Roland's horse this time, faded as I stepped into the
mudroom and flicked on the light. Past few days, I'd taken
over exercising the horses. Mr. Digby had enough to do.
Everyone—other than me—had enough to do, preparing for
the big visit. Papa would be getting the Zamoranos from the
airport today. Nanny was probably still bossing Caitlyn in the
kitchen. They'd prepared guest bedrooms yesterday and gone
shopping, Nanny trying out a motorized shopping cart. She
lived for this kind of stuff.

I would've loved to help Caitlyn with things, run errands
or whatever, but she avoided looking at me whenever I came
near, so I took the hint and made myself scarce.

With the toe of my boot, I nudged the boot jack out from
under the bench against the wall and sat down to work my
riding boots off. In the past, I'd leave my boots and shoes
wherever they fell, but I didn't want Caitlyn to have to pick
them up—grumbling about me all the while—so I stood them

neatly against the wall with the other shoes and boots and grabbed my white sneakers.

Not sure what to do with myself, I stepped into the hallway in my socks, sneakers in hand. I'd left my car parked out front, so maybe I'd go for a drive. Or maybe I'd just go upstairs and play video games. First, I wanted to check on Caitlyn. She'd be in the kitchen. How exactly was this visit gonna work anyway? She wanted to meet Selena, but I wanted to spend time with Selena too. Did she have to be so annoyed with me? Couldn't we go back to being friends?

I strode down the front hallway, peeking into Papa's study as I passed, finding him gone. Maybe Caitlyn sensed that I felt more for her than just friendship. A girl like her, she wouldn't want to lead me on. But sometimes . . . the way her emerald-green eyes glowed . . . I could almost believe she liked me the same way I liked her.

Stupid, really. She deserved so much better. She likely had a list of qualities that she wanted in a man. I likely had none of them.

I rounded the corner by the foyer, deciding to get something to drink. A good excuse for stepping into the kitchen, but I'd hardly had anything to drink all day. Caitlyn might not be overjoyed to see me, but I'd just say hello or maybe just nod and head straight for the fridge. That shouldn't bother her.

At dinner the other day, I'd had to struggle to avoid staring, her in that pretty dress. I'd allowed myself a split-second glance. Until she'd tasted the meatloaf and looked all mortified. So it needed a little salt. Big deal. It was great otherwise. The woman had skills in the kitchen. Then I couldn't resist looking again, when she'd practically burst with joy at the news of the Zamoranos' visit. Man, she was pretty when her face lit up like that.

Halfway there—a double crash came from the kitchen, something glass shattering.

Some rescue impulse kicking in, I bolted the rest of the way. Almost to the doorway, I forced myself to stop—though the socks on my feet had me sliding a few more inches. Would my appearance on the scene make it worse, make her self-conscious? So she dropped something. No big deal. But it might've been a big deal to her.

"Oh, no!" Caitlyn said in a tight, pathetic voice.

I shoved my feet into my sneakers and pressed my back to the wall in the hallway, taking a breath, fighting the urge to swing into the room and make everything right. She wouldn't want me to. She could barely stand to look at me, didn't trust me, didn't want me, didn't need me.

"Ow!"

My head turned on its own. She'd hurt herself. Maybe cut herself on the glass. Nanny wasn't in the room, or I'd have heard her by now. She was alone, probably feeling overwhelmed.

Glass scraped and a plastic grocery bag rustled. "What a mess, what a mess," Caitlyn whispered, her voice strained. "Oh, what a mess."

My heart wrenched. I couldn't take it anymore. It wouldn't matter if I helped her just this once. I swung into the room but couldn't see her until I neared the bar counter.

She sat on her knees, too close to a mess of glass and sloppy food, salsa and applesauce maybe. Tears streamed down her pink cheeks, and her hands, her entire body trembled, making my entire body ache to help. She scooped broken glass covered in salsa and applesauce into a plastic bag. Not noticing me yet. Eyes squeezed shut, she wiped her face with the back of her hand and let out a pitiful moan.

"Hey, are you all right?" My first words to her in days. I stood a distance away, one hand stuffed in the front pocket of my jeans, almost afraid to just jump in and help, afraid she'd reject me.

When she looked up, she gasped. Probably thought she was alone. More tears. More trembling.

I crouched, the big ugly mess between us. "Let me get that." I picked up a broken piece of glass and dropped it into the bag. Then I saw red on her skirt . . . blood on her knees, the sight stabbing me in the heart. She had too much pressure on her. She needed help. "Hey, you're bleeding," I said, frozen with a shard of glass in one hand.

She glanced at her messy hands then at me. Then she followed my gaze, bowing her head to see her knees, there in the middle of the mess. She wiped her skirt before she seemed to notice it. "Blood," she whispered.

Enough of this. She needed me. At least right now. And something deep inside compelled me to take care of her. Taking charge, I grabbed her arms and pulled her up. "Go take care of that," I insisted. "Get washed up. I'll clean this. It's no big deal."

She gazed into my eyes for a moment, confusion etched in her brow, then she nodded and shuffled off sniffling.

Wanting the job done before she returned, I retrieved a dustpan from the broom closet next to the pantry and shoveled the mess into plastic bags. Then I tied the bags off and took them to the garbage cans outside the laundry room. I didn't want to leave anything for her to deal with, so I washed the dustpan in the utility sink, shook off the excess water, and returned it to the broom closet. Then I ran two rags under the faucet, wiped up everything else, and tossed the rags into a dirty clothes basket.

I came back to appraise my work, finding it spotless but wet, so I grabbed a dishtowel and dried it up. As I closed the broom closet, I felt Caitlyn's presence in the room and turned.

My heart fairly stopped in my chest, and I had to force myself to breathe.

So beautiful. Hair hanging over her shoulders, curls resting on her chest. She'd changed into a breezy white sundress with short sleeves, a thin waistline, and a ruffled hem that flounced about her calves. With her gaze shifting from me to the floor, she stepped to the counter and stood in the exact spot where she had dropped the jars. "Thank you," she whispered as if in a dream.

Determined to lighten her load, I came up beside her and grabbed a notepad and pen from a drawer. "You need salsa and applesauce. What else?"

She made no reply, so I turned to her and . . . sucked in a breath, blown away by the look of love and longing in her eyes. Before I could exhale, she threw her arms around my neck and pressed her lips to mine.

Warmth. Longing. Love passed between us, my heart beating out of control, my mind stunned. I wrapped my trembling arms around her waist and pulled her closer. A faint moan escaped her as she rubbed my neck, toyed with my ponytail, and kissed me with a passion I'd never imagined possible between us.

A low voice came from the hallway and the sound of boots. Papa.

We pulled away from each other. Mildly panicked and seeing stars, I snatched the pen and leaned over the notepad.

Papa came around the corner, a cell phone to his ear. He gave us a casual nod.

"So, what else do you need at the store?" I tried to appear calm, though my heart still flip-flopped in my chest. She loved me.

"Um, um . . ." Caitlyn wiped her mouth and ran a hand through her hair, not too good at composing herself.

I scribbled my number on a scrap of paper and placed it in her hand, a thrill shooting through me when our hands touched. She loved me. "That's my number. Call me when you think of what you need." I gave her a little smile and held her gaze until Papa turned around from the fridge.

She nodded and watched me head for the laundry room to leave through the side door.

I stepped outside and shuddered as fresh air hit my sweaty chest and neck. With my head in the clouds, I walked along the side of the house toward the circular driveway, overwhelmed with something entirely new to me.

Caitlyn Summer loved me, and my life would never be the same.

Caitlyn

A cool sweat covered my body as I whacked a head of lettuce with a huge knife. *Oh my goodness, what have I done?* In my defense, I'd woken with a horrible headache and an overwhelming "to do" list and my high-school klutziness dogged my every move. Dropping those jars on the floor . . . *ugh.* I could still hear the thunk and the shattering glass. And suddenly I was a pile of fragile nerves, so vulnerable, really not myself at all, and then . . . Jarret came to my rescue.

When I'd come back from cleaning myself up and saw the sparkling clean floor—and the nice clean dishtowel on the floor too, but whatever—and Jarret West ready to help with anything else I wanted, all rationale, all self-control, everything just simply shut off. And I just lost my mind.

I minced a section of the lettuce, chopping quickly like those cooking show chefs, which was probably not a good idea. With my track record, I'd probably cut off a finger and need more than a bandage, like the ones on my knees. At least the skirt of my dress covered my knees so no one would notice.

I glanced down at my white cotton summer dress. Probably not the best choice for someone working in the kitchen. What was I thinking? I sighed, perfectly aware of what I'd been thinking. After I'd washed up and stood gazing at outfits in my closet, my only thought was, which dress would look best on me . . . for Jarret? *Oh my.* I took a breath, huffed, and grabbed a bowl. After scraping the diced lettuce into the bowl, I brought a plump tomato to the cutting board.

Seeing the nice clean floor . . . *Thank you,* was all I intended to say, but then suddenly my arms were around his neck, my lips on his mouth. I couldn't get close enough to him. A roll of duct tape wrapping us together wouldn't have sufficed. I wanted to belong to him, and him to me.

I stopped chopping the tomato and slapped a wet hand to my forehead. What did he think about this? About me? Sure he'd kissed me back—and oh, what a kiss . . . so warm and manly—I slapped my forehead again to stop my train of thought. Certainly I'd shocked him. And right now he was probably laughing to himself, thinking how silly and vulnerable and off my rocker I was.

As I grabbed a little bowl for the tomatoes, our elaborate dinner menu scrolled through my mind. Enchilada casserole today, pan-roasted chicken and vegetables tomorrow, something different for every day of the week for breakfast, lunch, and dinner— Oh, panic!

I froze with the knife in one hand and the bowl in the other. I forgot the drinks. When we'd gone shopping together, Nanny left me in charge of getting them. I'd gotten everything else but never even looked at the drink list.

Anxiety building, I rinsed my hands, almost dried them on my apron but reached for a towel instead, then went to Jarret's little note. *Call me,* he'd said.

My hand shook as I stared at the note. Jarret West's phone number. He wanted me to call him if I needed anything else. He was out shopping for me now. I breathed and shook my head. Okay, I could do this.

Forcing myself into action, I picked up the landline and dialed his number then stood trembling as both a hot flash and a chill swept over me. The phone rang once, twice, and then—

"Hey, Caitlyn." His voice on the phone, so low and confident, so masculine. "Need something else?"

"Um. Yes, we need drinks, actually, lots of drinks, maybe juice and tea and water. Do you think they drink pop? I don't know." The words poured out, my voice so whispery and weak with a little underlying tremor.

"Got it."

Before he could hang up or say something else, I forced out, "Hey, um . . ."

"Yeah?"

Then a very long pause. I had to apologize. First, I'm not talking to him, then I'm mauling him in the kitchen. What could he be thinking? "Um, thanks for your help, and I just wanted to say . . . I'm sorry for, you know, for what I did just before you left. I don't know what came over me."

"What, for kissing me?" Amusement in his tone. Then a bit stern. "You'd better not be sorry about that. You're not gonna erase it. It happened. It was good. You like me and I like you."

I didn't know how to respond. He liked me. Jarret West liked dorky old me. What did this mean going forward?

"Got it?" he said. "'Cause I'm not hanging up until you agree."

CHAPTER 22

Jarret

H er kiss . . . the impression of it on my lips. Imprinted in my mind. I didn't ever want it to fade. Caitlyn Summer kissed me, Jarret West. Miracle of miracles. Head still in the clouds and helium expanding my heart, I stood next to her on the front porch with Nanny, waiting for Papa to come home with the Zamoranos.

I straightened from leaning against a porch beam and dropped my hands to my sides, the hand closest burning to grab her hand. Did she want me to hold her hand? Would she want me to kiss her? Not now, of course, with Nanny sitting on a teak patio chair behind us and with company coming over. Maybe not later either. She probably wished she hadn't done it. But she did. She kissed me.

The sound of tires crunching over gravel distracted my thoughts.

Caitlyn's eyes shifted toward me with a look of anticipation, joy, and solidarity.

I smiled back, everything so surreal. We didn't have to hold hands or kiss or anything. She liked me and that was enough.

As Caitlyn shifted her focus to the visible part of the long gravel driveaway, the silver Lexus appeared. She grabbed my hand—her touch warm and alive—then released it and bounced on her toes. "They're here!"

My heart thumped harder now, probably more from her touch than from the arrival of our guests, and my zipper-neck polo shirt felt too warm for this hot summer evening.

Papa drove the long way around the paved circular driveway, parking with the passenger side to the house. The second the car stopped, a passenger door flew open. Selena shot from the car just as Caitlyn bounded down the porch steps, and the two squealed each other's names and flung themselves into each other's arms. As if they were long-lost best friends.

"You two haven't even met before," I shouted, laughing to myself as I descended the porch steps.

Selena tore herself from Caitlyn and wrapped her arms around me for a quick hug and an air-kiss on each cheek. I tried kissing her cheek but got her silky black hair instead.

"You haven't changed a bit," she said, standing at arm's length and looking me over.

"Uh, really, I have."

"Mmm." Her eyes held that playful, sort of taunting, gleam that I remembered from the summer our family visited hers in Arizona. "You'll have to tell me about that later."

The other car doors swung open and happy greetings filled the air. Mr. Digby—I hadn't noticed him until just now—assisted Nanny down the porch steps. After a round of hugs, handshakes, and hellos, we all traipsed back inside, ladies first, men loaded with luggage. Mr. Digby brought up the rear, hefting three suitcases, one in each hand and one tucked under his arm, until I trundled back down the porch steps and took two from him.

"That's right nice of you, boy." Mr. Digby gave me a pleasant look, one I always thought bordered on a smile.

Nanny and Caitlyn offered to show everyone to the guestrooms so they could freshen up and drop off their luggage, unpack if they wanted to. Caitlyn and Selena chattered and giggled all the way down the hall and into Selena's room, which was right next to Caitlyn's.

Then we all met up in the great room for drinks and appetizers: shrimp cocktail and homemade jalapeno poppers, more savory aromas from the kitchen drifting to us.

Señorita Kemina carried a glass of wine to an armchair and sat gracefully with her legs crossed at the ankles as she spoke to Papa about old times. She had to be in her late forties by now, maybe even early fifties, but she looked good, at peace and self-assured. Señor Juan sat on the end of the couch nearest her. Tall and with wide shoulders, he'd aged well too. A few streaks of gray in his tidy black hair, a speckle or two in his trim mustache. He was dressed in severe Western style, complete with bolo tie and studded belt. Little Rosa sat next to him, tucked under his arm, glancing shyly from face to face. Not so little as when I first met her. Probably turned twelve already.

The conversation never lulled, Papa and the Zamoranos updating each other on their lives, the Digbys asking questions and sharing their own little stories. Selena helped Caitlyn bring each person a drink. Caitlyn even brought me a Coke before I told her what I wanted.

I mostly sat listening from a chair in the corner, feeling a bit like Roland the Loner because I had nothing to say, just wanted to take it all in, thinking about what they all had and how it came to be, and what I hoped to have one day.

Papa had grown up next door to the Zamoranos, his parents close friends with Señor Juan's, him close to Juan.

Despite the difference in wealth—Papa's family dirt poor and theirs quite rich—they'd developed strong bonds. After Papa had gone off to college, Mama, a troubled teen, was sent from Mexico to live with the Zamoranos—to keep her out of trouble. When Papa returned home at Juan's request, she and Papa met and fell in love, a good strong love that even death couldn't break, despite their differences in culture, upbringing, and experience. They had their faith in common. And love.

After a dinner of the best Mexican enchilada casserole I'd ever had, Papa led the Zamoranos on a little tour of the house, and the Digbys retired for the evening. Selena, Caitlyn, and I remained behind, the girls like two starving hobos scraping whatever they could from the bottom of the casserole dishes.

"I should've made more," Caitlyn said after licking a spoon clean. "I thought two big casseroles would be enough."

Selena giggled. "It was enough. We're just pigs."

"I hope you make it again soon. It's my favorite," I said, leaning back in my chair to see Caitlyn past Selena, who sat hunched over a casserole dish with one leg folded under her. We all sat on the side of the table closest the kitchen, and dirty dishes stretched from one side of the table to the other.

After a final scraping of the casserole dish before her, Selena pushed it back. "Let's go explore the grounds." She looked from Caitlyn to me, her expression playful.

Caitlyn wilted. "I have to clean up." Then she sat up straight, practically bouncing in her seat. "I'll come find you when I'm done. Which way do you plan to go?"

I loved that about her. She didn't wallow in self-pity, except maybe for a few seconds here and there. She saw light not just at the end of the tunnel but right in the middle of it too. That hope probably helped her get through everything.

"We can't go without her," Selena said to me with a whack to my arm as if I'd assigned Caitlyn the chores. Then she stacked a few dirty plates and shoved them into my space. "Let's help her."

"Oh, chores," I groaned, but I wouldn't have wanted it any other way.

Caitlyn

Something about horseback riding reminded me of beginning a relationship. The height off the ground and the movement of the horse beneath me had me exhilarated in one moment— experiencing a raw sense of freedom—and fearing for my life the next. Not that I thought the graceful, powerful creature would throw me. It's just that my balance and ability to communicate with the horse needed improvement.

"Lighten your grip," Jarret said with a glance toward my hands clenching the leather reins. He rode beside me on Desert. "You look great, comfortable. How do you feel?" He smiled but not in a flirty way, just a man on his horse smiling at a fellow horseback rider.

"I love it." I smiled back, glancing so as not to turn my head too much and inadvertently shift my balance.

Selena, Jarret, and I had been riding the horses every day. The first time, I'd been too nervous to ride alone, so I climbed up with Jarret again, which made me even more nervous. He'd spoken to me continuously, his masculine voice in my ear, telling me everything he was doing and why, reminding me of things Roland once taught me. All the while, I couldn't stop thinking about our kiss, how his lips felt pressed against mine, how his curls felt under my fingers, how his hands made me feel as they'd caressed my back and pulled me close—

Anyway, I'd ridden alone ever since, me in a helmet and a borrowed pair of riding breeches, getting more comfortable every day.

"We're going to a movie later, right?" Selena twisted around in the saddle to look at us, her manner always so easy on a horse. She wore her hair up today in a bun on top of her head, a few dark strands having fallen loose since this morning.

"If you guys want to," I hollered back. "Chores are done, thanks to you both, so I'm free." They'd been helping me every day with my chore list, which had increased a bit due to our guests. I'd protested as strongly as I could, since I was the one getting paid for the work, but they'd insisted. Working together . . . it made everything so fun. After chores, we spent the rest of the day at play, taking walks, having picnics here and there, eating out, shooting pool, even trying out archery—which I couldn't get the hang of. And daily grooming and horseback riding. This was quickly becoming my favorite summer.

"What do you guys wanna see?" Jarret said. "Hopefully not some chick flick."

"Oh, not the romantic type?" Selena shot back.

"I don't need to watch a romance to be romantic,"—his gaze connected with mine— "do I?"

Even with the wind on my face, my cheeks burned. This was the first flirty thing he'd said to me since the day of our kiss. As he and I had stood on the porch waiting for the Zamoranos to arrive, I'd worried that Jarret would try to act all boyfriendy with me in front of everyone. To my great relief, he didn't—with the exception of an occasional lingering glance. Even horseback riding, he sometimes rode alongside Selena and other times me, like now.

Maybe he'd changed his mind about liking me that way, but I couldn't forget what he'd said when I'd tried to apologize for kissing him. *"You'd better not be sorry about that. You're not gonna erase it. It happened. It was good. You like me and I like you."*

CHAPTER 23

Jarret

I shoved my hand into the toilet to retrieve the bolt cap that had fallen inside. I'd only bumped the stupid thing while wiping the base of the toilet, and it had popped off. Then I couldn't get it back on, so I'd whipped it to the floor with a mini burst of anger. It bounced. Somehow ended up in the toilet.

Big rubber gloves protected my hands, but I still cringed. Could there be a worse job than cleaning a bathroom? But Selena said she'd clean the bathroom by the guest rooms, and Caitlyn was taking two other bathrooms. So . . . seemed right that I should take the upstairs one that only I used.

Fishing the cap out, I again tried fitting it over the bolt. It still wouldn't seat, so I left it sitting loose and stripped off the wet gloves as I stood up.

"Nice work."

Everything in me came alive at the sound of Caitlyn's voice.

She stood in the doorway, one hand on the doorframe, her hair falling in a silky red sheet over one shoulder. She and

Selena had been experimenting with their hair, probably used a blow dryer and flat iron on it today. Looked nice. Though her typical look appealed to me more: untamed curls with a hint of frizz that gave her a halo in the sunlight. Made me think how appearances didn't matter so much to her. For whatever reason, I found that attractive. Maybe because I'd too often been a slave to appearances.

"Thanks."

A cute little smile appeared on her face. I wanted to pull her into my arms and plant a kiss on that cute little mouth.

"So are you done?" She leaned against the doorframe.

Snapping from my appreciation of all things Caitlyn, I gave the room a quick scan and decided it looked good. "Guess so. As long as it meets your standards." I grinned, not holding her gaze for too long, not flirting, then I turned away, ran the faucet, soaped my hands and arms clear up to my elbows, rinsed.

She giggled. "You surprise me."

"Oh yeah, why?" I yanked the hand towel from the hanger and faced her, standing too far away for my liking.

"I never imagined you'd be willing to clean a bathroom."

After drying my arms, I wiped the water I'd just gotten all over the sink and hung the towel back on its hanger—which I never usually bothered doing. Then I peeked into the hallway, leaning past her to see who was around. No one. So I turned back to her—standing only three feet away now—looked her in the eyes and melted inside. "I'm willing to do whatever it takes to spend time with you."

Oops.

That slipped out. I'd been fighting the impulse to flirt for days, ever since she kissed me. If she'd fallen for me simply from our conversations, from us getting to know each other, maybe I risked messing things up by flirting.

Lord, don't let me mess this up. I wanted to get to know her. I wanted to see her. She didn't really date though. She practiced courtship. How was it different from dating? Would I have to talk to her father before I could see her? I couldn't imagine that going well. Would I have to move out if we started courting?

She'd glanced away at my comment, blushed, bit her bottom lip, maybe thinking about our kiss. Maybe thinking I was coming on too strong.

"Well, not *anything*," I added. "I wouldn't kill anyone."

A big smile popped onto her face before she subdued it. "That's good to know."

"Or steal or, you know, break any other commandments. But most anything else. Is my original line losing its impact now?"

She laughed. "Come on. Selena's waiting for us in the kitchen."

I glanced down at my shirt. "We're visiting some of your friends, right? I should probably change." Tempted to find a shirt that matched, I took in her outfit—casual blue shirt and a long, flowy skirt with an ombre fade from midnight blue to white. I could find something dark blue.

"Okay, we'll wait for you in the family room." She started for the stairs.

"Oh, hey, do I know them?" I almost couldn't believe she didn't mind showing up at a friend's house with me. Granted, both Selena and Rosa were coming tonight, so it would hardly seem like we were a couple. But still.

"Yes, you know him."

"Him?" Unease slithered into my chest. I knew whom she meant before she said his name. Of course *he* was the friend.

"Peter. He's home for the weekend, so I thought it would be nice to drop by. I can't wait for him to meet Selena. Plus, Roland will be there. I mean, I'm sure he'll stop home to see your father, but he's staying there for the weekend."

"Oh. He never told me. I-I'll go change." I backed into my bedroom, expressionless, nodding. Everything was okay.

That's the look I wanted to convey, anyway. Not the irritation and apprehension I really felt. After closing the door, I ripped off my t-shirt and flung it across the room with a harsh whispered complaint. Not satisfied with that, I snatched the pillows off my bed and whipped them across the room too.

Nothing worse than cleaning a bathroom, I'd thought. Well, I was wrong. This would be worse.

Caitlyn

Cars filled the parking lot on the bed-and-breakfast side of the Brandts' house, but we'd pulled into an empty driveway on the residence side. Peter said his parents and his younger brother, Toby, had gone out shopping and bowling. A bit of anxiety snaked through my chest as I knocked on the door, Selena, Rosa, and Jarret behind me on the front stoop. I couldn't wait for Peter to meet Selena, but how would he react to Jarret coming along?

The door opened, boisterous voices and laughter escaping before Dominic's cheerful tan face appeared in the doorway. "*Bienvenidos, amigos.* Come on in." All through high school, he'd always worn his hair in his eyes, but now the top stood up in styled tufts, the sides smoothed back. It looked good on him.

He stepped aside, gracefully motioning us in. To his credit, he gave Jarret the same welcoming smile that he gave us girls. But the gears were likely turning, trying to decide what Jarret and I had going on. Had he told anyone about seeing us at the Thai restaurant? Of course he had. He couldn't help himself.

"I am Dominic. You must be Selena." Dominic greeted her with a friendly nod then turned to Rosa. "And you?"

"This is my sister, Rosa," Selena said, squeezing her sister's hand.

"Welcome, Rosa. You have the honor of being the youngest *chica* here."

Rosa gave him a shy smile then stepped further into the house, dragging Selena with her.

"And you are looking lovely as usual." Dominic gave me a loose embrace, a peck on the cheek, and a quick once-over. Then he turned to Jarret for a fist bump. "Hola, bro. How have you been doing since I saw you last?"

"Yeah, fine. Since you saw me last." Jarret bumped fists with him and gave a nod, no smile, a bit of attitude in his eyes, maybe bracing himself for Peter or maybe wondering the same thing I was wondering. Who had Dominic told about seeing us together?

"Hey, there you are!" Peter shouted from the dining room. In our few months apart, since I'd last seen him over Christmas break, he'd grown more like his father in appearance, more the rugged lumberjack in stonewashed jeans and t-shirt, his sandy hair styled similar to Dominic's: long and unruly on top, short on the sides. His jaw even had a bit of stubble, hard for me to get used to since I'd known him since childhood. Childhood friends should not grow facial hair.

Peter left a loud group in the dining room—a couple of his friends from high school and two girls I didn't recognize—and came to greet us still standing just inside the door. His huge smile froze when his eyes shifted toward Jarret, who stood behind me. Then the smile fell, crash landing with a smug scowl. "Oh. You're here."

Jarret gave him a mildly hostile grin. "Yes, I am. Better get used to it." He blew past all of us, strutting through the little foyer and into the restaurant-style dining room. Roland, in black cargo pants and a dark gray button-front, got up from one of the three booths under the windows and met Jarret at the end of the long table in the middle of the room.

"Nope." Peter, his color deepening, watched Jarret with a hard glare. "Definitely *not* something I wanna get used to." He turned to me. "Why is he here?"

"Oh, pu-leeze," I said with my weariest expression while dusting imaginary lint from my shirt—oh, not imaginary. I'd worn the blue top because it matched my maxi skirt, but it sure collected lint. "Just be nice, okay? You can handle a little visit, right?"

Peter pursed his lips and twisted them to one side as if thinking it over, then his eyes shifted to Selena and Rosa.

I introduced them, and Peter managed a polite smile and handshakes.

Then Selena's attention shifted to something behind Peter, and her face lit up. "Oh, there's Roland!" She bounded to the dining room, flung her arms around him, and gave him an air kiss on the cheek—which had turned a lovely shade of pink as soon as he'd seen her see him. Rosa approached the two of them shyly, probably feeling a bit out of place, not knowing anyone.

Dominic returned to the group in the kitchen, which now gathered near the bar counter, where the Brandts always set out breakfast and dinner for their bread-and-breakfast guests. Snack food filled the counter now. I couldn't tell what exactly. Smelled like cheese sticks or maybe hot poppers and definitely popcorn.

"Hey." Peter grabbed me by the arm and dragged me around the old loveseat and into the front room. Someone had hung LED string lights over the big picture window. A retro video game image was frozen on the TV, something with boxes with eyes and a few mushrooms and trees in front of a blue sky.

"Are you really hanging out with Jarret West?" Peter said.

"Did you expect me to leave him out while we all came over here?" I folded my arms across my chest. "Roland's his brother. I'm sure they'd like to see each other."

"Oh, don't give me that." He propped one hand on a hip. "It's not just today I'm talking about. Dominic saw you two at a restaurant. I mean, I know you're living at his house and he's home for the summer—both points kind of disturbing on their own—but now you're hanging out with him? Don't tell me you're seeing him."

"We're friends. Something wrong with that?" My conscience stirred with my declaration of friendship. Jarret and I had kissed. He'd told me he liked me. And I . . . How did I feel about him? I pushed the question away. I'd have to analyze it later.

"Yeah, there's a lot wrong with that," Peter carried on, his eyes, posture, and tone all displaying his brotherly protectiveness—albeit overboard and uncalled for. "Maybe you're thinking friendship, but what's he thinking? Name one girl Jarret's been 'just friends' with."

"I never paid attention." Gosh, now that he mentioned it . . . I glanced at Jarret, who stood with his feet shoulder-width apart, exuding confidence with his straight posture and easy manner as he spoke with Roland and two of Peter's other friends. He was "just friends" with Selena, though, right? And me.

"Well, you won't find one. Jarret has girlfriends, not friends who are girls. So maybe you're thinking about it one way, but he's definitely got other plans."

"Don't be ridiculous." I dismissed Peter's accusation. "I'm certain he does not think of me as a potential girlfriend. Have you ever seen him date a girl like me?" I flung my arms out and glanced down at my skirt, a long, flowy white-fading-to-blue thing that almost hung to the floor. I'd probably trip on it before the night ended, especially once I kicked off my sandals and lost an inch.

But it wasn't just my clothing choices that made me not Jarret's type. His girlfriends tended to be serious about themselves, confident in ways that just didn't matter to me, and gorgeous. So maybe I didn't need to worry about the kiss or his declaration that he liked me. To Jarret, it was fun but done. No future between us.

"Maybe he's bored with his regular type and you're conveniently at his house, so he thinks *why not?* Maybe he sees you as a bit of a challenge, huh? Something to grow his already enormous ego? Getting a girl like you to like him would prove that he could have *any* girl."

I hadn't thought of that. Could it be true? *No.* I shook my head and gave him an exaggerated annoyed face. "Let's just enjoy the evening. Selena is here, all the way from Arizona. Haven't you always wanted to meet her?"

"Look." He grabbed my arm and stuck his face close to mine. "If you won't heed my warnings, you'd better be ready to start a family young and don't expect help from the father of your unplanned baby. He's not gonna stick around."

My arm tensed and I made a fist, the steam of intense anger bursting inside my head and chest. Then I twisted from his grip and shoved him hard. I didn't like his accusations about Jarret, but I couldn't tolerate his accusations about me.

Recovering from my shove, Peter shoved back. "You know I'm right."

"You don't know anything!" For my next move, I went all twelve-year-old boy on him, looping my leg around his and tugging hard, while simultaneously shoving him back. The strategy didn't work the way I'd hoped, me dropping him to the floor, because of my excessively long skirt. Instead we got tangled up together and both landed on the carpet between the coffee table and the window, both wrestling even as we went down, both grappling to get the upper hand. His moves hard and unyielding. My moves as nasty as I could make them—pinching, poking, twisting his flesh, and even tickling.

"Hey!" Jarret shouted, darting from around the couch.

Peter and I released each other, both of us looking up at Jarret and the fire in his eyes. Okay, we were acting like kids.

Really inappropriate for our age. And not something others might understand. Or do. Especially not a girl. I was s-o-o-o not Jarret's type.

"Sorry," Peter mumbled, reaching for my hand, but Jarret swooped in first.

In one smooth move, he yanked me to my feet and wedged himself between me and Peter. "What d'ya think you're doing fighting with a girl?"

Peter, with cheeks redder than I'd seen them in years, shook his head and let out a long sigh. "Yeah, my bad. But can I say, she started it?"

Jarret shook his head, the tension in his body making me fear he might jump in where I left off.

"Let's just go sit down." I ran my hands through my hair, hoping to tidy it, and scanned my skirt for necessary adjustments as I strode to the dining room. Oddly, the scrap with Peter left me feeling refreshed and youthful, not necessarily childish. Okay, maybe childish but still pretty good. Peter knew where I stood on this. Right?

Selena and Roland sat talking in the middle booth, her smiling and leaning and gesturing in that excited way of hers, and him serious. As I approached, Selena looked up then checked me out from head to toe.

Something must've been out of place, but I didn't want to try to locate the problem and draw more attention, so I just sat down next to her. Rosa sat across from me, next to Roland. I hadn't seen her over the seatback as I'd approached the booth.

Rosa giggled, covering her mouth, likely having just seen me scrap with Peter.

"What happened to you?" Selena reached up and fixed my hair.

"Oh, nothing important."

With dark brows lowering over his gray eyes, Roland glanced over his shoulder, probably also wondering what had happened to me. He combed a hand through his wavy dark hair. Every other guy seemed to sport a fade nowadays, but he wore his hair exactly the same as in high school.

In the next moment, Jarret came over and dropped into the booth, sitting next to Rosa and across from me, leaning his arms on the table, a little gold chain glittering on his chest. He threw me a warning look. He didn't want to be here.

Peter strode over too, swagger in his steps and a crooked grin on his face. I wasn't going to slide over in the booth to make room for him. He carried a big bowl of popcorn and a plate of fried spring rolls to us, then he dragged a chair from the long table and positioned it near the end of the booth. "So, Jarret, how's college life treating you? Meeting a lot of hot girls there?" He bit into a spring roll and chewed, staring intently at Jarret.

Jarret sat back in the booth, disbelief in his eyes as he turned to Peter. He wouldn't be used to Peter's unique personality or the little games he played. They'd never been friends. Would likely never be friends.

"Seeing anyone?" Peter offered a smile, the challenge in his eyes diminishing the friendliness of it.

Worried how Jarret would answer, I sucked in a breath and tried not to show panic. Jarret hadn't been acting like my boyfriend. And he'd only made one or two comments in the past few days that might indicate he had any attraction to me at all. He wouldn't say—

"No, Peter, I'm not." His gaze hadn't left Peter's face, hadn't strayed to mine, giving anything away.

I released the breath and grabbed a handful of popcorn. "Okay, Peter, time to switch gears." I kicked him in the shin. Then I slid the plate of spring rolls so Selena and Roland could reach them.

Peter's hand dropped under the table, maybe so he could rub his shin. "Between girls right now, huh?" Eyes back to Jarret. "I remember how you were in high school."

Jarret's only response came in the form of a sharp look with an underlying threat. How much self-control did he possess? Maybe Peter was working on revealing that answer.

"Peter, that's enough," Roland said from his corner in the booth. "Let's just have fun."

Jarret's expression mellowed as if he'd decided not to let Peter bother him. He grabbed the bowl, scooped up a handful of popcorn, and shoved a few pieces into his mouth.

"You ever hear from . . ." As if trying to remember a name, Peter shifted his gaze to the ceiling.

Tossing another piece of popcorn into his mouth, Jarret's eye twitched. Maybe he suspected where Peter was going with this.

"Ah, yes." Peter leveled his gaze at Jarret. "Zoe. Ever hear from her?"

That did it. Irritation ripped across Jarret's face and fire blazed in his eyes. He squeezed the rest of his popcorn in a fist, which he then pounded on the table. "You want to take it to the mat?" He nodded over his shoulder, toward the front room.

A smile of satisfaction came to Peter's face. He raised his hands, palms out. "Chill, brother. Just having a conversation."

Little Rosa, squished between the West brothers, giggled. It might've been a nervous habit. She shouldn't have to put up with this. We should all be having a good time. Why wasn't there any music? Why wasn't anyone playing games?

Jarret's eyes shifted to me for one split second. He likely saw the tension tying me into a rubber band ball. In the next second, he took a breath and his expression leveled out. "I got it. You want help finding a girlfriend. Sorry, Peter. Can't help you there." He released the popcorn he'd smashed in his fist, and it fell like confetti on the table in Peter's space.

While everyone burst out laughing, Jarret relaxed against the seatback.

Brushing popcorn from his arm, Peter gave a crooked grin as if impressed with Jarret's reply but not done with him yet.

As his mouth opened again, I grabbed his arm and slid out of the booth. "Peter, it's time for some music. It's too quiet in here."

At that moment, Peter's other friends—the ones standing around the bar counter—burst out laughing over their own conversation, contradicting my statement about it being quiet, but it worked. Peter got up, and we went into the living room together.

I wanted those two to get along, felt some deep need for it, actually, but they seemed so diametrically opposed. I could only imagine how this night would go if Jarret and I were officially together.

Jarret

Peter shoved the coffee table aside, put on some '80s tune, and started dancing like no one was watching. I admired that. He didn't care what anyone thought or how dorky he looked. He didn't have a huge ego dictating what he could and couldn't say or do or even wear, like I sometimes did. Though I'd never wear what he had on, a t-shirt with some schematic symbols and the words "I only give negative feedback."

Actually, I knew he hated me, but I liked that Caitlyn had a friend so intent on protecting her. And I could hardly blame him. He wouldn't know that I'd changed. A lame tattoo—or a dorky t-shirt—could fade away sooner than a bad reputation.

Dominic and a couple of Peter's other friends, the girls, danced their way to the living room. Caitlyn brought Selena and Rosa out there too. Peter shoved the couch toward the dining room to make more room, everyone laughing and having fun. Caitlyn's moves, so playful and carefree, held my gaze for a moment, until I realized Roland was watching me.

"You going out there to strut your stuff too?" I teased.

Stuffing his hands into the front pockets of his black cargo pants, he shook his head. "I gotta use the bathroom."

I shuffled to the hallway and leaned back against the wall, waiting for Roland to come out and listening to the next song, something else from the '80s. Not a bad tune. I could dance to it, but no way would I be busting out with Peter's lame moves, arms swinging every which way as he jumped up and down.

The bathroom door creaked open, and Roland appeared in the dimly lit hallway, his eyes shifting from me to the view of the dancers and back to me. "Oh, hey."

"Hey." I didn't really need the bathroom. Just didn't want to join the others, so I continued leaning against the wall.

Roland didn't move past me. The shifting of his gray eyes said he was working up to saying something to me.

Guessing his concern, I decided to beat him to it. "You're worried too, huh? Think I'm gonna bust some moves on Caitlyn? Compromise her virtue?"

"I didn't say that." A hint of worry colored his expression. Challenging me never came easy for him.

"You were gonna say something. You came back this weekend for a reason when you could'a spent it with your girlfriend. Where is she, by the way?"

"With her family. They don't live around here."

"And you're not staying at home because . . ." I already knew the answer. Roland knew how Papa felt about boys in the house this summer.

"I don't know." He lifted one shoulder and watched the dancers.

"So tell me what you think. I'm hanging out with Caitlyn. You worried?"

Moody gray eyes snapped back to me. "Should I be?"

I shrugged. Then I pushed off the wall and stood next to him in the middle of the hallway, both of us watching the others in the living room. I didn't want anyone to hear me, but I needed him to say something, to confirm what my inner voice told me several times a day. Maybe then I could stop feeling this way about her. Maybe give up on the pipe dream and face reality. "Aren't you gonna tell me I'm not her type, she's not my type, she deserves someone better than me?"

I stared until Roland looked me in the eyes, my little brother who always wanted to do the right thing, who hesitated to confront others but, when it got down to it, would tell the truth even if it would make life rough for him. "Look, Roland, I know all that's true, so you got nothing to worry about. Just be honest with me."

His eyes flickered. He probably wanted to look away, but he didn't. He also didn't reply.

"I don't deserve a girl like her, do I? We could never be more than . . . just friends." There. I'd said it. Now he only needed to confirm it. And I'd be good. At least I hoped I would.

Roland dropped his gaze to the hallway floor and bit his bottom lip. "Actually, Jarret"—eyes back to me— "you know Caitlyn and I stay connected. And I admit I was kind of worried at first, especially when I got the impression she's starting to like you."

"She likes me?" A smile forced its way onto my face. I didn't want to look so eager, so pleased, but I couldn't hide it. Then I thought better of it. "I'm sure she doesn't. She's just nice to everyone, cares about everyone." The kiss had been a mistake, some impulsive reaction to me helping her in a moment of stress.

"I know her, Jarret. She's starting to like you." He stared toward the crazy dancing in the living room, a little smile on his face. "And I was worried about it at first, but . . . you're not that guy anymore. You're different. You should have a girl like her." He nodded, as if confirming his conclusion, and then walked away, back to the dining room, where he sat in a chair facing the living room and watched the lunatics thrashing to the music.

But I just stood there for a moment, the prison bars of my past shifting a bit, widening . . . letting me out?

Next thing I knew, I was strutting to the living room to "Walking on Sunshine" by Katrina and the Waves. Everyone looked as I came around the couch. Peter even made room for me, mouthing the words of the song to me as he danced. "I don't want to spend my whole life, just waiting for you . . ."

And we all danced. Me with my simple hip-hop moves that wouldn't make me look like too much of a dork; Peter some out-of-control rocker; Dominic, Rosa, and Selena with their quick Mexican huapango steps between moves; and then Caitlyn . . . all smiles and laughter and joy. And red hair sailing through the air as she twirled one way and then another, free as a bird, breathtaking, heart stopping, pure . . . and maybe, possibly one day . . . mine.

CHAPTER 24

Caitlyn

Mesmerizing rock formations and beautiful pine-covered hills rose up across the valley before us. Jarret, Selena, and I had ridden the horses far today, beyond the West property and the farmland behind it, following one dirt road and then another, finally taking a trail that wound up an incline to a granite rock overlook. Jarret brought along firewood and snacks for the horses. Selena and I brought trail mix, cheese sticks, apples, and water. And now we sat under a slight overhang with a little campfire at the edge of a twenty-foot drop. At the foot of the cliff, the pine-covered land sloped down gradually, allowing a shadowy view between tree trunks. Further away, a few dirt roads snaked around grassy and treed areas, and blue hills stretched across the distant horizon. So beautiful.

A hint of melancholy tempered my peace and joy. In another day, this would end. Selena and her family would return home. I knew it couldn't last forever, but two weeks did not feel long enough. Would we ever see each other again?

"I'm mixed up. Which direction is your house?" Selena shielded her eyes as she peered about. A few fluffy clouds floated along, their shadows drifting across the landscape below. And a breeze blew the strands of hair that had freed themselves from her ponytail, all messed up now from the helmet she'd worn.

"That way." Jarret stood up wiping the seat of his jeans and pointed behind the granite overhang. He gazed with her for a while. "Can't really see it." After a pause, he said, "Didja know gold was discovered out here?"

"Really?" Selena said. "So not just California and Arizona, out here too?"

"Yup. In the 1860s, Sioux Indians told some missionary priest about gold that came from the Black Hills. Father de Smet. The Sioux called him Friend of Sitting Bull because he got along with their war chief, I guess, persuaded him to negotiate with the government for some treaty that helped them keep their land."

"Wow, Jarret the Historian." Selena smiled, amusement in her eyes.

"Eh, read up on it once. That was, like, fifteen years before George Custer and the Black Hills Gold Rush. They didn't find much around here but more up north." He returned to my side, sitting a foot away from me, glancing at me as he rested an arm on one raised knee.

Something sparked inside me at his glance. I shifted my gaze to the flames flickering in the campfire, flames sneaking down to the deep places between branches, growing, spreading, lapping, consuming everything. Had I ever felt this spark for Roland? Or was this something new?

"So lovely out here. I never imagined." Selena shuffled between Jarret and the campfire then plopped down on my other side. "Someday I will take my husband out here."

I laughed. "I thought you didn't have a boyfriend."

"Not yet, but I will. And I'll marry someday. When I'm ready." She reclined back on her arms, one knee up, the other leg stretched out. "I wish Roland could've stuck around longer."

"Yeah." And I wished Ling-si could've come too. Having given up my "no phone calls" rule, I'd been calling her every day with updates. Now she wanted to meet Selena. And Jarret. "Roland has summer classes," I explained.

"And a girlfriend," Jarret added.

"Mmm." Selena sat up and pulled the hairband from her hair, shiny black locks cascading down her back. Then she reached behind her head and gathered her hair up again. "I was wondering . . . and maybe you don't want to answer, but why did you and Roland break up?"

My stomach leaped.

Jarret's face jerked toward Selena or maybe toward me. Then he gazed back out again, maybe pretending not to care.

I didn't mind that she asked, but I didn't know how to answer right away, so I lost myself in the captivating beauty around me for a moment longer while I tried to gather my thoughts.

Jarret took a breath and made a move to get up. "I'll go check on the horses. You can have your girl talk."

"You don't have to go." I reached for his hand but only brushed it with my fingertips, his hand turning over to welcome mine. Not ready for that—although he apparently was—I tucked my hand back under my leg, sitting cross-legged. His maturity pleased me. In a reverse situation, I wouldn't have thought to excuse myself. I would've been too eager for the answer. "I was just thinking how to reply."

"I mean," Selena said, "that boy is handsome and sweet with an air of mystery, and if we lived closer to each other . . ." She waved her eyebrows, dropping the hair she'd been gathering for a new ponytail, and we both laughed.

Jarret shook his head, a slight grin on his face. "Trying to make me jealous all over again?" He peered past me to Selena.

"Like the summer you boys visited us? You're so competitive." She laughed again. Finally remaking her ponytail, she reclined back again. "But if you don't want to talk about it, Caitlyn—"

"No, I don't mind. First, I'll just say, everything you said is true, and I do love Roland."

Jarret's Adam's apple bobbed and he nodded, not looking at me, his jaw clenching.

Oh, I probably shouldn't have started with that declaration. "But we weren't actually seeing each other. I always felt we had some unspoken plans to enter courtship once we were ready, but as we grew closer, we became more like siblings than . . ."

"Lovers?" Selena offered.

"I don't know why or how it happened, but I-I . . ." A sudden wave of sorrow overtook me. Running a hand nervously through my hair, I had to force the rest out. "I hope it's not something in me, like maybe I'm not made for romantic love." I gave Selena a weak smile, still trying to contain the emotion, but I couldn't look at Jarret.

In the next instant, his hand was on mine, squeezing, comforting, as if he wanted to communicate something to me. So I looked at him, just a peek and a little smile, something sparking inside again the instant our eyes met.

"What about you, Jarret?" Selena leaned forward to see him on my other side.

A final squeeze and he drew his hand back. "What about me?"

"Why'd you break up with your girlfriend? What's her name?"

After holding Selena's gaze for a long moment, he turned away, sucked in a deep breath, and exhaled. "Her name's Rylee. She's just not the one for me."

Selena laughed. "Oh, come on. You can do better than that. Caitlyn poured her heart out, and that's all your gonna say?"

I smiled to encourage him, the wave of emotions having subsided. I wanted the answer. And, unlike him, I had no intention of stepping away so they could talk.

"Eh, Rylee argued a lot, with her friends anyway. Always a little on edge. And she didn't want kids, like, ever. And—the deal breaker—she didn't like Mexican food."

"What?" Selena screeched. "Who doesn't like Mexican food? I can totally understand dumping her. But"—she pinned him with an accusing glare—"Jarret West, I sense there's more."

He took another breath, shaking his head. "Yeah, okay. But this stays between us." After we nodded to assure him, he said, "She wanted . . . things I'm not giving away anymore. Not till I'm married."

"Ohhh." Selena dipped her head. "Wow, you have changed."

Now I suspected the real reason he came home this summer. It wasn't about his favorite professor. It was about something immensely more important. "Is that why you didn't go on the field study? Was she going to be there?"

"Yeah. I broke up with her at the airport. Pretty rotten thing for a guy to do, I know, but I hadn't figured it out until then. Or maybe I didn't have the courage to break up sooner. Or I thought I could still make it work, stay on the right path and keep her for a girlfriend. I don't know." He sunk his head in his hand then looked up to the sky and cracked his neck. "I was hoping to complete my bachelor's next year. Now I'll be a field study short."

"You put your soul over everything," I whispered, watching him wrestle with the choice he'd made. I was proud of him. And fairly amazed. Jarret West was waiting for marriage.

CHAPTER 25

Jarret

L ate afternoon under an overcast sky, Caitlyn and I watched Papa's silver Lexus disappear down the gravel driveway. A smile frozen on her face, Caitlyn waved until a moment after the car disappeared and the crunching over the gravel faded. Then her hand fell to her side, and she wilted. "I'm going to miss Selena. All the Zamoranos, really. They're such a nice family, so fun."

"Yeah, me too." My hand tingled to hold Caitlyn's once she'd swung it to her side, but I resisted the urge. Still not sure she'd welcome the gesture.

The day the Zamoranos had arrived, we'd stood together— hands almost touching—overflowing with anticipation, excitement, and the promise of good times ahead. Now, again standing side by side with our hands almost touching, I didn't understand the stirring in my chest. A different kind of anticipation. I had so much I wanted to say to her that I thought I might explode like Mount Vesuvius on that fateful day. At the same time, fear stirred inside. Something closer to what the unsuspecting residents of Pompeii might've felt the day before Vesuvius erupted. The mixed emotions struck whenever Caitlyn turned my way, her eyes holding some distant look.

Maybe it was simply my own fears. It had been so easy with Selena here, all of us doing everything together. What would things look like with her gone? Could Caitlyn and I return to what we had before, talking together every chance we got, watching a movie on TV now and then, maybe riding the horses?

But that kiss . . . I ran my tongue over my lips, which no longer remembered it but longed to be reminded. And I couldn't stop thinking of what Caitlyn had said when trying to explain how she and Roland had become more like brother and sister: *I hope it's not something in me, like maybe I'm not made for romantic love.* She was made for love, and maybe she would find that love with me.

The front door on the porch behind us squeaked, shifting my thoughts to the present. Mr. Digby helped Nanny into the house.

"I guess it's just you and me now." I started to smile.

Caitlyn turned to me with a little crease between her eyebrows that made her seem lost. But as she met my gaze, her expression changed, and the emotion in her eyes threatened to level me to the ground. My thoughts returned to her kiss in the kitchen. And as she searched my face, my lips burned, and I fought manfully to resist pulling her into my arms.

In the next moment, the mood passed, and she breathed. Then she turned toward the house. "Well, I'd better get inside. See if Nanny needs anything and then head to my room." She shuffled toward the porch.

"But it's so early. We could make a bonfire out back or something, sit around and eat junk food and miss Selena together." I held the door for her. I really wanted to talk to her, get some things out in the open, see where we went from here. "Maybe we could even make some plans. Summer's only half over, y'know."

She smiled, some faraway look in her eyes. "Sounds nice, but I just need to rest for the evening."

Caitlyn

As Mr. West's car disappeared from view, a bit of sadness enveloped me. The past two weeks had been so magical, the three of us together, getting to know each other, enjoying each other.

"I guess it's just you and me now." Jarret's deep voice rumbled through me, shaking me from my low mood, his statement heavy with promise and adventure and hope.

I turned to him, something wonderful stirring inside me, and glimpsed a sweet little smile that faded as our eyes met. Another look replaced it, something calling deeply to me, beckoning me to step into Jarret's world. Moments and emotions flashed in my mind. The hungry desire and neediness when I'd kissed him in the kitchen . . . the thrill of possibilities when contemplating my future while on the roof . . . Jesus waiting for my answer, tugging at my heart in the prayer closet.

My gaze shifted to his lips, the attraction so overpowering. The instant before I reacted to my impulses, a trembling seized me inside. Was I ready for a one-on-one relationship with Jarret? What would it look like? Suddenly I pictured my best friend from high school and her big pregnant belly. She must've felt this way around him, unable to control her desires. Maybe all his girlfriends did. He had some manly charisma about him, something irresistible.

I breathed and turned away before succumbing to my passion. Then I made my excuses and moved toward the porch, my feet almost unwilling to carry me.

"But it's so early," he said, coming up beside me, opening the door for me . . . such a gentleman. "We could make a bonfire out back or something, sit around and eat junk food and miss Selena together."

I stepped inside, trying to avoid looking into those deep brown—captivating—eyes.

"Maybe we could even make some plans. Summer's only half over, y'know."

"Sounds nice, but I just need to rest for the evening." Despite my best efforts to keep my eyes on the hallway I planned to go down, I glanced at him.

Confusion and maybe a hint of pain flashed across his face, wounding my heart. But I needed to step back. Needed a day or two to gain perspective. I'd looked forward to this "working retreat" so I could find myself, not lose myself even more.

But here I was, feeling so out of control around him.

"All right. See ya," he said.

I shuffled down the hallway, lifting a hand to my lips. If he'd tried to kiss me, would I have let him? A stirring inside me said I would've. What type of relationship would we be starting then? Us living here together under the same roof. I finally understood how intense emotions could lead a person down the wrong path.

CHAPTER 26

Jarret

The next morning, Sunday, pounding on my bedroom door woke me up. The door opened and Papa stuck his head into the room. "G'morning. We'll be heading off to Mass in a bit."

With a groan and a stretch, I rolled over and lifted my head from the pillow to see the clock. "Why so early?" I flopped my head back onto the pillow. For the past two Sundays, we'd been attending the later Mass. I liked sleeping in.

"Guests are gone, Jarret. It's time we get back in the saddle."

All showered, dressed in my Sunday best, and ready to go, I met Papa and Nanny by the mudroom door. "Did anyone wake Caitlyn?"

"Oh, her parents will be by in a bit, Jarret. They'll go to the last Mass, I presume." Nanny squeezed her gray curls into shape and smoothed her dress. "I think she'll be spending the day with her family."

Yeah, that made sense. She always spent Sundays with her family, except for the past two weeks, so it shouldn't have surprised me, shouldn't have increased the foreboding weaseling into my chest.

The day dragged without her. Video games, snacking, and a visit to the horses. No riding. Wasn't in the mood. I couldn't even call or text her. She had my number, but she'd only called me from our home phone. So I didn't have hers.

Caitlyn

Shortly after a dinner of pierogi and asparagus, while Mom and I cleaned up in the kitchen, Dad stepped from his den and stood between the dinner table and the kitchen bar counter. "Hey, so who wants to build a fire?" he said with a playful grin. He'd recently brought home and cleaned up a black iron fire pit that a friend from work had given away.

"I want to start it," Stacey said, jumping up from the living room floor. After clearing and wiping the table, she, Andy, and David had been building a space station or something out of Lego bricks. Now they all raced for the sliding door to the backyard, arguing over who would get to do what.

Knowing they'd want to roast marshmallows, I grabbed the bamboo skewers from a low cabinet. Suddenly I was picturing Jarret and me sitting in the backyard holding marshmallows over the little fire. I shook the thought from my head. My parents would never warm up to him as my boyfriend. Would he even want to come over here? Our house was like a closet compared to his.

"Can we roast marshmallows?" Priscilla came around the corner—her hair all curly in some experimental style—and she opened a cabinet and pulled out a bag of jumbo marshmallows.

"Sure, honey," Dad said. "Don't we have some bamboo skewers somewhere?"

"Got it, Dad." I handed the skewers to Priscilla.

"We'll be out in a bit." Mom rinsed a plate and set it behind other plates in the dish drainer. Once the sliding glass door slid shut, she said, "I wanted to talk to you about Stacey."

A hint of guilt teased me. Should I have told Mom about Stacey sneaking off with her friends to that touristy town twenty minutes away? Maybe Mom found out.

"She's been so sullen lately, not going anywhere unless we force her to." She rinsed the last of the silverware and set them in a holder in the drainer. "Not so long ago, she was leaving without permission and coming home late."

"Maybe she had a falling out with her friends." Or—I hoped—she realized girls willing to shoplift weren't the friends for her.

I opened a cupboard to put glasses away, and a packet of duck sauce from Chinese takeout fell out. My thoughts went back to the Thai restaurant, to me and Jarret searching the menus, and I smiled. Then I paused. Why didn't Jarret want people to see us together? I never did ask him. Was he embarrassed to be seen with me? What was my reason for hiding? Was I embarrassed to be seen with him? We didn't really seem like the perfect fit . . . not from an outsider's perspective.

"I do think she's starting to enjoy the parish youth group, though, although we still have to convince her to go," Mom was saying, along with a few other things I missed.

"Yeah, Fire Starters was a lot of fun. Maybe she'll make some friends there." I struggled to remain connected to our conversation. If Jarret and I were to see each other, would he want me to meet his friends? Would I introduce him to mine? What would they all think of us as a couple? Would they think he'd changed or that I had, like poor Sandy in the movie *Grease*?

Jarret

Monday morning, I woke early, deciding to resume my workout schedule. An hour later, invigorated from my workout, I headed upstairs for a shower. The vacuum cleaner blared in some distant part of the house, Caitlyn busy with her chore list. After my shower, I trundled downstairs and to the kitchen to the same hum of the vacuum cleaner in some other part of the house. An hour later, after eating leftover Swedish meatballs and pasta and cleaning up after myself—which I'd started doing lately—the hum of the vacuum cleaner ceased.

My heart seemed to thump in my throat. I was done in the kitchen but didn't want to leave. She'd have to come here to make lunch for Nanny. Searching for an excuse, some reason to still be in the kitchen, I opened the fridge and stared inside.

Soft footfalls. Then a sweet voice. "Oh, hi, Jarret."

"Hey." I turned around twisting the lid from a bottle of juice. Then I lifted the bottle to my mouth, identifying the type of juice in the nick of time. Prune juice. No thanks.

She giggled as I shook my head at the bottle and returned it to the fridge. "Not your favorite, huh?" She joined me on this side of the bar counter, turned on the water, and washed her hands.

"Yeah, I don't know why we have it in the house. Does anybody like prune juice?"

"Sure, some people do." She opened the freezer and read labels on the serving-size containers of frozen leftovers.

I went around the counter and sat on a stool, started fidgeting with the napkin holder and a saltshaker. I hated feeling so nervous around her. "I was thinking of making a snack run in a bit. Thought you might want to come with me."

"Oh, no thanks. But I appreciate you asking." She drew out three containers and had to stop others from sliding.

Strike one. I wanted to ask why but decided against it. I'd been called controlling before, and I didn't want to be that way with her. She didn't need to explain everything to me. "You wanna catch a movie later?"

"No, I can't. Today's a busy day."

Strike two? Or maybe I could still make it work. "I could help with chores."

"Oh, that's okay." She brought the stack of containers to the bar counter. "I'm taking these to the Digbys' suite. We'll have lunch there. Then Nanny's therapist will be coming over, and she wants me to stick around for that."

Definite strike two. Although I didn't see how those things would fill her whole day. Why couldn't she watch a movie later? I redirected my thoughts. "How's Nanny been doing?"

Caitlyn's mouth twitched. "I guess she accidentally twisted her leg last night, and it really hurt, brought back all the pain in one of her still-healing hips."

"Oh, that's rotten." Okay, Nanny really needed her then. Maybe she wasn't trying to avoid me.

"Yeah it is. Well, see you." Containers in hand, she darted around the bar counter and to the doorway.

I couldn't get myself to try a third time. I didn't want to strike out with her. Maybe we'd cross paths later anyway. Or . . . maybe she'd been rethinking us. Could it be the courtship thing? Maybe she was afraid I wouldn't go along with it, ask her father for permission or whatever. Like he'd ever say yes. But I'd sure try. If she wanted me to.

As I strode through the house, heading for the garage, doubts crept in. Maybe, over the past two weeks, I'd said something that made her change her mind about me. Maybe I'd flirted too much with Selena. Or I'd revealed something about myself that she just couldn't live with. I tried thinking over past conversations, but nothing stuck out.

Maybe her thoughts had returned to the kiss, just as mine had, and she regretted it, wanted us to remain friends. And maybe she was right. She deserved better. I didn't even have a job.

I spent the day at a distant mall just for something to do. Saw "help wanted" and "we're hiring" signs all over the place on my way there and back. My thoughts kept turning to Caitlyn no matter how I tried to distract myself. Home now, kicking off my shoes in the mudroom while trying to keep a grip on all my shopping bags, I thought I heard her voice.

Easing open the mudroom door, I spotted her. And every muscle in my body tensed.

She stood at the far end of the hallway, outside the open door to the Digbys' suite. Speaking with a guy. Some blond dude with short windblown hair, might've been a little older than me. Dressed in khakis and a white polo shirt. Bulging biceps. Who was this guy, and why was he in our house?

Wait—I put the brakes on my jealousy. Dude had to be Nanny's therapist.

Kind of late for a therapist to stop by the house. What was it, almost dinner time? How often did Caitlyn see this guy? Was this the reason she couldn't watch a movie with me tonight? Had to leave her evening free for him?

Chill. She's just doing her job. Nothing to be jealous about.

The dude handed something to Caitlyn, a little card with his phone number maybe. Had she given him her phone number too?

She nodded, staring at the card. He sidled up to her and pointed to something on the card.

The sight too much for me, I gritted my teeth and turned away, strode toward the back of the house, wrestling with jealousy. Turned the corner and finally breathed. Of course he was the therapist. And of course she didn't give him her phone number. She'd have no reason to do that. And jealousy had no place in a relationship.

While trying to control the direction of my thoughts, my heart thumped harder, and breaths came quicker. Did she even want a relationship with me? Could I become the man she deserved?

Caitlyn

"We really appreciate you making time in your schedule to see Nanny today." I flashed a smile, trying to wrap up the conversation with Dwight. He'd squeezed Nanny into his schedule today after she'd called about her new pain. So I was thankful, but still . . .

My attention had left him three heartbeats ago, when I'd heard the door to the mudroom ease open and the rustle of shopping bags. And in my peripheral vision, I'd glimpsed a figure. It had to be Jarret. Mr. West said he'd be home later and not to worry about making dinner for him.

"If the pain gets worse or she can't get through a couple of reps of each exercise, as we discussed . . ."

Jarret hadn't moved, just stood watching me. And Dwight. Had he met Dwight before? If not, he was probably wondering about the handsome, well-muscled blond talking to me. Certainly he would notice that we stood outside the Digbys' suite, and he'd figure that this was Nanny's therapist.

". . . you can call me anytime." Dwight handed me his card.

I stared at it, still aware of Jarret in my peripheral vision.

Dwight stepped closer, saying something about using a second number, looking with me at the card I held. Then he pointed to the number on the bottom of the card. His cell phone maybe.

I nodded. "Okay, thanks."

Once Dwight returned to the Digbys' suite, I turned toward Jarret . . . just as he rounded the corner at the end of the hallway. My heart sank with a little ache. Should I go after him? No, probably not. I had too much to sort out in my mind before I really talked to him again.

I headed down the front hall. After getting something to eat, maybe I'd find a quiet place to pray and think. My "retreat" had taken quite a different direction than I'd planned. I needed to come to terms with my feelings for Jarret. I couldn't avoid him for the rest of the summer. And I didn't want to. What did I want?

As I neared the kitchen, the rustle of plastic bags stopped me. Jarret had come the other way through the house to the kitchen. I put one hand to the wall and listened. A utensil clanked on a plate. He must've been making himself something to eat.

I slumped against the wall and sighed, returning in my mind to earlier today. *You wanna catch a movie later?* I did want to watch a movie with him, but I'd had to say no. We'd spent so much time together for the past two weeks, just after I'd kissed him. Going out to a movie, just the two of us, would feel like more than friendship. It would feel like dating.

Frustrated at the situation I found myself in, I leaned my head against the wall and rolled it from side to side. I couldn't imagine Jarret practicing courtship with me, didn't even know how to broach the subject with him. And how could it possibly work with both of us under the same roof?

A bar stool squeaked. Jarret taking a seat to eat his dinner alone.

Grief trickled into my heart. What would be the purpose of us courting anyway? A summer fling before we both returned to colleges on opposite sides of the country? I'd promised myself that I'd only court a man whom I might one day marry. Was that how I felt about Jarret? Could I see him as my future husband and the father of my children? Maybe I had to seriously think about that.

CHAPTER 27

Jarret

D ressed in denim-blue chinos and a faded-blue-and-white-
striped button-front shirt, my goatee trimmed to
perfection, and my hair at its best—although pulled into a
ponytail to avoid coming across as vain, I hesitated to step into
the kitchen. Why was I about to put myself through this
again?

I shoved a hand into the hair on my forehead and shook
my head at the ceiling. This was the last time. If she told me
no, I was done trying. I couldn't blame her, really, but after
she'd kissed me, I just thought . . .

Argh. Not allowing another internal debate, I took a
breath and swung into the kitchen.

Afternoon sunlight streamed in through every window in
the laundry room and kitchen, making everything glow and
giving me hope. Two spray bottles of cleaners and a big bowl
sat on the otherwise clean bar counter. Caitlyn, her hair in a
loose braid, washed the refrigerator door, but she must've
heard me enter the room. She stopped and turned.

"Good morning . . . or afternoon." Her smile further gave me hope. "Did you need something from the fridge? I'm done cleaning it. Cabinets next." She held up the cleaning rag.

"Uh, no, actually, I wanted to ask you something." Anxiety crawled every which way inside my chest like a bunch of ants. I leaned my hands opposite her on the bar counter and bowed my head a bit, eyes on her. Then I took my chances, forcing myself to just say it. "I'm having withdrawals from not seeing you much these past few days."

She gave a little smile, her eyes flicked downward, and a rosy pink came to her cheeks. "I miss seeing you too," she whispered. Then she bit her lip and turned away, dropped her wash rag into the sink, balled her hands into fists, and turned back.

Just then my phone buzzed in my pocket, and on impulse I set it on the bar counter. Then I wished I hadn't. Rylee's name and image flashed on the screen. I quickly rejected the call and sucked in a breath to combat the sick feeling flooding me.

Caitlyn's eyes shifted from my phone to me. Yeah, she'd seen Rylee's name and picture.

I squeezed the end of the countertop, bracing myself for the rejection I now sensed coming.

"There's something I really need to do," she said, her eyebrows turning up with a worried look. "So I can't see you today."

Strike three. I was out. Only, it seemed like she held the bat, and my heart was the ball. And she'd sent it sailing clear out of the park.

My final hopes escaped with an exhale. I pounded a fist against the edge of the countertop, even as I nodded to show her I understood. Though I didn't understand. Or maybe I did. Really not sure. Would her answer have been different if Rylee hadn't called me just now? "All right. See ya. I'm gonna head out then."

I turned to go. No final glance over my shoulder to see if it mattered to her. The kiss had meant nothing, or at least not what I'd thought it meant. She liked me as a friend, but even that may have been stretching it. Whatever. We couldn't be.

Caitlyn

The attitude in Jarret's steps as he strutted from the kitchen reminded me of the Jarret I knew in high school, the one all the girls fawned over. The one that only went out with "hot" girls.

Conflicting thoughts and images held me in place for a moment. When he'd said he missed me—not just missed me but *having withdrawals*, as if he'd become addicted to being with me—the longing in his eyes had stabbed my heart. Then he'd sounded resigned, almost expecting my rejection, but angry at the same time, with that fist pounding the edge of the marble countertop.

But what else could I have said? I didn't want to hurt him, but I didn't want to lead him on either. I needed space to think.

I forced myself back into action, grabbing the washcloth I'd dropped in the sink and running it under water from the faucet, wiping down the nearest cupboard.

Jarret had given me even more to think about when his phone rang. I'd recognized the name that flashed on the screen. Rylee. His girlfriend from college, the one he told Selena and me about. I'd only glimpsed her picture on his phone, but it was enough to see that she was pretty in that "hot" girl sort of way. Tanned skin and black hair with a blue streak on one side. Makeup to emphasize her sultry eyes and pouty lips.

I wasn't at all like the girls he dated, not "hot" in any sense of the word. Why would he want anything to do with me? And if he'd broken up with her, why was she calling? Maybe they'd become friends again. Or maybe she was hoping they'd get back together when they returned to college.

Water dripped down my arm as I scrubbed the next cupboard door. After summer, I wouldn't likely see Jarret again. We'd both get back to our real lives. I didn't want a casual summer fling. My heart twisted and turned, making my eyes water and my nose run. What did I want?

Jarret

Pulling my keys from a pocket, I strode straight to the garage and took off in my Chrysler 300. As I turned onto Forest Road and glimpsed the neon sign of the Forest Gateway B&B, Peter Brandt came to mind and a sneer came to my face. I could punch him right now, though none of this had anything to do with him. It had to do with Caitlyn. She didn't like me the way I liked her. Wasn't anybody's fault. Except maybe my own.

After driving aimlessly for an hour, sunlit scenery on less-traveled roads doing little to lift my mood, I returned to town, to the city center, and pulled into an angled parking lot across from Saint Michael's Church.

An old man sat on a park bench in the quiet park before me. A middle-aged woman walked a white-and-tan poodle on the sidewalk, right past my car, or actually the dog walked her. A glance in my rearview mirror showed the empty parking lot of Saint Michael's school. Was Stacey still going to the Fire Starters meetings? Was she growing in her faith, giving God a chance?

My soul stirred, maybe God calling, so I decided *why not* and got out of the car. I hadn't been alone in a church in a long time, and I had nothing better to do. Stuffing my keys into a pocket, I waited for a minivan to pass and crossed the street, my eyes on the old church. Made of dark granite stones and with carved cherry-stained wooden doors, it stood waiting for me at the top of wide front steps.

I grabbed the door pull and yanked, but the door jerked back, and something clanked and rattled on the other side of it. Figuring someone was on their way out, I stepped back.

The door opened a few inches . . . then wider, revealing Father Carston with his snow-white hair and beard and his tan smiling face. "Well, hello, Jarret. Come on in." He held the door and ushered me into the otherwise empty church. "I was just locking up a bit early. Heading out for a special Mass in Rapid City this evening. A friend's anniversary of ordination."

"Oh, should I go?" I jabbed a thumb over my shoulder, toward the doors. "I was just gonna—"

"No, no." He waved his hands as if to erase my suggestion. "Stay as long as you like. Just check that the door's locked when you leave. I won't be back till late, reception after the Mass and all that."

I remained in the back of the church, weighed down by unworthiness, while Father checked on *whatever* in the vestibule and then exited through a side door. The door clicked shut and the knob rattled as he ensured it was locked. Then stuffy silence and holy longing enveloped me, beckoning me forward. I dipped a finger in the holy water font and crossed myself, leaving a big drop on my forehead.

Wash me more and more from my guilt, Lord. Cleanse me from my sin.

Eyes on the candle flickering in the red holder above the altar, the pain of rejection heavy in my soul, I proceeded down the middle aisle. Stained-glass-window angels and saints, illuminated by the light of the early evening, watched me in the dimly lit church, along with Our Lady of Grace on one side of the altar and Saint Joseph on the other. My eyes shifted to the tabernacle and the presence of the Lord.

Remember, Lord, your creature, whom You have redeemed with Your Blood.

Reaching the front of the aisle, I meant to genuflect, slide into the first pew, and just sit there, but the presence of my Lord Jesus overwhelmed me, and I fell to my knees. My keys clanked to the floor, slipping from the stupid front pocket of my chinos, but I ignored them for now. Sorrow for my sins and the mercy of God swirled through my heart and mind. My weakness and failings meeting His perfections: strength, holiness, mercy, love.

The pain of rejection resurfaced, and I found myself speaking aloud. "Lord, when I came home this summer, I hadn't meant to fall in love."

For the past few years, I'd grown to hunger for a woman that would help me be a better man, someone that I could help too. But I didn't attract that kind of girl. Caged by the sins of my past, I attracted girls who wanted to take me by the hand with them on the wide and easy road. I didn't want that road anymore.

Caitlyn's last rejection . . . I couldn't blame her. She had to be cautious, tread carefully when letting guys into her life. She didn't deserve a guy like me. She deserved someone stronger, someone holy, someone without a past like mine.

For I know my transgressions . . . my sin is ever before me.

"I know you've forgiven me, Lord," I prayed, my voice wavering, my heart weary, "but it's forever a part of my past. And everyone knows it. And most people probably don't get it, that I've changed. Papa. Caitlyn. Maybe even Roland. They think I'm always a step away from falling. And maybe I am . . . if I take my eyes off You for too long."

My heart ached, self-pity and loss and longing and everything desperate in me trying to surface. I groaned and bowed forward, sitting on my knees, clasped hands to the floor. I didn't deserve a girl like Caitlyn, and she deserved so much better. "Help me get her out of my heart . . . and send me the one you've prepared for me."

A long moment later, I straightened on my knees, and my focus shifted to Our Lady of Grace. She stood so close to me, there on one side of the altar, with her head bowed humbly and eyes on me, her arms out at her sides and hands open as if to welcome me in a hug, to comfort me despite my failings. I didn't deserve to have her for my mother. I'd failed her.

I climbed to my feet and thumped toward her. My most recent failures haunted me vividly with every step, seeming to magnify as I drew closer to the statue of my all-holy Mother . . . fighting with Papa and rejecting his will, tossing shots back in the bar with Kyle, overconfidence and pride, spending too much time with Caitlyn before I knew she wasn't seeing Roland, and the jealousy rising at the sight of Caitlyn with the therapist, and other things . . . Impressions of sins that I didn't fully grasp squirmed inside me, making me sick with remorse.

Stepping behind the wrought iron stand of flickering votive candles, I knelt at her feet.

Sorry, Holy Mother. So, so sorry. I've let you down even though I promised . . .

I reached into my shirt at the collar, grabbed the cord of my Brown Scapular, and yanked it off over my head. Giving it a goodbye kiss, unable to lift my eyes to her, I draped the cord over her hand and bowed my head to pray.

Before I could form a thought, something brushed my arm and pattered softly to the marble step before me. I opened my eyes to find my scapular by my knees, and the sight brought joy, like little explosions of grace in my chest. She didn't want it back. She wanted me to wear it.

Hands trembling, overwhelmed with her love, I pulled the scapular on over my head and tucked it inside my shirt. "Okay, then. You won't give up on me. I won't give up on you."

When I looked into her eyes, the weight of my sins lifted as she communicated—magnified—the reality of God's love for me. His unwillingness to give up on me.

Sometime later, I got up from the floor. The flickering candles in the front and back of the church provided the only light, my witnesses, the stained-glass-window angels and saints, having turned darker shades of reds and blues as the sun set. With a final genuflection toward Jesus in the tabernacle, I backed down the main aisle then turned and strode to the door.

After stepping outside to a warm evening and the setting sun winking through the leaves of the big tree next to the church, I gave the door a good tug, making sure it was locked. Then I strode toward the street, somewhat renewed, ready for a do-over in my life. I'd get a job or something for the rest of the summer and stop feeling sorry for myself. I'd accept whatever level of friendship Caitlyn wanted. I could do this.

I stopped at the crosswalk, finding the traffic much busier now. Couldn't believe how much time I'd spent in the church. And I stuffed a hand into my pocket for my keys.

Then dread washed over me, bringing a heatwave. And I looked back at the church—the locked church. My keys had fallen out of my pocket, and I'd left them there in the main aisle.

CHAPTER 28

Caitlyn

"What is he doing?" I stood holding one porch beam, peering into the woods behind the stable, curiosity driving me mad.

Mr. Digby disappeared down the same path for the third time this morning—that I knew of. I'd first noticed him while sitting out here enjoying my breakfast . . . and hoping to catch Jarret returning home. Jarret had stayed out all night. I knew this because I checked the garage five times: three times last night and twice today. No red luxury car.

The second time I noticed Mr. Digby's odd behavior I'd been shaking out throw rugs next to the mudroom stoop. And now the third time . . . I had no reason to be checking on him except for my own nosiness. This time and the last, he'd carried things out there, one cardboard box and something smaller, a dish or little container maybe.

I watched the woods for a moment more, then responsibilities called me back inside. I clicked the door shut behind me, trundled off to the laundry room, and gathered supplies in a pail. I hadn't cleaned Jarret's bathroom Monday because the guest rooms kept me busy, so I decided to do it today. Mr. West didn't really want me doing it, but I wanted to . . . needed to. Jarret's sad eyes lingered my mind from when I'd rejected him. I didn't want him to think I hated him.

Where could he have gone last night? Where was he now? And why did it bother me so?

Jarret

"Sir, I need to see some ID?"

The commanding voice sucked me from a troubled dream. Cushions against my shoulder. A crick in my neck. A cool breeze on my cheeks and bare arms. I did not lay in my own bed.

My eyes snapped open. I pushed a pillow made of some stiff acrylic fabric off my abdomen.

A man in a tan uniform—oh, a police officer—stood over me, one hand near his baton, the other turned up. "ID please." Another officer stood at the ready some yards away in the backyard of—

Where was I? The memory of last night rushed into my mind as I pushed myself up on the outdoor sofa on the back porch of the rectory. Locked out of my car, I'd strolled through the park across the street then waited back here for Father to return, but then I'd fallen asleep. By the time I woke, it was late, the rectory dark, so I decided to go back to sleep and wait till he opened the church in the morning.

"Just a second." I stuffed a hand into my back pocket, not finding my wallet. I'd left it and my cell phone in the car. "Uh, actually, it's in my car." Praying last night, I'd sensed difficulties lay ahead for me, but I hadn't expected this.

"What's your name? And what are you doing here?"

"Name's Jarret, uh, West. Just waiting for the church to open."

"Is that right?" He smirked. "We've had some break-ins in the area. We're going to need to ask you a few questions, Jarret West."

Caitlyn

Cleaning supplies rattling in the pail, I climbed the steps. Jarret's bedroom door hung half open, creating a rectangle of natural light on the hallway floor. I stopped. Could he have come home very late and left early? I shuffled toward his room and stuck my head inside.

Such a fancy room for a guy, with purples, gold, and dark gray, and that little bit of blue here and there. Like in the bedspread. Which I'd turned down to tuck him in . . .

No, I was not allowed to revisit that memory. I was just looking for clues. His bed was made and the curtains open. Dirty clothes lay in a pile on the floor, more clothes strewn across a nearby antique chair. A clutter of things on the dresser. He needed a maid, but I couldn't really tell if he'd spent the night here.

Shaking my head—oh, I needed to stop being so nosy—I crossed the hall, slid the pail onto the vanity, and set to work in his bathroom, dusting shelves and wall décor first.

Maybe I should talk to him instead of letting questions build. Wouldn't that be the mature thing to do? I could start by explaining that I wasn't ignoring him, I just needed time to sort out my feelings for him.

My face burned at the thought of that conversation. Maybe he didn't think about me as a girlfriend. He'd only meant he missed me as a friend. Did friends have withdrawals when they didn't see each other? Friends sure didn't kiss friends back the way he'd kissed me . . .

Forcing that thought from my mind, I hung the dust rag on the edge of the pail and took out rubber gloves and window cleaner. After covering the huge mirror and little window with blue droplets, I grabbed a new cleaning rag.

Where had he gone after we spoke yesterday? Where had he spent the night?

The only answer I could come up with had to do with Kyle. But he'd mentioned staying with some other friend last time he didn't come home, the night he'd lost his job. Who was that other friend? Another high school buddy like Kyle?

Done with the mirror and window, I set the pail on the floor and scrubbed the sink, making the chrome shine and removing every drop of water with a microfiber cloth. Then I sprayed cleaner inside the shower stall and, letting it soak, started on the toilet.

In the next moment, footsteps pounded up the stairs and keys jangled.

Sucking in a breath, I straightened and turned toward the half-open bathroom door.

Jarret's hand struck the door, swinging it open all the way, and he bolted into the room but skidded to a stop when he saw me. "Oh, hey." He stood a mere three feet away in rumpled clothes, denim-blue pants and a striped button-front shirt, a few curly strands hanging free from his ponytail, shock on his face—so handsome even when unkempt.

Tingling with nervousness and not ready for an encounter with him, I gave a final wipe to the toilet and tossed the cleaning rags into the pail. "Sorry, I—"

"No, I'm sorry. I'll use the one downstairs."

"No, you can use this one." I shoved the pail of cleaning supplies into a corner, stripped off the rubber gloves, and moved past him, my heart beating so hard he could likely hear it.

"Are you just getting home?" I turned as I stepped into the hallway, trying to keep disappointment from rising, but a hint of annoyance may have been detectable in my tone.

"Uh . . . yeah." His eyebrows twitched. Either he really had to go, or he didn't want to explain further.

"So you were out *all* night?"

He stared at me, blinked a few times, and then nodded. "Yeah."

Disappointment bubbled up into anger, shoving thoughts into my head, and now one was spilling out of my mouth. "Out with Kyle?" The suspicion in my tone—*oh my. Lord, help me.*

"Uh, no. Just kind of had a strange night." One eye twitched and his head shook with some look of disbelief, maybe because of my questions but maybe because of whatever happened last night.

"Were you out drinking?" I blurted before I could stop myself.

He let out a scoffing laugh. "No, I wasn't drinking. Is that what you think of me?"

My heart thumped angrily inside me as conflicting emotions collided and more unreasonable suspicions filled my mind. "So who were you with?" I folded my arms across my chest to hold myself together.

"No one." His innocent expression didn't convince me. "Not really."

"Oh really?" I sounded super snotty, the way Priscilla did when Stacey had done something mean and lied about it. But how could that be true? Out by himself all night? Doing what? Staying where?

A little grin played on his lips, and he quirked a brow. "You think I was with a girl," he accused.

My cheeks burned. He thought I was jealous. "No, I don't." I turned away and started for the stairs. "And it's none of my business," I said on my way down, mortified at my behavior.

"Hey," he said, followed by something I missed.

I nearly tripped with my hurried departure but caught myself with a hand to the railing. What was I doing? How could I have spoken to him like that? But I cared for him, my feelings stronger than I'd realized. I didn't want him running away at the first sign of conflict. This was the third time he'd stayed out all night. The first time, he came home drunk. Not his fault, he said. The second time, after losing his job, he'd left to avoid his father. Didn't stay to talk with me or even come back to talk with me. And this time . . . because I wouldn't go out with him . . .

I wanted him to be a man I could rely on even when I struggled to understand myself. *Lord, please help me. Temper my feelings for him or show me if I can trust him.*

Jarret

Exhausted from a rough night's sleep on the patio furniture behind the rectory and a rude awakening by police officers, I opened dresser drawers to find a comfortable t-shirt and workout shorts. Turning toward the bed aggravated the crick in my neck. I should take a hot shower and go back to sleep.

Nah. I wouldn't be able to sleep at this time of day. Maybe I needed some coffee.

I smiled to myself. Father Carston had offered me coffee and something for breakfast in the early hours of the morning. After he'd rescued me from the police.

While one officer was asking me twenty questions and not believing my answers, Father had come around the back of the house with a pleasant grin and a mug of coffee. "Good morning, officers. How are you doing, Jarret?"

"You know this man?"

"Yes, of course. He's a parishioner. Saw him at the church just last night. Is there a problem?"

The officers had briefly explained then decided there was no problem and, with a sincere apology and a *no thank you* in reply to Father's offer for coffee, had gone on their way. I'd rejected Father's offer for coffee too, but I did hit him up for confession. So much had filled my mind last night, I needed to give it over to Jesus in the sacrament. It felt good unloading it all, getting a fresh start.

I changed out of my rumpled clothes, whipping the denim-blue chinos into the corner. Never wearing those again. Stupid shallow pockets.

As soon as I dressed in the shorts and t-shirt, I regretted it. Didn't really want to hang around the house and risk bumping into Caitlyn. After all our conversations, she didn't trust me or seem to know me at all. *Were you out drinking? . . . So who were you with?* The accusation in her eyes said she assumed I was with a girl. I'd really thought we were starting to get to know each other. But I sure didn't understand this change in her. And she obviously didn't believe the changes in me, the good ones that had taken place over the years. Despite the things I'd told her, she saw the old Jarret. Just like everybody else did.

I marched to the closet and grabbed black riding pants and a gray polo. I'd been a fool for hoping. We'd had fun though. And even if I couldn't have tomorrow with her, I wouldn't trade those yesterdays.

Caitlyn

Sometime between preparing lunch and accompanying Nanny—in her wheelchair today—back to her suite after lunch, remorse overcame me. I had to apologize. I hadn't even given Jarret a chance to explain. I'd allowed all my insecurities to surface and jumped to ridiculous conclusions, as if I hadn't gotten to know him at all these past few weeks. As if he were the same old Jarret from high school.

After closing the door to the Digbys' suite, I wandered through West Castle, peeking into one room after another. I checked the basement and even went upstairs—Oh! I'd neglected to rinse the cleaner I'd sprayed in the shower. After correcting that situation, and still not finding Jarret in the house, I stepped outside through the veranda and approached the stables.

Male voices came from inside the stables, and a horse snorted. Then a loud, "Giddyup," and a horse catapulted from the stables.

I stumbled back, though I stood a good ten feet away, and my heart raced as I watched Jarret mounted on the horse, leaning forward a bit, reins in hand and seat out of the saddle, moving in sync with his horse as it galloped away.

"I imagine that boy'll be gone fer awhile." Mr. Digby stood beside me with his hands on his hips, maybe having come from the stables, but I hadn't noticed him approach.

"Oh, that's okay." I turned to him, flustered. I'd come to speak with Jarret, and he knew it. Did he also know how much I liked Jarret? Just to feel less stupid, I blurted, "Did you need help with anything?"

Mr. Digby tilted his head to one side, squinting at me. "Sure could use some help in the garden, but I've gotta take care of something first. I'll meet you over there."

As he returned to the stables, I started toward the garden but then stopped as I neared the front porch. What did he have to take care of?

I turned in time to see him disappear down that very same path. Ready for a bit of investigating, I dashed back toward the stables, racing through the lawn, my eyes on the entrance to the horse path. A bit winded, I reached the tree line and stopped to peer around. Not seeing him, I stepped into the woods and crept down the trail, watching my step to avoid snapping twigs.

Not far in, I spotted him about twenty feet away.

Mr. Digby squatted by something, his back to me. "I reckon it's a fledgling," he said . . . to me? He straightened and glanced at me over his shoulder.

Since he obviously noticed me, I closed the distance between us.

"Too many feathers for a nestling." He gazed down at a fat bird standing before us just to the side of the horse trail. "Can't fly yet. Just hops around. Thought maybe it was injured."

"Oh, it's adorable!" I remained a couple feet back even though my fingers ached to touch the cute, downy thing. It just stood there, its little beady eyes shining up at us.

"Been checking on it now and then. Watching to see if its parents are feeding it. Haven't seen 'em yet. Sure would hate for other wildlife to find it before it gets the hang of things." He rubbed his wrinkled, clean-shaven chin. "S'posed to rain later. Gave it a little place to stay dry or hide if he needs it." He pointed to a cardboard box on its side on the ground, surrounded with a barrier of sticks and branches, a dish of water nearby.

My heart melted at his kindness. Mr. Digby wasn't so strange after all. All those times I'd glimpsed him heading into the woods this morning, he'd been trying to protect a baby bird.

--*

While rainclouds hung on the horizon, late afternoon sunshine warmed the top of my head as I picked another plump tomato from one of almost a dozen healthy plants loaded with fruit and dropped it into a basket of tomatoes. My discovery about Mr. Digby and the baby bird had me thinking about why I wanted to become a detective. I really wasn't very good at figuring out things—or people.

"So many cucumbers, I reckon we ought to take some up to the church." With pruning shears in a gloved hand, Mr. Digby harvested the cucumber vines growing on the trellis he'd built around the garden. The trellis kept the bunnies out and gave the vegetables something to grow on.

"That's a good idea." I wiped sweat from my brow with the back of my arm. We'd already gathered peppers, squash, and green beans, talking while we worked. Since Mr. Digby tended to mumble, I worked close to him. I loved listening to his stories and insights, and I regretted not getting to know him sooner.

Apparently, the baby bird was not the first wild animal he'd cared for. He'd once cared for a baby skunk! Another animal had injured the little thing, and he couldn't find the mother, so he'd nursed it back to health and sent it on its way. While I'd known he cared about his work, I hadn't realized his love for nature and life in every form. He was a good man through and through.

If I had been any kind of a detective, I wouldn't have let his odd behavior stand in the way of getting to know him. A classroom definition came to mind. *A good detective needs the ability to analyze complex problems and to use critical thinking to reach logical conclusions based on evidence rather than rumor, reputation, personal opinions, or prejudice.* Maybe my desire to become a detective stemmed from something I'd realized only subconsciously about myself: I needed to learn to look deeper at myself, so I could find direction for my life, and at others, so I could discover the real person beyond reputation or appearances. And stop jumping to conclusions.

"Here you go." Mr. Digby traded me a pair of garden gloves for my basketful of tomatoes.

After weeding and watering, we took several of each vegetable to the main kitchen and a few more to the Digbys' suite, then we loaded the rest into Mr. Digby's big black car, and I rode with him to Saint Michael's Church. On the way home, as we turned onto the long gravel driveway, Mr. Digby said, "Care to join us for dinner? Nanny's made a nice shepherd's pie."

CHAPTER 29

Jarret

A warm breeze blew a lock of hair into my face, so I turned into it. Storm clouds gathered north of the overlook, blending in with the blueish mountains along the horizon. No threat to me. A sunset stretched across the western horizon, tinging the few clouds on that side of the sky with pinks and golds. A possible threat. I should head home before it got too dark for me and Desert to pick our way along the rocky trails.

I'd been standing out here long enough, for almost an hour, on the granite rock overlook that I'd taken Selena and Caitlyn to . . . not even a week ago. I stood where Caitlyn and I had sat side by side, at peace—maybe even enthralled—with each other and the world. Everything had felt so good. So right.

With a sigh, I shoved a hand into my hair and bowed my head. Now she wanted nothing to do with me.

After a moment of soaking in self-pity, I opened my eyes. Weathering patterns had produced crevices and pits in the granite I stood on, some with a few strange plants growing in them, others that would likely pool when it rained. I grabbed the only loose piece of granite I could find on this jagged rock formation and whipped it out as far as I could. It sailed over a tree at the foot of the cliff I stood on and disappeared in the evergreens further down the slope. Not making a sound. Thus giving me no satisfaction. I shuffled around the outcropping, shoving my boot against the uneven folds, hoping to find something else to throw.

Still toeing folds and crevices atop the outcropping, I glimpsed something dark and flat wedged in a long crack. I crouched to pry it out. Rubbing my index finger raw, I finally got it. Some rusty old knife . . . like a table knife, not a hunting knife. Very old.

I sat down with it in my hand, knees up and supporting my arms. Maybe it once belonged to one of Colonel Custer's men. They could've been right here, using this granite rock as a lookout. That thought sparked something inside me, and I peered back at the crack where I'd found it. Maybe I could find other things up here. The fork that went with the knife? I smiled to myself.

A distant rumble of thunder drew my attention to the northern horizon. A white line zigzagged through the gray sky above the mountaintops. The clouds had grown, covering more sky and heading my way.

I turned the knife over, studying it. I did like archaeology. Papa's adventures over the years had sparked my interest— some told through photos, artifacts, and stories, others I'd experienced from tagging along, even as a troublemaker. But the love of archaeology, I owned it now. I liked the travel and seeing new things. Working with a team out under the elements. Uncovering old things, like secrets and treasures, and discovering the stories behind it all. I liked some of the planning and research too. And I could handle the boring prep before fieldwork and the paperwork that came after. This was what I wanted to do.

Peace over my career choice settled in my chest as a drop of rain struck my nose. At least I had direction for one part of my life. I'd leave the rest in God's hands.

A quiet moment passed, a few more sprinkles hitting my arms, and I thought about standing up and throwing the knife, seeing how far I could get it, trying to make the leaves move on some tree, but . . . nah. I got up, brushed off my seat, and crunched down the trail, back toward Desert. I'd keep the knife. Let it remind me of this day. I was pushing ahead with my education in archaeology. Maybe even getting a master's or doctorate and as many field studies as I could. Definitely had to see Pompeii. Then I'd see what doors God opened next.

Desert whinnied and shook his head, not in greeting so much as in warning. And as I took to the saddle, gray clouds hid the sun and a hard rain fell. I should've worn a cowboy hat. Guess the rain was closer than I'd thought. "Let's go, Desert. We got a long, wet road ahead of us. Then I gotta have a word with Papa."

Caitlyn

I washed the last dinner plate, set it in the dish drainer, and wiped off the Digbys' little table, while they sat talking on the couch. Conversation and shepherd's pie with this sweet couple brought peace to my troubled soul, but it also helped me realize a few things about myself.

As much as I wanted to please God in my daily work and relationships with others, I drew a line that kept me from really getting to know others, especially those who seemed a bit odd or had a bad reputation. Looking at myself and others a bit superficially, I'd simply tried to rise above my feelings and be "kind" without ever risking a glance at what cross or challenges might've made a person disagreeable. All this time at the West house, I'd been pleasant to Mr. Dibgy but still neglected to really get to know him because of his eccentricities. A little investigation would've revealed the gems of his personality.

I hugged them both goodnight and headed for the door.

I wouldn't have gotten to know Jarret at all if not for his vulnerable moment that I'd felt obliged to help with. Only then had I discovered his loneliness and how he missed his mother. When I'd forced myself to befriend him in the days that followed, I'd discovered even more, his goals and hopes and hints of how he felt about his troubled past. The more I came to know him, the more I came to—

A bit shocked by my train of thought, I shook my head and stepped from the Digbys' suite into the dimly lit house, muted light streaming from open doors down the front hallway, brighter light from Mr. West's study. As I closed the door behind me, movement on my left made my heart leap—so near I gasped and goosebumps popped out. I flung a hand toward the light switch on the wall, I thought, but bumped a cold hand instead.

The light flicked on, revealing Jarret West beside me, wet as if he'd just emerged from a dunking booth. A gray t-shirt clinging to his muscular torso, damp curls lying flat against his forehead. "Sorry, didn't mean to scare you."

"Oh, no, I just wasn't expecting . . ." An urge to fetch him a dry towel and heat up some soup scrambled my thoughts. I wanted to care for him the way Mr. Digby cared for the fledgling.

"Got caught in the rain."

"Oh, right. Rain." I forced my gaze to his face, to brown eyes aglow with purpose.

"I'm on my way . . ." He pointed down the hall, maybe to his father's study.

Realizing with a blush that I blocked his way, I moved aside. "Yes, of course. I'm . . . goodnight."

As he moved past, he smiled. And an arrow pierced my heart, stirring up feelings of longing, concern, regret—and determination. I had to take a deeper look at myself and at him and possibly us. I didn't want to keep the world at a distance, to keep him at a distance, so I had to become an investigator. And I couldn't put it off any longer.

I fetched Mr. Digby's chore notebook and a pen from my room and proceeded to the little prayer closet.

CHAPTER 30

Caitlyn

Tummy growling for breakfast, I traipsed down the hall on the way to the kitchen. A prayer lingered in my mind, St. Augustine's prayer: *Lord Jesus, let me know myself. Let me know You.*

After prayer and introspection last night—and a solid list of pros and cons in the Digby notebook for every possible vocation—I'd grown in conviction about my future. My education in police science and criminal justice would develop my ability to know myself and others, regardless of where life took me. And since I believed God planted seeds, desires within a girl to guide her toward her vocation, I felt certain God called me to marriage and motherhood. The who and when and how of it all, I left in His hands. I'd ended with the prayer, *Lord, show me who Jarret really is. If we are meant to be more than friends, give me a sign.*

In the days ahead, I would seriously think over what qualities I'd like to see in my future husband. But for now, I needed to speak with Jarret. First, I would apologize for doubting him and for not giving him a chance to explain. Then I'd tell him why I'd been avoiding him lately, how I'd needed to sort out my feelings because I really liked him a lot.

My stomach flipped at the thought of admitting that, of saying the words out loud. To him. I still harbored a bit of fear that he did not return the feelings. But I planned to come before him humbly and honestly. If he liked me too, we would have much to discuss. If he didn't like me that way, I would have to get over my feelings for him.

I passed through the foyer and got halfway to the kitchen when a wonderful coffee aroma met me, making me think of waffles and donuts and apple turnovers and fruit pie. Who was up this early? Maybe I wouldn't have to search for Jarret at all. We could talk over breakfast.

Male voices came from the kitchen, a congenial conversation.

He wasn't alone then. So no talking over breakfast.

"No guarantees on the accommodations there, but we'll make do."

"I don't know, Pop, I'm kinda hoping it'll still feel like a vacation. A little whirlpool in my bathroom, good food, a good view . . . air-conditioning, at the very least."

They both chuckled.

After a brief mental preparation and a hand through my hair, I stepped into the kitchen.

Jarret and Mr. West sat on stools at the bar counter on the end by the coffee pot, each with an empty plate and a coffee mug. Mr. West, on the furthest stool, faced me. He tipped his cowboy hat and smiled with his very blue eyes. "Morning, Miss Summer."

Jarret, who'd been facing his father, glanced at me over his shoulder. Turning back toward the counter, he said, "Some bacon if you want it," and he pointed to a few strips of bacon on a nearby plate.

"Oh thanks." I came around the bar counter, my heart kicking into overdrive for some reason. I liked seeing them getting along, but what were they doing up so early? Neither one made a habit of eating breakfast.

Two dirty skillets sat on the range, one with solidifying bacon grease and the other with remnants of scrambled eggs. The bread, butter, and egg carton all sat out on the countertop, so I slid two slices of bread into the toaster and grabbed two eggs. Then I turned on the burner under the cleaner of the two skillets. "You should've let me know you wanted an early breakfast. I could've made it."

"Ah, we aren't entirely helpless in the kitchen," Mr. West said. "Jarret ain't half bad at fixin' bacon and eggs, and I'm a pro at making coffee."

"Yeah, if you like it thick enough to stand a spoon in." Jarret lifted his mug and gave his father a lopsided grin.

Mr. West chuckled and brought his mug to his mouth.

I cracked two eggs into the skillet, took the used spatula, and leaned against the far counter so I could face the men. "So what are you two doing today?" I risked asking, stealing a glance at Jarret. It would feel too weird apologizing in front of Mr. West, but I could at least show him I was sorry by being extra nice.

"Running a few errands," Mr. West said. "Likely be out all day."

"Oh, together?" I liked the idea of them working together, especially after all the strife when Jarret first came home this summer. But all day? When would I be able to speak with him alone?

Jarret looked up from his coffee mug, some sullen, moody expression now coloring his face. "Yeah, and then I'm leaving in a couple of days, going to hang out with Papa at an opal mine in Brazil."

"What?" The question slipped out as a high-pitched whisper, and the spatula started to fall from my hand. I regripped the spatula just as the toast popped up.

"Sounds like your eggs are up too high," Jarret said before draining his mug.

"Oh!" I turned down the skillet and shoved the spatula under an egg with its curled, overcooked edges. My toast was going to get cold before I could—

Jarret came around the bar counter, dropped the toast onto a clean plate, and proceeded to butter them. Coming to my rescue.

"An opal mine, huh?" The spatula didn't slide under the second egg easily, but I flipped it anyway, turning it into an odd-shaped, unappetizing little thing.

"Yeah. An opal mine."

"In Brazil?"

"Yup. Brazil."

"Well, that sounds fun." I plated my eggs and forced a smile, my eyebrows all out of control.

"No, it doesn't." His brown eyes held mine for a long moment, communicating something . . . what was it?

My heart melted and twisted, and I imagined it turning into some odd-shaped little thing just like my eggs. I didn't want him to go. We needed to talk even if he didn't like me as more than a friend, even if he didn't want to spend the rest of the summer with me. I hadn't apologized. Not even for the luggage on his first day back.

CHAPTER 31

Jarret

Sweat trickled down my chest and back as I worked with a few young Brazilian dudes at the "opal mine" doing grunt work with a pick and a shovel. This in no way fit my vision of working in an opal mine. First off, there was no mine. My idea of a mine was something cool and damp underground or in the side of a mountain. Here, someone had found a few opal nuggets and the landowner had called on Papa—apparently, he had contacts everywhere. They'd found an alluvial deposit in a stream, Papa had said, which he'd instructed them to dry wash and sieve on screens. Then they wanted him to come out and find the primary deposit, the veins in the base of the sandstone stratum.

Standing in direct sunlight in the area we'd dug out, four feet below ground level, I swung the pick into sandstone under a layer of volcanic ash and pulled out clumps of dirt. No signs of opal.

Once we got out here, Papa had organized everything. We went over maps and the lay of the land and tested the alkaline and acidity of the environment, looking for specific combinations of minerals, finding the right geological conditions that favor opal formations so he could locate the opal field. Then he had an area cleared for opening the mine. Used to be a lake or pond, he'd said. And I got stuck doing a little tedious shaft sinking with a pick and shovel. In the "mine."

I cleared excess dirt from my work area, flung the shovel aside, and wiped the sweat from my forehead with the back of my dirty arm. *Great.* Now I'd transferred gritty dirt to my forehead.

Second reason this didn't fit my vision, I'd expected better weather. This was Brazil, after all, one of the best places to visit because of its temperate climates. Guess I'd never considered how large the country was and how the northwestern part was a tropical jungle and part of the Amazon rainforest. We were nowhere near the ocean with its mild temperatures and pleasant breezes. Instead, we got highs in the low nineties and humidity so thick you could see it. Not even a breeze most days. And with the land we worked stripped of all trees, no shade.

I turned toward Leandro, a twenty-year-old dude with short black hair and something hawk-like about his eyes and eyebrows, who now worked about ten feet away from me. "Any of you find anything yet?"

Leandro squinted up at the sun and then smiled at me, nodding. Obviously didn't understand a word I said.

Which brought me to my third point. None of these dudes I worked with spoke English. They spoke Portuguese or something. So I was left to my thoughts every day or mumbling to myself until I met up with Papa in the evenings.

I swung my pick hard and yanked out more dirt, clawed at something that looked like a stone but turned out to be nothing.

Papa and I went into the nearest city one day, driving down a red-dirt road through a flat green landscape of shrubs and grasses until we reached a depressing city of mismatched buildings painted in colors I never imagined a business would use, like lime green and purple.

Before stopping at the store, we ate at some dinky restaurant with a makeshift awning over outdoor seating. And I happened to think about Papa's lady friend and fellow archaeologist, Miss Anna Meadows. He hadn't mentioned her in a couple of years, so I decided to ask.

Papa hesitated before replying, his piercing blue eyes staring over his coffee mug. "She's been conducting research in Southeast Asia for the past two-and-a-half years."

"Thought you guys were gonna get married." I'd been a senior in high school when he'd hinted at it.

"Yeah, I never proposed." His eyes clouded over, memories likely surfacing. "She had her heart set on her work, and my heart had turned to you boys. Couldn't see myself taking off for Asia while you three were still getting your feet wet."

"Well, our feet are pretty wet now, so . . ." I hated the thought of him letting love slip away over us. How long would he wait before he felt ready? Certainly he wouldn't wait till we all settled down.

Papa's lip curled up in a melancholy smile. "Not yet, son."

As I swung the pick again, my stomach growled, my muscles complained, and my attitude sank all in one instant. Not worrying about the dirt, I sat on the ground in my cargo shorts and tank top and leaned my back against the area I'd just dug out.

Leandro did a doubletake and said something, gesturing, maybe wanting me to get up. He sounded encouraging, so I nodded and started talking to him.

"You know, Leandro, my father used to say man was made to work, and when you give yourself to it, especially when it's a hard row to hoe, you get back not only the fruit of your labor but something inside, something strong and good." I tapped my chest with the side of my fist.

After a moment's hesitation, Leandro imitated my gesture, tapping his own chest with his fist. Smiling. Then gesturing for me to keep working.

"Yeah, okay." I got back up and gave myself over to my work. I had to admit I did like swinging a pick. And even though Leandro didn't speak English, I liked working next to him. So I started talking to him, telling him all about myself, including my troubled past and this crazy summer and about Rylee. And Caitlyn.

As my strength waned toward the end of the day, my Brown Scapular shifted against my sweaty chest, making me think of the Blessed Mother accepting her share of suffering at the foot of the cross. I should've been doing that too. My suffering paled in comparison. It was just work. Jesus worked. Why shouldn't I? My job was sweaty and grueling, but Papa was right. There was something good about work.

"You know, Jarret," Leandro said, struggling with the r's in my name.

The pick nearly slipped from my hands as I pulled it back for a swing. I looked at him, standing frozen for a second. "You . . . you speak English?"

"*Sim.*" Leandro reached into the loose dirt he'd just attacked with his pick. "You accept bad things from the Lord, why do you not accept good?"

"Wh-what?" Sounded like a Bible verse but not really. Maybe with the order switched.

"You dink you are no good for dis *senhora*, you are only worthy of bad things. But maybe God brought you together." Leandro's gaze shifted to my section of the dirt wall, then he pointed. "I dink you have something."

I looked to where he pointed, my mind whirling and the word "unworthy" playing on a loop in my head. Leandro knew English? I'd told him everything from my rocky past to why I'd broken up with Rylee and then about this summer and how I felt about Caitlyn, including how I didn't deserve her.

After a moment, my eyes focused on a long stone stuck in the dirt. I pried it out with my fingers—a milky nugget with a play of color inside—and my heart thrilled. The word "unworthy" faded, the word "loved" replacing it, along with a revelation. The same God who loved me into existence, also loved me at every moment of the day and wanted only good things for me. I deserved suffering and pain because of my sins, but God wanted to give me good.

A verse I must've heard before came to mind: *For I know the plans I have for you, declares the Lord, plans to prosper and not to harm you, plans to give you hope and a future.*

CHAPTER 32

Caitlyn

After the last Sunday Mass, I knelt in the emptying church, offering a final prayer of thanksgiving, hope expanding my heart and bringing a big smile to my face. Sunday Mass— especially after a nice thorough Saturday confession—had a way of renewing me like nothing else could. Jesus would never stop loving me. He had a hand in all that happened in my life. And I could trust Him. The thought of what tomorrow held— known to God alone—left me with a sense of excitement and adventure. If I opened my heart to His will over my own, the mysteries of life would unfold gradually to something beautiful that I would've never imagined. I trusted that.

And finally, Lord, thank you for my West Castle retreat and the discovery of the little prayer closet. I'd visited the prayer closet every day for the past week, regaining perspective and waking from the fantasy that Jarret liked me as anything more than a friend. If he had, he wouldn't have left for Brazil.

My smile turned into a cringe as I remembered how I'd interrogated him a couple of days before he left for that trip. And I still never apologized. I just couldn't find the right words. A part of me wished we could've spent those days together, doing things that "just friends" do, but it was all for the best. I'd needed the time to get over my feelings for him.

My smile returned. *Mission accomplished.*

Since I'd once promised myself I'd never court a man that I wouldn't consider marrying, it had helped for me to make a list of the virtues I wanted in my future husband. So I'd turned to the middle of the "chore notebook" that Mr. Digby had given me, and I'd started yet another list—*Oh, I hope Mr. Digby doesn't want the thing back. I could always rip out the pages . . .*

First item on my list: I wanted a man with deep faith, someone who would inspire me and help me grow spiritually. Jarret was not that man, though, admittedly he had some degree of faith. But I also wanted to help my future husband grow, so he had to be humble and open to my help—and need me. Jarret did not fit those points either, although he did take my advice about getting a job. Anyway, he would be hardworking, faithful, gentle, and have a heart for others. Again, not really Jarret. So, case closed. My feelings had no choice but to bend to reality.

Lord, help me find my future husband one day. Until then, I would focus on my education and fulfill my dream to become a detective.

With a final Sign of the Cross, I genuflected and strolled outside to sunshine and joyful chatter. Stacey leaned against the big tree in the front lawn of the church, her knee out and foot propped behind her . . . and the long shorts under her skirt showing. Was she eating a donut? She must've grabbed one from downstairs, not staying to socialize—which was the whole point of Donut Sunday. Oh wait! A girl her age, also carrying a donut, came up to talk to her. A new friend?

I continued weaving past groups of parishioners who stood on the front and side lawns of the church. Oh wait, some of them had donuts too.

"Look. They brought the donuts outside." Stacey came up beside me with a greedy grin, her new friend no longer with her. She pointed to a long table with a thin white tablecloth by the side door of the church, all set up with donuts, coffee, and juice.

"Oh, that's nice." I walked with her to the table, my tummy growling.

"Hello there, Summer girls," Mrs. Bellamy, the parish secretary, greeted us with a smile as she arranged little paper plates then handed us each one. She wore an artsy midnight-blue-and-red dress that complemented her graying pixie-style hair.

"Hey . . ." Stacey smashed her empty paper plate against her skirt at the hip, her other hand sinking into the pocket. "When you see Jarret, give him this." She pulled out a long chain with a lobster claw clasp on one end and a key ring on the other.

I shook my head, dumbfounded by her request, and refused to take it from her. I grabbed a chocolate donut with sprinkles on top instead. Why would my fourteen-year-old sister want to give twenty-something-year-old Jarret anything? Certainly she didn't have a crush on him.

"Would you like some coffee?" Mrs. Bellamy held a Styrofoam cup toward me. Her manicured fingernails matched the red swirls on her dress.

"No thanks." I glanced at Stacey, who still held the chain out to me. "I'm sure Jarret is fine stuffing his keys in a pocket. I can't see him wearing that." A big chain hanging from his pocket—seemed a little too punk for Jarret's "hot and trendy streetwear" style.

"Are you talking about Jarret West?" Mrs. Bellamy smiled at Stacey then at me. "That young man could probably use one of those." She nodded, chuckling.

I shook my head again, doubly dumbfounded. "Why do you think that?"

"I came to the rectory a week or two ago and found police cars pulling out." She pointed toward the rectory. "Apparently, they'd found Jarret asleep on the couch on the back porch, slept there all night."

"What?" My face scrunched up, my mind struggling to process what she said.

"Poor boy dropped his keys in the church the night before, didn't realize it until he'd left but couldn't get back inside because Father had locked up early. Went to an ordination in Rapid City, didn't return until late. Anyway, Jarret fell asleep on the couch, waiting for his return." She laughed. "By the time he woke up, he thought it was too late to knock on the rectory door, so he just went back to sleep on the old couch. Can you imagine that?"

No, I couldn't. Jarret spent the night on the rectory porch—a week or so ago?

"Wait. What day was this?" Even as I asked, I realized the answer. This was the night that I'd interrogated Jarret about. When I'd asked who he was with, he'd said, *No one.* And that was the truth. Jarret, rejected by me, hadn't gone out with friends . . . he'd stopped by the church to pray. Father had left him there after locking up. Trusting him. I should've trusted him too.

Stacey, with two donuts on her flimsy plate, and I walked back to the big tree in the front lawn.

My appetite faded. I didn't want my donut anymore. As Stacey stuffed half a donut into her mouth, I realized there must be more to her story too. "Stacey, why did you get that for Jarret?" I pointed to the chain that now draped from the waistline of her skirt to her pocket.

"He can't keep a hold of his keys, is why." She laughed with her mouth closed, making a scraping sound in her throat.

"Did you see him that same day, when he dropped his keys in the church?"

"No." Her lip curled up and one eye narrowed as if she thought the question absurd. "Saw him on the first day of Fire Starters. He was over there." She pointed to the park across the street.

"What were you doing at the park on the first day of Fire Starters? Mom said you went to it."

She shrugged, dropped her empty plate onto the grass, and reached up to a low branch. Hanging from the branch, she walked up the side of the tree in her flats, but then her feet slid back to the ground. "I was gonna skip, but he talked me out of it. Said I'd like it." Then she grinned. "He did a pullup on a branch, and his keys fell out of his pocket."

I stood there stunned. "You saw Jarret, and he talked you into going to Fire Starters?"

She nodded. "He went with me, stayed for the whole thing. You gonna eat that?" She pointed to my donut then reached for my plate.

"You can have it." How could I eat anything with these revelations? Was this the night Jarret lost his job and didn't come home?

The skin on my arms prickled and my head grew light. It *was* that night. I'd spoken with Mom earlier that day . . . about Stacey. Jarret helped my sister when she'd been tempted to skip Fire Starters and even attended with her. I could hardly believe it, but then again . . . he wasn't the boy I knew in high school. But where did he go after?

"Hey, Stacey, do you know where Jarret went after the meeting?"

She stared at me for a second then started backing away. "Yeah, Fred invited him over for a campout or something. I gotta see if Paula can come over." And she took off.

Fred was one of the nicest boys I'd met in Fire Starters, faith-filled even as a teen.

I spent the rest of the day in a daze over lunch and pleasant conversation with my family, the Brandts, and Stacey's new friend, Paula, at our house. A game of Uno with my sisters and Paula and Peter's younger brother, Toby. Dinner with the family. Then as the sun crept toward the horizon, Dad drove me back to the Wests' house, and I realized: God had given me the sign I'd asked for. I could trust Jarret West.

--*

The Digbys relaxed on teak patio chairs on the front porch. Music came from a little speaker on the table between them, some old country song. A pitcher of lemonade and two glasses also sat on the table.

"Welcome back, dear," Mr. Digby said, waving his lanky arm as my dad drove off. After working with him in the garden for the past several days, I recognized his smile, the slight curve of his lips that he offered way more often than I'd realized before—back when I thought the man did not smile at all. And I actually felt quite close to him, just as I did with Nanny. His concern for that baby bird—which learned to use its wings two days later—helped me to see the real Mr. Digby.

"Did you have a nice Sunday?" Nanny asked as I climbed the porch steps. A crocheted blanket covered her legs, despite the warm temperature.

"Yes, it was lovely," I replied, though still in a daze. I'd been so wrong about Jarret. Mr. Digby too, for that matter.

I recognized the song now: "You're My Best Friend" by Don Williams.

"Have a seat if you like." Mr. Digby motioned to the patio chair next to him. "I can get you a glass. Got plenty of lemonade."

Before I could answer, the house phone rang, a quiet sound traveling from the kitchen, down the long hallway, and through the screen door. And if I'd been speaking, I would've likely missed it. "I'll get that."

I opened the door and raced down the hallway, even though I suspected the caller would only want to sell me something or ask my opinion of various politicians. As much as I enjoyed the Digbys' company, I really wanted to sulk alone this evening. So maybe I could come up with an excuse before returning from the phone call.

I snatched up the phone on the fourth or fifth ring and pressed the receiver to my ear. "Hello?"

Silence greeted me but not a dial tone, so I said hello again.

Still no answer but other sounds came through the phone, soft sounds, not like a call center but more like the outdoors. "If anyone's there, I can't hear you. Maybe the connection is bad. You can try to call back." I waited a moment then hung up.

Halfway back through the kitchen, I stopped. What if it was an important call, like, one from Mr. West or . . . Jarret? I returned to the phone to check the caller ID. The number didn't look familiar. Or did it?

I sucked in a breath and held it, then I yanked open the junk drawer where I'd shoved Jarret's cell phone number. The scrap of paper lay under a box of toothpicks. My pent-up breath released. The numbers matched. Jarret tried to call. What if something was wrong?

I picked up the phone and called him back.

He answered on the first ring with a hesitant, "Hello?"

The sound of his low, manly voice set my heart to thumping. "Hi, Jarret. Did you just call?" Regret surfaced, along with respect and a hint of awe. Jarret prayed, like, really prayed, like, probably even on his knees all alone in a church. And he helped my sister, somehow talked her into giving the youth group a chance. My gaze dropped to the floor where I stood. Jarret had helped me too when I'd really needed it.

"Uh, yeah, I did."

"Oh, I couldn't hear you. Maybe the connection was bad."

"No, I . . . I just didn't say anything."

"What?" A jolt of anger shot up, squashing all those nice thoughts to the side. Why would he— "You heard me say hello and just let me keep babbling like that? What's that about?" I was one second from slamming the phone down and ending the call. So maybe he prayed and helped my sister, but he obviously didn't call to actually speak with me. "Why would anybody—"

"I just needed to hear your voice."

My breath caught and my anger dissipated like steam under sunlight. "You *what?*"

"I wasn't sure you'd want to talk to me. Didn't think I could take the rejection."

"Oh," I whispered and then all breathy said, "It's good to hear your voice too."

"Yeah?"

"Yeah." I gave him a moment to say something else, but he didn't, so I filled the silence. "How are you? Is everything okay?"

"Yeah, it's all right. Except I miss you."

"You do?" I bit my lip. How did he mean this? I didn't want to jump to conclusions. I'd done enough of that already. In fact, maybe this was my opportunity to apologize.

"Yeah, I do. And there's something I need to say to you."

"Oh, I have something to say to you too."

"Okay. You first."

Did I want to go first? Maybe he would say something that would change what I wanted to say. No, that wouldn't be possible. I owed him a few apologies. "So . . . I want to tell you I'm sorry."

"Sorry for what?"

"Well, to start with, for piling your luggage in the middle of the hallway, you know, when you first came home. And then for all my snotty remarks in the days that followed, but mostly . . . for doubting you and speaking so harshly before you left. You told me you don't drink, and I should've believed you."

"Eh, I probably deserved all that. Is that it?"

"There's one thing more. After Selena left and I was avoiding you, I probably should've explained why." My throat seemed to close up, and my mind drew a blank. Did I really need to explain this to him?

"So . . . are you gonna tell me why?"

"Yes. Just give me a second." I tapped my head. Did I really need to? Okay, just out with it. "I was starting to get feelings for you, and I just wanted to step back and figure them out."

"Feelings . . . like . . . you like me?"

"Right. Those kind of feelings."

"Like . . . you like me more than Peter?"

"Well, not in the same way." Was he going to force me to spell it out?

"Hm. Like, more than you like Roland?"

I let out a sharp sigh of impatience. "Yes. And not in the same way. I told you we became close like siblings, so not like that. Do you really need me to say more?" I paced back and forth, gripping the phone, pressing it to my ear. "I-I was starting to feel something every time we were together, something too strong, and I was, maybe, afraid of my feelings—I really like you, Jarret. I mean, I did. I did like you." Heat washed over me. I said way too much, didn't I?

"You don't now?"

"I . . ." *Oh my.* How *did* I feel now? I'd tried so hard to get over my feelings for him. In fact, as I'd made my list of what I wanted in a husband, I'd succeeded. Right? But now, after what I'd just learned about him today . . .

"Well, I hope you still do 'cuz that'll make what I have to say easier." He paused, and then his next words spilled out. "I want to see you, Caitlyn, or court you or whatever it takes. I'll move out if I have to. Find a permanent chaperone, whatever. I'll talk to your father right now if you want. Just gimme his number." Another pause while my head spun, then the clincher. "I think I'm falling in love with you."

Happiness filled my heart to overflowing, tingling down my spine and bubbling out in laughter. "Okay, then, let's see each other. When are you coming back? We can talk to our parents together."

We spent another twenty minutes on the phone, hope, excitement, and a new sense of adventure filling me. He told me about his experiences in Brazil and how they'd found what they'd been looking for, some primary deposit or something, and how the Brazilians could handle the rest. So he'd soon be coming home. And I told him about the baby bird and working with Mr. Digby and how Nanny was improving again.

"When you get home, let's discuss the specifics of our courtship before talking with our parents," I said, wanting to be prepared for the questions my parents would throw at us. I wanted them to know we weren't entering into this lightly.

"You mean setting rules, right? Well, that's fine as long as—"

"Hello?" I listened to the silence on the other end of the phone for a few seconds. His phone must've died. As I finally hung up the landline, peaceful happiness floated in my heart, opening to something I once would've never considered possible. I would soon enter courtship with Jarret West.

CHAPTER 33

Jarret

Since the phone call with Caitlyn, I'd been walking on air. My hope-filled mood got me through the final days in Brazil and accompanied me on the plane ride and the drive into town, even as rain welcomed us home. But as Papa turned down our driveway and our house eased into view, rain pelting the turrets and battlements, doubts crept in. Maybe she'd changed her mind. Or after seeing me for a couple of days, she'd come to her senses.

Then the front porch came into view, along with Caitlyn in a long peach-colored dress, her red curls hanging over one shoulder. She clung to a porch beam and peered in our direction. When she saw the Lexus, she bounced on her feet and her hands came together, reflexive type actions that brought a smile to my face.

"Well, there's Caitlyn," Papa announced, pulling onto the circular driveway. Just then the front door swung open, and Nanny stepped outside with a cane, Mr. Digby behind her.

"Yeah, there she is." My heart raced, threatening to leap from my chest and go on ahead of me. I hadn't told Papa about Caitlyn yet, since we'd decided to discuss things before talking to our parents. But my impulsive nature warned me Papa was about to find out.

Papa no sooner shifted into park when I flung open my door. My mind had me going to the trunk for my luggage and playing it cool, but my heart had me racing through the rain, around the car and toward the porch.

Caitlyn descended the steps, the skirt of her long dress billowing out, and we collided in a hug on the sidewalk, our arms fitting naturally around each other, hers around my neck and shoulders, mine around her back and waist. We'd probably have rules about hugging, but today we exchanged a good solid hug where for one moment our hearts beat against each other and we breathed into each other's hair.

I didn't want to let go, but we probably had an audience, so I released her and eased her arms from around my neck. We stepped away from each other. The look in her emerald eyes as a few raindrops came between us turned my heart to mush and made my lips burn for hers. But I wouldn't let myself kiss her. Not yet anyway.

"Welcome home," she whispered then her gaze shifted to some point behind me.

The trunk popped open, and Papa's boots clomped on the driveaway, but I couldn't tear my gaze from those gorgeous green eyes and her sweet little smile. Finally home. Finally with her. And we were finally gonna start something together. Me and her. I could hardly believe it.

"Well, that was some how-d'ya-do." Papa came up beside me, his suspicious blue eyes shifting from me to Caitlyn and back to me. Then he shoved a suitcase between us. "Let's get our stuff in the house, shall we?"

After greeting Nanny with a hug and a kiss on the cheek, I grabbed the rest of my luggage from the trunk. I assumed

Mr. Digby would help with all of Papa's stuff, so I tossed my stuff on my bed, changed my clothes, and went to meet Caitlyn.

As I stepped through the double doors to the family room, she started to get up from where she sat cross-legged in the overstuffed chair near the suit of armor in the corner.

"Don't get up." I glanced over my shoulder before the doors swung shut. Papa would come looking for me soon, curious about that hug. Best we didn't start hugging all over again.

"I made food." She smiled, tucking her feet back under her.

I sat on the end of the couch nearest her. Plates of snack food filled the coffee table between us, including pigs in a blanket, veggies and dip, eggs rolls, and a bowl of chips. And a Coke on ice.

"If you're too tired to really talk about anything today—" she started to say.

"Nope. I'm not too tired for this conversation."

She blushed and pressed her lips together as if trying to keep from smiling. "So where do we start?"

I glimpsed a notebook tucked between her leg and the arm of the overstuffed chair. "You got a list there or something? I don't have a clue how this goes, so you'll have to teach me."

Her blush deepened. She let her hair fall over her face as she turned for the notebook. Then she sat with her head down and a curtain of red curls hiding her face. "I wrote a couple of things down. Is this going to be all too strange for you?" She peeked up.

"No way. I'll do anything." I shook my head, and an unbidden scene played out in my mind, something I would not let happen, me sliding off the couch and coming around to her on the chair, kneeling before her and sinking my hands in her mane of red curls, pulling her toward me and enveloping her lips in mine—

"Jarret."

I snapped from my thoughts and spun to face Papa, who stood behind the couch.

"You got something you need to tell me?" While he worded it like a question, his eyes, all narrowed up, commanded.

Caitlyn and I looked at each other, her with the hint of a smile, not seeming too bothered by Papa's question. Me with a mild degree of panic. I didn't want him to know until we came to tell him ourselves.

I threw her a look which she may not have understood, trying to warn her that we had to tell him now. Keefe, my twin, always understood my looks and read my body language. Maybe she would someday too.

"Jarret?" Papa said.

Caitlyn glanced at Papa and back to me. Then she nodded, a little nod that seemed to say she gave me permission to tell him. Maybe she did understand my look.

"Why don't you have a seat?" I motioned for Papa to join us.

He grabbed a pig in a blanket and sat on the couch adjacent me. "So let's hear it."

While my mind told me to ease into the conversation, my mouth blurted, "We want to see each other."

"Yup. Figured that's what that hug meant. When did this happen?"

I shrugged and shook my head, something of my old attitude taking over and probably apparent in my eyes, some fear that he'd start judging me and not give me a chance. I wasn't worthy of a girl like her, and we all knew it.

You accept bad things from the Lord, why do you not accept good?

Okay, I had to change my way of seeing myself and also my way of seeing Papa. Sure, I made mistakes now and then, but I wanted to follow the right path. I really tried. And not that I deserved anything at all, but God didn't will bad in my life. He meant all things for my good. Even Papa, while not perfect, meant good for me.

"We just started talking about it while you guys were in Brazil," Caitlyn said, swinging her feet down and sitting more like a lady. "Jarret called. Well, and then I had to call back. But, I mean, we've been getting to know each other all summer, talking and all that. Then when Selena was here, we all spent time together, the three of us. But we haven't . . ." She blushed again. Her hands went to her knees and her eyes to me for a moment. Then, as if gaining strength from that one glance, she continued. "I mean, we didn't consider seeing each other until . . . you guys went to Brazil. Not really." And she blushed again, maybe thinking about our kiss—like I was now.

Papa nodded and helped himself to three more pigs in a blanket. "So how's this gonna work?"

"We're gonna practice courtship," I said, heat riding up my neck. I could hardly believe I was saying it, much less preparing to practice it. Would we have to tell everyone that's what we were doing? We'd want her parents to know, of course, and Papa, but did Peter and Roland and every other friend need to know?

"And how does that work?" Papa took a bite and chewed.

"I got no clue. She was getting ready to explain it to me."

Caitlyn nodded, a smile stretching across her face.

After munching his snack while staring at some point on the floor, Papa looked at her and then me. "Well, I guess I'd better let you get to it." He got up and shook a pant leg over his boot. "After you've had your talk, let me know how this works. And I'm sure you'll be talking this over with the Summers."

"Yeah." I'd be asking her father for permission. And I still couldn't fathom him giving it.

As Papa left the room, I stared after him, stunned. I wanted to run after him and say, *Wait, you don't care that I'm about to see Caitlyn? You aren't going to tell me that she's too good for me, or that I'm a bad egg?* But I didn't need to run after him. Papa was okay with it. He must've trusted Caitlyn and maybe trusted me on account of her.

"Well, that went well." Caitlyn pulled her legs up again, tucking her feet under opposite knees, then she slid her notebook onto her lap and flipped open to a page in the middle of it. "I don't really know where to start."

"I do." I grinned. "Let's talk about kissing."

CHAPTER 34

Caitlyn

"Let's go see your father one more time." Standing in the kitchen, across the bar counter from Jarret, I turned a page in my notebook so I could review the rest of the notes we'd made together. Courtship notes for me and Jarret. Oh my goodness, this was so surreal. This morning we'd spoken with his father again. After dinner we planned to tell my parents.

"Why, so we can kiss?" Jarret leaned toward me, sliding his hands across the bar counter, a sly grin on his face. He peeled my hands from the notebook and laced our fingers together. "Oh, wait . . ." He released my hands and backed up, clasping his hands behind his head, his biceps bulging from under the short sleeves of his t-shirt. "Am I allowed to hold your hands?"

Trying not to giggle—boy, he was cute . . . and trying so hard—I stepped to the zucchini on the cutting board and picked up the knife so I could finish dinner preparations. "Courtship isn't just a list of rules." . . . although I did like my lists, and we'd filled several pages with them last night. "It's about two people getting to know each other without the distraction and temptations that come with physical intimacy."

"You sound like a book." Jarret folded his arms on the counter, watching me work.

"Well, I have read a lot of courtship books. But it makes sense, doesn't it? So for example . . . if we hold hands *all* the time, we'll grow comfortable with that, but we'll also want to get closer and maybe start putting our arms around each other."

He turned up a hand and shook his head, obviously not getting it.

"Once we get comfortable holding hands all the time and draping our arms over each other, as we grow closer together, won't we want more? What comes next? And then what after that?"

"Can we just draw a line in the sand?"

"Maybe that works for some people, but I just want us to get to know each other without pressure." I finished slicing the zucchini into little half-inch-thick circles.

"There won't be any pressure. We already decided no kissing unless we're around others. Let's just hold hands whenever we want."

"Aren't we only spending time together with a chaperone?"

"Or at public places. Where I get to hold your hand." He gave me a crooked grin.

I added oil to a skillet and turned on the burner. The chicken and baked potatoes would soon be done.

Jarret sighed and spun my notebook toward himself. He flipped back a few pages to one of our lists. "Okay, so we get to know each other by hanging out with the Digbys, my father, your family, Peter . . ." He huffed. "That's gonna be a fun day."

Our list included a variety of activities so we could get to know each other in different circumstances, including praying together, game nights with my family, double dates with friends, volunteer work, cookouts and other outdoor events, walks and horseback riding, making meals together, group activities, even shopping . . .

In addition to listing activities, we also listed subjects we should discuss, like faith, marriage, children, work . . . While writing that list, we made each other important promises about communication. He agreed never to drive off when he was upset. I agreed not to give him the cold shoulder when I didn't understand his actions.

"You're not ready to tell your parents, are you?" Jarret flipped to another page in the notebook. "That's why you want to talk to Papa again. He was pretty easy, but just because of you. He trusts you and knows you won't tolerate any funny business from me."

After scraping the zucchini off the cutting board and into the skillet, I stood opposite him at the counter and grabbed his hands, lacing our fingers together, which brought that sly smile to his face. "Yes, I'm ready to tell them."

"Do they know we're coming over, or are we making a surprise visit?"

"I told them I was coming over with a friend."

"A friend?" He squeezed my hands and released them.

"If I'd said your name, they'd have all this time to wonder what we wanted and to jump to conclusions."

He shook his head. "So we're going to try shock treatment instead."

I nodded. *Please, Lord, go with us.*

––*

Jarret and I climbed the front porch of my house. Dad's voice traveled through the screen door as he shouted at one of my siblings to stop playing by the neighbor's garden. Since I'd spent the past month and a half at West Castle, visiting home only on Sundays, and then the previous months at college, I almost felt like I should knock. But I did still live here, as the smallest room in the house packed with all my belongings would testify.

With a rush of nervousness, I yanked open the screen door, which screeched to announce us, and I stepped inside with Jarret behind me.

"Hi, Dad." I stopped in the middle of the front room, and Jarret came up beside me sorting through the best place for his hands, pockets, hips, finally deciding to drop them to his sides.

Dad turned from the back patio door and glanced from me to Jarret. "Hello there, Caitlyn. Your mother said you were bringing a friend. You meant Jarret, huh? That's a bit of a surprise." He shuffled toward us, offering a hand to Jarret. "You still driving that cherry red Chrysler?"

"Yup." Jarret shook his hand and nodded over his shoulder. "It's parked right there in your drive."

The back patio screen door slid open and eight-year-old David stepped one foot on the track, his big orange-and-blue plastic archery bow in hand. "Andy's still over there looking for arrows. I told him we only have five now."

While Dad shuffled back to the patio door, Mom stepped from the hallway with a stack of kitchen towels and washcloths and swung around the corner, into the messy kitchen. "Oh, hi, Caitlyn. Your sisters are out this evening—" Midway through the kitchen, she stopped and turned around, her eyes open wide now. Then she forced her normal company smile onto her face. "Sorry, Jarret, I didn't realize you were standing there too. How are you doing?"

"Good, thanks." Jarret glanced to Dad as he returned from the patio door. "They're playing archery, huh?"

"Yeah, with those suction cup arrows the wife picked up at a garage sale, never stick to the target." He chuckled and swiped his unruly hair off his forehead as he looked Jarret over again.

"If they really like archery, bring 'em on over to our house. We've got a couple of youth sets and a foam target. No suction cup arrows."

"Oh, got those steel tips?" Dad tilted his head, looking interested.

"So what are you kids out doing?" Mom said, coming from the kitchen now. Seeing the two of us together, she likely suspected something. Dad probably did too, but he didn't mind putting a bit of small talk before the discovery. He'd talk to anyone about cars and sports, and even kids' games.

Jarret made the slightest jerk back at Mom's question, but then he turned with all calmness to Dad. "Actually, Mr. Summer, I'd like to speak with you."

After a moment's hesitation, a smile crept onto Dad's face. "Should I be worried?"

"Don't be silly, Dad." My face burned. I hadn't thought of this. The last time Jarret had come to our house—how many years ago?—I was a freshman in high school. How could I have not prepared for this? Dad's thoughts went directly to the day Jarret had come to our house to see his pregnant girlfriend, my best friend, who had temporarily moved in with us. Dad had talked to Jarret about following rules if he wanted to see her. This was horrible.

Dad and Jarret stood facing each other across the room, like two gunslingers ready for a showdown. What was I thinking? Dad would never approve of our seeing each other.

"Caitlyn," Mom said, maybe noticing the panic on my face. "Would you like to help me in the kitchen? I didn't get around to the dinner dishes yet."

"Is there somewhere we can talk?" Jarret said to Dad as I went mechanically to the kitchen.

"Sure, Jarret, step into my office," Dad said.

Jarret

"Mind if I ask you a personal question or two, Jarret?" Mr. Summer leaned back, the stuffed faux-leather rocker creaking as he settled. A big TV screen hung on the wall opposite his chair, but he'd angled the chair toward me before sitting down.

"Um, sure." I sat across from him in his little "office," on one end of an old crushed-velvet loveseat, trying to keep my palms dry. My gaze kept shifting to the cluttered shelves behind Mr. Summer, to the DVDs and old VCRs and the books and miscellaneous junk stacked on top of things. To anything but his probing eyes. When I'd asked to start courting his daughter, he'd said, *I was afraid of that.* And I'd had no response.

"How many girls have you seen since Zoe?"

"Uh . . ." I slid a glance to the closed door, wishing that Caitlyn would come through. "I don't know. Why?"

"Really? You don't know. Can you give me a ballpark?"

A little huff escaped me, and my face warmed, the room suddenly stuffy, my palms practically dripping. "You want an actual number?" *Lemme think.* Zoe was my first real girlfriend. I dated someone a couple months after she broke up with me. Chantelle. Her brother didn't like me. I'd told myself I wasn't dating in my senior year but ended up seeing two girls. One for a week, another for a month maybe. Did one-offs count? Took a girl to homecoming. Another one to prom. And then at college—

"If you haven't got enough fingers, I can help." Mr. Summer held up his hands and wiggled his fingers, a mirthful arch to his bushy eyebrows.

"No, I, um . . ." I actually touched my index finger as if ready to start counting, but the names and faces of past girlfriends flitted in my mind randomly.

Just then the door flew open. "Dad, don't be ridiculous." Caitlyn stormed into the room with scrunched up eyebrows and a scowl. Madder than I'd ever seen her. And cute, cute, cute.

She plopped down on the loveseat next to me, grabbing the sweaty hand I'd been counting on. An angry growl rumbled in her chest. "Jarret had the courage to come over here and ask your permission to court me. He's trying to do things the right way. Not just in this, but he has been for years. He's changed. You're not even giving him a chance. How many girlfriends?" She huffed. "What difference does that make?"

Mr. Summer listened to his daughter rant then he leaned back and started rocking in the chair. "I think it makes a big difference, honey. How many of those girls practiced courtship? Because the world's standards are quite different from ours."

"None of 'em," I said. "I've only known one girl to practice courtship. Your daughter." I set my jaw, the black snake of my ego now rising. I struggled to subdue it, had to keep it from rising any higher, had to keep it from a sudden strike. Its poison would only come back on me. "And that's why I'm here, asking you now." Caitlyn's defense of me, her support, freed my tongue. "We've set rules and boundaries and all that stuff, and we want to get to know each other better. I'm not gonna take advantage of her."

"Forgive me for judging, Jarret, 'cause I really do like you, but I'm not sure you're the best man for my daughter. And with your living arrangements, I mean, you're right there under the same roof." He paused. "I don't want her getting hurt."

Caitlyn, so free with emotion around her family, tilted her head back and let out an exasperated groan.

I rubbed her hand, trying to calm her and myself. Could I really blame him for his apprehension? Would I feel any differently in his shoes . . . a guy with my history asking to see my daughter? And we'd talked about alternative living arrangements, but she didn't like the idea of me staying with friends, and Nanny still needed her at the house, so . . .

Caitlyn jumped up from the couch, releasing my hand, and stomped to her father's side. Cupping a hand to one side of her mouth, she whispered in his ear. Then she backed up, hands to her hips, and looked at him as if checking that he understood what she'd just told him. He opened his mouth to speak but then laughed. What had she told him?

Mr. Summer shook his head. "I don't know, Caitlyn, that's a mighty strange request."

"Please."

That simple word, the way she said it with humility and insistence, always worked on me.

"Well, okay." Eyes shifting to me, Mr. Summer sat forward in the rocking recliner as Caitlyn returned to my side.

I wanted to ask her for an explanation, but Mr. Summer was looking me over, rubbing his hands together, readying himself to comply with Caitlyn's request, I assumed.

"Jarret, I've got kind of an odd request."

"O-o-o-kay?"

"Open your shirt."

He . . . wanted me to do what? I shot Caitlyn a look for help, desperation shooting through my eyes. This was getting strange.

"Just do it," she said with that confident smile.

I shook my head in disbelief and reached for the top button, shoved it through the buttonhole, next button, next . . . and by the time I got to the fourth button, I understood why.

"Well, I'll be." Mr. Summer stared at the ratty old scapular on my chest. "How long have you been wearing that thing?"

"Since the summer before my senior year."

He nodded and leaned back, sinking comfortably into the padded chair. "Well, whaddya know?" A pause. The gears moving. "That's just after Zoe, huh?"

I nodded, satisfied that he now started to understand me—I'd changed since high school, been trudging on a different path, a harder path but the only one worth the journey. I rubbed the cord of my scapular between my finger and thumb, humbled by the way Blessed Mother had come to my rescue just now.

Thanks, Blessed Mother. I should've known you'd have my back. My devotion to her made my courtship with Caitlyn possible. In more ways than one.

"You can button that up now." Mr. Summer waved a finger. "No need for the gratuitous display of your buffed up chest. You put a lot of work into that body, huh?"

"Dad." Caitlyn let out a weary groan and collapsed against the back of the couch.

CHAPTER 35

Caitlyn

"**P**ull into the B&B parking lot." I pointed to the gravel parking area off the addition on the right side of the Brandts' house. "Toby's birthday party will be out back." The neon pink sign of the Forest Gateway B&B stood in stark contrast to the natural, peaceful shades of their house and landscaping. Just as my nerves today at the thought of telling Peter about us stood in contrast to the joy I'd experienced courting Jarret for the past month or so.

Jarret and I had adapted well to our courtship rules. We intentionally avoided each other during the day. I focused on Nanny and chores, most of which Nanny now did with me. After his morning weightlifting routine, Jarret worked with his father on research and planning for upcoming assignments. He also spent more time with the horses and Mr. Digby, which made my heart happy because of my new fondness for the old man but also because Jarret thrived on physical activity, which horse riding and grooming provided.

We never spent time at the house together without Nanny or Mr. Digby or Mr. West nearby. And although we traveled to and from places alone, which allowed for some of our deepest conversations, we only went to public places, like stores, church, busy parks, and Fire Starters meetings. My family came over a few times for cookouts and games, my siblings just loving Jarret's attention as they learned archery and the basics of horseback riding. And we'd visited my family for dinner and card games a few times too.

My favorite moments occurred on the quiet evenings on the front porch with the Digbys, reminiscing and talking about things of little importance while we listened to old-time music. One evening, "Ain't No Mountain High Enough" by Marvin Gaye and Tammi Terrell came on and . . .

As the unique drum pattern started, Jarret jumped up with a crooked grin. He took my hand and tugged me from my chair. "Dance with me," he said in that bossy way of his. Then he offered his right arm and guided my left hand to his muscular bicep.

Happiness rippling through me, I let him escort me down the porch steps and out into the grass, both of us barefoot and walking in step to the slow beat of the song. As the lyrics began, we turned to each other, and he offered me one hand and then the other. He lifted our clasped hands overhead and turned me so we faced the same direction, our right hands then resting by my right shoulder and left hands out, and we walked a few steps before he spun me around and brought me, laughing, back to him.

Then I rested one hand on his shoulder, and he held my back, our other hands clasped, and he leaned toward me and sang a few lines in my ear. My heart melted at the sound of his manly voice so close to me, making me awash with tingles.

He dropped his gaze to my lips and then glanced at me, as he always did, for permission it seemed. And we moved toward each other hesitantly until his lips found mine. And his kiss . . .

so sweet, so powerful, like a burst of love with a promise of passion, but we kept the passion at bay—unlike our first kiss in the kitchen.

When that song ended, "Annie's Song" by John Denver began. And we continued dancing barefoot in the grass, him gazing into my eyes and the Digbys watching us as we swayed and sang and the sun sank behind the trees and our souls melted together in some surreal moment that I never wanted to end.

Jarret said something, yanking me from my thoughts. I only heard him say, "I'll just park on the grass," as he pulled up next to Roland's black Avenger. Cars filled the rest of the gravel lot. As he shut off the engine, he slid a glance my way. "You've told Peter about us, right? Or is this gonna be a big surprise?"

"Well . . . he hasn't been home, and I thought it would go over better in person."

He huffed. "You sure about that?" Then he leaned back in the driver's seat and stuffed his keys into the front pocket of his denim shorts, the keychain Stacey had given him draping down. Gray athletic shoes and a forest-green tank top completed his look.

We didn't match at all, not that it mattered, but I wore a gray t-shirt, soft coral pink skirt, and white sneakers. "Peter will be fine. You guys got along last time we saw him, remember? Everyone dancing at his house . . ."

"We weren't courting then." Jarret reached for the door handle and looked at me, his brown eyes roving over every inch of my face. "You know he's not gonna approve. That's not gonna change things, is it?"

While we had definite rules about kissing, I lunged toward him and planted a quick one on his pouty lips, making him smile and then lick his lips. "It might take a bit of work," I said, "but I'd like you guys to get along. He'll always be my friend. He's like a brother to me."

Jarret rolled his eyes and sighed. "You've got a lot of friends that are boys. Not sure how I feel about that."

Saving that discussion for some other day, I grabbed our giftbag from the backseat, and together we strolled out into the lawn.

Toby, now fifteen, and a group of children from ages eight to sixteen, some with obvious special needs, stood in two groups under a shade canopy on one end of a mowed-lawn bocce ball court in the middle of the wide backyard. Mom sat with Mrs. Brandt and other adults in camp chairs nearby. A few kids played by the trees that bordered the back of the property. And on the furthest side of the yard, kids formed a sloppy line to throw beanbags at a stack of cans—probably a game that Peter had set up.

I couldn't see Dad, but a mixed group sat on the big deck that came off the B&B, around a table with a blue plastic tablecloth and colorful balloons. A smaller decorated table held gifts and another one, food.

"There's Roland," Jarret said, eyes on a group around a picnic table further back. Then he suddenly squeezed my hand and stopped walking.

"What's wrong?" I couldn't see anything out of the ordinary. A few friends from high school stood in a circle by the picnic table, including Dominic and Fred and some girls. Peter wasn't among the group.

Roland, sitting at the picnic table, saw us and bumped Ling-si's arm with his own, the way he used to bump me when he wanted my attention. Ling-si sat with her back to us, talking with some of my girlfriends from high school. She wore her jet-black hair loose today and falling halfway down her back.

"What's she doing here?" Jarret said, his voice strangled.

"Who?" I looked again, glancing from girl to girl.

Ling-si turned toward us and, glimpsing me, her hand shot into the air, her mouth opened with a huge smile, and she waved. "Caitlyn," she shouted and took off running toward us. Never one to hide her ethnicity, she wore a Chinese-style shirt with a cherry blossom print and olive-green capris.

Jarret exhaled and turned to the sky, his hand trembling for a second. "Never mind."

Anxious for them to meet, I pulled him forward and we met Ling-si in the middle of the lawn. I handed the giftbag to Jarret and hugged her as if we'd not seen each other in years.

Still holding my arms and bursting with excitement, she backed from the hug and glanced at Jarret. Then she pursed her lips, eyes as wide as they could go, and she fanned herself, which made us both laugh.

Getting control of myself, I stepped aside to include Jarret, and I introduced them.

"She talks about you all the time," Jarret said, shaking her hand.

"Probably not as much as she talks about you," Ling-si said, her dark eyes glittering and dimples popping out on each side of her smile.

"Mm. I hope it's all good stuff, although . . ." He shook his head and threw a few glances between us. "I'm sure there were days . . ."

Ling-si fell against my shoulder laughing.

Roland strolled up beside her and greeted Jarret with a fist bump that Jarret turned into a quick hug. Then Roland mumbled something, and both West boys turned to look behind Jarret.

"I'm taking this to the gift table." Jarret walked off with the gift bag before I could reply.

In the next moment, Peter joined our circle, standing casually with a hand on one hip. "Well, here you are. And I see you brought a friend." He glanced toward the deck as Jarret mounted the steps with the gift bag. "Or I guess, he brought you."

"Oh, you mean Jarret?" I hugged Peter since I hadn't seen him in a while, even though I knew he'd just leave his one hand on his hip and give me a slap on the back with the other.

"So you guys seem quite chummy." Peter pinned me with an accusing glare.

I played with a lock of my hair. *Why did Jarret have to wander off now?* "You know, don't you?"

"Yeah, I heard. *Some* of my friends don't keep secrets from me."

"I didn't say anything," Roland mumbled. Ling-si laughed on his shoulder.

Peter shot him a look. "Yeah, I know. You're one of my friends who *does* keep secrets from me. I had to hear it from someone else." His accusing eyes shifted back to me. "Should've heard it from you. *Hey, Peter, I'm dating the guy you despise most.*"

"I wasn't keeping a secret, just wanted to tell you in person. And you shouldn't *despise* anyone."

"Oh, hey," a guy said, "what a surprise." A young man with windblown blond hair and dressed in a peach polo shirt with white trim stepped into the group—wait, Nanny's physical therapist, Dwight? He pushed in between Roland and Peter, looking at me. "I didn't know you guys knew each other."

"You know Dwight?" Peter grinned at me.

"Well, yes, he's Nanny's therapist," I said, confused. "How do you know him?"

Peter explained how Dwight had worked with Toby for a time, helping with his unusual gait, and how Toby had grown fond of him and now texted him daily—after somehow getting his number from their mother's cell phone.

"You got a minute?" Dwight's brows lifted with a hopeful expression. "There's a little boy you should meet. He's got Down Syndrome. Wants to become a detective when he grows up. You said that's what you're studying for, right?" Dwight flashed his handsome smile.

"Um . . ." I turned to see what kept Jarret. He stood talking to my father near the snack table on the back deck, not even looking this way. So I turned back to Dwight. "Okay, sure." And then to Ling-si, "Would you tell Jarret when he comes back?"

She nodded. Peter continued grinning. And Roland's gray eyes flickered with worry.

Jarret

After dropping our giftbag on the crowded gift table and chatting a moment with Caitlyn's father, I stepped off the deck shifting gears, preparing for Peter and his sarcastic remarks about me seeing Caitlyn. Taking a few strides toward the group, I stopped. Roland and Ling-si hadn't moved from where we'd met up with them on the lawn. Peter had joined them. But where was Caitlyn?

Peter caught me standing in place, looking around, a big grin stretching across his ugly mug, so I continued toward the group.

A trace of the dread I'd felt when first seeing Ling-si returned. From behind she looked just like Zoe—silky black hair that I'd run my hands through hundreds of times, slender body that I knew too well. At the sight of her, a dozen condemning thoughts had plagued my mind, along with a vivid memory of past sins and the hurt I'd caused.

"Well, there he is, Jarret West, girl magnet." Peter lifted a fist in welcome as I drew near the group of three: him, Roland, and Ling-si.

"And there's Peter Brat." I bumped his fist a little harder than I typically did then I glanced at Roland to see where Caitlyn had gone.

Roland nudged Ling-si.

"Oh yeah." Ling-si smiled up at me with her pretty almond-shaped eyes and dimples. "Caitlyn's over there." She pointed to a group on the far side of the grass bocce court. "That one guy wanted her to talk to a little boy about . . . something." She looked to Roland, opening her eyes wide, probably wanting help with a better answer, but Roland gave a little headshake to tell her she'd done fine.

"Who's *that one guy?*" Trying to appear unfazed, I looked to where she pointed. Caitlyn stood next to a blond dude—in a pink polo shirt—and a couple of mom-aged women, all of them focused on a boy maybe eight years old.

"Wait a second. Don't you know him?" Peter folded his arms across his chest, standing smugly. "That's Dwight. He's your nanny's physical therapist. Caitlyn knows him. And he seems to know her pretty well too. Knows she's going to college to become a detective, which is why he brought her over to meet that little boy."

I didn't let it bother me that he'd called Nanny "your nanny" as if I were a child, but the comments about Dwight knowing Caitlyn "pretty well" dug in. How often did Dwight come to the house anyway? Turning away, pretending I didn't care, I said, "Dude's wearing pink."

Peter glanced. "Well, it's more like peach but"—he looked me up and down—"not every guy has a muscle-shirt body." He lifted his folded arms and glanced down at his own soft belly on his otherwise stocky, fairly strong body. Then he peered off in Dwight's direction for a long moment. "Of course, Dwight could probably make it work. Bet he's no stranger to the gym."

"The pink sure ain't doing him any favors." My gaze shifted to someone galloping toward us, Peter's brother, Toby. He had to be fifteen or sixteen, but his big innocent eyes, floppy haircut, and rounded belly made him seem way younger.

"Hi, Jarret West." He stopped a little too close and cocked his head to one side as he stared. For whatever reason, he'd always had some strange fascination with me. Maybe he'd first seen me with my identical twin, Keefe. That could've been a bit of an anomaly for him.

"Hi, Toby." I offered my fist, and he bumped it. "Happy birthday, man. How old are you?"

"Jarret to play bocce ball with Toby, right?" He pointed at me, maybe in case I wasn't sure he meant me.

"I thought you guys already formed teams." Peter stepped between us, his back to me. "Wouldn't be fair to add players now."

"Sure, I'll play," I said, just because it seemed to bother Peter that he'd asked me. Then I headed for the court, and Toby kept up, alternating between galloping and walking.

Roland and Ling-si sat in the grass and watched while I played on Toby's team and Peter played on the opposing team. Caitlyn's sister Stacey, in a red South Dakota Coyotes t-shirt and a white baseball cap, volunteered to referee. She clipped a little measuring tape to the long keychain she wore that matched the one she'd given me. As the game got going, Caitlyn and Dwight strolled over engaged in conversation. Her eyes flitted to me a few times as they drew near. He watched only her.

When my turn came and I stepped to the pitch line, Peter shuffled over within earshot. "Do you think Dwight realizes she's seeing anyone? I wonder if she's told him."

Undaunted by his remarks, not even glancing, I made a controlled underhand throw, not too hard and not too light. My bocce landed closest to the Jack, the target ball, like within three inches, so the turn went to Peter as the next player on the opposing team. "Your turn, Peter Brat."

Peter threw, bumping one of his team's bocce balls further from the Jack and bumping mine directly into it. They cracked together and bounced away from each other, but we were still the inside team. So his team got the next throw.

With the throwing of the last bocce ball, our team—Toby's team—gained three points, and just about everyone on both teams congratulated everyone else, even though we were playing to twelve points and still had a while to go. The special needs kids had a unique sense of sportsmanship that rubbed off on the rest of us.

We all strolled to the opposite side of the court, Peter by my side rambling on about Dwight's education, job, looks, and income.

Caitlyn smiled at me as I passed her. Dwight was still talking, one arm folded over his muscular chest, the other arm gesturing as he spoke. The sight of him next to her ruffled my feathers a bit, but I didn't want to show it.

"You have to admit they look good together," Peter said as we neared the shade canopy.

"Because they're both wearing pink?"

Peter laughed.

I hated to admit he was right, but they did look good together. And not just because her pink skirt matched his shirt or because they both had innocent smiles and light hair, hers red and his blond. Everything about this guy said he was a good man. Hardworking, educated, nice . . . comfortable following the right path probably from the beginning.

"Your turn, Jarret," Toby said in a singsong voice as he handed me a bocce ball.

After my throw, Peter took a turn and the game rolled on. His throws seemed mainly aimed at spocking—hitting— whatever bocce I threw last. And while his team gained three points in this frame, we had nine by the end of the next few frames.

"Game's about over, Peter, my boy. Then you'll have to go bug someone else."

"You tired of talking to me? I'm hurt." He made a sad face.

"All you're talking about is Dwight, trying to convince me that I should step aside. Sorry, dude, it's not working. I'm not giving her up."

As Toby approached the pitch line, I stepped to his side. He had a habit of throwing hard, like he might do in bowling, but our opponents were the inside team with three bocces in good positions—thanks to Peter's throw, which knocked our only good bocce down court to where the rest of our team's balls had gone. "Hey, you see the Jack?" I pointed to the little white ball we were all supposed to be aiming for. "It's not far down the court this time, so don't throw so hard, okay? You just got to get it over that blue ball." I pointed out the opponent's bocce that blocked the Jack. "Go easy." Maybe Toby could turn it around for us.

Toby stared from me to the court, hopefully understanding, but then he said, "No" and tossed the bocce with a bowling swing.

As his bocce joined the rest of ours, I slapped my forehead and tried suppressing a groan. I wanted to win, if only to show Peter up, but now all our balls were down court, and I had the last throw. With a sigh, I traded Toby places, stepping up to the pitch line, and glanced at Peter, ever by my side.

Standing hands on hips, Peter grinned and waved his brows. "Good luck."

I had one possible play but no clear shot to accomplish it. I had to toss my bocce over the one blocking the Jack and hit the Jack hard enough to push it down court at just the right angle. After a bit of evaluation—and with a hope and a prayer—I changed my strategy and made the throw.

"No way! This isn't pool," Peter shouted. The rest of the players cheered and exchanged high fives and fist bumps, as did the audience that had been growing with each frame. "You should've called the shot first."

My shot struck the bocce blocking the Jack, sending the Jack at just the right angle down to the grouping of our three balls at the far end of the court, gaining us exactly what we needed to win. "Your brother's team won, aren't you happy?" I turned to Caitlyn, who stood cheering—still next to Dwight. Roland and Ling-si had gotten up from the grass and stood with them. I started toward them.

"You win every game you play, don't you?" Peter, keeping to my side, said it as a statement rather than a question. "Then what, you move on to the next game, huh? Just like you do with girls."

That remark stopped me in my tracks and a familiar wave of hot anger washed over me, blinding me to every other thought.

"I know you want to pummel me, so whaddya say I challenge you to a duel," Peter said as I turned to him. "You win and I'll stop bothering you. In fact, maybe I'll work harder at giving you a chance. But if I win, you have to listen to me for the rest of the night and really consider what I'm saying."

A breathy laugh escaped me as I tried releasing my anger, not really succeeding. "A duel? Using what?" My family had swords, but I didn't think he did.

"Wait here." Peter dashed off in the direction of the shed near the back of their house.

Caitlyn appeared by my side, the rest of the group approaching. "Good game. I didn't know you played bocce ball."

"So how often does *he* come to the house?" I blurted, indicating Dwight with a tilt of my chin, the anger floating above me now but not gone.

"What?" Caitlyn's smile faded. She glanced as Dwight, Roland, and Ling-si joined us. "Have you and Dwight ever actually met?" She introduced us.

"Oh, hey, nice to meet you." Dwight, with a genuine smile, stuck out a hand. "Your house is incredible, all medieval castle on the outside and modern conveniences on the inside. Nice."

"Yeah, thanks. How much of the inside have you really seen?"

Caitlyn shot me a look.

"Just the Digbys' suite really. Is the rest much different?"

"You'll have to take him on a tour sometime," I said to Caitlyn even though I wouldn't want her to actually do it.

"Maybe I will," she said with a fiery glare.

Peter jogged back to us, panting, and handed me one of the two bamboo sticks he carried. He dropped a head guard at my feet.

Judging by the length of the handle, I assumed the bamboo stick required a two-handed hold, so I gave it a try and sliced the air a few times to get the feel of it.

"What are you doing?" Color came to Caitlyn's face as she glanced between me and Peter.

"Just having a little fun," Peter said. Then he proceeded to explain how to grip the "shinai" and basic kendo techniques. "Kendo has four target areas: head, wrists, torso, and throat. That's how you score a point. Score two points, you win."

"I'll figure it out." I didn't need his lessons. I had more than enough experience fencing with my brothers over the years—though we hadn't competed in a while. How different could this be?

Someone close to the house, maybe Mr. Brandt, shouted, "Pizza," and most people migrated toward the deck. We wouldn't have an audience. Not that I cared.

"Let's go eat," Caitlyn said, a pout on her face. "The pizza's here."

I looked at her but didn't answer. I needed to do this, and I didn't want her to talk me out of it. I even liked Peter's terms. If I won, he'd accept me seeing her. If he won, I'd listen to him. Part of me wanted to listen to him. Part of me believed him.

"We'll join you in a few minutes," Peter said to her. "This won't take long." Then he shifted his eyes to me, a grin of challenge spreading on his face.

Caitlyn huffed, shook her head, and turned away.

Dropping the shinai to my side, I grabbed her arm and leaned close so Peter wouldn't hear me. "You're not gonna be mad, are you?"

Without making eye contact, she huffed again, tugged her arm from me, and stomped off with Ling-si, joining the migration of guests heading for the deck.

"She'll get over it. Come on." Peter, already wearing the head guard and peering at me through the steel grill, tapped his shinai to mine.

I pulled the head guard on, tugging the heavy cloth over my head and shoulders, and picked up the shinai.

With his weapon at his side, Peter moved to about ten feet away from me and made a little bow.

I shook my head. I was not bowing back. But I gripped the bamboo stick with both hands and angled it toward him.

He did the same then stepped close enough to touch the tip of his shinai to mine. Then he went right into action, swinging with an aim to tap my wrist.

I blocked him, lunging close, and we crossed weapons. "I know you don't like me, but why can't you respect her choice?" We shuffled along together, our bamboo sticks pointing to the sky, neither of us able to make a move locked like this.

"She's not thinking clearly." Quicker than I thought possible, Peter twisted his shinai away and swept toward my head.

Blocking at the last split-second, I guided his weapon to my shoulder instead, and we locked our hands and the handles together.

"I sure don't understand it"—Peter grimaced through his mask—"but you seem to have a way with girls. Even girls like her." He pushed away from me. Our weapons clacked together, crossing, sliding, clacking again.

I stepped back to regain my balance.

He must've seen my move as an opening. He attacked low, swinging for my abdomen.

A rush of adrenaline saved me, my body reacting instinctively with a block and a follow-up strike to his wrist. "That's a point, right?" I said, taking steps back and repositioning for my next move.

"Yeah, that's a point." Peter swung the shinai through the air, not near me, just to release his irritation, likely. "Lemme ask you one thing."

"Go for it." I stood ready for his verbal as well as physical strike.

He lunged into action, initiating an attack, lifting his shinai overhead then swinging with a combination of long and short cuts, our shinais cracking together. "Was she just convenient," he shouted through swings, "staying at your house and all, a little something to do for the summer, or did you think of her as a challenge? I mean if you can even get someone like her to like you—"

My temper spiked with my next swing, and it cost me. I fell back on fencing moves, which didn't work in kendo, and in the next moment, his bamboo stick cracked my wrist. And his next swing tapped my throat, where my heart seemed lodged and thumping out of control.

Enraged, I let my shinai fall to the ground, and I lunged for him with my hands. He brought his bamboo stick up between us and I grabbed it, turning it horizontal, and shoved it at his throat—which the fabric of the face guard covered. We both crashed to the ground, me on top, pressing the shinai toward his throat, him holding it back, keeping it from actually making contact.

"Face it. You're not good enough for her," he spat through the grill of his face guard. "Look at you. You can't even control your temper. If you think you love her, you'll let her go before you hurt her."

"Jarret, stop." Roland was suddenly upon me, snaking his arms underneath mine and yanking me up.

I didn't resist his efforts. Once on my feet, I tugged the face guard off and whipped it to the ground near Peter. "I'm outta here," I shouted, and then quieter to Roland, "Take Caitlyn home later, will ya?" I stomped toward the parking lot, barely glimpsing the gathering on the patio and a few stray observers elsewhere in the lawn.

"Not a good idea, Jarret," Roland called after me.

But I didn't turn back. I dropped into the driver's seat of my Chrysler 300, backed out of the parking lot, and sped away. Peter won, but I didn't need to listen to him for the rest of the evening to know that he was also right. I wasn't good enough for her.

CHAPTER 36

Caitlyn

"**H**e left without me?" I stood peering across the lawn at the parking lot, looking for a red car even though Peter just assured me Jarret had left. Feeling a bit disconnected with reality, I dropped my gaze to the mound of food on the paper plate I held: several slices of pepperoni pizza, a scoop of macaroni salad, green Jell-o salad, and two brownies. My appetite waned as emotion rose, some weird mix of anger and hurt stabbing my belly.

"Why would he do that?" I said to no one in particular. He'd promised he wouldn't drive off when faced with challenges. Had he broken his promise already? But then . . . when he'd asked me how I felt about him sword fighting with Peter, I hadn't answered, just gave him the cold shoulder. And I'd agreed not to do that anymore.

"He told me to take you home when you're ready," Roland said coolly. He gazed out toward the parking lot with me, probably wishing he could make Jarret reappear.

"What do you expect from him?" Peter said. A dark red color had come to his cheeks a moment before he'd told me the news, a hint of guilt in his eyes.

"Where do you think he went?" I said, my voice weak and whispery.

Roland shrugged. "Probably for a drive."

"Come on. Let's sit down and eat." Peter motioned for us to follow him, breaking my trancelike state. "Who knows, maybe he'll come back."

Roland, with his jaw tight, took a deep breath and shook his head. Avoiding eye contact with everyone, he walked with me and Peter toward the picnic table at the back of the house.

Nearing the table, I moved closer to him. "What's the matter, Roland? What happened that made Jarret leave?"

"Peter happened." He shot Peter a cold glare.

Before Roland could explain, Ling-si ran up behind us, two plates of food in her hands. "Who won the sword fight?" Then she looked here and there. "And where's Jarret?"

"Jarret's a sore loser. He took off." Peter reached the picnic table first and cleared a few young children away before plopping down.

Ling-si sat next to me and Roland across from her, on the end opposite Peter. He mumbled something to Ling-si about Jarret going for a drive.

"You know, Caitlyn"—Peter grabbed a slice of pizza from my plate, which I'd pushed to the middle of the table—"maybe you feel like things have been going well between you and Jarret, but all that wears off over time and the real person comes out. Who is the real Jarret West? Well, today he was tested. And found wanting."

Roland shook his head, his jaw even tighter now.

"Every girl in high school had a crush on him," Peter continued, "and even when he dumped one for another, they didn't see the real him. I don't get it. He's got, like, some supernatural power over girls."

"Don't be stupid," Roland said.

"Should I try to find him?" I said to Roland, who only shrugged.

"Who are we talking about?" Dominic came over with a can of pop and a plate of chicken wings. He sat on Peter's other side, making Peter slide toward the middle of the bench.

"But it's different between them," Ling-si said, coming to my and Jarret's defense. "Caitlyn didn't start off attracted to Jarret, like every girl in high school, as you say." She turned to me. "You didn't start liking him until you got to know him, once you started talking every day. Right?"

"Yes, that's right." As attractive as he was, I didn't see him that way until after I started to see the good things in him.

"Okay, so what do you like about him?" Ling-si said before biting into her pizza.

"Why don't we talk about his weak points instead?" Peter said. "Talk about the things you don't want to see in him but you know are there. Like him taking off and leaving you here. Who does that?"

"This is like a trial without the defendant," Roland blurted, slamming his fist on the picnic table. He hadn't touched the food Ling-si brought him.

Peter grinned. "Why don't you stand in for him, Roland? Although I don't see how you can after the crappy way he's always treated you."

"He's changed," Roland said, loud and clear. "You saw it yourself his senior year. He stopped picking fights in school and became the defender of every nerd and outcast, including me."

A few other friends joined us, some squeezing onto the picnic table benches, others standing nearby. A few of them gave their assent to Roland's statement.

"But he was still quite popular with the girls," Peter added.

"That's not his fault," Roland said. "And it doesn't mean he was taking advantage of them."

Dominic lifted a finger, his expression showing reluctance to speak, although we all knew he liked to share everything. "I've heard rumors."

"You can't believe every rumor you hear," Roland snapped, "and you really shouldn't be spreading them. Just because *you* haven't changed since high school—"

"Easy now." Peter batted Roland's arm with the back of his hand.

I returned in my thoughts to Ling-si's question. What did I like about him? Jarret West was not the egocentric man I first thought he was. And while he certainly wasn't perfect, he truly cared about doing the right thing. When he messed up, he admitted it and worked to fix things—maybe not right away, but eventually, and sometimes sooner than I was able to admit my mistakes. Plus, he learned from his mistakes and turned them around for good, even helping others as a result of what he'd learned, like helping Stacey when she wanted to skip Fire Starters.

Over the course of this summer, he'd shared so much about himself with me, making himself vulnerable and trusting me. And he wanted to know everything about me, making me feel special to him. I discovered his faith, and I shared my faith, and I felt like we had this partnership on the spiritual journey. He needed me and I needed him for all the right reasons. I didn't want this to end. Not ever.

"I think I should go find him," I said, just realizing the others had continued Jarret's trial, some praising him, others pointing out flaws.

"What?" Peter shook his head in disbelief. "Weren't you listening? This is the perfect excuse—or reason—to cool things off with him. Besides, summer's almost over and where does that leave the two of you? You're both going back to college, where he'll likely meet his next—"

"Not if he loves her," Ling-si said. *"Nothing can break the invisible thread between two people who are meant to be together."* After repeating the Chinese proverb she'd once shared when explaining her parents' love, she looked me in the eyes. "True love will last while you're both away at college."

Roland leaned across the table toward me and spoke in a low voice, though everyone nearby could likely hear him too. "I guess you just have to ask yourself: do you love him?"

"Thank you, Roland and Ling-si." I stood up giving Peter a hard glare across the table. "Peter, I'm going to give you the benefit of the doubt—which is more than you're doing for Jarret—and I'm going to decide that you mean well. You're just trying to protect me. But, Peter, you're being a jerk. Jarret is not the same as he was in high school. Or I wouldn't be seeing him."

I reached across the table, took Roland's hand, and sucked in a breath, ready to act on my resolve. "Roland, can you give me a ride?"

Jarret

I jogged a few steps down the path that ran behind the stables. Then I walked a few steps, jogged a few steps, walked . . . filling my lungs with warm, end-of-summer air, exhaling through my mouth . . . releasing hopes, longings, goals, and the dreams I hadn't been able to firmly wrap my mind around anyway. Letting it all go.

Five minutes ago, the jeweler had texted me: *Custom order ready for pick up.*

Okay, it was ready but I wasn't. Not anymore.

Running now . . . my heart thumped to a steady beat while thoughts raced erratically through my mind, anger colliding with regret, condemnation battling hope, weakness approaching mercy. *Help me, Lord. Show me the way.*

Walking now . . . trees and angels stood as witnesses to my anguished state, along with squirrels skittering along branches and—some stupid fly dive-bombing me. I waved the fly away.

Why had I taken off? Why couldn't I have simply accepted defeat . . . and condemnation? None of it mattered. None of it changed who I really was. But I'd promised Caitlyn.

When you face difficulties, please don't leave. Talk to me.

Okay, I will. From now on. I promise.

But here I'd done it anyways. Actually, I'd started driving off but then slammed on the brakes and swung around, making an illegal U-turn in the middle of the empty street and heading back. I'd eased on the brakes as I neared the Forest Gateway B&B parking lot, but I couldn't get myself to face Peter so soon, so I just turned down our driveway and decided to head back over on foot. The walk would give me the time I needed to cool down . . . and man up.

If Caitlyn wasn't ready to give up on me, we'd have to talk about this. About the way I handled conflict. What was I supposed to do when emotions exploded in my head and rational thoughts escaped me? I didn't want to say things—do things—I'd regret.

I could see her point too. She didn't want to sit wondering where I'd gone and worrying what trouble I might get into. Maybe she wouldn't mind me driving off so long as I texted her now and then to let her know where I'd gone. Once I gained some level of control, we could talk.

Jogging again, I studied the view before me, the play of light on leaves and branches, the beauty of it all, so peaceful while my mind swirled with a hundred opposing thoughts and emotions.

Peter's comments, questions—condemnations—came as no surprise and braced up the critical voice too often in my head, the one that caged me and stole my hope, the one Caitlyn had freed me from.

I'd really lost my cool though. Shouldn't have thrown Peter to the ground and tried to force his bamboo stick to his throat. He'd won. And in many ways, despite his attitude, he was right. It wouldn't kill me to listen to him.

As I slowed to a walk and the thumping of my shoes quieted, a new sound came from behind me. Horse hooves clomping down the trail. I turned, expecting to see Mr. Digby.

A horse and rider emerged from around a curve in the path. Red flyaway curls glowing in patches of sunlight, a coral pink skirt draping on either side of Desert . . . *Caitlyn?*

Not sure I could trust my eyes, I stood motionless, just breathing as she drew near. Then I backed off the path to let the mirage pass.

Desert bobbed his head and snorted, stopping before me. Caitlyn said nothing, just reached out to me, inviting me to join her on the bareback saddle pad. Mr. Digby must've helped her with that. How had she guessed I'd returned home?

Three heartbeats later, she said, "Get on the horse." She tried suppressing her smile, but a dimple popped out.

"I'll need that stirrup." I touched her white sneaker with one hand, the stirrup with the other, and eased her foot out of it.

She covered her mouth and stifled a laugh. "I guess I'm not as smooth as you were the first day you invited me for a ride."

Lord, I love this girl. I shoved my shoe into the stirrup, bounced on my other foot, and swung up behind her. The conflict in my mind and all the self-loathing dissolved, hope and determination to make things right replacing it. Caitlyn, my helpmate. I wanted to wrap my arms around her and hold her tight, but I rested my hands on my thighs instead. "I took off in my car. What made you think to look for me here?"

"You promised you wouldn't leave when things got rough. So I figured you came home to settle down. You're on your way back, aren't you?"

"Yeah." The way she understood me pleased me at some deep level. My arms went around her waist, and I sank my face in her hair before I could stop myself. I resisted the urge to confess my love for her, but I had to tell her soon. It was raging like a fire in my chest.

She transferred the reins to one hand and rubbed my arm with the other. "I'm sorry I ignored your question before you and Peter had your little sword fight, or stick fight, or whatever. I should've told you what I was thinking."

With a final squeeze, I drew my arms back and rested my hands on my thighs again. "Yeah, I'm sorry too. But I've come to realize something about myself . . . sometimes I need to back away and cool down before I talk to you. How can we make that work?"

She smiled over her shoulder, sunlight turning her green eyes into jewels. "Just tell me what's going on. And talk to me afterwards. And I'll try to do the same. I guess I ignore you when I'm not sure how to react. Maybe next time I can at least tell you I need time to think."

"We're gonna make it work, right?" I spoke close to her ear, emotion deepening my voice. "'Cause I don't want to lose you."

"Yes, we are."

I wanted to kiss her. To hold her close to my heart. To relish the physical and spiritual and emotional and everything about her. But most of that would have to wait. A part of me liked waiting. It made me stronger, more in control of myself, which meant I had more of me to give. Maybe, before summer's end, I'd feel ready to ask her the deepest question in my heart.

We rode the rest of the way in silence. Desert needed little urging to get his hooves wet in the stream that ran parallel Forest Road. Then he clomped across the road, through the

Brandts' front yard, and soon we emerged from the parking area of the Forest Gateway B&B.

The younger guests—minus Toby—played with a huge ball in the backyard, and the adults sat in lawn chairs nearby. All heads turned toward us, several squeals filling the air and a few kids stating the obvious. "That's a horse!"

"You're going to be the hit of the party," Caitlyn said, glowing with happiness as I dismounted and helped her down.

Roland strolled toward us, the hint of a smile on his face. Then he shot a worried look toward the deck.

A few people still hung out there—still no sign of Toby. Peter gathered Toby's presents from the birthday table, stacking them in his arms, ripped giftwrap all around him. When he looked up, he did a doubletake, and a book and a box slid back to the table.

"Why don't you and Roland see who wants a little horse ride?" I handed her Desert's lead.

She gave me a nod of confidence, maybe knowing what I intended to do.

"You came back, huh?" Peter studied me, blushing the way he did when about to rip into me.

"Disappointed?" I bounded up the deck and stood adjacent him at the cluttered table.

"That's not a strong enough word." He added a box of fireworks to his armful of gifts and reached for another box on the table.

I smiled. "Yeah, well, come up with your own word. I just wanted to come back and tell you I'm sorry."

"Wha—?" The color drained from his face and his mouth hung open. He glanced over my shoulder, maybe at Caitlyn and Roland and the horse.

"Look, Peter, I know you just want to protect her. I like that about you. Sorry I knocked you to the ground and tried to kill you with your bamboo stick."

His mouth twitched, a smile threatening to emerge. "It's a shinai. And you couldn't kill me if you tried."

Pleased I'd found the strength to apologize to my archenemy, I nodded. "Okay, then. Are we good?"

"Maybe. You still gotta listen to me for the rest of the night. Those were the terms."

"Yup. Start talking."

Peter handed me a few of Toby's gifts, and we took them inside. Toby sat at a desk in his bedroom, playing with miniature bowling pins and using his hand as a pinsetter while a bowling game played in a loop on his laptop. He'd probably had enough of people for one day. I could relate. Peter could invite him to take a horse ride later.

After Peter and I cleaned up the mess on the deck and the kids all had a turn on Desert, a bunch of us gathered around the bonfire Mr. Brandt built, and we spent the rest of the night sitting around it and talking. Peter, Roland and Ling-si, Dominic and his girlfriend, Fred, and a few other kids that I'd met when attending Fire Starters in my senior year. And me and Caitlyn. And for whatever reason, Peter didn't criticize me once or try to tell me I was wrong for Caitlyn. It was all good.

CHAPTER 37

Caitlyn

"What's the matter with Jarret?" Stacey leaned across the kitchen counter, sliding her folded arms toward the plates I'd set out for the crumb cake, giving me her typical sneaky grin.

"What do you mean?" Worry flickered through me, but I pushed it away. If something were wrong, he'd tell me.

Still, he had been acting strange lately. A few days ago, he took me to dinner at an expensive restaurant. We'd both dressed up, him in a suit jacket and me in a turquoise blue dress with a sheer overlay with little black flowers. The way his eyebrows twitched every now and then and he gave me long piercing gazes, I'd thought sure he had something on his mind, but he hardly spoke all evening. The next day, we'd taken a long walk in the woods behind his house. He kept dropping my hand and wiping his on his jeans then taking a deep breath and turning toward me, but again hardly speaking.

"He went out back to see what Andy and David were up to," Stacey said, "but now he's walking back and forth on the side of the house."

"He's what?" I spun toward the kitchen window. There he was, in black chinos and a green-black-and-gold-patterned button-front shirt, walking past the window and talking to himself. He typically wore casual attire when visiting my family. Why had he dressed up today?

"Want me to go ask him what's wrong?" Stacey said.

"What? No." I turned back to her and the crumb cake, which she was now picking at. "I'll talk to him later. Actually, why don't you tell everyone to come inside for dessert."

She smiled, her eyes sort of goat like, in my opinion, and she dashed for the sliding glass door.

I cut the cake into squares in the pan and shoved a spatula under the first one. Maybe Jarret was upset because summer was almost over and we'd both be returning to college. We planned on talking on the phone every evening and returning home on holidays to see each other. He'd have to fly—which would get expensive—but I could drive. Except I didn't have a car. Maybe Roland wouldn't mind driving me.

"Hey, where's that man of yours?" Dad came over, stood on the opposite side of the bar counter, and slid a plate of cake towards himself.

"Outside, I guess," I said just as the sliding glass door opened and Jarret stepped inside. What did Dad want him for?

"There you are." Dad swiped his unruly hair off his forehead, tugged his t-shirt straight, and met Jarret by the dinner table. "Caitlyn's working on dessert, I know, but you gotta minute?"

"Yeah, sure." After tossing me a concerned glance, Jarret followed Dad into his den.

Within ten minutes, the rest of us polished off the dessert—barely saving one piece for Dad and one for Jarret— and my sisters and I moved to the front room to play a game of Parcheesi, while my brothers went back outside. Distracted, I kept violating the rules, trying to pass blockades and such, and Priscilla was getting annoyed with me, while Stacey found it funny.

Twenty-three minutes later, Jarret emerged from the den without Dad and came into the front room. He stood at the end of the coffee table, staring down at the gameboard for thirty seconds then said, "Take a walk with me," all cute and bossy-like.

We strolled without talking down empty sidewalks under a pretty blue sky, the sun creeping toward the horizon and making the lower half of the sky blush. A mom and two toddlers passed us on the sidewalk, leaving the playground ahead empty, so we sat on the swings.

While Jarret moved his swing only a little, keeping his black boots on the ground, I walked myself back in my sandals and kicked off. I wanted to ask him what Dad wanted with him but decided not to pry. I liked it better when he offered information, and he seemed on the verge of telling me something. So I continued building momentum, tucking my feet under as I swung back and reaching into the air with my feet as I swung forward, but not going too high since Jarret wasn't really swinging with me.

Since he didn't seem ready to speak, I talked about little things, like my upcoming college courses. As much as I didn't ever want to be apart from him, I looked forward to learning new things and earning my associate degree. Would I really get to be a detective some day?

A few minutes later, Jarret got up from his swing and stood looking at me and biting his lip, so I slowed my swing down. Then he reached for the chain and stopped it. Maybe he was ready to tell me what was bothering him.

I placed my hands on my lap and waited. Whatever it was, we'd get through it together.

In the next moment, he dropped down directly before me to tie his shoe—oh, not to tie his shoe. The blood seemed to drain from my face. The intense, somewhat nervous look in his Coca-Cola brown eyes startled me at first . . . then it set fire to my heart.

"Caitlyn, I love you." The nervous look faded, determination and hope and a bit of insistence replacing it. "And I want to spend the rest of my life with you, have a family with you. You make me want to be better than I am. And I know I can make you happy."

My heart like a helium balloon lifted higher with every word. My mind floated above me, watching the scene play out, and my body turned light as feathers . . . Was this really happening?

"I want you to be my wife." He took my right hand from my lap and pressed a little ring to my palm.

I closed my fingers over the ring. The emotion constricting my throat wouldn't allow me to speak and my eyes welled with tears, so I slid from my swing, gripping the ring tightly in one hand, and knelt with him on the ground.

His mouth trembled as he gazed at me, waiting for my answer.

Still unable to speak, I wrapped my arms around his waist and rested my head on his chest.

He wrapped his arms around my shoulders and stroked my hair . . . just as I'd stroked his that one fateful night, the night I'd developed compassion for him and inadvertently opened myself up to discovering the real man.

My mind raced through the entire summer from the moment he returned home and made a pile of luggage, to the night he called me "beautiful" and I sang him to sleep, to the chores we did side by side as we got to know each other, and our first kiss, then to the joyful days with Selena and our courtship. The difficult times came to mind as well, the misunderstandings and challenges and hurt feelings and the way we'd resolved each one. This was a man I could grow with, one who needed me and whom I needed, *the* man I wanted to make a covenant with.

Once my voice returned, I gazed into the eyes of the man who made me feel so cherished, so loved, so needed. "Yes," I whispered, my heart offering a prayer of thanksgiving to God. I would've never given Jarret a chance, having known only the mistakes of his past and not the man he'd become. And I would've missed out on him, on us, if we'd not had this summer at West Castle, where we could really get to know each other.

"The way it all worked out, Jarret," I said, choked with emotion, "your father offering me the job and you not going on your field study because you wanted to avoid temptation, I think God brought us together."

"Yeah, me too." He eased us apart and turned my hand over. "You haven't looked at your ring."

I opened my fingers. A beautiful opal with iridescent strokes of red, orange, and pink sat between two diamonds on a gold band. It was lovely, so lovely. And the opal . . . "Did you . . . ?"

He nodded, love and pride in his eyes. "This is the first opal I found at that mine. They let me keep it." He took the ring from me and slid it onto my ring finger, his fingers warm against mine. "I wanted it for you."

"We're getting married." I gazed at the ring on my finger, still stunned by it all. My parents might not be too happy about it, but we'd face that challenge together. "I can't wait."

"Yeah, me too." With a finger to my chin, he tilted my face to his and dropped his gaze to my lips. Then he kissed me with passion, our hearts and hopes melting together at the promise that the two would become one.

May he grant you your heart's desire
and fulfill all your plans!
~ Psalm 20:4

Did you enjoy this book? If so, help others enjoy it, too! Please recommend it to friends and leave a review when possible. Thank you!

Every month I send out a newsletter so that you can keep up with my newest releases and enjoy updates, contests, and more. Visit my website www.theresalinden.com to sign up.

ABOUT THE AUTHOR

Theresa Linden is the author of award-winning *Roland West, Loner* and *Battle for His Soul*, from her West Brothers series of Catholic teen fiction. An avid reader and writer since grade school, she grew up in a military family. Moving every few years left her with the impression that life is an adventure. Her Catholic faith inspires the belief that there is no greater adventure than the reality we can't see, the spiritual side of life. She hopes that the richness, depth, and mystery of the Catholic faith will spark her readers' imagination and make them more aware of the invisible realities and the power of faith and grace. A member of the Catholic Writers Guild and CatholicTeenBooks.com, Theresa lives in northeast Ohio with her family.

Made in United States
Orlando, FL
28 November 2023

39602568R00176